# SPECTRE
## THIRTEEN
### A CHARLIE WALKER NOVEL

# NICK POBURSKY

BAMBOO FOREST
PUBLISHING

ISBN: 978-0-9910079-8-1

Published by Bamboo Forest Publishing

Visit us Online at:
www.bambooforestpublishing.com

*In memory of Floyd and Samantha Pobursky.*

*I will miss you both.*

# PROLOGUE

"WAKE UP, MARTIN," she said, softly. "Wake up."

And Martin opened his eyes.

At first, he didn't understand where he was, but when the dense fog of unconsciousness finally burned away, it all came back to him.

▼▲▼

He'd been out late at Splitsville, drinking like he always did on Tuesday nights—hell, drinking like he did *every* night—when he met her: tall, redheaded, full-chested, and willing to talk to him. The first three traits on that list were great, but it was the last one that made all the difference.

Martin Ramos was just north of forty and lived alone. He had no family, no friends, a job he couldn't care less about anymore, and a drinking problem. His existence was a sad one, and he knew it.

As a result of his sad existence, Martin went to Disney Springs every night for two reasons: to drink, and to stare at the asses and chests of every female that happened to walk by. It was an ever-evolving roster of all-stars and it never got old.

So, typical of his daily routine, he'd been at Splitsville, drinking and admiring the overabundance of skimpy clothing, when she approached him.

He was well into his fourth gin and tonic and had worked up a serious buzz when she gracefully sat down on the stool beside him and offered her name.

"I'm Rebecca," she purred. "And you look lonely."

For a moment, Martin's gaze was lost in the cleavage that was spilling out of her skin-tight tank top.

"I'm Martin. And... uh, no, actually," he said, finally pulling his eyes away from her chest. "I'm here working."

"And what kind of work would that be?" she asked.

"Security," he told her, only half lying.

In truth, Martin was a high-ranking officer in resort Security, working directly under Charlie Walker, the big boss himself. Martin hated Walker. After all, Martin had been groomed for the position from the start and then, all of a sudden, Walker booted some psychopath out a window and the job was just handed to *him* instead.

Martin had seen the seen the bodies and countless shell casings in the parking lot of Bay Lake Tower. He'd been close enough that night to hear the gunfire from Monorail Red and he'd seen the fear and grief caused by Walker's actions on the face of every single Guest who'd witnessed the carnage he'd been a part of. And worst of all, he'd seen the red wreckage that was Spencer Holloway's body splattered across the pavement beneath Bay Lake Tower. What kind of madman would do that to a person? And *this* was the guy they put in charge of everyone's safety? Ridiculous.

There wasn't a day that went by that it didn't piss him off.

But the most infuriating part was that Walker made it so hard to hate him. He wasn't a bad guy; he treated everybody well and with respect, and was a legitimate warrior. But none of that could trump the fact that he'd stolen Martin's future from him without a moment's hesitation.

"Disney Security?" Rebecca asked. "That's hot."

"Yeah. Plainclothes," he lied, casually brushing his shirt aside to reveal the badge clipped to his belt. At one point he'd had a handgun clipped next to the badge, but Walker had taken it from him when he'd found Martin drunk in his office, lazily spinning the loaded weapon on the desktop. Martin had protested, but Walker told him that he could either take his gun or his job. Then he'd had the nerve to tell Martin that he was being irresponsible and that he could seriously hurt somebody.

Asshole.

"They let you drink on duty, huh?" she asked, playfully, gesturing toward his nearly empty glass.

"I do whatever the hell I want," he declared. "As long as I get the job done, they stay off my back."

Again, not true. After the handgun situation, Walker had been on his case about his drinking problem for months. It took everything he had to hide his trips to Disney Springs from the shrewd ex-detective. Yet another reason Walker could go to hell.

"Can you tell me what you're working on—or is it top secret?" she joked, brushing a hand along his bicep. He quickly tried to flex, but she doubtlessly felt his lack of muscle and he cursed himself for letting alcohol potentially ruin this opportunity for him.

Luckily, Rebecca seemed not to notice—or care.

"There have been some assaults in the area lately. Essentially, some asshole's been touching women in places they shouldn't be touched in public."

If it were four months earlier, this would have been true. That situation had come to an abrupt end when Walker himself had come down to the Springs after being tipped off by that little Habst fucker. Martin had helplessly watched from the bar as Walker struck the man with a swift two-knuckle punch to the solar plexus, thrown him to the ground and cuffed him, with Habst laughing his ass off the entire time. Yet *another* instance of Walker stealing Martin's glory.

"I don't know if I'd mind that too much," Rebecca said with a wink.

"Oh, really?" he asked, shifting gears. His eyes wandered down past her waist, investigating the miniscule yoga shorts she was wearing. "That stuff turns you on, huh?"

"Maybe."

"These are on you," she informed him, ordering two gin and tonics.

"Yes, ma'am," Martin obliged.

So, for the next forty-five minutes, their conversation went from one thinly veiled innuendo to another. Constantly, Martin had to reassure himself that this was really happening. Every time he looked at Rebecca he wondered how someone so unrealistically gorgeous could ever have any reason to talk to a chubby middle-aged drunk like himself.

"You know how to get to the Comfort Suites off 192?" Rebecca asked him.

"Of course."

"Good. Take me there," she ordered and stumbled drunkenly toward the exit. After picking up the tab, Martin hurried after her.

▼▲▼

"Ah, there you are…." Rebecca whispered.

She sat on a chair before him and seemed to be completely naked. She held something in her hand but Martin's vision was too blurred to make out any specific details.

He tried to sit up, but found that he couldn't move.

"Don't try to get up, baby. It'll be a little… hard."

She laughed, and there was an edge to that laugh that made him nervous.

He shook his head a few times and eventually his vision cleared enough for him to see the horror that sat before him.

Rebecca was covered in blood.

"Oh my god, are you alright?" he asked.

"I'm perfectly fine. More than fine, actually."

She *was* completely naked, sitting with her legs crossed, twirling a sleek black knife between her fingers. She wore black nitrile surgical gloves.

"What the fuck is going on here?" he demanded, instantly on guard.

"This is your blood," she told him, smearing it across her chest with the blade of the knife, her other hand sliding down between her legs as her entire body shuddered with pleasure. "Does it look good on me, baby?"

Martin began to panic. Weakly, he fought against his restraints but it did him no good.

"You're fucking crazy!"

"I know," she admitted with a laugh. "And I'm also fucking impatient. So, let me tell you what's happening before your time runs out."

"Why can't I move?" he interrupted, testing his bonds once again to no avail.

"I tied you up, dummy. Now, what I've done is made very small, very precise incisions in your femoral and carotid arteries, as well as a matching incision on your jugular vein. Your life force is currently seeping out into these cute Minnie Mouse mugs I bought in the gift shop downstairs. If the flow isn't stopped, you'll lose consciousness in about ten minutes, and then there will be no bringing you back. That'll be the end of Martin Ramos. And if you die, I will drink your fucking blood, Martin—I'll drink all of it. You'll have been a major disappointment. And I bet that won't have been the first time you've disappointed a pretty lady, huh, little guy?"

"Why are you doing this?" he asked, fear making his voice quiver.

"All in due time," she chided. "Anyway, there is a way to save yourself. Answer my questions truthfully, and I'll make sure you don't bleed to death. Sound like a good deal?"

"Whatever you want, lady, just stop the fucking bleeding!"

"Not until we're done talking! Okay, first question. Do you work for Charlie Walker?"

"Walker?" he asked, confused. "Yeah, I work for him. I hate that asshole. Why?"

"Good boy. I want a little information about Mr. Walker, and I believe you're going to tell me everything I need to know...."

▼▲▼

"It's right this way, Detectives," said the medical examiner.

Orange County detectives Anthony LeCarre and Jimmy Bell followed the ME along a brightly carpeted hallway to a room on the fourth floor of the Comfort Suites in Kissimmee.

*We really don't need a goddamn tour guide*, thought LeCarre. It was clear which room he and his partner were needed in, as it was obstructed by a circus of activity. Everyone from local PD, to medical staff, to hotel representatives and security—and even a few reporters—were swarming the scene, trying to look like they were doing their respective jobs. A murder this close to Disney property was a big deal and everyone wanted to be part of the story.

LeCarre stepped under the tape first and began barking orders.

"Everyone whose title does not start with the word 'detective' get the hell out of my crime scene before I pitch you out the fucking window," snarled LeCarre, the senior detective by two decades.

Silence fell upon the scene, and immediately people began to file out.

"Not you, Alan," he growled at the medical examiner.

The ME stayed but fidgeted awkwardly, unsure of where to stand.

"Great," LeCarre sighed. "Now that our crime scene has been thoroughly contaminated by all of these mouth-breathers, I suppose we should sift through what's left."

LeCarre saw things he'd never seen before in all his years on the force. What he saw upon entering that room would haunt him for the rest of his days.

The remains of a man lay sprawled across the bed to his left. If he hadn't known it had been a man beforehand, he may have thought it was just a pile of meat. The poor soul had been flayed from head to toe. A slim, black knife protruded from the ruin of its forehead.

"Jesus Christ," Bell uttered, gagging and turning away. The poor rookie lunged for the bathroom and barely made it before retching up his breakfast.

"How long has he been dead?" LeCarre asked the ME.

"We estimate the time of death as being approximately midnight. His body was discovered by the cleaning staff a little before three this afternoon."

"Cause of death? Did he bleed out?"

"He definitely didn't bleed out. Cause of death is acute frontal lobe trauma caused by a knife. Preliminary examination suggests that he was alive when he was... uh... skinned."

LeCarre stepped closer to the corpse, oblivious to the sounds of his partner's retching coming from the bathroom. He knelt beside the bed and looked over the bedspread. There were bloodstains, but not nearly enough to account for the amount of blood this man must have lost.

"If he didn't bleed out, then where's all the blood?" LeCarre asked, genuinely curious.

"That's the strangest part, Detective. It's gone. He's been drained."

"*Drained?*" LeCarre asked, incredulous.

"Check the dresser," offered the ME.

LeCarre stood and moved to the dresser where he found three porcelain

Minnie Mouse mugs arranged in a line. A small amount of blood pooled in the bottom of each, almost as if they were the last sips of wine that someone had neglected to drink.

"There can't be but a half-gallon total between all these mugs, doc. Where's the rest of his blood?"

"I… I don't know, Detective. It's just… gone."

LeCarre stood still for a moment, thinking. Why would a killer take that much blood with them? Why was this man skinned alive? More importantly, *who* was this man? The medical examiner might know.

"I guess the question of the hour is: who was he?"

The ME cleared his throat.

"Martin Ramos. Forty-two years old. No next of kin. History of alcoholism. Works for Disney Security. Second in the chain, right under Charlie Walker."

"Walker?" LeCarre perked up, recognizing the name of the famous head of Security over at Disney. "Interesting."

"What's interesting?" asked the ME.

"Walker's maybe the most widely recognizable detective of our time—a guy known for solving some of the most gruesome murders imaginable. And you're trying to tell me that his second-in-command just gets carved up like a goddamn Thanksgiving turkey out of the blue? That doesn't seem right."

"I don't know what to make of it, either, Tony," admitted the ME.

LeCarre nodded.

"Has anyone tried to contact Walker?" he asked.

"I called his office just before you arrived but apparently he's on vacation. I apprised them of the situation with Ramos and I would imagine that they'll notify him shortly if they haven't already. But I could call him now if you'd like."

LeCarre thought about that for a moment.

"No," he said. "That'll be alright. I'll speak to him personally. If you could, inform his staff that they are not to contact him until I have spoken with him."

"Of course, Detective."

LeCarre had worked the Walker/Holloway case three years ago and he remembered that clusterfuck all too well. Mostly, he'd helped clean up all the dead bodies and spent shell casings that the young detective had left in his wake. He'd sifted through the almost liquefied remains of Spencer Holloway to ID the body after the old man had been tossed from Bay Lake Tower and shook hands with the pavement. He knew about Walker's reputation as a smartass know-it-all with a propensity toward violence. More than once, he'd heard reports of units coming to the parks to pick up some shoplifter or drunk that'd had the living shit beat out of them by the hotshot ex-detective. He'd seen the YouTube video of Walker busting a man's arm to relieve him of the knife he was brandishing. However, Walker was untouchable because anybody with the right amount of brass considered him to be a national hero twice over.

*Fuck that,* he thought. *This has something to do with Walker. Nothing this theatrically gruesome has happened anywhere near Disney property without Walker's name attached since that poor girl got her arm mangled by that tattooed freak a decade ago.*

LeCarre shelved that line of thinking with a deep sigh.

"Bag and tag that knife," he ordered, "and send it to the lab for prints ASAP. I want to know the minute a match is made."

The ME did as instructed, even though it wasn't his job to do so. It was all the same to LeCarre. The faster the job was done, the faster he could catch the asshole that did this.

*I will catch him,* he thought. *And god help him when I get my hands on him.*

▼▲▼

An hour and a half later, the medical examiner rushed to catch LeCarre and Bell in the parking lot before they got into their cruiser to leave.

"Detectives!" he shouted.

"What is it?" LeCarre asked, stopping to lean against the open driver side door.

"We have a ninety-eight percent print match on the murder weapon."

"Good. Who is it?"

"It's… you're—you're never going to believe this."

When the ME spoke the name, LeCarre shuddered.

He hadn't expected this. He *didn't* believe it.

It was so improbable as to be absurd.

And yet he couldn't help but smile.

# ONE

IT WAS HARD TO BELIEVE that three entire years had passed.

It seemed like just yesterday Charlie Walker had stood in this very spot, gun in hand, ready to take the fight to the group of mercenaries that had taken his wife and daughters from him.

It was surreal.

Everything that had happened since then weighed heavily on his mind: losing his badge; packing his family up and moving to Florida for his new job; the whole Habst fiasco—all of it.

For a few moments, he simply breathed deeply the scents of the early spring and let it all sink in.

He strolled casually, just outside Bay Lake Tower at the Contemporary Resort, and made his way to the exact spot that Spencer Holloway had met his brutal end. He visited this spot every year on the anniversary and simply stood for a while, pondering the horrible events that had brought him here and all the great things that he'd gained because of it.

He'd met some of his closest friends that day, and he'd learned that courage came in many different packages, whether in the form of seasoned CIA operatives, a university professor and mother of two, or even in two little girls who were only upset that their vacation had been ruined. Charlie had surrounded himself with unique and wonderful people and there was never a day he wasn't thankful for it.

As he made his way back toward the parking lot, he refused to think about how close he'd come to losing everything, and instead focused on how much he'd gained. It brought back his trademark grin.

Life was good.

Pulling his car keys from his pocket, Charlie thought back to one of the more recent major changes he had made since his move. One day, on a whim, he'd been on his way home from training at the shooting range when he'd driven past the local car dealership and something had caught his eye in the showroom.

Two hours later, he'd traded in his piece-of-shit Toyota, and left with a brand new Shelby Mustang GT350 in shadow black. He'd bought it directly off the showroom floor and watched happily as the porters had to remove glass panels from the building just to get it outside. When he'd gotten home with it, Meghan had stood on the porch with her eyes wide open while the girls argued over who would get to ride shotgun.

"Did you get your car washed?" Meghan had joked with a smirk. "Something looks different about it."

"Yep. I washed it clean out of our lives. You mad about it?" he'd challenged playfully.

"Only if you can't fit the three of us in it right this instant," she'd said, kissing his cheek and heading toward the passenger door.

*I've got one hell of a wife*, he thought.

He laughed aloud in the parking lot remembering how worried he'd been about coming home with his new purchase.

Getting behind the wheel, he depressed the clutch, tapped the ignition button, and was instantly reminded just how great an impulse buy this had been.

With a screech of tires, and the furious growling thunder of more than five hundred horsepower, Charlie left Bay Lake Tower behind, in much better spirits than he'd been three years previous.

▼▲▼

Just as Charlie was merging onto Buena Vista Drive, his iPhone chirped. It was a text from Habst.

Yo dude, you around?

He frowned, wondering why Habst would need him on the last day of his vacation.

Coming back from BLT. Should be home in twenty. What's up?

Just call me, man, Habst replied.

"Hmm...." Charlie wondered aloud, navigating to Habst's contact info and pressing the call button.

Habst answered on the first ring.

"Hey, dude," he said, sullenly.

"What's up, Habst? Couldn't bring yourself to let me have one uninterrupted week of vacation?" Charlie joked.

"Yeah, sorry, it's just that—I heard something just now and I think you should know."

"What is it?"

"Hector told me he was in Security when they got a call. Apparently it was some county medical examiner or something. Martin's dead, man. Someone killed him. I'm sorry."

"What! How?" Charlie demanded.

"I don't know how. That's just what Hector said he heard."

"Why hasn't anyone called me?"

"That's the weird part, dude. The same guy called back not long after and said that nobody in the office should tell you about it until some detectives talked to you first."

"Son of a bitch," Charlie spat. "Where are you?"

"On my way to Trader Sam's."

"Hector with you?"

"Yeah. You coming?"

"I'll be there in ten."

He disconnected without another word, dropped a gear, and sped off toward the Polynesian Village Resort on the warpath.

▼▲▼

Habst and Hector were seated at the bar with their backs to Charlie when he arrived. The place had just opened a few hours ago and was already packed, but they'd saved him a seat. A glass of Lagavulin sat on the bar in the empty spot—a whisky they didn't serve, but Charlie guessed Habst had pulled a few strings.

He sat, sighed, and took a long, slow sip of the peaty Scotch.

"You were there when this call came in?" he asked Hector.

The big man nodded.

"Yeah, boss."

Charlie didn't know Hector well enough to trust him without reason, but Habst trusted him, and Habst's opinion carried weight in Charlie's mind. He decided to give the big man the benefit of the doubt.

Habst, specifically, had bonded very quickly with Hector, though Charlie suspected he'd latched onto the big man for a skewed kind of support after a series of life-changing events that had left him in a strange place.

Habst's girlfriend, Monika, had abruptly split up with him earlier in the year. When Charlie had asked him about it, he only grumbled something about a football player from UCF and a senior prom and dismissed it offhand.

Charlie figured the roots of that situation may have run deeper, however. Not long before the split, Habst had vacated his Vice Presidency and given the position to Tricia Meyers—a decision which Charlie had fully supported. Tricia had the disposition, experience, and humble beginnings to be successful.

Habst had been very vocal about his distaste for his old position. What he'd thought would be a dream job had turned out to be nothing more than endless tedious decision-making, an inbox full of emails from people whose vacations had been "less than magical," and an onslaught of handshakes with legions of wealthy people who'd never heard of Purell.

More often than not, Charlie would find Habst sitting on a bench on Main Street, vacantly staring at the names on the second-story windows. So, when Habst had come to Charlie to tell him he was handing the job over to Tricia, he hadn't been surprised in the least. In fact, he'd been relieved. He could tell the job had been taking its toll on his friend.

Habst's last act as Vice President was, by Charlie's estimation, the most Habst thing Habst had ever done. He had created a brand new position for himself in which he essentially took home a sizable paycheck and was able to do nearly any job in the parks he wanted at any time—at *his* discretion. He'd titled this new position "Progress Coordinator." Surprisingly, nobody had argued the decision.

For the first time in a long time, Habst's mood had started to improve.

On the flip side of that coin, now that Habst was free from most responsibilities, he was slowly becoming a thorn in Charlie's side, just like he'd been years ago when Charlie first started as head of Security. Still, Charlie let a lot of little things slide; Habst had experienced a myriad of life-altering changes in a short period, and Charlie figured a little mischief might be the best kind of therapy.

Habst didn't seem too broken up about any of it, though, and spent much of his newfound freedom drinking with Hector in the resort bars or—oddly enough—working Custodial.

Hector Lynch himself was a large Hispanic man, even though his last name suggested otherwise. He was burly, muscular, and intimidating, but always smiling and ready with a joke. He'd worked Maintenance for the last six months and spent a lot of time in the Security offices. He worked hard, kept mainly to himself, and Charlie liked him.

To Charlie's surprise, Violet and Katie also liked Hector quite a bit, and talked with him frequently when Charlie brought them to the office.

Charlie took another sip of the Scotch and got down to business.

"Alright, Hector. Tell me everything you know," he requested, calmly.

"Well," Hector began, hesitantly, "there isn't much more than what Habst already told you."

"I want to hear it from you," Charlie said. "Everything you heard."

"There was a call, said someone killed Martin and that nobody was supposed to talk to you about it until after the cops did. And here I am talking to you. Could I get in trouble?"

"There's absolutely no legal reason you could get in trouble for talking to me. I've got your back. Now, did you hear where Martin was killed?"

"I don't know, but I read on my news app that they found a body over at the Comfort Suites off 192. They didn't say who it was, but I bet it was him."

"Good man," Charlie complimented him, draining the rest of his Scotch. "How the hell did you get Lagavulin here, anyway, Habst?" he asked, looking at the empty glass as if it were an alien artifact.

"You just gotta know people, mon," Habst declared in a poor Jamaican accent, winking at the pretty bartender who smiled back at him from across the room.

She sidled over to them when she noticed Charlie.

"If it isn't Charlie Walker. Here on business?" she asked, drying off a glass with a terry towel.

"Nope. Vacation," Charlie half-lied, putting up a casual front. "Stopped in to have a drink with these two idiots," he said, playfully, slapping Habst on the back. Habst lazily raised his beer in a mock toast and began to flirt with the bartender.

Charlie sat back, tuning out and thinking about what Hector had said. Should he go to the Comfort Suites and find out if it was Martin's body they'd found? If he did, they most likely wouldn't let him anywhere near the scene and they definitely wouldn't release any details to him. After all, he was a civilian now. He couldn't just go barging into crime scenes demanding information. Sometimes he missed being a cop.

Suddenly, his phone began to ring, snapping him out of his thoughts. It was Meghan.

"Hey, babe," he answered. "What's up?"

"Charlie, there are a couple of cops here at the house. Detectives."

Charlie froze.

"Tell me you didn't let them inside."

"Hell no. I know better than that. They're out on the porch. But they're looking for you and they won't tell me what's going on."

"I'm actually working on figuring that out right now. Long story short: Martin Ramos was murdered, and my staff were warned not to speak to me—and I don't know why. I need to talk to these assholes. Tell them to take a walk around the block. I'm coming home. I'll be there in fifteen minutes."

After hanging up, Charlie pulled two twenty-dollar bills from his pocket and threw them down on the bar.

"Their next round's on me," he said to the bartender. "I've got to go."

As he stood, he leaned in close to Habst and whispered, "That was

Meghan. Apparently, there are two detectives standing on my front porch. It's about time I found out what went down and why the fuck they tried to keep me in the dark. Don't get too drunk, I might need you."

"Aye, aye, captain," obliged Habst. "I'm a phone call away."

With a quick nod, Charlie left the bar and headed home.

**S**URE ENOUGH, a blue unmarked cruiser was parked at the curb in front of his house. Charlie revved his engine to make his presence known as he glided to a stop in his driveway. Two men sat on his porch steps, and both of their heads snapped up at the bark of the Shelby's motor.

Before exiting the car, Charlie unclipped the holster containing his Walther, and stowed it in the glove compartment. The last thing he needed right now was to be hassled over his weapon, even though he was licensed to legally carry it.

"Can I help you gentlemen?" he asked, stepping out and locking the Shelby with a chirp of the alarm.

Neither man spoke immediately, but the elder of the pair eyed Charlie from head to toe as he made his way over to them.

"You're smaller than you look on TV," said the older man, breaking the silence.

"Depends on how big your TV is," Charlie quipped. He cleared his throat. "Again, can I help you gents? Two large men sitting on the porch of a house with a pretty lady and two little girls inside seems pretty suspicious. Maybe you could help put my mind at ease."

The younger man shot a glance toward the police cruiser, half confused by Charlie's apparent lack of attention, and half outraged by his subtle insult. The man began to speak, but the older one cut him off.

"I'm Detective Anthony LeCarre and this is my partner, Detective Jimmy Bell. We're here on a matter of police business."

Charlie took a slow breath and gave a small shrug. He'd already pegged LeCarre as the type who overestimated his own accomplishments and afforded himself a generous helping of theatrical gravitas. There were dozens of idiots just like him back in Detroit. Charlie knew that playing counter to LeCarre's tough-guy act would work to his advantage, so he did what came naturally: he made a complete mockery of the situation.

"Sadly, guys, I haven't been a police officer in a long time. I wish I could help you out, but I'm just a regular guy these days. But, I mean, if you guys need a few pointers or anything…."

LeCarre bristled, but maintained his composure.

"We didn't come here for your help, damn it—"

"Oh, are you here to swear me back in? I do kind of miss being a police officer."

"We came here to—"

Charlie cut him off again, deciding to take control of the situation earlier than he'd planned.

"You came here to tell me why you stopped my office from informing me that one of my employees was murdered. That's why you're here, right?"

LeCarre exchanged a quick glance with Bell.

"You didn't think I'd find out?" Charlie asked with a condescending laugh. "Well, I did. And I'd really like to know why I wasn't informed immediately."

LeCarre puffed his chest out and Charlie knew the show of bravado was incoming. LeCarre simply *oozed* an obvious need for validation and a desire to be the alpha male.

"You weren't informed immediately because you didn't *need* to know. The death of an employee is both tragic and unfortunate. However, as lead investigator, it's up to me when the details of such a case are released to the public. Like you mentioned, you are no longer a police officer. Your involvement is unnecessary and I felt that, if you were notified before we were able to fully work with the scene, you could potentially cause problems for us."

Charlie kept all emotion from his face and remained calm when he spoke.

"Then tell me why you're on my porch, or get the hell off my property."

LeCarre smiled.

"I was just getting to that. But first—if you'd be so kind, Mr. Walker— please place your hands behind your head. You're under arrest. Jimmy, cuff him."

Charlie was genuinely surprised.

"What! You can't—"

LeCarre cut off his protest.

"You have the right to remain silent…." the older detective began as Bell cuffed Charlie's hands behind his back.

Walker offered no resistance and was deathly silent as his rights were read to him, but LeCarre caught his first glance of Walker's fabled intensity.

Never had he seen a look like that before and it nearly made him stumble in his well-rehearsed recitation. Walker was a head shorter than LeCarre, and easily thirty pounds lighter, but nevertheless was intimidating in his own way. His presence and power were undeniable.

Suddenly, LeCarre realized he was no longer looking into the eyes of the well-liked, sarcastic head of Security at Disney. Rather, he was looking into the eyes of the man who had taken on twelve mercenaries, an assassin, and a psychopath to save his wife and children. He was looking into the eyes of the detective that had brought a demonic mass murderer to justice in Detroit and taken a bullet to the throat in the process. He was looking into the eyes of the man who had beaten a hardened mercenary to death with his bare hands after that man had assaulted his wife.

Momentarily, LeCarre wondered if he was making a mistake.

*You can't think like that*, he reminded himself, shaking his head.

Charlie spoke up, calmly and steadily, after LeCarre was through with the Miranda warning.

"Thank you for reading me my rights, Detective. That was very nice, really brings me back. But you haven't told me what I'm being arrested for."

Bell spun Charlie around and shoved him roughly toward the back of the police cruiser.

After Charlie was loaded into the back seat, LeCarre paused with his hand on the open door.

"For the murder of Martin Ramos," he said.

And slammed the door shut.

# THREE

VICTORIA HOLLOWAY WAS SITTING at the kitchen table in her one-bedroom apartment in Alexandria, Virginia, drinking Wild Turkey, and thinking about her life.

As far as strange lives went, she was probably a forerunner in the competition for the strangest life of all time.

And it had started at birth.

She had been born a twin to her brother James, and their father was a professional criminal.

Not the ordinary, knock-over-a-liquor-store, steal-your-mom's-car criminal, but an honest-to-god mastermind. He'd had a wife and children only as a cover for his illegal doings.

One day, their father had decided to kill their mother and put the twins up for adoption. Family life had no longer served his needs, and so he'd moved on. Just like that.

Victoria had ended up with a kind and loving family just outside Boston, while James had gone to a family in Cleveland.

After graduating from college with a degree in criminal justice, the then-twenty-two-year-old Victoria had applied for a position with the Central Intelligence Agency. She'd been accepted, and her future was secured.

James, on the other hand, had been an enigma. He'd left his adopted family at sixteen and disappeared. From what Victoria had read in the Company's files, James had spent his entire adult life as a vagrant drifter, moving from state to state, never staying in one place for long.

He'd *had* to move often. He was killing people.

She sighed, thinking about her lost brother. By the time James had finally come face to face with Charlie Walker, he'd become one of the country's most infamous serial killers. Walker had killed him in a firefight while trying to protect James' next intended victim.

Ironically, it was this event that was the catalyst for a series of events that would lead her to eventually become close friends with the man who'd killed her brother.

Walker's slaying of James had consequently brought him to the attention of her estranged father, Spencer Holloway, who had by that point graduated from criminal mastermind to full-blown psychopath.

Having made his fortunes and gained his infamy, Spencer Holloway had spent the latter years of his life pursuing talented individuals and challenging them to lethal mind games. The prize for winning was to be their lives. He'd been mostly successful in these challenges until the day James' death had led him to Charlie Walker.

Three years ago, during one of these challenges, Charlie had killed Spencer Holloway... but that's another story altogether.

Victoria held no animosity toward Charlie for what he'd done—in fact, the opposite. Her brother and father were monsters, and she'd vowed to put an end to their atrocities but was always one step behind them, Charlie had simply helped expedite the process she'd already begun years before.

So now she was close friends with the man who had killed every remaining blood relative she had. Charlie's kids referred to her as "Aunt Vee" and she loved those girls as if they were her own daughters. Charlie's wife, Meghan, had become an unofficial sister to her and was one of the only real girlfriends she had.

The world works in mysterious ways.

She had just taken another sip of her Wild Turkey when her phone began to ring. She set down her glass and checked the display.

Speak of the devil.

Meghan's name and picture were on the screen.

"Hey lady, what's—?" she began, but Meghan cut her off.

"Vee, Charlie's been arrested."

"What!" Victoria was immediately on her feet. "Why?"

"Murder. They're saying he killed this man Martin that works—worked—for him. He didn't do it, Vee. You know that."

"I know. I know," Victoria said, placing a hand to her brow and thinking. "When did this happen?"

"Not five minutes ago. Two detectives showed up looking for him and—"

"You didn't let them in, did you?" Victoria interrupted.

"Jesus, no. Why does everyone keep asking me that? Anyway, they showed up looking for him but he was out, so they sat on the porch waiting while I called him. He came home not long after, they talked for a few minutes in the front yard and then, next thing I knew, they were cuffing him and throwing him into the back of a police cruiser.

"One of the detectives came back up to speak to me before they left. They said he was arrested for the murder of Martin Ramos. I asked what proof they had but they wouldn't say. They just said, 'We have evidence.'"

"That's bullshit, Meghan. Who was this guy—this Martin Ramos?"

"He was a Security specialist that worked right under Charlie. Decent enough guy, but I honestly think he hated Charlie. Charlie's friend, Habst, told me that before Charlie took the head of Security job, it was supposed to go to Martin."

"Shit."

"What?"

"Motive," Victoria explained. "Professional competition is common in cases like these."

"He didn't do it, Vee!"

"I know he didn't do it! But these detectives have a motive to work with. If they have *any* kind of evidence at all, they can combine it with that motive and make a case against him. But there is a little bit of good news."

"What?"

"Well, if they don't have enough evidence to charge him—and I don't think they do—then they can only hold him for a maximum of forty-eight hours. Then, by law, they have to either charge him or release him. But I'm not going to let it get that far."

"God, Vee, this is awful. What can I do?" Meghan asked.

"You can give me a half hour. I've got an asset in your area and I'll send him to you. Something's not right and I think you and the girls should have protection."

"Okay. And then what?"

"And then I'm going to mobilize the team and we're all coming down. We'll get Charlie out one way or another, and then we'll figure out who put him in there and why."

"Can you do that—just grab the team and go? There isn't a bunch of approval processes or anything like that?"

"Let's just say my boss owes me some favors and I've got some vacation time I need to burn. Sit tight, girl, help is on the way."

And with that, Victoria disconnected and sent a single group text to the members of X-ray Team:

Pack your shit. The Walkers need us. We're going to Disney World.

# FOUR

TWENTY-FIVE MINUTES LATER, Meghan was sitting at the kitchen table, idly sipping on a cup of coffee when there was a knock at the front door. Violet and Katie sat nearby and both girls glanced up at the sound. Zeus, their faithful German shepherd, slowly made his way to the front door, hackles raised and ready for action as always.

Meghan stood and picked up the Smith & Wesson Bodyguard that lay on the table before her. She'd grown too cautious over the last few years to leave herself unprotected.

"Wait here," she told the girls. "Zeus, guard."

Upon Meghan's command, Zeus turned away from the door and moved to stand in front of the girls.

When she looked out the peephole, she saw a face she recognized from Charlie's office. Habst's friend, Hector Lynch, stood on the porch, patiently waiting. Confused, Meghan cautiously opened the front door a few inches. Hector stood several feet away from the door with his hands out to his sides to show that he was not a threat.

"Hector Lynch. What are you doing here? Where's Habst?"

"It's alright, Mrs. Walker, I'm here to help. You don't need that three-eighty—at least not for me."

Meghan, growing increasingly wary, wondered how the big Hispanic man even knew she held a gun—it was hidden from view behind the door.

"What—"

"Victoria sent me. I came as fast as I could."

"Victoria? But—"

"Long story short: I'm a member of X-ray Team. And my name isn't Hector Lynch. It's Hector Vega. The boss-lady sent me down here six months ago to watch out for you guys. She said she'd feel better with one of her own nearby. I'm supposed to stay here until the rest of the team get here. I could stay outside if you'd feel more comfortable, it's no problem."

"No, no, come in," she said, opening the door and letting the big man in. "It's just a lot to process right now."

"I understand. But you've gotta be getting used to the Company's ways by now, eh?" he teased.

"You guys are definitely a hard bunch of people to pin down," she admitted, "but I guess that's the point."

"You hit the nail on the head, Mrs. Walker."

"You can call me Meghan. X-ray Team is family."

He nodded thoughtfully, and then a look came over his face that she recognized from the other members of X-ray Team: the look of an experienced CIA operator getting ready to work.

"First thing's first, we need to secure the house. Lock all the windows and doors, and clear the rooms. Keep that Smith & Wesson handy, just in case."

Meghan nodded and they began moving throughout the house, locking it down. When she arrived back in the kitchen, Violet and Katie looked up at her with mild confusion, but complete calm. The girls were always calm. Sometimes it was eerie.

"Uh, Mom, what the heck is going on?" Violet asked.

"I don't know. But Aunt Vee has sent someone to watch over us just in case. She and the others are coming down to get your dad out so they can figure out what's happening."

Violet gave a quick nod and returned her attention to her phone. Katie had already become engrossed in whatever game she'd been playing moments before.

Hector walked into the kitchen and confirmed that the house was clear and secure.

"Hey, Vega," Violet said, without taking her eyes off her phone. "Sup?"

"The usual, little bird. Just with some extra weirdness thrown in today."

Violet made a little grunt that seemed to mean she somehow understood exactly what "the usual" was for Hector Vega.

Meghan was dumbfounded. It took her a moment before she could speak.

"Violet Ann Walker, how on earth do you know who this man is?"

"What—that he's from Aunt Vee's team? I've known that for months," she declared with a dismissive wave of her hand. She never once looked up from her phone.

"How?" Meghan prodded a few moments later, after it became clear that Violet wasn't about to volunteer any more information.

Violet set down her phone and looked up at her mother.

"We caught him spying on us."

"What?"

"We've seen him at Dad's work, and a couple times with Habst, so we recognized him. But one day we saw him in a car when we were at the park down the street. Then a few days later we saw him at the mall when we went shopping with you. Then again a week later outside the library."

"And how did you figure out who he really was?" Meghan asked.

"After a while, we started taking pictures of him each time we saw him. Then I sent the pictures to Aunt Vee and told her that this man was following us around. She *had* to tell me who he was at that point."

Vega chimed in, sounding a little embarrassed.

"Victoria called me one day and chewed me out for being made. Imagine my surprise when she told me I'd been made by a couple of little girls. I thought I was a pretty good shadow until these two figured me out and called my boss on me."

"We talk to him sometimes when we visit Dad at work," Katie admitted. "But Aunt Vee said we had to promise to keep it secret. You and Dad weren't supposed to know who he was."

Meghan took a deep breath and then sat down at the table next to her daughters.

"I swear to god," she said, exasperated, "that you two take after your dad and Aunt Vee more than you do me. I've got two spies-in-training living in my house."

Violet perked up at that declaration and gave a little tilt of her head and a smirk. She'd been considering that particular career pathway for a while.

"You've got to admit, they're good," Vega joked, and Meghan couldn't help but laugh.

She knew what she was getting into when she married Charlie. Being a detective's wife would never mean a normal life. But this? This was something else. Spies and killers had become a part of her daily routine.

Suddenly, Vega reached into his pocket and withdrew his vibrating phone.

"It's her," he said, and Meghan knew he meant Victoria.

"Hey... Yeah, it's clear... Yeah, she knows *now*... She called them spies-in-training," he laughed. "Sounds about right... When?... Okay, we'll be here." He disconnected the call and turned to Meghan. "She says they'll be here in the morning. They're already gearing up."

Meghan nodded and sighed with relief. She'd feel much safer with Victoria and the rest of the team around. Aside from Charlie, she trusted X-ray Team more than anyone else on earth. If the girls recognized Vega and had confirmation from Victoria that he was on the level, then she trusted him too.

"What do we do now?" she asked.

"We wait for the boss-lady—and hope no one tries to kill us in the meantime."

FIVE

CHARLIE SAT IN A CELL, and he had almost nothing.

His belt, keys, phone, shoes, socks, sunglasses, and wallet had been confiscated when he'd been processed. All he'd been left with were his clothes, his wedding band, and his watch.

He'd been fingerprinted, photographed, and unceremoniously shoved into the little eight-by-eight closet, all while LeCarre watched with a shit-eating grin plastered on his face. That smug smile meant that the idiot detective thought he'd finally made his big break: he'd caught the fallen hero who'd turned to killing his own employees. Ironically, that thought made Charlie want to break the detective's jaw.

Shaking his head to clear it of these unproductive thoughts, he tried to sharpen his frustration into something useful, but he couldn't make sense of the situation. They still hadn't told him what evidence they'd found that had them so convinced he'd killed Martin Ramos, but they also hadn't charged him and he'd been locked up over three hours. By his guess, it was maybe ten or eleven o'clock. He figured they'd let him stew in here until morning, when they'd come to try and pry a confession from him.

*Good luck, assholes*, he thought.

After another hour, he began to grow restless. He stood and began to pace his windowless cell slowly. He wanted to sleep, but his rage kept him wired and his curiosity kept his mind in constant motion. He had nothing to go on, so he made no useful connections and no revelations came to him. He may have been a great detective, but even Sherlock Holmes couldn't solve a mystery without a single piece of evidence.

Finally, he decided to physically wear himself out, in hopes of being able to sleep. He alternated between sets of pushups, sit-ups, and bodyweight squats until he was too exhausted to stand.

Sweating and breathing heavily, he lay down on the Spartan cot, folded the meager wool blanket and placed it over his eyes to block out the light. After what seemed like an eternity, he finally dozed off.

▼▲▼

"Get up, Walker. It's eleven o'clock in the morning and the detectives are ready for you to talk."

The blanket was pulled from his eyes and his world exploded with blinding whiteness. Coarse hands pulled him from his cot and manhandled him to his feet. He was shoved roughly into a dirty hallway where he was unceremoniously ushered into a plain room with a table and a few chairs. They didn't bother to cuff him to the eye bolt attached to the table top.

A cup of coffee was set out before him and he fell upon it like a lion upon its unlucky prey. It was cheap, burned coffee from an old machine, but it tasted like nothing he'd ever had before. He drained the cup before the detectives came in to meet him.

"Hello, Charlie. Have a good night?"

"Cut the shit, *Tony*, and get to your point," Charlie offered calmly, staring into the bottom of his empty Styrofoam cup.

LeCarre took an aggravated breath and looked over at Bell, who put up a hand to calm him down. He gave the older detective a look that seemed to say, "Don't let this guy get under your skin." But Charlie could tell he was already embedded deep. LeCarre wasn't used to rebellion, it threw him off balance and that's exactly what Charlie wanted.

"You think you're hot shit," barked LeCarre.

"I think *you're* out of your depth. And stalling for time. Either charge me, or open that door. I've got to make arrangements for Martin."

"You're not going anywhere."

"Then let's hear it," Charlie urged, crushing the Styrofoam cup in his fist and letting it fall to the floor. He leaned back in his chair, tipping the front legs off the ground.

"Why did you kill Martin Ramos?" LeCarre asked him.

"I didn't."

"I believe otherwise."

"So you keep saying. And yet you've got nothing but a hunch to go on. What—do you think just because Martin didn't like me that I murdered him?"

"No. I think you killed him because of whose prints we found on the murder weapon."

"You found my prints? That would be impossible," Charlie said, truthfully.

"No," LeCarre said, and motioned to Bell, who slid a single piece of paper toward Charlie. "Not yours."

For a moment, Charlie didn't realize what he was seeing.

It was a small file with basic information. It contained a name, an address, an age, and a few other small details. It also contained a picture taken at an elementary school, a set of fingerprints taken during a field trip to a local police station in Michigan, the description of an expensive black automatic knife, a name, and a single number followed by a word. It was the name and the number that terrified him to his core.

```
Violet Ann Walker. 98% match.
```

The realization hit him all at once.

"No," Charlie gasped, and then began to panic.

VICTORIA WAS DEATHLY SILENT as she piloted the big, black Lincoln Navigator toward the Orange County Sheriff's office. Somewhere inside they were holding Charlie Walker, and she wasn't leaving until he was a free man.

She had the entirety of X-ray Team with her—minus Vega, who was still guarding Meghan and the girls.

As she looked in the rearview mirror, she saw her team, stone-faced and prepared to do whatever had to be done.

She saw Jen-Jen, calmly picking at her nails with the gleaming silver knife she always carried. McCoy sat silently, looking at the well-worn laminated picture of his daughter—an item he was never without. In the passenger seat next to Victoria sat the giant Hawaiian, Kalani. As usual, he was feasting on some new monstrous fast food creation—this time a McGangbang. And in the very back of the Navigator sat one of their newest members who'd come onboard as a package deal with Vega. April Simms was the team's sharpshooter and medic, and she was one scary little girl. She could shoot the fleas off a dog's back at a thousand yards and put ten rounds through a hole the size of a dime from three hundred yards as fast as she could pull the trigger. Without exaggeration, she hit what she aimed for and never missed, and this had made her an invaluable asset for X-ray Team over the year and a half she'd been with them.

"Everyone hang back when we get there," Victoria said. "Me and Big Kahuna will head in and try to get Charlie out the legal-ish way. If something goes wrong, then we'll adjust our plans on the fly, but we *will* get him out. One way or another."

If she had to bust her friend out of lockup, she would. Charlie was family, and she needed him to know he was never alone. Someone had set him up and he deserved the chance to find out who it was.

"Boss," April spoke up. "What's the big deal about this guy? I mean, I get that he's your friend and all, but would you really break laws to get him out of jail? You're asking us to potentially assault American cops. On American soil. That means court-marshals and prison time if we're caught. And we're not even supposed to be down here. Hell, we could get court-marshaled or shitcanned just for being here."

"The big deal is that the Walkers are as much family to me as you guys are. You weren't there when my dad tried to kill them. Charlie was ready to give his life to save his wife and kids, but in the end he won, and now I never have to worry about my dad hurting anyone again. Someone is playing a sick game with Charlie, and if there's one person on this planet I would trust to figure out who that is, it's Charlie himself. He can't do that if he's stuck in a cell."

"I didn't mean anything by it, Vee. You know I'd follow you into hell if you asked. I just wanted to make sure it's worth it."

"I promise you it's worth it. Otherwise I wouldn't have pulled you off leave."

"We'll get him out, *wahine*," Kalani promised between mouthfuls of food. "Little *braddah* is tough; he'll last until we can get him."

Victoria nodded solemnly and they drove the rest of the way in silence.

When they finally reached the Sheriff's office, she and Kalani stepped out of the car into the searing midmorning Florida heat.

After clipping her CIA badge, ID, and sidearm to her belt in plain view, Victoria unbuttoned two buttons on her shirt and pushed her bra up as far as she could to put more cleavage on display. In her experience, something so minute could make all the difference when trying to get her way.

Kalani checked his magazine and chambered a sleeper round before holstering the weapon beneath his trademark Hawaiian shirt.

When all of the theatrics were in place, she spoke.

"Let's go get our brother out of there, big guy."

# SEVEN

**W**HEN THE DOOR BURST OPEN, Charlie expected anything but what he saw. Victoria and Kalani strode in confidently, flanked by two flustered officers who had clearly been trying to bar them from entering.

"My apologies, Detectives, but you're relieved," Victoria notified them in the most authoritative voice Charlie had ever heard her use. "Please leave the room."

"Excuse me?" parried LeCarre.

"*Excuse me?* I'm sorry, did I stutter? I said, 'You. Are. Relieved.' This is a Central Intelligence matter now, Detectives. It is no longer your jurisdiction. Please leave the room," she repeated.

LeCarre and Bell exchanged baffled glances and then stared daggers toward the flustered officers standing in the doorway behind the two CIA agents.

One of the officers shrugged apologetically.

"I'm sorry, Tony," he said. "They check out. Orders just came through from Langley. Walker is officially the CIA's problem now. I don't know how this adds up, or why, but it's legit. We can't even appeal it, we have no choice but to comply."

"You've got to be fucking kidding me!" bellowed LeCarre, slapping the table and springing to his feet so forcefully that he sent the cheap folding chair crashing into the wall hard enough to dent the plaster.

Victoria dramatically placed a hand on the butt of her sidearm.

"I am most certainly not kidding, Detective. I'd appreciate it if you'd calm down and show some professionalism. If you're going to pose a threat to me or anyone on my team, be aware that we are authorized to use force against all aggressors, foreign or domestic."

If Charlie hadn't still been so shocked by the file Bell had given him, he would have laughed. He knew Victoria couldn't shoot a detective in a police station. But he also knew that she loved to lie to get her way and that she was very good at it. Her bluff paid off. Bell placed a hand on LeCarre's shoulder and he seemed to deflate.

"This ain't over," he said, angrily pointing a finger toward Victoria.

"I'm afraid it is," she corrected. "Now please step outside so that I can speak with my prisoner."

With a lingering glare, LeCarre left the room and Bell followed, slamming the door behind him.

After a quick pause to make sure they'd really left, Kalani blocked the door's small window and Victoria rushed around the table and slammed into Charlie as he stood, hugging him so fiercely and intensely that he thought she'd crack his ribs if she'd been any stronger. Regardless, he gently returned his old friend's embrace, rested his chin on top of her head, and closed his eyes.

"I'm so sorry, Charlie," Victoria said. "I'm so sorry this happened."

"It's okay, Vee," he whispered. "There's nothing you could have done. There's nothing *I* could have done. But there's something you need to know...."

She released him and took a step back.

"What is it?"

"The weapon that killed Martin Ramos. The reason these detectives suspect I killed him is because of whose prints they found on it."

"Yours?" she asked.

"No," he answered, his voice like gravel. "Violet's."

"What!" exclaimed Victoria and Kalani in unison.

"Someone's fucking with me, Vee," Charlie growled, fresh anger bubbling past the surface of his calm.

"Why?" she asked.

"I don't know. But I mean to figure it out. And when we find who did this, we won't be making any arrests."

▼▲▼

"Get me Mr. Walker's personal belongings, please. He is being taken into CIA custody," Victoria barked at the confused receptionist sitting near the interrogation room. She snapped her fingers twice. "*Now.*"

The girl leapt to her feet and hurried away down a dimly lit hallway. Within minutes, she returned with two large plastic bags filled with Charlie's things.

"Thank you."

When Victoria reentered the interrogation room, she quickly tossed the bag to Charlie, along with a set of handcuffs.

"Put the cuffs on and get ready to move. No, leave your stuff in the bags—even the shoes. The way I see it, at some point someone here is bound to recognize me or Kalani from when we fought Chaos Squad, and by the time they do, we need to be long gone—those orders are only *semi*-legitimate." She looked at Kalani, "Big man, grab the bags and get Charlie into the Navigator. I'll finalize the transfer, grab whatever evidence they have, and be right behind you. Go now!"

With that, Kalani roughly shoved Charlie through the door into the hallway and he stumbled before the big Hawaiian's hand caught him by the bicep and guided him toward the exit.

"Get moving, asshole," Kalani barked, putting on an overly dramatic show for the whole station. "I ain't got all day to deal with scum like you."

Charlie tried not to laugh as he stepped through the glass double doors into the blinding morning sunlight and yelped when his bare feet touched the searing blacktop.

Kalani laughed.

"It's the black Lincoln over there. Hurry up, *braddah!*"

Charlie moved as quickly as he could over the burning asphalt and hopped into the door that McCoy had opened from inside. Once he was seated, he looked around at the familiar faces of Jen-Jen and McCoy, and his eyes landed on a thin, dark-haired girl he didn't recognize. *New blood*, he remembered Victoria saying when she and Kalani had come to visit the previous year.

"Well I'll be damned," Jen-Jen said, throwing an arm around his shoulders. "You still look pretty good."

"And I'm still married," he parried with a laugh.

Jen-Jen gave him a quick kiss on the cheek, reached lower behind his back, and suddenly his handcuffs fell open and he was free.

Kalani appeared in the front passenger seat and tossed Charlie the two bags full of his possessions.

"Welcome back to the land of the free. You can put your shoes on if you want."

Charlie laughed and opened the bags.

"It's good to see you guys again," he said, reaching into the first bag and retrieving his shoes. "You've got a new member. Care to introduce us?"

"This little hellion is April Simms. Resident sharpshooter and medic. She's one scary bitch."

Charlie offered his hand and she graciously shook it.

"I've heard a lot about you," she said.

"Probably lies," Charlie joked. "Especially if you heard them from 'The Poor Man's Dwayne Johnson' over there," he said with a jab of his thumb toward Kalani.

April laughed. Kalani only shrugged and took a bite out of a burger that had materialized in his hand.

"Sharpshooter, eh?" Charlie noted. "She steal your job, McCoy?"

It was McCoy's turn to shrug.

"Kid's good," was all he said.

As Charlie reached into the second bag to retrieve his phone, he laughed at the fact that, in the three years he'd known McCoy, this was the first time he'd heard him utter more than a single word at a time.

As his hand closed around his phone, it brushed against something unfamiliar and caught his attention. Ignoring his phone for the moment, he withdrew the other item from the bag.

It was a neatly folded piece of heavy white cardstock.

"What the hell is this?" he asked.

"You didn't get booked with that?" Jen-Jen asked.

Charlie shook his head.

"Haven't stopped by the Hallmark store in a while," he joked, unfolding the card.

At first glance, he noticed that the text was handwritten in a familiar dark reddish brown. He recognized it immediately. The handwriting was sloppy this time, but clearly the same as the threatening notes X-ray Team had received the previous year.

Interestingly, the tone was inconsistent, erratic—almost childlike. And yet it was chilling all the same.

The Holloway bitch came for you.
If she hadn't, you'd have never seen this, would you? So, she did come for you.
Did she bring everyone? McCoy? Jennings? The Hawaiian? Yeah, I'll bet they're all with you. Even the new kids.
Good.
This will be fun.
I made you a promise last year, didn't I? Did you think I wouldn't keep it? You're dead. All of you.
But dead isn't enough. It's obviously the endgame, but it just isn't enough. Soon you'll see what I mean.

Love,
Thirteen

"What the actual fuck?" Charlie said, staring at the card in disbelief.

"What?" everyone else asked in unison.

Charlie handed the card to Kalani and let him read it.

"Oh man," he groaned, passing the card around. "It's Thirteen. She's finally trying to make good on her promise."

Jen-Jen sighed, McCoy cracked his knuckles, and April remained silent.

Charlie felt frustration bubbling. He loved these people—they were his friends—but they should have found Thirteen by now.

"It's been a year, Kalani. A fucking *year*! How have you not found her?" Charlie snapped.

Kalani looked down at his hands for a moment before speaking.

"We never looked," he admitted.

"What?" Charlie asked, incredulous.

"Listen, *braddah*, it's not as simple as you think. We're the CIA. We pursue threats abroad. We're not even legally *allowed* to operate on American soil without a domestic agency attached. The only reason we got away with it last time was because you were a Detroit cop. We barely slid by on a technicality. This time, we're all here off the books. If Margrave finds out about this, we could be fired. Maybe even court-marshaled."

Charlie cast his eyes down and said nothing, regretting his outburst.

"I know it's a shitty situation, and we fucked up," Kalani continued, softly. "But we're here now. And we're not leaving until this is done. We're not going to let anything happen to you or Meghan or the girls."

Charlie nodded. Kalani had let him off the hook easy.

"I'm sorry," Charlie apologized. "It's just frustrating. Chaos Squad was a nightmare—a nightmare I thought was over when we sent them all to hell. It's not easy knowing that there's still one of them coming for us. And it isn't just me and my family that are at risk. It's you guys, too."

April cocked her head to the side and was about to speak when the driver's door opened and Victoria climbed in.

"Ready to go home?" she asked, shoving a box into Kalani's chest. She almost immediately picked up on the somber vibe. "What? What happened?"

Kalani handed Victoria the card. She read it and then gazed out the front window for nearly a full minute before speaking.

Victoria thought back to a year earlier, when she and Kalani had visited Charlie in his office and told him about Thirteen and the threat she presented....

*"There have been some developments."*

*"I hate when you say* developments, *Vee. Just tell me what's going on."*

*She sighed.*

*"Someone's hunting us, Charlie."*

*"Hunting you? Why?"*

*"Not just X-ray Team. All of us—including you."*

*"Why?"*

*"Because I dropped the ball back when we first met. Remember when we said that Chaos Squad was a twelve-man unit?"*

*"Yes. And now it's a zero-man unit. We dealt with them."*

*"I was wrong," she admitted, shaking her head. "When Chaos went AWOL on Blackwater, they were* thirteen *men strong. Well, twelve men and one woman."*

*"She calls herself 'Thirteen'," Kalani broke in. "And she's one crazy bitch. We've read the reports on her and they're bizarre to say the least."*

*Victoria picked up where Kalani left off.*

*"Real name: Rebecca Jane Altamont. She was court-martialed for attempted murder during her time in the Army Rangers. Apparently, one of her superior officers made some unwanted advances, and she literally bit his throat out in response. On-base surgeons were barely able to save him. Though the defense ruled in her favor, she was dishonorably discharged.*

*"After that, she disappeared for a few years before turning up in a brand new Blackwater unit. You know Chaos Squad's story as well as we do. Anyway, sometime between Chaos Squad going rogue and ending up working for my ex-Dad, Miss Altamont parted ways with her former brothers.*

*"Now, this girl is clever. She'd managed to scrub her name from every Blackwater digital record, which is why we didn't know she existed. However, after the incident with my Dad, Blackwater turned over all of their hardcopy records to us. She hadn't been able to get to those, and that's how we learned about her existence."*

*"So, you've known about her for over two years and haven't done anything?" Charlie asked, incredulous.*

*"Honestly, she wasn't high on our list of priorities. She didn't have anything to do with the events that took place here a couple of years ago, and she hadn't been heard from since Chaos went off the grid. Now it looks like she's got a new team—and she's pissed."*

*"So, why are they hunting us?"*

*Victoria exchanged a nervous glance with Kalani.*

*"You'd better look at this," she said, reaching into her bag and pulling out a sheet of folded white cardstock. "Each member of X-ray that was involved in the Chaos Squad takedown woke up this morning with these notes sitting on our bedside tables. This one is mine. We've gotten some new blood on the team, but only me, Kalani, McCoy, and Jen-Jen got these notes. We don't know how they got in; no security camera caught anything—they're fucking ghosts."*

*Charlie unfolded the note and inspected it. It was written entirely in a dark reddish-brown ink that was meant to represent dried blood.*

*"She's coming for us, Charlie. It's time to prepare for the worst."*

▼▲▼

"So I guess we know who killed Martin Ramos," Victoria said, without looking back.

"She said that 'dead isn't enough.' What do you think that means?" Charlie asked distractedly, seemingly more to himself than anyone else.

Victoria sat in a thoughtful silence for a while. She thought about the condition in which Martin Ramos' body was found: mutilated, skinned, drained of blood. She had a good idea what "dead isn't enough" meant but she needed Charlie functioning at full capacity. If he became distracted by the thought of horrible things happening to his family and friends, then it might hinder his ability to find Thirteen and deal with her. If he hadn't made the connection yet, then she wasn't about to enlighten him.

Suddenly, she slammed the Lincoln into gear and peeled out of the parking lot.

"Who gives a fuck?" she barked, in a clipped tone. "It doesn't matter what she meant. We only have two things to worry about. Find her. Kill her. Fuck the rest."

Charlie couldn't help but agree. For years it had been his job to ask why. It had been his job to *find out* why. But not anymore. He was no longer a detective. He was a civilian with a vengeful ex-mercenary hunting him, his family, and his friends. Whatever Thirteen's plans were for them before they were killed didn't matter. What mattered most was protecting his family and sending Rebecca Jane Altamont to meet her team in hell.

"I'm not Detective Walker anymore," he admitted, as much to himself as to everyone else. "I'm done reacting. Let's *act*. Let's find her *before* she makes her move."

"I can dig it," Kalani said with a fist pump.

April looked upon Charlie and saw something far different than she'd expected—something far different than even the man she had met just minutes beforehand. She saw not a detective, not a father or husband, not a security officer or a civilian. She saw a stone cold warrior, just like the rest of them. She began to understand why X-ray Team held this man in such high regard.

"We're not just going to turn the tables on her," Charlie said. "We're going to flip them in her fucking face and make her wish she'd stayed invisible. No games this time. Let's hunt this bitch and put her in the ground."

And, just like that, X-ray Team and Charlie Walker were back in action.

# EIGHT

WHEN VEGA AND MEGHAN heard the crunch of tires on gravel, they hurried to the front door and peered through the peephole to see a large black Navigator parked behind Charlie's Mustang.

"That's them," Vega told her. "Charlie's in there. But don't go outside. Let them come to us, just in case. And remember, Charlie only knows me as 'Hector from Maintenance' so it'll be a little jarring for him to find me here."

Gun in hand, Meghan nodded and waited.

Violet and Katie quietly stepped into the hall from the kitchen and Vega was the only one to notice them; Meghan's attention was still firmly on the Navigator outside.

"*¿Que pasa, amigas?*" Vega greeted, with a casual nod of his head.

"English, Vega," Violet commanded with a giggle. "I don't start Spanish for two more years."

"Fair enough," he agreed. "Sup?"

"You know, the usual," Violet joked.

"Is that Dad?" Katie asked, with a small nod toward the driveway.

"It is," Vega confirmed. "And Aunt Vee and Kalani and everyone else."

"Cool," she grinned. "I knew they'd bring him home."

Vega slowly nodded his head, still a little mesmerized by the peculiarity of these girls. The novelty of their ability to take high-pressure situations in stride still hadn't worn off. Here was an armed, combat-trained CIA operative and the girls' only acknowledgment of that fact had been an offhand joke from Violet. He still found it incredible.

Finally, the door opened and Charlie stepped through. Ignoring Vega, he scooped Meghan up and wrapped her in a tight embrace while the rest of X-ray Team filed in behind him.

Vega stood back, next to Violet and Katie, and watched his team in silence.

April approached him and shot him a stern, icy look. He matched her gaze, held it, and lifted his chin to look down upon her, all business. For a few moments they simply stayed this way, each daring the other to back down. Eventually, April's stony façade crumbled and a wide, bright smile broke out on her face. She sprung forward and grabbed Vega in a crushing embrace that rivaled Charlie and Meghan's nearby.

"I missed you, you jerk," April whispered.

"Yeah, I missed you, too," he admitted, kissing her for the first time in months. "But have you seen my sunglasses anywhere?"

"Why—?" she began, but caught herself. "You're about to make a pale-girl joke, aren't you?"

"No… yes."

She sighed. "Get it out of your system."

Vega laughed. "I was just going to say, have you seen my sunglasses anywhere—*because*—the blinding whiteness of your skin is burning my retinas out of my skull."

"Ah. A timeless classic. That's really the best you've got?"

"For now," he said, with a wag of his finger. "For now…."

When Vega glanced up, he saw that Charlie had let go of his wife and was now staring directly at him.

"You're not really Hector Lynch from Maintenance, are you?" he asked with a smirk.

Vega shook his head.

"Hector Vega, X-ray Team, Central Intelligence Agency."

Charlie shook his hand.

"The team filled me in on the way over. Thank you for what you've been doing for us. I know the risk you've been taking."

"It's nothing," Vega assured him, trying for modesty.

Charlie cocked an eyebrow at him and smirked, almost identically to Violet.

"Habst is going to be pissed," he said.

Vega shrugged.

"He'll get over it. Besides, I haven't arrested him for his, uh, hobbies."

"That's true."

"So," Victoria broke in, "now that we're all here and not imprisoned, what's the plan?"

Charlie sighed. He'd been thinking about that and he knew that none of them would like it.

"First thing's first: I need to see the evidence and I need to see that crime scene. I need to see where Martin died. And I can't have those two asshole detectives getting in the way while I'm doing it."

"I don't like it," Victoria admitted.

"It's the only place we know for sure Thirteen has been. It's our best shot for picking up her trail."

"Ugh. Why are you always right?" Victoria spat begrudgingly.

"I sold my soul to the devil for eternal bragging rights," he shot back.

"I'm still not convinced you aren't the devil himself. Come on. The sooner we get to that hotel, the sooner we can find Thirteen and finish this. Big Kahuna, you're with me and Charlie. The rest of you, stay here and make sure these three ladies are safe and happy. We'll be back soon with whatever 'Motown Sherlock' can dig up."

REBECCA JANE ALTAMONT, also known as the ex-Blackwater mercenary Thirteen, sat in a corner seat at Jock Lindsey's Hangar Bar in Disney Springs. She was sipping on a Hail Marty, reading a beat-up *Harry Potter* paperback, and waiting for confirmation from her team that those Company meatheads had liberated Charlie Walker from his false imprisonment.

*Hail Marty*, she thought. *They consider this a cocktail? It's just expensive bourbon and an ice sphere. It is good, though.*

As she took another contemplative sip, she glanced at the table next to her. A young couple sat with their feet kicked up on the low table, which they didn't bother to remove even when the waitress brought their appetizer of stacked pretzel rings.

*Fucking savages.*

As the couple began tearing into the soft pretzels, she decided that she hated them both with a burning passion. For some reason, they were unable to chew with their mouths closed and the cacophony of slurps and lip smacks was almost too much to handle.

*These two did the rest of the world a favor finding each other*, she thought. *Trash attracts trash.*

Doing her best to ignore the disgusting couple that was—now that she thought about it—*far* too close to her, she went back to her book and was able to finish almost an entire paragraph before a kid in his late teens approached her. His flat-bill hat was cocked to the side at a forty-five-degree angle and the waist of his shiny metallic jeans rested squarely atop his knees.

*This clown doesn't have a clue.*

"What brings a stunning female like yourself to a place like this so early?"

She'd been in the building thirty minutes, and this was the second time she'd been approached. It was as annoying as it was predictable.

"Fuck off," she said without looking up from her book.

"But I—"

"Fuck off," she repeated, this time with the shortest of glances over the top of her thick-rimmed glasses.

"Damn, girl. I just want to—"

"Listen," she snapped, slamming her book shut so forcefully that half the people in the bar turned to look. "This place has been open for less than an hour. You're the second guy who's come over here to practice ignorant pickup lines. Understand something: this isn't fucking eHarmony. If I wanted to be here with somebody, I would be here with somebody. Now would you please be respectful enough to let me enjoy my book and my drink in peace? Thank you."

Without another word, she opened back up to where she left off and continued to read while the dejected kid sighed and sauntered out the front door, probably heading toward one of the other bars to see if there actually were any desperate, slutty vacationers to pick up on a Thursday afternoon. Thirteen could hear whispering coming from the couple at the table next to her and was able to focus on it closely enough to hear what was being said.

"What a bitch," the girl whispered. "She didn't have to be so mean to him."

"Look at her, though. She just *looks* like a bitch, doesn't she?" the boyfriend responded. "I mean, I bet she's like that to everyone just because she can be."

"Some people are awful. That whore is probably only decent to rich guys who have money to spend on her."

Finally, unable to contain her anger, Thirteen's head snapped up and she locked eyes with the girl, who didn't have time to look away.

For a tense few moments she stared at the girl before suddenly sliding across the upholstered bench to sit directly beside the young couple. Thirteen's thigh was pressed against that of the boyfriend's but he was shocked into silence.

"Close your mouths, you fucking mutants," Thirteen demanded in a vicious whisper. "I've spent the last ten minutes listening to you slop down your food like a couple of goddamn pigs and you somehow have the stones to call *me* awful?"

"Listen, we didn't mean to—"

"Not another word, little girl, or I will carve your eyes out of your skull and feed them to this mongoloid boyfriend of yours. If you think I'm lying, I suggest you take a look at what's in my hand."

Somehow, a razor-sharp knife had materialized in Thirteen's hand and the tip was placed directly against the boy's crotch.

"Here's what you're going to do: You're going to stand up, apologize to everyone in this building for being disgusting freaks, pay your check, pay *my* check, tip the waitress generously, then you're going to leave and never come back. Ever. Understand?"

The couple exchanged nervous glances, but nodded.

They did exactly as they were instructed and Thirteen settled back into her seat to watch them hurry out the front door. In their haste, they nearly collided with a slim, heavily tattooed man wearing a dark, sleeveless denim vest over a black T-shirt. If it weren't for the man's lightning reflexes, the pair would have slammed directly into him. The intriguing man made his dodge look casual and effortless, and Thirteen couldn't help but take notice.

The man stopped in the doorway and crossed his arms, amusedly watching the couple hurry away. Thoroughly entertained, he scanned the room quickly before his eyes landed on Thirteen and he casually made his way over to her.

Without a word, he took a seat across from her at the low table and smiled.

Thirteen smiled back, her book forgotten at her side.

"Alfie," she greeted warmly.

"Rebecca," he replied in kind, with a small bow of his head.

"I've missed you, old boy," she teased, playfully mocking Alfie's English accent. "Where on earth have you been?"

"Oh, here and there," the Englishman replied. "I've news."

"Do tell," she said, leaning forward.

"Your boy is free. The clowns are with him."

Thirteen clapped her hands.

"Perfect!"

"What now?" Alfie asked, lazily eyeing an attractive girl that had just entered the bar.

"Walker's got some work to do before we can continue, and we'll have to give him time to do it. So, now you buy me a drink, and we relax for a little."

Alfie cocked an eyebrow.

"Buy *you* a drink? Please. *You* owe *me*."

Thirteen laughed.

"Fine, fine," she agreed. "Anyway, I just got a free drink from that happy couple you passed on your way in."

"I assumed there was a story there."

"There is, but I'm not telling. They needed to be taught a lesson."

"They *walked* out of here," he pointed out, a sudden darkness bubbling up beneath his casual expression. "Did you not teach them this lesson?"

Thirteen shrugged playfully.

"Do you think I should have been harsher?" she asked.

"My dear, I think you can still *be* harsher. They can't have gotten far. Forget the drink. There's entertainment to be had."

Alfie stood.

"Shall we?" he asked.

"Oh, we shall...."

Alfie turned to leave and Thirteen got her first good look at the vest he was wearing. Across the back was a chaotic cartoon drawing of a headless ghost standing before a stack of toppling hatboxes. The ghost was in the process of tearing apart an AT-AT Walker from *Star Wars*. A large stylized logo was embroidered below the artwork.

"Spectres?" Thirteen asked, tracing the lettering with her finger.

"That's us now," he told her. "Do you like it?"

Thirteen bit her lip.

"You steal that name from my little project?" she asked.

"I figured it fit with the theme of the operation," he admitted with a shrug. "And the artwork was Patrick's idea. I believe his exact words were, 'All these barmy *social-club* arseholes have got senseless fuckin' artwork, so why don't we get somethin' that really *means* somethin', bruv?'"

Thirteen cocked her head.

"He said all that?"

"I may be paraphrasing." Alfie pointed to the exit. "Are we still planning on educating? They're getting away."

Thirteen palmed her knife, thumb on the button that would snap open the blade.

"Let's go have some fun."

*WHAT IN THE ACTUAL FUCK just happened here?* thought Habst. He'd been sitting at the bar at Jock Lindsey's, alternating between long pulls of his third beer and small sips of his second Red Bull. He'd been waiting to hear from Charlie but he hadn't heard anything yet and it'd had him on edge. He'd told himself that he would wait—that he wouldn't just call Charlie—for a couple of reasons. One: he hadn't wanted to seem like he cared. He had a reputation to maintain, after all. And two: he really hadn't wanted to interrupt if Charlie was somehow helping the police with their investigation into Ramos' murder. It would have been the smart move; knowing who Charlie was, the police should have requested his help right off the bat.

He'd stared at his phone on the bar top and had fought the urge to pick it up and call his friend.

The previous night, Hector had gotten a phone call and had suddenly bolted from Trader Sam's with no more explanation than: "We'll talk about it later, *hermano.*"

Weird.

Habst hadn't slept, and instead had just driven around thinking about Ramos and why someone would want to kill him. Unsurprisingly, he'd come up with too many reasons. A shorter list would have been reasons why someone *wouldn't* want him dead. The guy was a piece of shit.

*Unproductive line of thinking, man,* Habst had thought. *Unproductive but true.*

So he had found himself at Jock Lindsey's right as they were opening and had decided to head inside and drink until somebody told him what the fuck was going on.

He'd been sinking beers for the better part of an hour when the hot redhead had almost made some guy cry and then immediately went batshit crazy on some couple in the corner. He'd become equal parts aroused and terrified. He couldn't hear what she'd said, but he could hear the vicious, hissy tone of her whisper and he watched in astonishment as the couple had immediately stood, apologized to everyone in the bar, and called themselves "disgusting freaks" before hurrying out the front door.

Habst had never seen anything like it, and he'd seen some ridiculous things in his life. Hell, Charlie Walker was one of his best friends and if ridiculousness followed any one person, it was *that* man.

After the couple's bizarre—and admittedly hilarious—apology, Habst's attention had been drawn back to the redhead. There was something about her that he just couldn't put his finger on. Something *wrong*. And he was afraid he'd never figure it out, because she so easily distracted him. The way she'd bitten her lip and looked over the rim of her glasses at the tattooed guy that walked in as the couple rushed out made him wish he could *be* that guy—if only for a second.

Still, something wasn't right about her.

As he'd watched the tattooed guy take a seat at the redhead's table, Habst had decided to become a little more proactive. Maybe it was the caffeine or the alcohol or the lack of sleep, but he'd sensed something was off about this woman and he'd *needed* to know what it was.

Habst had grabbed his beer and his Red Bull, and stretched, acting as if his seat had suddenly become far too uncomfortable to tolerate any longer. He'd yawned, stood, then stepped on his untied shoelace and stumbled, sloshing his drinks but recovering without incident. The redhead and her friend hadn't seemed to notice so he'd casually made his way to a high-top table closer to the pair. It was a risky move, but he'd seen Charlie do something similar many times, albeit with a bit more finesse.

"I assumed there was a story there," the British dude had said as Habst had sat down.

The redhead had played coy, telling the man that she'd taught the couple a lesson.

At that point, their conversation had taken a much darker turn, with the man suggesting the redhead be "harsher" to the couple, whatever that meant. She'd seemed to agree and then they had both stood, said a few more things Habst didn't quite catch, and left the bar. He'd thought he had caught a glimpse of a folding tactical knife in her hand, a knife not unlike the one Charlie carried with him every day.

And then it had dawned on him what "harsher" meant.

▼▲▼

He threw a couple of twenties on the table and rushed out the door, hoping he wasn't too late to catch up to them.

No, there they were!

Roughly a hundred yards to his left, the redhead and her tattooed friend in the ridiculous Disney gang vest were making their way past The Boathouse. He lost sight of them as they rounded a corner.

"This is *so* stupid," he whispered to himself, and yet he still hurried to follow them. He needed to know what they were up to.

"You are *not* a detective!" he scolded himself, as he caught sight of them again just past Chapel Hats.

"You're not Charlie!" he repeated over and over again until he stopped in his tracks.

"Charlie!" he exclaimed, pointing a finger to the heavens in triumph.

This was as good a reason as any to call Charlie. Investigation be damned, someone was about to kill two people on Disney property and he could actually do something to prevent it!

Charlie picked up on the third ring.

"Habst, I don't really have time to—"

"No, no, listen, man!" Habst interrupted. "Some bad shit is about to go down and you're the only person I trust to deal with it."

Habst hoped that Charlie would listen, and not just brush him off. Thankfully, Charlie—forever a cop, no matter how many years or miles between him and the job—answered immediately, "Tell me, brother. I'm listening."

Habst let out a sigh of relief.

"Okay. I just left Jock's, and I think this hot redhead and some British dude are about to kill a couple of people."

There was silence on Charlie's end of the line for a few moments but then he asked, "How sure are you?"

"Very. I really don't have time to explain, but I saw them threaten two people at Jock's and then follow them out of the building. I think the girl had a knife. Either way, dude, I'm fucking following them and I've never done shit like this before and I don't know what to do."

Habst could hear voices in the background but couldn't make out what they were saying. Charlie must have had him on speaker and it sounded like he was with a couple of other people.

"I'm in the middle of something big, man. It's a long story, but I'm in some serious shit. Those detectives charged me with Martin's murder. They arrested me last night. You remember my CIA friends, X-ray Team? They busted me out. But I can't come to the Springs. Not yet. I've got to clear my name first. If someone recognizes me there, this whole thing could go south and there's more at stake here than just my ass."

Habst was confused, but didn't question Charlie about his situation. Instead, he questioned him about his own, "So what should I do?"

Charlie didn't miss a beat.

"Stay on them, but don't be seen. I'm sending someone to you—someone from X-ray Team. He's at my house, so he's only a fifteen-minute drive from you."

"Okay."

"If something happens, though, do *not* intervene. Do you hear me?"

"I hear you," Habst said, apprehension coloring his words. "But what if—"

"Habst, promise me you won't try anything. Don't be a hero."

*Fucking hypocrite,* Habst thought. *Who the hell are you to talk about playing the hero?*

Instead, he said, "I promise."

In his heart, he knew he was lying. Even though he wasn't a fighter like Charlie and he didn't have years of specialized training or even much muscle to speak of, if it really came down to it, he figured he could take a hot redhead and some hipster British dude. He couldn't just stand by and let them kill two innocent people.

"Thanks, buddy. And listen, when our guy from X-ray gets there, don't be too hard on him, alright? He was just doing his job."

Habst didn't know what that meant so he shrugged it off. With Charlie, pretty much everything was a big mystery, but it always turned out okay and he fully trusted the ex-cop. Even though it sometimes annoyed him, Charlie *was* usually right.

"Okay," he agreed.

"I'll knock this out on my end and find you as soon as I can. Be safe."

They disconnected and Habst glanced toward the redhead and the British guy who were pretty far ahead of him.

He sighed.

Time to be a hero.

# ELEVEN

EGA ENDED HIS CALL with Charlie and Victoria, and sighed. April wouldn't be happy about this.

But he had no choice.

A few moments earlier, Charlie had told him that Habst was tailing two people through Disney Springs and suspected they were about to kill an innocent couple. Charlie, still unable to resist acting like a police officer, had asked Vega to find him and do whatever he could to prevent the murders. However unlikely, there was a possibility the people Habst was following were involved in Martin's murder, and they couldn't let a lead slip away. So Vega had agreed to find Habst and assist.

"Baby," Vega whispered, sidling up next to April. "I've got to go. That was Charlie and the boss-lady."

April didn't seem shocked. She smiled sadly as she looked up at him. "What's going on?"

"My friend, Habst—remember I told you about him?—well, he's in some trouble, and there's a possibility it could be connected to what we're dealing with here. Charlie and Vee asked me to find him and help him. I couldn't say no."

She placed her hand on his chest, over his heart.

"I understand. We'll be okay here. Just get him and come back to me, alright?"

He nodded.

"It'll be easy. I'll be back in no time."

"Don't get killed," she joked.

He shrugged.

"Go!" she commanded, playfully, shoving him lightly.

And he went.

▼▲▼

It took Vega sixteen minutes to get to Disney Springs. He pulled out his iPhone and checked his "Find My Friends" app, hoping that Habst had reception and could be located. Habst's approximate location was, luckily, somewhere inside the parking structure that Vega had just arrived at. Unfortunately, the structure had five stories and Habst could be on any one of them.

Reversing out of his spot, Vega decided to cruise the lot and look for him. Charlie hadn't given him a description of either the suspects or their intended victims, so Habst was the only lead he had.

After searching the fourth floor and still not seeing anyone even slightly resembling Habst, Vega decided to text him.

Sup? he sent.

No reply. Usually Habst was glued to his phone and replied almost instantly. Even in the middle of the night when he was asleep. It was weird.

This time, nothing. That could mean trouble.

Vega's heart started to beat a little faster, and he pressed the gas pedal to match, heading for the ramp to the top deck at speeds that were far too high for a parking structure.

The top deck itself proved to be mainly empty, with only a small concentration of vehicles near the stairs. He didn't even see any people.

After making a slow circuit of the deck, he was just about to head back down the ramp when he saw a man stand up from behind one of the cars near the stairs. He looked to be in his early thirties, with a beard, heavily tattooed arms, and a dark vest.

*Probably one of those Disney gang weirdos,* he thought, but then he noticed something about the man that struck him as odd. He seemed as if he were convulsing. His upper body shook violently as he stared red-faced toward the ground. Vega was too far away, though, to be able to see any real detail.

Vega angled his car in the man's direction, trying to get closer and, once he could see a bit better, realized that the man wasn't convulsing at all. He was shaking from effort; his face was red from physical strain.

He was stomping on something. Hard.

*Shit.*

Vega threw the car into park, jumped out and rushed low to take cover behind the nearest car. The concentration of vehicles near the stairs was thick enough that he hadn't yet been spotted by the man, so he figured he'd be better off approaching with stealth. He hadn't yet drawn his gun, in case this was somehow a misunderstanding, but he could have it out and ready without a moment's hesitation.

He crouched silently for a moment, listening. He heard a muffled cry and the thick, wet sound of impact coming from the man's direction and knew, without a doubt, that the some*thing* being stomped was actually a some*body*. He had to move.

Now.

He broke from cover and rushed around two more cars, silently coming to a stop behind an SUV, ten feet from the attacker.

He stepped out from around the SUV only to be stopped in his tracks by what he saw.

On the ground lay a man and a woman but he couldn't tell whether they were alive or dead. There was too much blood to make out any details. Crouched over the bodies was a redheaded woman with thick-rimmed glasses and a tactical folding knife that she was using to further mutilate the pair.

Behind her, the man he'd seen earlier was brutally stomping on a third body.

And that body was Habst's.

ABST HAD FOLLOWED THE REDHEAD and the Brit through Disney Springs and found himself at the entrance to the parking structure. He watched from fifty feet away as the pair followed their prey into the stairwell. He decided that it would be better to wait down here—where he could see the entire staircase—instead of following them and potentially being discovered. This way, he could see which floor they went to and then he could hurry up after them.

*Solid plan,* he assured himself.

And then he thought, *How the hell is this X-ray Team guy even going to find me?*

Before he could pursue that line of thinking, the redhead and her friend had made it to the top deck and disappeared from sight. He sprinted for the stairs and took them two at a time until he stumbled, winded, out onto the top deck—

—and saw no one.

"What the fuck?" he mumbled, looking in every direction. "Where did they go?"

There weren't many cars; maybe twenty in a loose group around the entrance to the stairwell. They had to be somewhere in that group. Assuming the redhead and the Brit had followed the couple up here, there were four people within twenty yards of him that he just could not see.

Until he heard the scream.

"Please!" the voice bawled followed by a choking sob.

Then there was no more sound.

Habst ran toward the cars, trying to pinpoint the source of the scream. He had no idea what he'd do when he found it. He had no weapons and no training, but people were being hurt and he couldn't just sit back and hope some CIA asshole showed up and saved the day. He was the only one with the opportunity to help.

He heard a scraping noise just a few cars away and corrected his course to head toward it. When he rounded the SUV nearest the noise, he was greeted by a nightmare.

Thick, dark blood glistened in the intense sunlight, throwing red reflections in every direction. It coated the pavement, and splattered the doors of the cars on either side.

He was so entranced by the sight of all the blood that he didn't register the wiry, tattooed man stepping up next to him. He never saw the fist that caught him in the chest with a sharp punch that stunned him so thoroughly his legs gave out beneath him and he crashed to the deck without a sound. Habst's attacker knelt beside him, concealing himself from the view of any potential onlookers.

Habst would have cried out then, but found that there simply wasn't any air in his lungs. Never before had he felt an impact like that simple, vicious punch. He writhed on the pavement, drool spilling from his lips, his world nothing but an ocean of pain.

In his misery, he saw the redhead crouched over the bodies, knife in hand. She looked down at him with a bemused grin and spoke.

"I know you," she told him, waggling the tip of the knife in his direction. "Pabst, right?"

"No, love," the Brit corrected. "Pabst is a shitty beer. This is *Habst*. Habst is a shitty person. He's Charlie Walker's little burnout buddy."

Habst was in too much pain to be offended by that.

"Right. Habst," she agreed. "What are you doing here?"

Habst coughed violently, trying to catch his breath, and his attackers laughed.

"You were following us, weren't you?" she asked, rhetorically.

The Brit stood.

Finally able to breathe, Habst opened his mouth to speak but was instantly silenced. The Brit's boot crashed violently down on his ribs and he could have sworn he heard a crack. The pain was so intense and focused that tears came to his eyes and he couldn't stop them.

The redhead smiled at him sadly.

"You fucked up, huh?" she said. "Thought you could be a hero like Walker? Save some innocent people from the bad guys, maybe?"

She pointed her knife at the two dying, bloodied bodies splayed out before her.

"You're a little late, hero. They're past saving. Bad guys won. And now you're being flattened beneath Alfie's boot. And there's nothing Alfie likes more than beating the life out of someone. Right?"

In reply, Alfie stomped Habst again, in the same place, and Habst felt something crack and give way in his ribcage. One, maybe two ribs broken for sure.

He tried to scream, but no sound would come out.

He coughed, felt something shift in his side, coughed again.

This was hell. He was in hell.

He laid his head back on the pavement and tried to focus on breathing when the impossible happened.

He heard a scuffling noise and used the remainder of his strength to lift his head. What he saw was, without a doubt, the last thing he'd expected.

His friend, Hector Lynch, rounded the corner of the SUV and, after a split-second pause, shot a quick front-kick toward the redhead. The tip of his boot caught her square in the hand holding the knife and the weapon went sailing free, bouncing off a side view mirror and clattering to the pavement.

Without skipping a beat, he rammed a knee into her chest, sending her crashing, dazed, into the sedan beside her, and simultaneously reached behind his back. Hector's hand reappeared holding a pistol which he raised toward the tattooed Brit.

Before he could squeeze the trigger, Alfie shot out an agile hand and slapped Hector's gun aside while delivering a swift left jab toward Hector's throat, looking to crush his windpipe. Somehow, Hector anticipated the blow, dropped his chin and instead caught a glancing strike to the side of his jaw.

Again, Hector brought the pistol to bear, only to be completely disarmed this time by a maneuver that was far too fast for Habst's dulled senses to even comprehend. Alfie tossed Hector's pistol away and threw two devastating rights that Hector blocked with a raised elbow. Alfie followed with an underhand left that slipped past Hector's guard and landed just beneath his ribcage. Hector didn't even utter a grunt in pain or surprise.

*Who the hell is this guy?* Habst wondered, seeing his friend in a whole new light.

Hector feigned left, but aimed two quick rights at the Brit's side, connecting with one before Alfie was able to put up his defenses. It staggered him back a step and made him cough, but Hector couldn't catch a break; the redhead was trying to stand and join the fray. To Habst's surprise, Hector noticed this, and immediately sat her back down with a closed-fist backhand that split her lip and drew blood.

Just as Habst thought Hector was gaining the upper hand—and was cocking back his arm for a fight-ending overhand right—Alfie struck with such speed and precision that Habst at first didn't understand what had happened.

It almost looked as if the Brit had reached out and slapped Hector in the ear—which may have been exactly what he'd done—and Hector dropped to his right and reflexively brought his hand up to cover it.

And then Alfie ended the fight.

He wasted no time in following up with an arcing punch that caught Hector square above the eye and drove him down to a knee. Alfie kicked Hector's foot out and, using the momentum of the man's fall, grabbed him by the shirt and sent him crashing headfirst into the SUV, unconscious.

*Shit.*

That was when Habst noticed the knife. It was almost *inside* his hand it had landed so close. Without thinking, Habst grabbed the weapon in an upside-down dagger grip and immediately drove it into the Brit's thigh, aiming for the femoral artery but not actually knowing where it was. All he could do was hope.

The Brit cried out and reached for the blade, pulling it free and tossing it to the pavement, out of Habst's reach. At the same time, Habst heard a voice from far away yell, "Hey! You alright over there?"

Habst saw the redhead's eyes widen, but the Brit didn't seem to notice, instead raising his good leg for another stomp that would have sent Habst to the great beyond if the redhead hadn't saved him.

"Alfie!" she rasped. "We need to move. Now!"

The Brit seemed caught up in indecision for a moment, but he lowered his leg and nodded. He moved over and helped the redhead to her feet.

Before hurrying away, Alfie turned and stood over Habst, looking down into his eyes.

"Be seein' you real soon, mate," he said.

Then his foot came crashing down into Habst's face and his world went black.

# THIRTEEN

CHARLIE LAUGHED.

The hall outside the room in which Martin Ramos was murdered was completely deserted. Every guest on that floor had been given a new room on another level and no officers were posted to guard the area. In fact, they'd even placed a single strip of police caution tape across the door that had actually assisted Charlie, Victoria, and Kalani in finding the room faster.

*LeCarre and Bell actually think I did it,* Charlie thought. *They've already shut down the crime scene.*

In a bizarre way, it made sense. The detectives did have Charlie's daughter's prints on the alleged murder weapon. Charlie hadn't seen the weapon itself, but he suspected he already knew what it was: a matte black Microtech Halo automatic knife. The very blade he'd taken from Spencer Holloway's assassin. He carried it every day, but it had been missing for a while. He'd thought he'd lost it while riding one of the *Harry Potter* rides with the girls at Universal the week before, but now he wasn't so sure.

In any case, none of that mattered. There *had* to be something in this room that could point him in the right direction. Thirteen had framed him for murder, and his best chance to clear his name lay behind that door.

"Open it," he said, and Kalani obliged.

From a small satchel, the big Hawaiian pulled out a strange device that looked like an old-school cell phone with wires attached to a plastic card. He inserted the card-shaped section into the door's lock and pressed a few buttons. Within a few seconds, the light on the lock flashed green and the door was open.

Charlie swatted the single pathetic piece of caution tape out of his way and carefully headed into the room, making sure he didn't disturb any potential evidence. Even though it had been years since he'd been involved in an active investigation, Charlie's instincts kicked in immediately and he was once more Detective Walker.

The scene beyond was horrific.

Even though the body had long ago been removed, the echoes of violence still remained. The bed still sat in place, coated almost entirely in dark brown dried blood.

"Jesus," Victoria gasped.

"This is no good, *braddah*," Kalani agreed.

"It could be worse," Charlie assured them. Back in Detroit, Charlie had seen things that were far more gruesome. Brutal murders and crimes of passion were a daily occurrence in the Murder City. In fact, Victoria's own brother had left behind scenes of carnage infinitely more repulsive than this, but Charlie loved Victoria as if she were his own sister, so he refused to dredge up such painful memories for her. Even so, he suspected she knew.

The coppery smell of blood permeated the room, but Charlie considered himself lucky that hotel staff had discovered the body before it had begun to rot. Nothing was more distracting than investigating the scene of a murder while being consistently distracted by the nauseating scent of rotting human flesh.

*The body. It.*

At once, Charlie realized how clinical and cold he was being. Regardless of the fact that this was a murder investigation, this was someone that Charlie had personally known. Whether or not they had gotten along was irrelevant. Still, there was nothing that could be done for Martin now except to find his murderer, and doing so would also clear Charlie's name. So if he needed to revert into the clinical, calculating detective he used to be, then he could live with the remorse that came along with it. It would benefit both him and Martin. So he switched off all emotion and approached this scenario as he would any other on the job.

"What are we looking for?" Victoria asked, bringing him back to the present.

Charlie took a moment answering.

"Anything that shouldn't be here," he told her. "Forget the blood, the evidence tags, or anything that *obviously* has to do with the murder. Imagine that this is a clean hotel room you'd just entered on the first day of your vacation. What doesn't fit? What would you think was out of place?"

"I'd say those Minnie Mouse mugs over there on the dresser," Kalani added.

"Good. What about them?" Charlie prodded.

"Well, there's dried blood in all three of them."

Charlie looked at them for a moment.

"Right. But what is it about the blood that stands out?"

Kalani looked at the mugs for a moment but shrugged.

"There's a line near the rim of the mug. They were almost full at one point," Victoria noticed.

Charlie nodded.

"Right," he said. "So where did rest of the blood go?"

"Down the drain?" Kalani offered.

"Maybe. Assuming that was the case, you'd figure they'd be emptier or have been rinsed out. Do me a favor. Check the rim of each glass."

"What am I looking for?" Victoria asked.

"Lipstick, lip balm—anything like that."

"You serious?" she asked, raising an eyebrow. "You think she *drank* his blood? Maybe she just poured them out and didn't rinse them. Murderers aren't exactly known to be neat freaks."

"Humor me," Charlie requested. "The fact that there is still blood in those mugs and that the mugs themselves are still here suggest that they've been left intentionally. They're meant to send a message. I've seen something like it before. This is Thirteen—she's an egotist and a psychopath. She wants to be known, she wants attention. Or," he paused, "she wants to test me."

Victoria's expression changed from that of suspicion to sympathy. Her own father had tested Charlie in a similar manner a few years previously and she didn't wish to press the issue. She did as he asked and, after pulling on latex exam gloves that Kalani had handed her, lifted each mug to examine it.

On each of the three mugs, she found exactly what Charlie had expected: dark red lipstick in the shape of a female's lower lip.

"My god," she muttered.

"What is it?" Charlie asked.

"You were right," she told him. "She drank his fucking blood—or she wanted it to look like she did. What kind of monster are we dealing with?"

Charlie rubbed his temples, trying to prevent the migraine he felt coming on. He'd hoped she wouldn't find anything, but feared that she would. His mental profile of Thirteen became clearer and he didn't like what he saw. She was unquestionably psychotic and that didn't bode well. Psychosis breeds unpredictability and unpredictability made it infinitely more difficult to develop a pattern that would allow him to locate her.

Out of the corner of his eye, he noticed something on the bottom of the mug.

"Wait!" he exclaimed.

With a quick look at the top of the dresser, Charlie noticed the thin layer of dust had left an imprint where the mug had been; nobody had even picked these mugs up.

Immediately, Charlie understood.

Once the detectives had the murder weapon, they'd disregarded any other piece of evidence, no matter how clear the implications could have been. Especially if—as Charlie had suspected—the weapon had extremely clear fingerprints on it.

"Incredible," he breathed.

"What?" Victoria asked, frozen, unsure of what he was getting at.

"Those idiots didn't even pick up the mugs. They're tagged with numbers but they haven't come to remove them yet."

"Why does that matter?" she asked.

"Because," he said, pointing to the bottom of the mug. "There's a message on the bottom."

Victoria flipped the mugs over and, sure enough, a clear message was revealed, one word on each:

WHERE
IT
ENDED

# FOURTEEN

ETECTIVE ANTHONY LeCARRE FUMED.

Never before had he experienced such fury. It consumed him.

He threw books across his office. Upended his chair. Shattered the "World's Best Dad" mug his son and daughter had given him years ago. He shoved reams of papers off his desktop. His office was a ruin when he finally paused.

"You done?" Bell asked.

"It's bullshit, Jimmy, and you know it is," LeCarre barked, pointing a finger at his partner.

"I know, but you're *this* mad about it?"

"This was our chance, kid. We fucking *had* him!"

Bell shook his head slowly as LeCarre righted his chair and took a seat.

"Tony, come on. This is Charlie Walker we're talking about. You seriously think he just up and murdered a guy out of the blue?"

LeCarre punched his desktop, hard.

"We found evidence!"

Bell sighed.

"We found his *daughter's* prints, man—not his. You think a ten-year-old girl killed a full-grown man and skinned him alive? If so, we'd better swing by the elementary school and arrest her, because she might strike again—and this time it'll be on our heads!"

LeCarre stared daggers at him.

"Is this a joke to you, Jimmy? This is funny? This could have been the single biggest bust of our careers and, instead, some CIA idiots show up and Walker disappears into the woodwork. That's fucked up."

"Yeah, it's fucked up," Bell agreed with a considerate nod, "but it's the nature of the beast. You want my honest opinion?"

LeCarre deadpanned, "I would love that, Jimmy. Because you haven't been completely candid so far."

Bell ignored the jab and continued.

"I don't think Walker did it."

LeCarre leapt to his feet.

"What!"

"You heard me, Tony. I don't think he did it."

"How? How could he not have done it? Everything points to him!"

"Exactly."

"What are you trying to say?"

"Look, Tony, I haven't been at this as long as you have, but I know when someone's fucking with me. This is just too easy."

"Sometimes you get lucky," LeCarre offered.

"Not *that* lucky. I think someone's setting Walker up. And we're the idiots that are helping them take him down. The guy's a hero, Tony. You know how many innocent bodies we'd have scraped up at the Magic Kingdom a few years back if he hadn't stopped those mercs?"

LeCarre sat down heavily in his chair, pinched the bridge of his nose between his fingers, and sighed.

"Not you, too. No. You can't be on the Walker bandwagon."

"I'm not on any bandwagon, Tony, I'm just trying to look at the situation with a little bit of logic."

"And what does your immeasurable sense of rookie logic tell you?" LeCarre snapped.

Bell cut him a sharp look, but answered.

"It makes me wonder why Walker's daughter's prints were on that knife. Why weren't his own prints on it?"

"They were. On the inside."

"What?"

"Maybe that knife didn't make it into that evidence box the CIA bitch took with her," LeCarre admitted with a dismissive shrug. "I had it taken apart to check and two of his prints were inside, near the firing mechanism. Looks like they were older, from the last time it was cleaned and oiled. It was Walker's own knife."

Bell nodded.

"Alright, still, what better way to frame a guy than to use his own knife?"

"True, that would work, but there would be no point framing him."

Bell tilted his head and bit his lip.

"Unless…."

"Unless what?" LeCarre asked, interested.

"Unless someone wants him out of the way for some reason."

"What kind of reason?" LeCarre asked, sitting forward.

"Who knows? Another attack, maybe? It would be a solid plan to put the guy with the best chance of stopping an attack behind bars for a few days. If they framed him, they know we'd eventually see through it, but he'd be benched long enough for them to pull off whatever they wanted. Tony, we could have actually been *helping* them by arresting him."

LeCarre sighed again. Bell was making sense, but he still wasn't buying into it.

"Alright, Jimmy. Let's say I believe you. What then? Where does that leave us? Who killed Ramos, and who's trying to frame Walker?"

"Honestly, I don't know. But we weren't very thorough in that hotel room. We just kind of took the knife, bullshitted with the guys, and left. The answer could still be there."

"I suppose it wouldn't hurt to go back. There could be something we missed."

"It's definitely worth a—"

Bell never got a chance to finish. The door burst open and a uniformed officer rushed in, clutching a phone to his chest.

"We've got two murder victims in the parking structure in Disney Springs; you two need to get there now!"

"How long ago did it happen?" LeCarre asked, hopping to his feet.

"Not long. Twenty minutes, maybe."

"Suspects?"

"Two. A Hispanic man named Hector Lynch, and some kid named Reginald Habstermeister. Both found injured and unconscious at the scene. Looks like there was a hell of a scuffle. There's damage to the nearby vehicles and blood everywhere."

"Habstermeister...." LeCarre wondered aloud. "Why's that name sound so familiar?"

"Because," Bell answered hesitantly. "It's Habst. Charlie Walker's pet informant."

LeCarre stood up straight, with the air of a man who's sure he's been right all along.

"Framed, my ass, Jimmy. This is no coincidence."

Y OU'VE GOT TO BE FUCKING KIDDING ME," Victoria snarled into her phone, causing Charlie and Kalani to take notice.

They had been driving to Bay Lake Tower, intending to head up to the scene of Charlie's final confrontation with Spencer Holloway, when Victoria had received a call from one of her contacts at the CIA. Charlie and Kalani had exchanged nervous glances; a call from the Company couldn't be good.

Victoria hung up.

"What was that about?" Charlie asked.

Victoria sighed and shook her head slowly.

"We should have gone to your friend when he called."

Charlie sat up and leaned forward, staring directly at her face, but she wouldn't meet his gaze.

"Habst? What happened to him?" he asked.

"He was found unconscious in a parking structure in Disney Springs—along with Vega and the bodies of a man and a woman."

"Goddamn it."

She stared straight ahead and didn't speak.

"Get us over there!" Charlie barked.

"No," she quavered.

"Why?" Charlie asked, trying to remain calm.

"It's too late to worry about Habst and Vega. The local cops have them in custody now. What are we going to do, go over there and start shooting the police? Do we try the CIA transfer thing again and hope they don't arrest us? No. We can't do anything for them. *Yet.*"

Charlie sighed. He didn't like it, but he knew Victoria was right. The only way out was forward.

"So we go to Bay Lake Tower—" he began.

"—and finish what we started," Victoria declared.

▼▲▼

"Annie, I need access to villa eighty-four sixteen. Can you make that happen?" Charlie asked the shy girl working the check-in desk.

"Oh, uh, Mr. Walker, uh, yeah. I can do that," she stammered without glancing up at him. She began tapping keys.

Charlie shot a glance back at Victoria and Kalani, impatient and worried. They returned it with identical looks of their own. Theirs was not a good situation to be in.

"Oh, uh, Mr. Walker? I can't actually give you access. Um, there's, uh, Guests staying in the room currently."

She looked up nervously.

Charlie paused and thought for a moment before responding.

"What name is the room booked under?"

Annie leaned in close to the screen.

"Looks like it's booked under the name 'Katherine Violet.' Is that someone you know?"

Charlie sighed and threw another quick glance at Victoria before turning back to the flustered Cast Member and giving her his detective face—polite, but all business.

"Katherine and Violet are the names of my daughters. That room is registered under a fake name; there's probably nobody staying in it. And if there is, it's someone I'd *really* like to have a few words with. Can you get us in? As a favor to me?"

Annie blushed, paled, returned to normal and squeaked, "Yeah."

"Thank you. I won't forget this," Charlie promised as he took a room card from her. "And call me Charlie."

"Okay, Charlie," Annie assented with a shy smile.

Charlie smiled back as he turned to leave but paused and looked back over his shoulder.

"Oh, and Annie? Don't tell anyone you saw me here. At least not for a few days, okay?"

She nodded vigorously and he walked away, headed for the elevators.

▼▲▼

"That girl has a *wild* crush on you, Walker," Victoria teased as they ascended the tower in the elevator.

"You think?" Charlie asked, considering it. "Old man's still got it...."

"Old man?" Victoria laughed. "You can't even be thirty-five yet."

Charlie simply shrugged.

"You two are both wrong. She wasn't staring at no *haole*. She was looking at me," Kalani boasted.

Charlie gave another shrug, with a nod this time.

Before there could be more boasting or teasing, the door to the elevators slid open and the three stepped out.

Charlie nervously glanced around. He didn't necessarily sense danger, but this entire building always gave him an uncomfortable feeling. As he reached the door to the villa, his sense of unease grew.

He glanced down to see a "Do Not Disturb" sign on the handle.

He leaned in close and placed his ear to the door. He remained silent for a long while, listening for any sounds of occupancy. The door was on the thicker side, but generally if the room was occupied, some sound would eventually filter through. Charlie heard no such sound.

"Sounds empty," he whispered.

With a shrug, he scanned the card, unlocked the door and began to turn the handle. Slowly, he began to open the door, but something in his periphery caused him to immediately freeze.

The door was open only an inch but barely visible near the floor was a line of thin black monofilament. It was sheer luck that a ray of natural light happened to reflect off the line and catch Charlie's eye.

"Shit," Charlie muttered, frozen.

"What?" Victoria asked.

"Trap. Kalani, give me your knife."

Kalani hesitantly handed over his tactical folding knife.

"You sure, *braddah*?" he asked.

"Yep. Look, the line is being pushed by the edge of the door. That's telling me it's activating something rather than deactivating something, if you know what I mean."

"A bomb?" the big Hawaiian asked.

"I don't think so," Charlie shrugged, wedging his foot against the bottom of the door. He knelt and held the knife over the line.

"Maybe you guys should take a couple of steps back, just in case," he suggested.

"Just cut the damn line already, Walker," Victoria snapped, urging him on with an impatient gesture.

He cut it.

And they all survived.

The door swung loosely inward until it thumped against something hard and came to a stop. Charlie looked up to notice that the closing mechanism at the top of the door had been disabled, allowing the door to swing freely without automatically shutting.

There was just enough room for Charlie to squeeze through and, when he made it inside and saw what the door was resting against, he nearly gasped.

He knew the door was trapped, but he'd never seen anything quite like this.

Standing on an elaborate tripod was a sort of vice clamp holding what appeared to be a well-used double-barrel shotgun, with the barrels sawn off to just an inch or so. A device made of several pulleys connected the monofilament from the wall near the floor to both triggers of the weapon, where the line was looped around in a slipknot, ready to fire both barrels into whatever unlucky bastard tried to open the door. With the hair triggers and shortened barrels, had Charlie opened the door another inch, he, Victoria, and Kalani would have been shredded to pieces by the close-quarters blast.

"Unbelievable," he muttered, staring at the weapon.

"What is it?" Kalani asked from the hallway. "Let us in, little man, I'm getting bored."

Snapping out of his daze, Charlie carefully swiveled the shotgun away from the door and moved the tripod so that they could enter.

"Jesus Christ," Victoria gasped. "What kind of person comes up with something like that?"

"I'm pretty sure you have a full dossier and psych evaluation on that exact kind of person sitting in the Navigator," Charlie offered.

"Fair enough," she agreed.

"Streak's still intact, though," Charlie joked, handing Kalani's knife back to him.

"What streak?"

"Every time I've entered a Grand Villa here, someone has tried to kill me."

Even though the joke was dark, Victoria and Kalani managed to laugh. It was the truth, after all.

"They haven't succeeded yet," Victoria pointed out. "You're lucky."

"I'll consider myself lucky when crazy people stop trying to kill me," Charlie countered. "Well, let's have a look around, eh? Stay frosty in case of more traps."

Victoria and Kalani nodded their assent and the trio made their way deeper into the room.

Over the three years since Charlie had last been in the room, not much had changed. The furniture was still in the same place, the décor largely untouched. The only difference was that the window through which Holloway had traveled to meet his end had been masterfully replaced.

After ten minutes of careful searching, they'd found nothing. No clues. No traps. Nothing so much as a single bedspread wrinkled.

Nothing at all.

"What the hell?" Charlie said, finally breaking the silence. "Nothing?"

"What was the point of this?" Kalani asked. "Did she think that the trap would take us out?"

"I don't think so. There's more to this," Victoria stated.

"What do we do?" Kalani asked. He was getting irritated; there hadn't yet been anyone to hit or shoot and it was starting get on his nerves. Thinking and mind games were Charlie and Victoria's jurisdiction—he needed to put a bullet or a fist into somebody *soon*.

"We look at the only clue we have: that fucked up shotgun mechanism," Charlie told them.

"Better than nothing," Victoria agreed.

Charlie made his way over to the trap and carefully turned the spindle on the vice clamp to remove the gun from its cradle.

For all appearances, it looked like any other well-used firearm. Old— maybe two decades or more. There were smooth spots on the grip and stock where the lacquered finish had been worn down to almost bare wood.

So, someone's prized shotgun then.

Charlie carefully examined the barrels. The edge of each was bright raw metal, too new to have been like that for very long. Someone had sawn off the barrels recently.

Turning the rifle over in his hands, Charlie was surprised to find initials engraved in the stock.

"S.H.," he read aloud.

"S.H.?" Victoria repeated. "Spencer Holloway?"

"Who else could it be?" Charlie asked.

"Sherlock Holmes," Kalani snapped from across the room, leaning against a wall with his arms crossed. "Stephen Hawking, Salma Hayek, Sammy Hagar—it could be *anybody*. How is this helping us?"

"What's the matter with you?" Victoria asked him.

"What's the matter?" he repeated. "We're getting our asses handed to us here, Vee. This Thirteen bitch is fucking with us, and we're just playing the game. Meanwhile, Vega and Charlie's friend are hurt and in police custody, and here we are trying to figure out some coded initials that might or might not lead to anything."

"We're trying, Big Kahuna," Victoria soothed, trying to calm him down. She understood his frustration. Someone was planning to kill them and every friend they had. It upset him that he couldn't face that threat head on. "I know it sucks, but we have to play her stupid game if we're going to find her."

"What if there's another trap?" he asked. "And then another? And another? How far do we go? Until it kills one of us?"

"We're on guard now. We can—"

"Fuck that," Kalani spat, heading for Charlie like a bull. "I'm not doing it."

Charlie remained silent, but instinctively took a half step back with his right foot to adjust his center of gravity.

Kalani reached out and snatched the shotgun from Charlie. The ex-detective didn't even attempt to hang on to it.

"I'm sick of mind games," Kalani growled.

Then he pointed the weapon out into the villa and pulled both triggers at once.

Neither Charlie nor Victoria flinched and, as it turned out, neither of them would have had much reason to.

Instead of the percussive blast of two shotgun shells discharging at once, there was a small pop, akin to a firecracker.

Nothing in the room was destroyed.

"Squib loads?" Charlie asked, bewildered.

"No," Kalani said, turning to them. "Look."

He held the weapon out to them.

Protruding from the barrels were twin flags on telescoping poles. It was like something out of a cartoon. Something that shouldn't be a part of real life.

"What the hell is going on?" Charlie wondered aloud, taking a step forward to examine the flags.

Both flags were identical, their meaning not immediately clear.

Stylized cartoon drawings of a farmhouse emblazoned both flags.

And that was it.

"What does it mean?" Victoria asked.

"It's just a house," Kalani guessed.

"No, it's more than that. I just can't remember why," Charlie said, pinching the bridge of his nose. "I know that house. It's here on Disney property somewhere."

"Is it the haunted one?" Victoria hazarded a guess.

Charlie glanced at her. "Not even close."

For a few moments, Victoria and Kalani were silent, letting Charlie work his way through his memories to find the location of this farmhouse.

"Wait!" Charlie exclaimed, startling both Victoria and Kalani. "The Land!"

"The what?" Kalani asked.

"Living with the Land," Charlie expanded, looking at his friends expectantly.

"No idea what that is, buddy," Kalani offered, as kindly as he could.

Charlie finally remembered that he was the only Disney nerd in the room, and realized he had to explain himself.

"It's a ride at EPCOT Center," he began. "A slow boat ride that takes you through some greenhouses and other agricultural stuff, but that's not important right now. The point is the farmhouse."

"What is it, and what's so special about it?" Victoria asked.

"As far as I know, nothing. It's a fake farmhouse early in the ride. But it has a kind of cult following on the internet."

"You serious?" Kalani asked.

"Dead serious. Last year Habst showed me this Reddit post that popped up from some guy claiming to have been Disney Security. I'd never heard of him, or any of these 'black polo and khakis' guys he talks about; and I run the show—so you'd think I'd know. But anyway, in the article, he explains that this farmhouse was actually a front for some kind of undercover child abduction ring. He claimed that there was some sort of sacrificial altar inside and that a door led down a set of stairs to some cells filled with old toys and other messed-up stuff. I'm paraphrasing, obviously, but you get the picture."

"Jesus," Victoria said in disgust. "Did you ever check it out?"

Charlie laughed.

"Really? Vee, I have killed *actual* terrorists in this place. Do you think I'm going to waste time going to see if there's a kidnapping cult hiding beneath a boat ride?"

"I just meant, did you ever go in the house to see what's there?"

"No. Habst wanted to go, but I wouldn't let him. And, shockingly, he actually listens to me when I ask him not to do things these days… for the most part."

"Looks like we're going in there now," Kalani concluded.

Charlie sighed—Kalani was right.

SIXTEEN

VEGA REGAINED CONSCIOUSNESS SLOWLY. He was in a small room—a cell—and he was not alone. On the adjacent cot lay Habst, still unconscious. And leaning against the wall was a gruff man in his mid-forties with a five-o'clock shadow and the telltale look of someone who hadn't slept in days.

"Good morning, Mr. Lynch," the man greeted.

Vega sat up.

"That isn't my name," he admitted immediately, rubbing his sore neck. His head ached worse than he could remember and he had a little trouble hearing out of one of his ears. All in all, he was alive, and he recalled every detail of his fight with the tattooed Brit. What seemed, at first glance, to be nothing more than a wiry tattooed hipster had actually turned out to be one of the most ruthless fighters he'd ever faced—and Vega had paid dearly for his underestimation.

*I will kill that son of a bitch if I ever get out of here,* he promised himself.

"Really? Then who are you?" asked the detective, not without a generous helping of condescension.

"Special Agent Hector Vega, field operator with the Central Intelligence Agency," he stated, matter-of-factly.

"A Company man, huh?" the man laughed. "We've been getting all sorts of you guys through the station lately. You wouldn't happen to know the bitch that came through here earlier, would you?"

Before Vega could mask it, he perked up at the mention of a previous Company agent. This man must have been referring to Victoria—there couldn't have been anyone else.

Surprisingly, the man stood straight up and cocked his head at Vega, clearly noticing his reaction.

"What did she look like?" Vega asked, already knowing.

"Dark hair, tits on full display, barking orders like she owned the place. Big-ass Hawaiian guy following her around. Familiar?" the man told him.

Vega was surprised that he'd given him any details at all.

"Yeah, I know her. That's Victoria Holloway. My boss. And Kalani. Two of my closest friends. Members of my team. *Mi familia*."

The man nodded.

"Well, your *familia* stole a murder suspect from me."

"We have that power," Vega informed him with a shrug.

"You do," the man agreed. "However, that suspect was part of an ongoing investigation. And they took him before we were legally obligated to release him."

"You didn't charge him, eh?" Vega asked, and the man looked offended.

"He was a murder suspect and—"

"Uh huh," Vega cut him off, rubbing the back of his neck. "But you didn't charge him. And you willfully let him go. Which means you didn't have anything concrete. But what do I know? I'm just a lowly Disney Maintenance grunt."

Vega smiled, tasting blood in his mouth and hoping it showed through his teeth.

The man took a threatening step toward him but Vega didn't move a millimeter.

"What do you know about Charlie Walker?" he asked, simmering.

"The man is a goddamned American hero," Vega declared, knowing it would enrage the man further.

"You think you're just going to walk out of here?" the man snarled, violently stabbing a finger toward the door behind him. "You're going to tell me every fucking thing you know about Charlie Walker and then you're going to prison for the murder of those two people. You think saying you're with the CIA is a get-out-of-jail-free card? I'll—"

Vega held up one finger and it silenced the man. For some reason, he still had his Company-modified Apple Watch. They hadn't taken it from him. *Idiots.*

He tapped the screen a few times, looked up at the livid man and simply said, "Yup."

The man looked completely flabbergasted. Vega almost felt bad for him.

Within thirty seconds, there was a knock at the cell door. A young officer entered.

"Detective LeCarre," the younger man said. "This just came in."

He handed the detective a piece of paper and Vega smiled as the messenger hurried out the door as quickly as he'd come in.

LeCarre's face reddened as Vega watched him read and reread the paper.

"What'cha got there?" Vega asked playfully, lifting his chin and pretending to peer over the paper.

"A request for the immediate release of Special Agent Hector Vega and Mr. Reginald Habstermeister."

For a split second, Vega had the mental image of LeCarre's hair bursting into flames and steam billowing out of his ears and nostrils. It took everything he had not to laugh.

Vega faked a gasp. "No way! Does it say anything else?" he asked, already knowing.

"Upon release, Special Agent Vega and Mr. Habstermeister are to be driven to a location of their specification within twenty miles of their current position," LeCarre read aloud, still fuming.

"That's interesting, huh?" Vega said, looking exaggeratedly perplexed.

"What did you do?" asked LeCarre, letting the hand holding the paper fall to his side, forgotten.

"You should be asking what *you* did," Vega told him. "You left me with a smartwatch. Come on. This device should have been removed before I was put in this cell. What *I* did is unimportant. What matters is, I am a law enforcement agent just like yourself, but unfortunately for you, I outrank you. I sent a quick distress code to my support at Langley. Those guys are scary good. Also, they have templates for letters exactly like the one you have in your hand. You think this is the first time a Company operative was detained while carrying out his duty? Not even close. Oh, don't forget to read the small print at the bottom where you can win a free trip to Gitmo just for telling anyone I was here."

Something in LeCarre's manner changed. He seemed to visibly deflate. The rage and helplessness disappeared and all that showed through was defeat. He sat down heavily on the cot across from Vega, near Habst's feet.

"Why are you here—why are any of you here? What does the CIA want with Charlie Walker?" he asked, quietly.

Vega considered this. His opportunity had come to clear Charlie's name, but he would be breaking protocol. On the other hand, this could exacerbate Charlie's situation if he didn't play it right.

Vega sighed.

"We want to help him," Vega admitted truthfully, testing the waters.

"Help him *what*?" LeCarre asked.

"Help him stay alive. Charlie and his family are in a bad spot and it's kind of our fault."

"I really don't understand," LeCarre told him, all of his malice replaced by genuine exhausted curiosity. Vega almost felt bad for him again.

"You remember those 'terrorists' Charlie fought a few years back—Chaos Squad?"

"I helped catalogue the bodies."

"Right. Well, they weren't exactly terrorists. They were ex-mercenaries hired to abduct Charlie's family and eventually kill them if their boss gave the word. That situation is irrelevant, but what really matters is that the team of twelve mercenaries had actually been a team of *thirteen*."

"We only discovered twelve bodies other than Holloway," LeCarre recounted.

"Exactly. The thirteenth? She'd been off doing her own thing since a few years before that, when she'd abruptly parted ways with Chaos Squad. Now, this thirteenth member, we only found out about her after the attack, but we dismissed her because she hadn't been seen in years. We shouldn't have done that."

"Why? Who is she?"

Vega paused. He was giving away too much sensitive information, but at this point he was too far along not to let this detective in on everything.

"Her name is Rebecca Jane Altamont. She calls herself Thirteen for obvious reasons."

"What does she want with Walker?"

"She says she wants him dead. And she wants my team dead. Even though I wasn't with them during the Holloway situation, she wants me dead. And, more importantly, she wants Charlie's entire family to die before him. She wants all of us to pay for the loss of her friends."

"You believe her?" LeCarre asked, leaning forward.

Vega nodded. "I do. Last year, everyone involved with the Chaos Squad situation woke up to a note from Thirteen in their bedrooms. All on the same night. In the notes, she explained that at some point in the future, she would come for us. All of us. And that she'd make us suffer.

"Nobody knows how she got in or out. Everyone's doors and windows were locked from the inside. I only know two things for sure: she's batshit crazy, and her team are top-notch professionals."

LeCarre pinched the bridge of his nose.

"How good?" he asked.

"You see this?" Vega gestured to the bruises that he assumed must be forming on his face. "I was a Ranger before I was discharged and joined X-ray Team. I know more ways to kill a person with my bare hands than you know song lyrics. And that little asshole she had with her in the parking garage fucking took me apart. He systematically dismantled me. I've never been so thoroughly disassembled in my life. They are *very* good."

LeCarre nodded.

"Why were you on that rooftop?" he asked.

"Charlie asked me to be there. He said Habst had overheard a woman talking about killing people that had gotten on her nerves. Habst had followed them. He'd tried to intervene when she attacked that couple, but by the time I'd found them, the couple was dead and they were beating the hell out of Habst. I drew my weapon on them, but like I said, they lit me up before I even realized what was happening. Put us both to sleep and disappeared. Next thing I knew, I was here.

"Listen, I know I'm pissing you off, but we're on the same side. Me, you, Habst, Charlie, my team—all of us. I tried like hell to save that couple but I was just too late. I couldn't even help my friend."

Vega gestured to Habst.

LeCarre nodded in understanding.

"Did you get a good look at the two of them?" he asked.

"I did. *We* did. And we did you one better than that. We marked them up. Thirteen now has a nasty split lip, and her manfriend has a knife wound to the thigh courtesy of Habst. Your perp had to have lost some blood on that rooftop. I suggest having it sampled, but it's your show."

LeCarre leaned back against the wall, staring at the ceiling, lost deep in thought. Vega understood; this was a lot for anyone to process, let alone the man who was building a case *against* Charlie Walker. He let the detective take the time he needed.

Eventually, LeCarre took a few deep breaths, sighed, and looked Vega straight in the eye.

"She framed Walker for Ramos' murder, didn't she?" he asked, dejected, already knowing the answer.

Vega nodded in confirmation.

"Full disclosure," Vega began, "I was sent down here to keep an eye on the Walkers; to make sure that they'd be protected when Thirteen eventually carried out her plan. I can tell you, with one-hundred percent certainty, that Charlie Walker did not kill Martin Ramos.

"I'll level with you; Martin Ramos was a world-class dickhead. Nobody liked him. *Nobody*. Except for Charlie Walker. That's just the kind of guy he is. He can see the best in people even when nobody else can. There'd be times when Charlie would learn that Martin had been down at the Springs drinking before a shift and, instead of firing him, he'd put him in the Security office watching cameras looking for some MacGuffin that would never come—all so he could sober up and keep his job."

"But it was Walker's knife that killed him—his daughter's prints were on it," LeCarre interjected.

"Which daughter?" Vega asked, out of genuine curiosity.

"Violet. It was an almost perfect print match."

"Not surprising. Like I said, Thirteen and her team are ghosts. Breaking into the Walker's house and lifting Charlie's pocketknife would be entry-level stuff for them. Getting Vi's prints on it would only be a matter of swinging by her bedroom on their way out of the house. I think that part was her idea of a joke. She was fucking with you—with all of us. Showing off."

LeCarre looked lost for a moment. He glanced around the room, not searching for anything in particular; he just couldn't meet Vega's eyes.

"That knife is missing from the evidence lockup," LeCarre admitted quietly. "A lab tech informed me ten minutes ago."

"Victoria took it, right? They had an evidence box with them earlier."

The detective shook his head and sighed.

"I made sure it wasn't in that box. I wanted more time with it."

Vega paused.

"Thirteen took that knife," he told LeCarre plainly. "I already told you that her people are ghosts. I don't know why they took it, but she must have plans for it."

LeCarre didn't speak

"I should have listened to Jimmy," he said to the wall.

"Who's Jimmy?"

"Jimmy Bell, my partner. He wasn't convinced. He knew Walker was being set up."

"Smart guy."

"He is, and he deserves a better partner."

Vega shrugged.

"But what I don't understand is, why would this Thirteen frame Walker? If she's so good at this stuff, she had to know any charges wouldn't stick to him."

"I think she does know. I just think she wanted Charlie out of the game for a little while."

"Why?"

"Because Charlie is the reason twelve of her closest friends are in the ground. He is the reason that their bomb never went off in the park and no civilians died. He is the reason the most ruthless band of private military contractors on the planet were reduced to dead amateurs. He humiliated her, and I think she means to make up for that."

"Another attack?" LeCarre asked, Bell's warning from earlier ringing true.

"We think so."

"Jesus Christ," the detective exclaimed, leaping to his feet, causing Habst to stir. LeCarre turned and opened the cell door.

Vega closed his eyes and sighed in relief; the fake Company letterhead he'd sent to the station had actually worked. It was a longshot, but it had paid off. He'd gotten the detective on their side.

"What do we do?" LeCarre asked.

Vega stood and locked eyes with the detective before answering.

"We help Charlie."

# SEVENTEEN

HEY, WE NEED TO MEET, ASAP, the text read. It was from Vega.

*Hector?* Charlie wondered. *How in the hell is he texting me? Isn't he locked up?*

Kind of busy. What's up? Charlie replied. By the way, aren't you in jail?

Habst and I got out. And anything you've got going on can wait. Trust me, this is huge. Meet us at Jock's. 20 minutes.

"Habst and Vega got out of jail," Charlie told Victoria and Kalani.

"What? How?" Victoria asked.

"Didn't say. Just said that we need to meet them at Jock's in twenty and that it's important. You think this is legitimate, or is it a trap?"

"Those detectives want you bad—it could be a trap."

"Vee, it's Hector," Kalani cut in. "If he needs us, we should go."

"But if this is just those detectives *using* Vega to nab Charlie, then we're all fucked."

"He's family, Vee...."

Charlie took a deep breath. It seemed as if the world was in no mood to be his friend today and, in that case, he'd at least make himself a worthwhile enemy.

"Fuck it, let's go," he decided. "Turn here."

Victoria looked over at him.

"Really?"

"I'm sick of running and hiding. Go to Jock's, let's get this over with, whatever it is."

Victoria replied with a quick nod and headed off in the direction of the Springs.

▼▲▼

Seventeen minutes later, Charlie, Victoria, and Kalani stood outside Jock Lindsey's Hangar Bar in Disney Springs. Charlie was a big fan of the place, but he couldn't help feeling an incredible sense of dread as he walked through the entrance. Something about this wasn't right.

As he scanned the room, he noticed how busy it was. Even though it was a Thursday afternoon, the place was already packed with vacationers drinking before heading out to one of the Springs' many restaurants.

He caught no sign of Habst or Vega in the main room, so he decided to head out onto the patio, which was themed like an old-timey steam-powered riverboat. Sure enough, Habst and Vega were there.

Along with the two detectives who'd been hunting him.

It was a trap.

"Shit," Charlie grunted, cutting a quick about-face and heading back into the bar. "Trap! Move, *move!*" he hissed at Victoria and Kalani and tried to usher them in the opposite direction.

It was too late; Vega had seen him.

"Charlie, Vee, wait!" he shouted, springing to his feet and heading after them. Strangely, the detectives and Habst remained seated and simply watched.

Vega caught up with him and Charlie stopped. Nowhere to run; the place was probably surrounded.

"What the hell is this, Hector?" Charlie growled with a sweeping gesture toward the detectives. "You killed us, man—*all* of us!—you know that?"

Charlie stepped directly up into Vega's face.

"It's not like that, I promise," Vega pleaded, hands up in a placating gesture.

Charlie bristled, not convinced.

"Then what is it like? Those assholes are trying to put me away for a murder I didn't commit, and you helped them. We weren't *done*, Vega. We didn't find them."

"Charlie," Vega whispered calmly, "they're here to *help* us."

*Help?* Charlie wondered. *Help how? By putting the dangerous serial killer, Charlie Walker, behind bars for the rest of his life?*

Without a word, Charlie brushed past Vega and strode directly up to the detectives. He took a seat on the bench beside them and sighed heavily.

"Here I am. You've caught me. What now?" he asked them, point-blank.

LeCarre laughed lightly and spread his hands in an exaggerated shrug.

"You tell me, boss. It's your show."

Charlie cocked his head to the side.

"What?" he asked simply.

"After your buddy Vega woke up back at the station, we had a little talk.

He explained your situation to me. All of it."

"*All* of it?"

"All of it. I know about the mercenaries, and I know about Thirteen. Before you start to worry: I've dropped all charges against you. Your name is now legally clear. I've also dispatched black-and-whites to patrol your neighborhood. I know you've got Company people with your wife and kids, but more backup is never a bad thing. I apologize for being an asshole. I was careless and impatient, and Thirteen took advantage of it."

"Are you being serious right now?" Charlie asked. "You sure you're not just going to whip out some flex cuffs and throw me in a cruiser?"

LeCarre pretended to consider this.

"Seventy-thirty," he joked, tipping his hand from side to side like scales.

"I'll take those odds."

They both laughed, but Charlie's mood faded as soon as he got his first good look at Habst. The kid was hurt, and it was brutally obvious. He sat almost completely upright, arm clenched protectively over his belly, dark bruises forming on his face and arms. Whatever he and Vega had gotten into, it hadn't ended well for either of them. Habst wasn't a trained special operator; he didn't wear his wounds as well as Vega, and Charlie felt for him.

"Habst, you all right?" he asked, leaning toward his friend.

Habst grinned.

"Couple of busted ribs, maybe, but I'll live. You should see the other guy."

Charlie grinned back.

"You mess him up good?"

Habst recoiled exaggeratedly.

"Oh hell no, the guy beat the living shit out of me *and* Hector. I was just saying that you should see him. Lots of tattoos, super-tight pants, stupid Disney gang vest. He's a real sight. Fucking hipster douchebag."

Charlie laughed.

"You get a good look at the girl he was with—Thirteen?"

"Oh yeah. Smokin' hot. Well, *before* Hector put his knee through her face. You should see her though, dude. Red hair, big ole round ass, perfect titties. If it wasn't for her boyfriend stomping me into a paste I'd have had a full tent pole situation happening.

"Focus," Charlie chided, snapping his fingers a couple of times. "Remember, she's trying to kill us all."

Habst faked a disgusted look.

"Doesn't mean she can't look good doing it."

Charlie grinned and shook his head in incredulity.

"You know, I always thought getting your ass kicked would maybe level you out a little bit. Turns out you're still a dickhead."

Laughter burst out of Habst and Charlie chuckled too. But Habst's laughter quickly turned into a sharp cough.

"Aw, don't make me laugh, dude," Habst said, laughing, coughing, and then spitting over the railing into the water. "Hurts."

"Don't worry, man. We're gonna get 'em."

Habst nodded. He could see that familiar look coming over Charlie. He'd always called it 'savage calm.' It was the look Charlie got every time he was centering himself in preparation for doing something super badass.

"I know," Habst agreed. "If there's one guy in the entire world they should be worried about, it's you. I'm fucking good, and you've never let me get away with shit."

Charlie grinned.

"Maybe you're just not as good as you think," he joked.

Habst shrugged.

Charlie turned toward LeCarre and Bell. Victoria and Kalani had joined them with Vega and were sitting beside the detectives.

"So, here we are," he declared, palms out. "Two cops, two civilians, and three CIA operatives. We have to catch a batshit crazy ex-mercenary murderer and her team of psychopathic hipsters before they hurt anyone else—and we have almost no information to go on. Sound like fun?"

"Well, when you put it like that…." Kalani mused.

"What have you been up to since you left the station this morning?" Bell asked, hoping Charlie had any sort of lead.

Charlie filled them in on where they'd been and what they'd done as quickly as he could. When he finished, both Bell and LeCarre looked embarrassed and a little ashamed for not finding the clues left by Thirteen at the crime scene.

"It's okay, gentlemen," Charlie told them. "You had the weapon. That's ninety-five percent of a case. I understand. However, that's a dead end. I know where we need to go next, and now that my name is clear, I can get us there."

"Where?" LeCarre asked, leaning forward.

"We're going to ride a ride at EPCOT Center," he stated with a grin.

# EIGHTEEN

WHEN APRIL'S PHONE RANG, it startled her.

She let out a little yelp and Violet and Katie both laughed, since she'd collapsed the Jenga tower they'd been building for the last fifteen minutes.

"Son of a bitch," she moaned, looking at the ruin of tiny rectangular blocks that lay on the table before her. She pulled her phone out of her back pocket.

It was Vega.

She desperately fumbled for the answer button, the game forgotten.

"Hector?"

"*Hola*, ghost," Vega said.

"What happened to you?" she rasped. "It's been hours!"

Vega chuckled.

"That is a very long story. And I'll tell you everything, but not now. There isn't time. Let's just say that I've met Thirteen and one of her people, and I paid for underestimating them."

April tilted her head and grinned.

"You get your ass kicked?" she asked.

"I got my ass kicked, and then I got *arrested*," he told her, laughing. "But everything's alright. I didn't get hurt too badly, I found Habst, *and* I got Charlie's name cleared. A couple of bruises is a small price to pay."

April was impressed.

"Are you coming back?" she asked. "I miss your face."

"I miss your face, too, but no. I've got to go with Charlie and some cops. They found a clue that might get us closer to catching Thirteen. Vee and Kalani are here, too."

April winced, but she understood. They were both Company operatives, and their duty came before all else. Even each other. It was the nature of the beast—but it was the life they both chose to live.

"Where are you headed?"

"Epcot," he chuckled. "Charlie Walker refuses to stop dragging Company agents into Disney parks.""And you're not bringing me along?" she asked, feigning offense. "You're a shameful excuse for a boyfriend, Hector Vega."

"No argument from me," he admitted. "But I've got to go, we're almost there. I just wanted to hear your voice for a little bit."

She felt her eyes tearing up, but blinked the tears away before they could fall.

"Be safe, *vato*," she pleaded.

He laughed, and then hesitated.

April listened to the silence for a moment before he spoke again.

"I love you."

It was the first time he'd ever said it. She didn't know how to react.

"I love you, too."

They disconnected, but April's mood had suddenly fallen to a record low.

If Hector felt the need to tell her he loved her like this, he must have thought there was a serious chance he may never see her again.

And it scared her to death.

The tears fell then, and there was nothing she could do.

# NINETEEN

NEED A WEAPON. Who has something for me?" Charlie asked impatiently, looking around the Navigator.

"Just got this stupid thing. I figure I can let a dumb *haole* like you have it," Kalani offered, with a wink.

He opened the glove compartment and handed Charlie a Wilson Combat Rapid Response folding knife. All matte black, sleek curves, and sharp edges. Charlie loved it. It was a more-than-adequate replacement for the Microtech that wasn't in the evidence box Victoria had taken from the station.

"Damn, Big Kahuna, this thing's mean."

Kalani nodded.

"I've got a present for you, too," Vega announced. "Asked Victoria to bring it down. Is it here?" he asked her.

"Under the back bench," Victoria told him.

Vega reached under the seat and felt around until he found what he was looking for. With a flourish, he produced a black plastic case with two steel latches and handed it to Charlie.

Charlie opened it and found a futuristic black handgun, three loaded magazines, and a black Kydex holster inside, complete with a matching magazine carrier.

"I know you love your Walther," Vega announced. "So we brought you an upgrade."

Charlie raised his eyebrows.

"Walther PPS M2 LE," Vega went on. "An updated redesign of the original model you carry. Better grip ergonomics, front and rear slide serrations, and a stronger mag release. Familiar, but better. It's not for sale to the public yet, but you know the CIA has its ways. And the Company gunsmiths have made some modifications. Hybrid tritium and fiber optic night sights, full Talon grip wrap, guide rod recoil reduction system, and it's loaded with one hundred fifteen grain low-recoil hollow point rounds."

Charlie whistled.

"Damn, Hector, this thing's mean," he said with the exact same inflection he'd used with Kalani.

He inspected the weapon, inserted a magazine, chambered a round, and was pleasantly satisfied. The action was smooth, everything was solid, the sights glowed like lasers, and the redesigned grip was beyond comfortable, especially with the rubberized Talon wrap. He did love his old Walther, but this new model was something else.

"*Gracias, esé*," Charlie said with a slight bow of his head.

"We're here," Victoria called out from the driver's seat. "Where should we park?"

"Head right up to the front by the bag check. I'm about to pull rank," Charlie replied with a smirk.

After a quick chat with a nearby Security officer, they left the car right where Charlie told them—with LeCarre and Bell parking behind them—and headed toward the bag check. Since none of them carried a bag, they waltzed right through. When they reached the gates, Charlie approached a Cast Member he recognized and explained their situation.

As far as the Cast Member needed to know, Charlie was escorting several law enforcement agents through the park for an unscheduled inspection—which was, more or less, the truth.

Within moments, they were inside EPCOT Center.

▼▲▼

"So what *are* we doing here?" Habst asked Carlie as they walked past Spaceship Earth toward the nexus of Future World.

"Promise you're going to be chill about it when I tell you?"

"Yeah, but my promises aren't usually worth much. So, sure. Fuck it. I promise," Habst grinned.

"We're going into the farmhouse in Living with the Land."

Habst's jaw dropped. "Wait, what?! We're actually going into the farmhouse?" Habst asked excitedly.

"That's what it looks like," Charlie agreed.

"Man, I've wanted to do this for a *long* time!"

"A year," Charlie pointed out. "That's a long time to you?"

"Year's a long time when you're a free spirit blowing in the wind," Habst joked.

"Right. The only thing ever blowing in the wind around you is a vapor cloud from a pound or two of weed."

"*Allegedly*," Habst corrected, with a glance at all the police and CIA operatives around him, and Charlie laughed.

"But seriously, man, you should wait outside," Charlie told him.

"What? Why?" Habst argued.

"Look at you. You look like you fell off the Monorail again. There could be traps in there. There probably *are* traps. This could get you killed."

Habst looked offended.

"Everybody's got to die sometime, right? I'm fine, man. And besides, I didn't *fall* off the Monorail. I was *carried.*"

"Whatever. You know what I'm trying to say. This is about to get real and I don't want you to pay for my mistakes. If I miss something—some... detail—you could get hurt. I can't have that, man," Charlie offered, honestly.

"You aren't my dad. You don't have to protect me. I've been through shit, too. And I've got to see this for myself. Even if there's nothing there, I've got to see it."

Charlie stared at Habst for a few moments as they walked. Then he nodded.

"Okay. But there will be someone with a gun in front of and behind you at all times. And you will touch *nothing*. You feel me?"

"How can I feel you without arms, Charlie?" Habst asked, tucking his arms behind his back, agreeing in his own bizarre way.

Charlie laughed and shook his head in exasperation.

▼▲▼

When they finally reached Living with the Land, Charlie approached one of the Cast Members working the ride.

"Hey, Mr. Walker!" the kid exclaimed, surprised and nervous to see the head of Security. "What can I do for you?"

"Listen, Andy," Charlie said, politely, "I need a boat for just me and my friends. After we board, I need you to change how you're loading. Send two empty boats, then one with Guests. Keep it going like that until we get back. Do you understand?"

"Are you getting off?" Andy asked.

"Yes. We'll be getting off to make a security inspection. That's why I need those boats to be empty—we'll need a ride back. And we can't have anyone see us get on or off the boat."

"We can just shut the ride down until you're finished," Andy suggested. "It's not been very busy tonight."

"No," Charlie disagreed. "It has to stay open and nobody can know. Understand?"

Andy looked nervous, but refused to turn down the head of Security for the entire resort.

"Definitely. I can make that happen for you."

"You're the best," Charlie told him, placing a hand on his shoulder. "I'll make sure you get a few extra vacation days if this goes smoothly."

Before long, they were off.It took less than five minutes to reach the farmhouse, but the slow pace and uncertainty of what lie ahead ground on Charlie's nerves. He was worried about what he'd find. He'd read through the Reddit post the previous year when Habst had shown it to him, but he'd simply laughed and shrugged it off as being written by someone with an overactive imagination gunning for a handful of upvotes and a little viral attention. The more he thought about it, however, the more he couldn't shake the feeling that Thirteen had been planning this and that the story held some grain of truth—that it was something she'd fabricated.

He began to mentally kick himself for not investigating it before, but the idea was so farfetched that he couldn't be faulted for thinking it wasn't real. What mattered now was making it through whatever lay beyond that unassuming front door. Whatever it was, he was ready for it. His family's lives depended on it.

"Okay, we're good. Move," Charlie commanded.Hurriedly, everyone stepped off the moving craft and onto the "lawn" in front of the house. Charlie drew his sidearm and held it at low-ready, hoping he wouldn't need it.

He ran low and fast to the steps. Carefully, he stepped around the animatronic dog, opened the screen door, and knelt before the front door, examining the handle. He was about to say that nothing seemed out of the ordinary when something at the door's seam caught his eye.

Upon closer inspection, Charlie noticed a bead of clear silicone sealant that ran around all four of the door's edges, effectively sealing it shut.

"What...." Charlie breathed as he leaned in close to inspect it more thoroughly.

"What is it?" Victoria asked.

"Sealant," he told her. "Someone wanted this room airtight. The rest of these set pieces are ancient, but this looks newish."

"I don't like this," Kalani said to no one in particular. "What would they want to seal in there?"

Ignoring Kalani, Vega spoke up, "You know, I remember hearing some guys from Custodial talking about cleaning show areas. They hit what Guests can see and then they move on—"

"—so they'd have no reason to even attempt to open this door," Charlie finished.

Carefully, he tested the handle, and it turned smoothly—with no lock—but the door did not open, most likely held in place by the sealant.

"Here's my guess," Charlie began with a deep sigh. "Whatever's in there has been there over a year. That post you showed me, Habst—that was Thirteen, or one of her boys. They're fucking with us. They knew I wouldn't go in back then, and they knew I wouldn't let you or anyone else go either. Whatever this is, it's an insult. It's a show of power. She's telling me I could have stopped this over a year ago."

Before anyone else could speak, they heard a full boat approaching.

"Fuck it," Charlie declared, holstering his weapon.

He turned the handle again, put his shoulder into the door and the sealant gave way with ease.

Then he took a step into hell on earth.

# TWENTY

**T**HAT'S THE FIFTH TIME I've seen them go by in the last fifteen minutes," Meghan said, watching a police cruiser slowly roll past the house. "What are they doing?"

"Watching," McCoy told her.

"Why?"

"Because they believe you now," April said, sitting on the couch and slowly running the blade of her knife along a whetstone. "Vega cleared Charlie's name. He must have done it well because it looks like they're making damn sure this place is secure."

"At least that's one less thing to worry about," Meghan agreed, dropping onto the loveseat next to Jen-Jen.

"Why does this stuff keep happening?" she asked, after a few moments of silence.

"What—terrorists, mercenaries, death threats? Stuff like that?" Jen-Jen asked in reply.

"Yep, pretty much that."

"Well, honey, I hate to break it to you, but your husband is a famous bad-guy killer and most of your friends are CIA special operators."

With a sad smile, Meghan nodded. Then she laughed, and a single tear rolled down her cheek which she quickly wiped away, hoping no one would notice.

"Sometimes I just wish we had a normal life."

"You don't mean that," Jen-Jen told her. "I know it's dangerous, but look at all the good things. You're a blazing hottie." She winked. "You've got Charlie, who's honestly lucky to have you. You've got Zeus, who is the world's biggest baby. You've got a couple of super weird-ass kids—"

"Hey!" cried both girls in unison, to which Jen-Jen only winked again and the girls giggled.

"—and you basically live in frigging Disney World. So what if the CIA has to come and kill a couple mercenaries every now and then?" Jen-Jen finished, nudging Meghan in the ribs.

Meghan couldn't help but laugh. To have her bizarre life laid out for her so plainly actually helped her to feel better.

"You know, now that you put it like—"

And the front door violently exploded inward, showering everyone in the room with splinters of wood and shards of glass.

"Move!" McCoy yelled, his gun already drawn. He fired two shots into the smoke that obscured the front doorway while April and Jen-Jen pulled Meghan and the girls deeper into the house, toward the stairs to the second floor.

McCoy rounded the corner in a hurry, followed immediately by two grenades that landed heavily on the floor behind him.

In too much shock to move, Meghan stared at the grenades, eyes wide, as McCoy pushed her further toward the stairs, kicking one of the grenades back in the direction it came from.

"Meghan! Close your—" someone yelled from behind her, but it was too late.

When the grenades exploded, it was as if the entire world ignited in brilliant white flame. The thunderous noise combined with the extraordinary whiteness of the detonations immediately blinded and nearly deafened her. She felt no pain, but she could feel impacts on the backs of her ankles from being dragged up the stairs by someone—probably McCoy.

How had he survived the explosions? Through the intense ringing in her ears, she could just make out what sounded like gunfire. She could feel flecks of debris hitting her face and arms, but she still felt no pain.

Had she been paralyzed? Could shrapnel have hit her spine?

If it had, then it would have ripped through McCoy to get there; he was between her and the grenades when they went off. If that had happened, how had he carried her up the stairs? No, it had to be something else.

Through the confusion, blindness, ringing, and disorientation, Meghan felt an extreme sense of nausea welling up.

Her vision was nothing but a hot white void, though she could feel some of the ringing in her ears subsiding—she almost wished it wasn't.

What she thought had been gunfire was indeed gunfire—and a lot of it. She could hear fully automatic weapons firing from somewhere far to her left—though it sounded less sharp than she expected—and answering fire coming from somewhere much closer.

She heard a man cry out in pain and prayed that it wasn't McCoy.

"Barricade, now!" Jen-Jen yelled, and Meghan heard something heavy slam onto the floor not far from where she lay.

Some of the gunfire had become muffled, and she assumed that X-ray Team had tipped the nearby bookcase in front of the staircase for cover. Meghan knew the wood would never stop a bullet, so she assumed X-ray was using it to hide themselves from view and block easy access.

*Smart*, she thought. *That staircase is the only way to get up here.*

"How many did we get?" she heard April ask quietly after the gunfire ceased.

"One," McCoy replied.

"Did you get a full headcount?" Jen-Jen asked.

"No," he replied.

"Fuck," Jen-Jen gasped. "Girls, you alright?"

"Yeah," Meghan heard her daughters confirm, and let out a breath she didn't know she'd been holding. *The girls were okay!*

"My ears are ringing bad, though," Violet said, irritated. "And I dropped my phone down there."

"Sorry, little one, it's theirs now," Jen-Jen said, sadly.

"At least Zeus was already up here," Katie said, and Meghan heard the jangling of his tags as he stalked around, growling low and trying his best to protect his people from this unknown threat.

"Where the hell did they go?" April asked. "And I don't want to be a buzzkill or anything, but ammo is finite. We can't survive another back-and-forth like that on what we've got."

"Dad's guns," Katie suggested.

"Yeah, he's got guns and bullets in a locker in the bedroom," Violet agreed.

"McCoy, you got the stairs covered?" Jen-Jen asked.

McCoy grunted in reply.

"Good, we're going to check the windows and then load up Charlie's weapons. Don't let them up those stairs."

"Is Mom okay?" Meghan heard Katie ask. She tried to speak, but still couldn't manage anything.

"Yeah, honey, she's okay. She was real close to those flashbangs down there so she's going to feel pretty sick for a little while, but I promise she's okay."

*Flashbangs*, she thought, glad that she wasn't paralyzed. *Jesus, that's what they're really like?*

After a few minutes of silence the ringing in her ears was nearly gone, and her vision was almost fully restored. She sat up against the wall and sighed lightly. McCoy turned and caught her eye. He gave her a quick nod before returning his attention to the staircase. It was the most concern she'd ever seen him show for her.

The girls quietly hurried over and hugged her, whispering that they were glad she was okay.

Jen-Jen and April came back with several loaded guns from Charlie's locker and enough ammo to fight a small war—which may well have been the case.

The two CIA agents knelt on the floor beside Meghan and addressed everyone.

"I've got bad news, and worse news," Jen-Jen announced. "The bad news? We are under siege by an unknown number of enemy combatants, and none of us made it up here with any communications devices. There could be one guy down there, or twenty, and we'd never know without going down—and that would mean certain death. They could be inside the house, or outside looking for another way to get at us."

Meghan sighed again. "And what's the worse news?"

"The worse news is that your front door isn't visible from the street. So, unless those cops rolling by decide to get curious and come up for a chat, they'll never know what's happening."

"What about the gunshots? The explosions? Surely one of the neighbors must have heard."

"Maybe, but I don't think so," April said. "I know it didn't sound like it, but those guys were using suppressors. And these houses are *really* nice. Not only are they relatively far from each other, but they're well insulated and probably have some sort of sound-dampening to keep out the noise of the local fireworks. The neighbors *might* have heard, but I wouldn't bet our lives on it. It's safest to assume we're on our own here."

"Damn," was all Meghan could think of in reply.

They all heard the slight crunch of a boot on glass coming from somewhere downstairs, and McCoy risked a glance over their makeshift barricade. After a moment, he knelt down and shook his head.

It was going to be a long night.

# TWENTY-ONE

MMEDIATELY, CHARLIE WAS STRUCK by the putrid scent of old death.
Of rot.
Of decay.

Musty, humid, and overwhelming, the unmistakable aroma of long-forgotten human remains assaulted Charlie's nostrils for the first time in many years.

But this was like nothing he'd ever experienced before.

This was worse.

This was hell.

"Jesus Christ," he choked, backing out of the farmhouse.

No longer caring about the ever-nearing boat full of Guests, he stepped back onto the porch, coughing.

"Jesus fucking Christ," he spat.

He was met with a chorus of confusion and curiosity. Everyone spoke at once and it overwhelmed him.

"What is it, man?" Habst barked, excitedly. He tried to slip around his friend, but Charlie placed a hand on his chest and shoved him back.

"No," Charlie said. "Not yet."

"What did you see, Walker?" demanded LeCarre.

Charlie blocked the room from view, refusing to let anyone enter.

"What's in there, Charlie?" Victoria asked, sternly.

"Someone give me a flashlight," Charlie requested, doing his best to remain calm. "Anyone have one?"

Kalani turned on a surprisingly bright penlight and handed it over.

Steeling himself, Charlie shone the light into the farmhouse.

The room was small, maybe the size of a standard bedroom, and mostly barren—aside from the four desiccated corpses lying haphazardly on the floor.

Their throats had been slit from ear to ear. Charlie could see the faint traces of large amounts of long-dried blood. It terrified him.

He stepped inside, kneeling before the largest of the four corpses. It was naked, and had been dead for so long that it was nearly mummified. Judging by its size, it had been an adult male. The form lying next to it had been a woman, perhaps the man's wife. And nearby lay the small forms of what had once been two children, probably not much older than his daughters.

"Mother*fucker*," Charlie growled, rage welling up inside him. "What kind of monster—"

"My god," Victoria breathed. "Oh my god…."

Charlie hadn't heard her approach, but there was nothing he could do. He let her inside. She knelt and put a hand on his shoulder.

"Charlie, I—" she began, but Charlie cut her off.

"I'm going to kill her, Vee," he said, quietly and plainly. "I'm going to make her pay for this."

Victoria didn't speak, just looked her friend in the eyes in the glow of the penlight. After a few moments, she nodded.

Charlie stood and shined the penlight around the rest of the room before the beam came to rest on a small wooden table neatly displayed against the back wall. A dusty package sat atop it in the form of a plain cardboard box. Angrily, he snatched the package from its resting place, toppling the small table in the process, and stormed out of the farmhouse, violently shoving the screen door open and nearly dripping over the animatronic dog on his way.

"Walker, what—?" began LeCarre, but Charlie thrust the penlight into his hand and made his way to the large tree with the swing and sat on the floor. Fishing his knife from his pocket, he flicked the blade out and cut open the package. Only then did he notice it said "Walker" atop it in dried blood, most likely the blood of the family that lay dead and forgotten inside the farmhouse for the past year.

He reached inside and found only a single item: a brown leather wallet.

Opening it, he glanced through its contents, noting that no cash or cards had been taken. Finally, his eyes landed on the ID.

Confused, Charlie read and reread every word on the driver's license. It was an unremarkable ID except for one detail. He recognized the man's name, but he'd never seen the face.

The name on the ID was of a former Westfield, Massachusetts resident named Robert Murphy. "Big Ginger Bobby"—or "Murph" as he was known among the Magic Kingdom staff. A massive red-haired Irishman, Murph was known for being quick with a joke, hot-tempered, and one hell of a bowler.

Except the man on the ID wasn't big or ginger at all. The man on the card was a short, thin black man with a shaved head, a well-trimmed goatee and large brown eyes. It took only a second for the facts to click into place.

"No...."

"What is it?" Victoria asked, sitting cross-legged in front of him.

Charlie handed her the ID.

"Go inside, tell me if this ID belongs to that man," he said calmly. Then he closed his eyes and leaned his head back against the tree.

For a while he waited, eyes closed, not paying attention to the raised voices coming from Habst, Vega, and the detectives. Not paying attention to the alarmed voices of Guests as a boat came and went. Flashes of light turned his darkened eyelids red momentarily as Guests took photos of the strange group of people. After a few moments, he heard someone sit in front of him and, upon opening his eyes, found that Victoria had returned. She handed him the ID.

"It's him," she confirmed. "Who is he?"

Charlie sighed deeply.

"I don't know," he admitted. "The Robert Murphy from Massachusetts that I know is a big Irish white guy with flaming red hair. Works at the Magic Kingdom."

Charlie leaned forward and stared into Victoria's eyes, waiting for her to make the connection.

"Oh, Jesus Christ, Charlie. Are you saying the guy you know killed this man and his family and took his place?"

Charlie nodded grimly.

"He showed up right around the time those people would have died. Vee, this guy has met my wife and kids. He's been inside my house. Hell, Habst and Hector know him. He's been a fake the entire time and none of us had any idea."

"What's his family like? His wife and kids?" she asked.

"I don't know if he even has any. Never really had an opportunity to meet them."

"This is insane. Shit like this just doesn't happen in real life," Victoria said. "I've seen some messed-up things in my line of work, but this is ice cold."

LeCarre approached and knelt by them.

"I've never seen anything like this," he admitted. "And I honestly don't know what to do."

"Call it in," Charlie recommended. "Those poor people have been in there long enough. The least we can do is make arrangements for them. I'll organize the shutdown of the attraction and have the CMs assist your people with anything they need."

LeCarre nodded and took a few steps away from them, pulling out his cell phone.

Charlie stood and made his way over to the house where Habst and Bell sat next to each other, each of them looking as white as a ghost. Kalani and Vega were inside the house and seemed to be scouring every inch of the place looking for clues.

"Is this what it's like?" Bell asked Charlie. The young detective's eyes were red, and his breathing was choppy. Habst stayed abnormally—but respectfully—silent, head down.

"It's sad, but this is how it is sometimes. And it's never easy."

"They were just kids, man," Bell said, just speaking without a real point. Charlie thought the man might be in shock.

"Monsters are real," Charlie told him.

"I've seen some sick things, Mr. Walker, but nothing like this. Who even thinks of something like that?"

"I know exactly who thinks of something like that. And when we find her, I'm going to—I'm going to make sure she goes away for a long time."

Then Bell surprised him. He suddenly stood and leaned in close to Charlie.

"This isn't right," he whispered aggressively. "We can't arrest her. With her resources and what she's capable of, I don't think there's a prison in existence that can hold her. It's crazy that I'm even thinking this, but it's up to us to make sure she doesn't get that far."

"Be very sure about what you're saying, Detective," Charlie warned in an equally aggressive whisper. "That's a road that only goes one way."

Bell looked him in the eyes and nodded.

"You guys killed Holloway and those mercenaries," he countered.

"They didn't give us any other choice. We *can* choose this time."

"What's the plan then—find her and let me slap some cuffs on her? Drive her down to the station? Put her in a holding cell?"

Charlie looked Bell square in the eyes for a long moment, getting the measure of the man. The young detective held his gaze.

"No," Charlie said, finally. "Choice or no choice, Thirteen is dead."

Bell closed his eyes and nodded. He was on Charlie's side, whether his partner was or not.

"So, what now?" Victoria cut in. "This isn't much of a clue."

"Sure it is," Charlie said, looking at the ID. "Thirteen is telling us to go to Murph's house."

"So, is that where we're going?"

"No," he said. "That is obviously a trap. A trap that, if we survive, will have another vague clue for us to find. I'm done playing her game—at least by her rules, anyway. Let's rewrite the rules."

"How?"

"We're going to see Murph in person at work."

"Why the hell would he be at work?" Bell asked.

"Why *wouldn't* he be there?" Charlie asked in reply. "Think about it. If Murphy doesn't show up for work tonight, I'll be notified—for some reason, I get emails about all absences. Thirteen will know that and I don't think she'd risk anything that could tip me off. Murph *will* be there. I'd imagine she plans to call him and tell him to bail once she's gotten us. And I bet she plans on us biting the dust at Murph's house."

"If he really is at work then he's not alone," Victoria offered. "And whoever's with him will be looking for you. We'll have no idea who they are."

"I don't care. We're going to find him, and I'm going to beat him until he tells us where Thirteen is. I'll kill anyone who tries to stop me. I'm tired, Vee, and I'm sick of playing games."

"You make it sound so easy," Victoria joked.

Charlie checked his watch.

"This time of day, the parks are relatively crowded. Gives us a good opportunity to get to him unnoticed. We should go grab him now—it's our best chance."

"You're the boss," Victoria told him. "Detective, you good with this?" she asked Bell.

"I'm good with whatever ends this," he said, with a glance over his shoulder at LeCarre.

"Then let's go get this motherfucker," Charlie growled.

# TWENTY-TWO

GRADUALLY, A STINGING, burning pain revealed itself near Meghan's left ankle. When she glanced down, she noticed a small shard of ceramic sticking out of her skin an inch or so above her heel.

"Damn," she said, inspecting the wound. The shock of the flashbangs must have worn off. Until now, she hadn't noticed that she'd been hurt.

"What's up?" April whispered, sitting close to Meghan and sharpening her knife once more.

Meghan nodded her head toward her ankle.

"Yikes," April gasped in mock surprise. "I can get you fixed up," she offered, reaching into the bag slung over her shoulder and pulling out a small red case. From this, she withdrew a roll of gauze, some tape, and some alcohol.

Within a few minutes, the ceramic had been removed, and the wound cleaned, sterilized, and expertly bandaged.

"Thanks, April," Meghan said, rotating her ankle to get a good look at the girl's handiwork.

"Marksman and medic," she muttered, with a shrug. "April of all trades."

"Marksmedic," Meghan joked.

April snorted a laugh that startled Zeus out of his nap. The big shepherd sighed, walked into the nearby bathroom, and went back to sleep immediately.

"I'm glad you're here," Meghan told April.

April glanced up at her briefly, but did not reply. For a split second, she looked like a vulnerable little girl and it reminded Meghan of her daughters. She wasn't used to seeing this side of X-ray Team's members.

After a few moments of silence, April finally spoke.

"You think they're okay?" she asked, referring to Charlie, Habst, and the other half of X-ray.

"We're under siege and you're worrying about *them*?"

April shrugged.

"We haven't heard from them in a long time. What if they were attacked, too?"

Meghan considered it.

"Well, if I had to pick any two people in the world capable of holding off an ambush on Disney property, it's Charlie and Victoria." Meghan's tone softened, "Hector will be okay."

"I hope you're right," April replied faintly.

Just then, a small creak came from Katie's bedroom at the far end of the hall. April's head swiveled toward the source of the noise, but McCoy was already on the move. His gun was leveled at the darkened doorway, and without hesitation, he disappeared inside.

Within seconds, the sharp report of a single gunshot rang out, followed by a meaty *thud* as a body hit the floor. A moment later, a suppressed assault rifle slid out into the hallway, followed by a pistol and a knife. McCoy reappeared shortly after, wiping a few droplets of blood from his face. Smoke still curled from the barrel of his gun.

"Company," he told April and Jen-Jen.

"How many," Jen-Jen asked.

"One," McCoy replied.

"Dead?"

McCoy grinned as he shook his head—the mercenary was still alive.

Jen-Jen stood and drew her knife, matching McCoy's wicked grin with one of her own.

"Let's have a little fun."

▼▲▼

Jen-Jen and McCoy stepped into Katie's bedroom and Jen-Jen clicked on a small lamp near the door. Immediately, her eye was drawn to the window, where an entire pane of glass had been silently removed using a diamond-tipped cutter that lay on the sill. She felt a momentary pang of regret as she noticed a bright red spray of blood had ruined a stuffed unicorn and coated the side of a night table near the bed. She made a mental note to get a replacement when this was all over.

The intruder lay in a slowly spreading puddle of his own blood, hands bound behind his back with a set of flex cuffs. McCoy had put a bullet directly through the man's left kneecap. He'd live, but he'd forever walk with a severe limp even if he found the best surgeon on earth for the repair job.

"Tsk, tsk," Jen-Jen scolded, kneeling before the man and casually tapping the flat of her knife blade against his Kevlar vest. "You're not their best guy, are you?"

The man tried to spit in her face, but nothing came out. He was losing fluids quickly.

McCoy gave the man a solid kick to the ribs for his trouble but, to their surprise, he did not cry out.

"Tough," Jen-Jen noted, half mocking him. "That's alright. I've met tough guys before."

Jen-Jen stared at him for a three-count before speaking again.

"Okay. You know why I'm here, you know why he's here, and you know why this knife is here. How about this? Let's skip all the clichéd movie threats and the 'I'm not tellin' you shit, lady' nonsense and have an adult conversation."

The man glared at her, still trying to look tough and intense despite his worsening wound.

"How many of you are left? Lie to me and I'll know."

The intruder said nothing.

Jen-Jen took a deep breath.

"Alright, that's how you're playing it. I'm going to ask that same question again, and if you don't answer me, I'm just going to start cutting shit off you. I'm taking everything that I can reach. And I feel like you're about to act tough again and test me, so I've already picked out my first part. So, after you're done screaming, you'll tell me."

"Cliché," McCoy whispered with a small chuckle. Jen-Jen ignored him.

"How many of you are left?" she asked the man again.

As she'd suspected, he stayed silent.

So she took his left ear.

It happened quickly. She reached in, grabbed a hold of the ear, and sliced it off in one clean motion.

And, as she'd suspected, he screamed.

*Good*, she thought. *Let them hear him outside.*

"Hello? Can you hear me?" she asked, speaking into his severed ear.

She laughed and casually tossed the man's ear onto his chest.

"So, now that we know who's who and what's what, maybe we can have a more insightful conversation. Keep in mind: I already have my next part picked out. And don't worry, it isn't another ear. I'll still need you to hear me. How many of you are left?"

For a split second, the intruder looked as if he might rebel again, but after Jen-Jen leaned forward with the knife, he broke.

"Three!" he blubbered through the pain. "There are… three more outside. Bloody hell… you lunatic!"

He spoke with an English accent, which she found interesting, but she filed that detail away for later.

"Five-man team," she noted aloud. "Who's in charge?"

The man glanced nervously from side to side, but answered.

"Guy named Montgomery."

"That a first name or a last name?" she asked.

"First name," he replied quickly.

"Then give me his last name," Jen-Jen demanded, slapping him lightly across the cheek.

"Summers."

"Your hit team is being led by a man named Montgomery Summers?" Jen-Jen asked, stifling a laugh. She grinned back at McCoy who also looked to be on the verge of cracking up.

"Laugh all you want... he'll kill you for this," the man insisted.

This time Jen-Jen did laugh.

"I promise ole Monty Summers will get his shot. But it'll end a little differently than you think. Anyway, back to business. What are your other three mates up to out there, guv'nor?" Jen-Jen asked, in an awful mockery of his accent.

"They were waiting for me... to make it inside. Once I drew your fire toward this room... they'd come round the other side of the house in the confusion."

Jen-Jen turned to McCoy. "You hear that? Get April and make damn certain that side of the house is clear. I can handle this asshole."

McCoy disappeared with a nod.

"Dead or alive?" she asked the man once McCoy had gone.

A look of confusion came over his face. She attributed it to blood loss.

"What?" he asked, his face paling and his comprehension fading.

"Were you going to try to take us dead or alive?" she elaborated.

He sighed.

"You, your friend, and the scary little girl with the knife: didn't matter either way," he admitted. "The wife and the two little girls were to be taken alive. And they still will be. When Summers comes in here, he'll—"

Rapidly, Jen-Jen placed a hand over his mouth, turned his head, and buried her knife to the hilt in the soft spot near the base of his skull. His light was extinguished immediately and the blood seeping from his wounds slowed to a stop.

She didn't need him anymore. The picture he'd painted was clear enough.

X-ray Team was to die, the Walkers were to be tortured.

All of them.

Even the little girls.

Although she'd just killed a man, it was the thought of those good people being tortured by these maniacs that turned her stomach.

That wasn't going to happen while she was still breathing.

She stood, left the room, and closed the door behind her, leaving the Englishman's cooling corpse behind.

▼▲▼

"Where's the guy that broke in?" Violet asked Jen-Jen as she made her way toward the other side of the house, where April and McCoy were checking to make sure nobody was cutting their way in.

"Sleeping," she lied, even though she knew the girl was far too smart to believe it. In a gesture far beyond her years, Violet didn't reply, only gave a somber nod of her head.

"Don't worry, little bird," Jen-Jen tried to reassure her. "This will all be over soon."

She winced.

Even to her own ears, Jen-Jen thought that sounded ominous.

"What can you see?" she asked when she found April carefully peering out a window in Meghan's office.

"Nothing. I can *hear* them, and I know they're out there, but I can't see them. These guys are good. If we don't think of something soon, we might be in trouble."

April sighed.

"We should close all the blinds," Jen-Jen suggested. "At least that way, we would hear them if they tried to break in."

April nodded. "Any warning is better than none."

It took them only a few moments to close all the blinds upstairs and, by the time they were finished, it was almost as dark as night. The only light came from the cracks around the blinds and a few lamps they'd brought into the hall.

"That should help," Jen-Jen commented. "And now we—" At that moment, the lights snapped off and the house was plunged into darkness. The assault team had cut the power.

Violet or Katie yelped from the hallway, but other than that, the house was deathly silent.

"That's not good," posited April.

"Nope," Jen-Jen agreed with a sigh.

Just as she and April reentered the hallway, the situation went from bad to worse.

From every direction, they were assaulted by the nightmarish sound of panes of glass shattering. First upstairs on the west side of the house, then downstairs to the south, then upstairs on the east. It went on for almost a full minute, sound never coming from the same place twice.

Then silence.

"What the fuck was that?" April whispered, craning her neck to make sure Meghan and the kids were still okay.

"That, my dear," Jen-Jen began, slowly drawing her sidearm, "was the sound of every window in the house breaking. This is bad."

Heavy footsteps sounded from almost every direction, upstairs and down. There were only three assailants left, but this coordinated attack made numbers irrelevant. If they couldn't see their attackers, and were unable to tell which direction they were coming from, they couldn't defend themselves.

Something came whistling out of a doorway at the end of the hall and struck April in the neck.

"What...?" she stammered, before slumping against the wall and sliding to the floor.

McCoy hurdled over the bookcase and launched himself down the stairs, attempting to catch any attackers off guard, but was struck by two projectiles and was unconscious by the time he hit the bottom of the staircase.

Jen-Jen brought her pistol to bear, but was struck in the left hip, then twice in the chest. She went down hard on her right side.

Slowly, a figure emerged from the bedroom at the end of the hall, stepping past Violet and Katie and headed toward Meghan. Meghan crawled toward Jen-Jen's dropped weapon, but the shadowy figure spoke.

"I wouldn't do that if I were you, miss."

Meghan ignored the voice and kept moving toward the pistol. She heard a metallic rasp as the shadow reloaded his weapon.

"I'd hate to have to splatter your pretty face across these walls," he threatened.

"Careful," another man warned, appearing behind the first. "We need her alive—for now."

"Relax, Summers, I'm just having a little fun."

Meghan stopped crawling. She caught Violet's eye and nodded.

"Zeus, hit!" Violet yelled, and the big German shepherd launched himself out of the darkened bathroom. He latched onto the figure's vest and dragged him to the ground.

"*Hit, hit, hit!*" Violet yelled.

The dog savaged the figure, causing the man's weapon to skitter away down the hall. He did everything he could to defend himself, but it did him no good—Zeus was too powerful. The man raised a forearm to hold the shepherd back, and Meghan swore she could hear the bones crunch as Zeus bit down with brutal force.

Just when Meghan had reached Jen-Jen's pistol and retrieved it, two small pops sounded out and Zeus stumbled dizzily away from the battered, but still breathing, attacker—weakly snapping at him as he went. Zeus staggered a few more uneasy steps, lightly rebounded off the wall, and then went down next to April.

Meghan tried to raise the pistol but two more pops sounded and she felt a stinging pain in her chest and shoulder. The last thing she saw before she started to fade was Violet and Katie kneeling with their hands in the air as two men dressed in black tactical gear moved swiftly toward them, futuristic pistols in hand.

She tried to call out to them but her voice wouldn't obey. Still trying to raise the weapon that now seemed to weigh thousands of pounds, she lost consciousness.

# TWENTY-THREE

"YOU'RE GETTING OLD, ALFIE," Thirteen teased, lightly pressing an icepack to her lip.

"Old," he scoffed. "Are you not the one nursing a split lip? You couldn't even be bothered to get up and help me."

"Please," she shot back. "You got stabbed by a stoner."

Alfie grimaced just then, but Thirteen couldn't tell if it was from the jibe or from the needle he'd just jammed into his thigh.

He sat on a sofa in an executive suite at the Swan, pants slung over the back of a chair, stitching up the knife wound in his leg.

"If you hadn't noticed, I was having a deep conversation with that Central Intelligence chap."

"Yeah, yeah," Thirteen purred, tossing the icepack onto the table and reaching for the bottle of gin she'd been nursing on and off for the past fifteen minutes. "Anyway, great idea to teach those two freaks a lesson. We really came out on top, there."

She took a long pull from the bottle.

"You may want to go easy on that, darling. We've still got a long night ahead of us."

"Don't you remind me about our night," Thirteen warned with a reasonable amount of venom. "Listening to you almost ruined this entire operation. What would have happened if that CIA asshole just shot you?"

"He didn't."

"I know he fucking didn't, Alfie! But what if he had? What if—because *you* thought it would be fun to kill a couple of idiots—this entire operation had been blown? What then? Do you even give a shit about all the work that went into this? All the money? All the time?"

Alfie suddenly became very focused on stitching up his injury, and didn't look at her as he spoke.

"We came out of it alright," he said quietly.

Thirteen jumped to her feet and slammed her bottle onto the table. She stormed over to where Alfie sat and glared down at him, one hand on her hip.

"Look at me when you talk to me, you fucking coward."

Alfie tied off his final stitch, cut the filament, and stood.

Only then did he turn his gaze toward her.

"I am," he said calmly, towering over her.

"Do I fucking look like I came out of that alright?" she rasped, gesturing to her lip. "How do I explain where this came from if some curious good Samaritan cares to ask? How do I—"

Alfie's hand shot out and clamped around her throat and he lifted her up onto her toes. He stared into her eyes and saw the fire there. It made him nervous, as it always did, but he loved it.

"It adds character," he pointed out, hand still clinched around her throat. "Get over it."

With his other hand, he slapped her hard across the cheek, then shoved her roughly away.

For a moment, he thought she may draw her pistol and shoot him dead, but then a wide grin broke out on her face and she charged him. Her lips pressed hard against his and he let himself be pushed back down onto the sofa.

Thirteen slid on top of him.

"Let me tell *you* how this evening is going to go," she growled.

# TWENTY-FOUR

JUST AS CHARLIE HAD EXPECTED, the crowds were starting to thicken as they made their way into the Magic Kingdom.

"I need to swing by my office, check Murph's schedule. Vee, why don't you take Vega, Kalani, and Bell, and see if you can put eyes on the bastard. If you do, shadow him. I'll take Habst with me."

LeCarre had stayed behind at Epcot to coordinate with the authorities he'd called in. Bell had told him they were going to Murph's house to see if there were any leads to follow up on and that they'd contact him before they made any other moves. Charlie expected LeCarre to protest, or at least be suspicious, but the man was visibly distracted and agreed without argument.

"I can dig it," Kalani chimed in, looking at Victoria for confirmation.

"Agreed," she declared with a nod. Bell stepped forward and asked in a low voice, "What are we going to do with him when we find him?"

"I'm going to ask him some questions," Charlie told him, simply. "If I like his answers, you get to put cuffs on him, stash him somewhere, and take him in when we finish with Thirteen. If I don't like his answers, or if he doesn't answer... well, then you might want to walk away for a little bit. Because I'm going to have my CIA friends ask him those same questions, and they won't be as nice as me. Then he'll go with them and the world will forget he ever existed."

Bell took a deep breath, but nodded. He was in deep now; he understood what they were up against and that there was no room left to be squeamish.

"You good with this?" Charlie asked, placing a hand on his shoulder. "You can go back with LeCarre and help out over there. Tell him I ditched you somewhere and you don't know where I am."

Bell shook his head, "No, I'm good. I'm just not used to operating like that. But it has to be done. Don't worry about me."

Charlie nodded.

"Big Kahuna, you solid?"

"Pshh," Kalani scoffed. "All day long."

Charlie looked over at Vega, who gave him a quick nod.

"Vee?" Charlie asked.

"Five by five."

"Then let's hit it," Charlie barked and headed off with the tired and injured Habst silently in tow.

▼▲▼

"You really do live for this shit, don't you?" Habst asked Charlie once they were in his office.

Habst sat in Charlie's chair as the ex-detective rifled through a couple of drawers in his filing cabinet. He hadn't told Habst what he was looking for.

"What do you mean?" Charlie asked without stopping his search.

"I mean look at you, dude. You're like a used car salesman on coke. I've never seen you with this much energy."

"I've got to finish this. We're all at risk until Thirteen is gone."

Habst lazily shook his head.

"Yeah, but you're actually *enjoying* this."

Charlie didn't answer.

"You *are*, aren't you? Man, I knew you were crazy, but I didn't know you were *this* fuckin' crazy."

Again, Charlie stayed silent and continued his search. "What's that all about? It's not for attention. Shit, you disappeared after everything with Sat-Com went down. I saw the news after you killed Holloway: they couldn't stop talking about you but they barely showed your face—so you must have dodged them left and right. So what is it?"

Suddenly, Charlie pulled something out of the back of one of the drawers and advanced on Habst.

"It's that I refuse to let innocent people get hurt because of me," he snapped, leaning over the desk for effect. "If you die—or Meghan, or the kids, or anyone on X-ray Team—it's because of me. If Thirteen is planning an attack on this place, and some poor kid loses their mom or dad—or worse, the other way around—then that's on me and I'm not fucking having it."

He flicked his wrist and a collapsible steel baton snapped open. He turned the weapon, testing its weight.

"Oh, shit," Habst sputtered, "is that the thing you hit that guy with in that YouTube video?"

"Nope. I gave that one away to someone who needed it more than I did."

"And you missed it so much you bought another one?"

Charlie laughed, "No, I took this one off a guy who thought it would be a good idea to sneak it into Hollywood Studios and kneecap the guy who's dating his ex. He got to walk out of there—eventually—and I got a new toy."

"Tricia hasn't tried to take it away from you?"

"She has *suggested* that I don't use it on the job. Same with the gun," Charlie added with a smirk.

"Is that what we came here for?" Habst asked.

Charlie shrugged. "We had extra time and I thought I might need it. Plus, we needed to check Murph's schedule. Come on, let's go."

Habst stayed in Charlie's seat.

"What's wrong?" Charlie asked, halfway out the door.

"I'm tired, man," Habst admitted, eyes cast downward. "I've definitely got some broken ribs, a loose tooth, and I'm really fucking tired. I'm going to sit this one out."

Charlie looked him over for a few moments before speaking.

"Are you sure?"

"Yeah, man. The whole commando action-hero lifestyle doesn't really suit me. Tried it earlier, didn't care for it. I'll leave that up to you and Hector and your meathead buddies."

Charlie laughed and nodded in understanding.

"I feel you. I'll call Vega and have him take you back to my house. That new girl on X-ray, April, she's a medic. She'll get you fixed up."

"Thanks, man. Hey, is she hot?"

Charlie sighed.

"Pretty sure that's Vega's woman you're talking about. You prepared to fight him?"

Habst laughed.

"He got beat up by a hipster earlier. I think my chances are okay."

Charlie couldn't help but laugh with him.

"Well, good luck with all of that," Charlie joked.

Habst nodded, leaned his head back on the chair and closed his eyes.

"I'll see you when this is over. Take care of yourself," Charlie told him, and then disappeared into the hall.

▼▲▼

On the way back to Charlie's house, in a Disney company vehicle that Charlie had gotten someone to loan them, Habst and Vega finally had the chance to talk for the first time since Habst had learned his friend was a CIA operative.

Breaking the silence that had been with them since they'd left the Magic

Kingdom, Habst laughed to himself.

"What?" Vega asked, glancing quickly toward his passenger.

Habst shook his head and grinned.

"I should have known," he declared melodramatically.

"That I was in the CIA?"

"Yep. The signs were there."

"What signs?"

"You couldn't fix a flat tire, let alone a broken ride system."

They both laughed, a great deal of tension easing.

"That's it then? You're not going to yell at me and tell me how pissed off you are that I lied to you?"

Habst laughed again.

"Are you kidding, man? Have you met Charlie? That guy will lie to your face, tell you about it a week later, and convince you it was for your own good and that it was your idea. No, dude, if I was going to get mad about secrets and lies and terrorists and all that kind of stuff I'd have moved far away from the Walkers years ago. Even their little girls are creepy supervillains."

Vega turned his head to look at Habst and, after a moment, gave him an understanding nod.

"So, we're good then?"

"Yeah, brother. We're—"

They didn't feel the first impact, it was so sudden. All they could comprehend was that gravity had come unhinged and that up and down didn't matter anymore. They were weightless and floating, surrounded by thousands of bits of shattered glass.

The second impact they felt. Hard.

The two men were thrown against their seatbelts and pulled hard to their right. Sparks flew past them and more shattered glass peppered their faces. When finally they ground to a halt, they hung in their restraints and realized that their car had been knocked onto its passenger side. Inches from Habst's face was the bare pavement.

"What the *fuck*?" Vega gasped, already attempting to free himself from his seatbelt.

Habst coughed once, pain blossoming in his wounded chest. He couldn't find the air to reply so he simply hung in place and fought the urge to pass out or vomit.

Vega freed himself, hung from the steering wheel, and lowered himself to his feet in front of Habst. He leaned down to free his friend, but the crunching sound of glass being tread on caught his attention. It had come from the far side of the car. Someone was coming.

Habst didn't know when Vega had drawn his gun, but it was in his hand when he silently stepped through the opening where the windshield had been and disappeared from view. A figure came around the hood of the vehicle, but Habst couldn't tell if it was Vega returning or if it was someone else entirely. Cautiously, he approached the opening, handgun drawn and aimed into the cabin.

Not Vega, then.

When the man came closer, Habst noticed that he wore a dark vest identical to the Brit who'd attacked them in the parking garage, but this was not the same person. This man was burlier, more muscular, and wore his black hair slicked back and shaved on the sides. He knelt on the pavement, ignored Habst, and searched the vehicle for Vega.

"Where's the driver?" he growled in little more than a whisper.

British, just like the other one.

"You just missed him," Habst coughed, spat. He pointed to his left, up and out the driver's side window. "You didn't see him? Flew straight up and out. Magic carpet, I think. This place is magical."

"Funny," the vested assailant said with a fake smile. Suddenly, his tone became exaggeratedly caring and sympathetic. "Listen, you've been in a horrible traffic collision. Your head ain't workin' right. You need an ambulance. I can understand how something like that could make your memory a little foggy, but I'll give you one more chance. See if you can remember where your friend is."

Habst opened his mouth to fire off another sarcastic reply and never regretted another decision more in his life. The moment he tried to speak, the sound of a cannon blast shocked the breath out of him and a warm, salty, coppery, gritty substance filled his mouth.

Vega was there, standing with the smoking barrel of his gun where the Englishman's head used to be. His would-be attacker was slumped against the hood of the car, dead; the contents of his head spilled across the hood, the dashboard, the spent airbags, and—to Habst's abject horror—on his own face and in his mouth.

Immediately, he vomited.

Violently.

Vega holstered his weapon, reached in, and carefully extracted Habst from where he hung from his seatbelt. He dragged him around and leaned him against the roof of the car, careful to avoid the spreading puddle of vomit. Habst threw up again, followed by dry heaves so powerful that it hurt Vega to watch.

"You alright?" Vega asked, hesitantly.

"*Am I alright?* That guy's fucking brains were in my mouth, dude!" Habst gagged again, another round of dry heaves brought on by the thought of what had just occurred.

"I'm sorry, buddy. Had to be done."

"Fuck you, Vega!" Habst grabbed the hem of his T-shirt and used it to wick away whatever blood and gray matter remained in his mouth. He violently scraped his tongue with the fabric until he accidentally gagged himself again.

"Why does this shit always happen to me?" he asked, slumping back against the car in defeat and slamming the side of his fist into the metal. "I probably have some kind of hipster kuru now."

Vega shrugged.

"Bad luck," he offered. "Very bad luck."

"No shit."

"I have a present, though," Vega said, and walked out of Habst's field of view. Within a few moments, he came back dragging a second lifeless body in a familiar black vest.

"Another dead body, dude? Come *on*," Habst complained, though he was far beyond being fazed by the sight of another corpse.

"Not dead," Vega replied with a grin. "And I'll bet he's willing to talk— but not here, we're drawing a crowd."

Habst glanced around. They *were* drawing a crowd. A handful of cars had pulled off to the side of the road, although nobody had gotten out to assist. Habst could see several of the people in the cars pointing phones toward him. Filming, he assumed.

*Great, this'll be on YouTube in ten minutes.*

He struggled to his feet and was finally able to survey the scene. The driver's side of the car was a complete wreck of twisted metal and broken glass. A large silver truck with a ram bar mounted to the front sat idling a few feet away. It was barely scratched.

"How did they find us?" Habst asked.

"I don't know," Vega admitted, hauling the unconscious man up onto his shoulder after having secured the man's ankles and hands behind his back with his own flex cuffs. "But we're going to find out."

The CIA operative nodded toward the idling truck.

"Get in. These guys owe us a ride. We'll take theirs."

Habst nodded and did as he was told.

Once inside, Vega put the truck in gear and sped off in the direction they were originally headed.

"Those people are going to call the police," Habst said.

"Probably already have. But that's good, we could use the backup. This is bigger than we thought."

Habst nodded thoughtfully, still in a sort of daze.

"Where are we going now?" he asked.

"We're still headed to Charlie's," Vega announced, but Habst could sense some tension behind his friend's words.

"That's a good thing, right?" he prodded.

Vega sighed.

"I didn't want to freak you out, but I tried to text April twice and got no reply. I have a bad feeling about what we'll be walking into."

Habst groaned, "No. I *just* left the Magic Kingdom specifically to avoid this type of stuff. And now you're saying we may be headed into action-hero shit anyway? Stop. Let me out. I'll get an Uber to the hospital where maybe I can die in peace."

Vega looked at him.

"I need you, man. I can't do this by myself. If something is happening there, then I'll need all the help I can get."

Habst thought about it. What was the worst that could happen? He could die? Hell, he'd already had another man's brains in his mouth. Dying couldn't be anywhere near as bad as *that*.

He took a deep breath, held it, then slowly let it out.

"Fine."

# TWENTY-FIVE

"WHAT TOOK YOU SO LONG?" Murph asked, his usual Irish brogue coming through thicker for effect.

He cradled his ribs on his left side and had a split lip, but he was not much worse for wear than the last time Charlie had seen him, a week or so earlier. The big Irishman sat on the floor of a Companion Restroom just outside the exit of Splash Mountain. This area of the park wasn't overpopulated, so Victoria had brought him here and notified Charlie of their location.

Charlie looked over the big redheaded man in silence.

*Should've beaten him worse*, he thought, understanding that Kalani had gone *extremely* easy on this man. He wondered whether or not Kalani had held back for Bell's benefit. The young detective stood in the corner, still seemingly ill at ease with all of this.

Murph looked up at Charlie and smiled.

"Well. On with it, then."

"You know why we're here."

"I do," he agreed with a nod. "But I'd thought you'd have been here ages ago."

"You knew we'd come for you here," Charlie stated, half a question.

"Only an idiot would have gone to my house. No, we knew you'd come for me here."

"I'm assuming by 'we' you mean you and Thirteen."

Murph shrugged.

"Me, Thirteen, and everyone else. You're predictable, *ex*-Detective."

Charlie crossed his arms.

"I'm done playing her games, Murph," he declared, calmly.

Murph chuckled, looking genuinely confused.

"Done? How could you be *done*? You haven't even gotten to the good part."

"I've been to Bay Lake Tower, I've found the bodies in The Land, I've—"

"That?" Murph interrupted. "That was a warm-up, boyo. The qualifying round. The fun stuff is yet to come." He laughed, hard.

Charlie risked a glance to his left where Victoria stood in silence. She caught his eye, but he found no reassurance there. Whatever Murph was getting at surely wasn't good.

"You think that was the *whole* game?" Murph continued. "You must be touched. Thirteen clearly thought too highly of you. The famous Detective Walker!" He roared with laughter again. "No. You haven't gotten to the best part yet."

"What are you talking about?" Charlie asked, kneeling down to Murph's eye level.

"What's the best part of *any* game, Charlie?"

Charlie remained silent.

"The prizes! Great games have great fuckin' prizes! Did you *win* anything at the hotels, or in the farmhouse? Nay, my friend, you did not."

Charlie swallowed. Suddenly, he began to worry that three members of X-ray Team weren't enough to protect Meghan and the girls. He had the overwhelming desire to simply leave without a word and rush back to them. He fought that urge, however, because more lives were at stake than just theirs, and this was his best chance to find out what was coming.

"Alright, I'm interested," Charlie said, playing along. "Talk to me about prizes. If you say I've still got to play, then what do I win?"

Murph looked comically taken aback.

"And ruin the surprise?" he asked, aghast. "I shall not. Although, I reckon I can give you a hint as to what your first game will be."

*This shit again*, Charlie thought, tiring of all of this.

"Fine. Show me."

Murph nodded toward Kalani but didn't take his eyes off Charlie.

"'The Mountain that Surfs' over there took my phone. If you'll kindly provide me with that, I can show you."

Charlie held his hand out and Kalani passed him the phone, but he didn't give it to Murph.

"Tell me how to unlock it and find what I need. If you're lying to me, I'm not handing you a chance to get a message to your people."

"Smart. Fine. To open it, you have to connect those dots on the screen in the shape of a cock and balls."

Charlie looked up at him.

"Are you serious?"

"As a fuckin' heart attack, mate," Murph spat with a curt nod.

Charlie sighed and held out the phone so that he could still see the display. "Do it."

As advertised, Murph scrawled the blocky phallic image between the dots and the phone opened onto its home screen.

"Jesus Christ," Charlie sighed, shaking his head at the absurdity of the situation. "Okay, what am I looking for?"

Murph gestured with his finger toward nothing in particular and said: "Click on 'Images & Videos'. There's a folder called 'Meghan Walker Nude'. What you're looking for is in there."

Charlie bristled, thinking Murph was joking. Yet, as ridiculous as it sounded, the folder was there. Charlie felt nervousness and frustration rising as he opened the folder. Inside was a single video clip. The thumbnail was indeed the back of a naked woman, but Charlie couldn't tell for sure who it was. With nothing left to do but proceed, he clicked play.

The video started with a close-up of a nude woman's back, just like the thumbnail image. Charlie began to feel his fury rising until the camera panned out enough to reveal a full head of red hair.

Not Meghan.

He let out an involuntary sigh of relief and hoped nobody else noticed. The woman turned toward the camera and, for the first time, Charlie got his first good look at Rebecca Jane Altamont. She stood with one arm covering her breasts and a wild smirk on her face beneath her thick-rimmed glasses. "So, you made it!" she said, a genuine smile on her face. "You found Murphy and his phone and here you are. Watching a video of a naked woman in the middle of a family theme park. That's not really something a good guy would do, is it?"

On screen, Thirteen laughed and Charlie glared up at Murph, who sat with the most innocent of smiles plastered across his face.

"Anyway, you've made it to the *really* fun stuff, now. This one won't be easy, and the prize is shit, but I'm sure you'll play anyway, because you've always got to show off. So, if you'll hand Murph his phone, we can begin."

She used the hand that had been covering her breasts to wave at him, exposing everything in the process, and the screen went blank. Momentarily confused by the overload of complete nonsense that had occurred over the past couple of minutes, he stared at the blank screen.

Until the door to the Companion Restroom banged open and he whirled around, dropping the phone.

In the doorway stood Thirteen, Alfie, and two other men in dark vests. They pointed strange-looking futuristic pistols at Charlie, Bell, and the CIA operatives.

Thirteen flexed her jaw and Charlie noticed that her lip was split—a parting gift from Vega.

"Hi, Charlie," she greeted quietly, eyes slowly glancing around the room.

Tense moments of silence passed as Charlie waited for an opportunity to disarm one of Thirteen's men. But none came, for there wasn't time.

Thirteen awkwardly seemed to snap out of a daze.

"Oh, uh, yeah. Shoot them," she ordered halfheartedly, and immediately her men began firing.

Victoria was hit in the thigh and chest, Bell directly over his heart, and Kalani was struck several times in the arms and torso.

Charlie was last, and even though he began to panic, he was oddly at peace. When the round finally took him, it was in the neck, not far from the scar left by James Holloway's bullet.

There wasn't much pain, but there was an intense, overwhelming feeling of nausea that passed as quickly as it had come. And then terrible exhaustion. His limbs weighed thousands of pounds, and he could no longer find the strength to hold them up. He began to collapse.

*This is what it feels like to die,* he thought, and then he slipped away.

# TWENTY-SIX

VEGA AND HABST ARRIVED at the Walker house to a scene of such absolute carnage that neither of them got out of the truck. Shocked into inaction, they could only look upon the disorienting display of chaos with equal amounts of horror and confusion. Something awful had happened here.

A police cruiser sat on the lawn, both front doors open wide, flashers blazing wildly, but no one inside. Every window in the Walkers' house was shattered. The front door was torn off its hinges and smoke lazily wafted its way out. Nothing but darkness could be seen through the window frames; the power must have been cut. From what they could hear, all was quiet.

"Oh my god," Habst croaked. "What happened here?"

Vega was silent. Again, his gun was in his hand before Habst could see him draw it. He ejected the magazine and counted his rounds before reinserting it into the weapon.

"This is bad, brother," Vega whispered. He leaned over and opened the glove box, checking for a weapon to give to Habst. As luck would have it, a small .22-caliber pistol lay atop the truck's papers. "Take this. Do you know how to use a gun?"

Habst held the weapon up and examined it in the glare from the streetlights.

"Just point and shoot until it goes click?"

Vega shrugged. "Yeah, pretty much."

He moved to get out of the truck, but turned back to Habst and reached for the weapon. Casually, he flicked off the safety.

"*Now* you're ready to rock," he said with a small nod.

Habst slipped out of the passenger door, attempting to smoothly make his way around the car like he always saw the action stars do in the movies, but he caught a heel on the running board and fell to his knees in the grass. With catlike reflexes, he sprang back to his feet before Vega rounded the corner.

"You good?" Habst blurted nonsensically, brushing grass off his knees. "I'm good."

Vega gave a small, slightly confused smile.

"That's great, man," he whispered, then gestured toward the house. "Business time. Stay behind me. Kill anyone you don't recognize."

"Kill them?" Habst asked. "I don't know if I can…."

"It's them or it's you. Don't let *them* make that choice for you. If it comes down to it, you empty that pistol into their center mass and don't think twice about it."

Without another word, Vega ran low and fast toward the front door. Habst struggled to keep up, but took cover opposite the darkened entryway from Vega. He'd played enough video games to know that doors and corners were the most dangerous places in a combat scenario—if that's what this was.

Vega pointed toward Habst, then to his eyes, and then to his own back.

*Watch my back.*

Habst nodded, and the pair slowly and quietly made their way across the threshold.

Once inside, the smell hit. Habst's nausea came rushing back in a heartbeat, but there was nothing left to expel.

Death.

It was a sickening charnel-house aroma that immediately overwhelmed them.

All attempts at stealth were abandoned the moment their eyes adjusted to the darkness.

It was immediately clear that Meghan, the girls, and the members of X-ray Team were gone. Or—if they were still in the house—they'd been reduced to bloody, unrecognizable remains.

Habst prayed to whatever entity would listen that Meghan and the girls were not among the dead that he and Vega were surely about to discover.

Through the haze of smoke and darkness, they could see a body sprawled in the middle of the living room carpet. But they'd smelled it long before their eyes had adjusted enough to see its shape. The coppery scent of spilled blood and fresh meat permeated the house, mixing with the aromas of spent gunpowder, cooling brass, and charred wood.

Vega pulled a small penlight from his pocket and clicked it on. Habst wished Vega had just left him in jail. This was too much.

This first body lay sprawled in the shape of da Vinci's *Vitruvian Man*, but the similarities ended where they began.

He was dressed in the tattered remnants of a suit of strange, futuristic tactical armor. He'd clearly died from the grisly gunshot wound that stared purple and angry from his cheek like a third eye. However, the horrors that had been committed to this man after his death made Habst wonder just what kind of world he lived in. Things like this simply didn't happen in real life. He hadn't been a part of the Holloway scenario, but he remembered it, and he couldn't believe anything then had been as bad as what he was seeing now.

"Look at him, Hector. Jesus Christ. What is this, man?"

"I don't know."

"This can't be real."

Vega knelt, inspecting the horrific scene.

Aside from the Kevlar vest, the man's sleeves and pant legs had been cut away. From a distance, Vega thought the man's limbs had been covered in small cuts from shards of the shattered glass that covered almost every surface in the room. Upon closer inspection, he was mortified to learn that the cuts were made deliberately by someone with a very sharp blade.

They were *words*.

Starting at the man's outstretched left arm and heading clockwise, he read.

"Once upon a time, a house of angels was beset by demons."

He moved to the right arm where the verse continued.

"Bravely they fought, and one by one fell."

Then to the right leg.

"Until the rest were carried away...."

Finally, the left leg.

"To hell."

Habst looked at his friend for reassurance, and it almost broke him to see a look of terror setting in on Vega's face.

"This is insane."

Habst was about to offer a kind word when he noticed something written on the floor above the head of the corpse. He motioned for Vega to shine his light on it.

Surprised they hadn't noticed before, the corpse's hands were pointing in either direction. Above the head, written on the carpet in blood, was one word:

CHOOSE.

Shining the light further into the room, Vega noticed that the corpse's hands were pointing to two doorways ahead of them, leading deeper into the darkened house.

Habst stood.

"We don't actually have to, do we?"

Vega sighed.

"Where did they take our friends, Habst? We have to know. We need to move forward."

"You know we're going to find some more shit like this!" he rasped, pointing toward the desecrated corpse.

"I know. But if this is one of Thirteen's games, then there will be some sort of clue."

"You do realize that Charlie almost got lit up by a fucking ancient shotgun on a tripod looking for one of those clues, right? What chance do a couple of jerks like us have? We're just begging to step into a trap, man, and you know it."

Vega turned toward Habst and lowered his voice to a particularly menacing snarl. He pointed toward the front door of the house.

"If you want to run, Habst, then run. Those people are your family—*my* family. Now, I'm going in there. And I'm going in even if there are traps, or dead bodies, or fucking zombies, or anything else this ridiculous day can throw at us, because *they* need me to. They need *us*! Now get your shit together, and let's figure this out and get these assholes."

After a pause, Habst nodded somberly.

"I'm not running, Hector. This stuff just isn't easy. This is some occult-level shit and I'm having trouble adjusting. But I'm good—I'm in. Let's do this."

Vega nodded back, satisfied that his friend was with him.

Carefully stepping over the corpse, he made his way toward the door on the left and stopped a few feet shy. He held out a hand to stop Habst.

Shining the penlight inside, Vega was only slightly surprised to find a dead police officer splayed out on the dining room table.

"Come *on*," Habst sighed.

The fact that the officer's head was missing barely registered as a shock to Habst's already-fried nervous system. Blood was everywhere. It coated almost everything.

Except....

Except part of the wall directly behind the stump of the dead man's neck.

"Vega, the wall over there," he pointed. "What is that?"

Vega illuminated the wall, and they found their clue. Or so they thought.

Written in the arterial spray of blood was another string of words.

"If your friends you wish to find, you mustn't lose your head," Habst read aloud. Something else was written below, and he took a step closer to get a better look.

"You're dead...." he read.

That was when they heard a sharp *click*, an accelerating mechanical whir, and the sound of metal grinding against metal.

"Down!" Vega shouted, throwing a shoulder into Habst and checking him to the floor.

But he wasn't quick enough to get them both out of harm's way.

From out of the darkness of the doorway to their right, a matte black circular saw blade came whistling through the air, narrowly missing the top of Habst's skull and slicing neatly across Vega's left pectoral muscle until it came to a springy, vibrating stop, embedding itself deeply into the drywall on the opposite side of the room.

Vega went down without a sound in a splash of blood.

Habst rushed to his friend, only to hear a similar *click* and the same mechanical whir. Immediately, he dropped to his stomach as another blade flew into the room, violently smashing into an armoire and shattering its contents.

"What the—!" shouted Habst. His brain was having trouble forming words to fit the absurd situation. Then he remembered Vega.

He crawled to his friend and found him breathing, but injured. The blade had cut Vega deeply across the chest, opening up a deep gash three inches across. It bled profusely, but didn't look to be life-threatening. Habst grabbed a thick cloth placemat from the floor, folded it, and pressed it to Vega's wound.

"Thanks," Vega coughed, pressing the cloth hard into his chest.

The CIA operative, bound and determined to find his friends and save Charlie's family, struggled back to his feet.

"Hector, man, we can't—"

"We chose wrong," Vega cut in. "We need to check the other room."

"What if there's another trap?"

"There probably is another trap," Vega hypothesized plainly. "Doesn't change what needs to be done."

Habst sighed, but climbed unsteadily to his feet and followed Vega back out into the front room, wary of more flying blades.

Passing the body of the man in shredded tactical gear, they followed his other hand toward another darkened room. Vega stayed clear of the doorway and shined his light in, but couldn't see much due to the angle. All he could see was a wall that led away from him. Something was written on it.

"Safe...." Vega read aloud.

"Yeah, I bet."

Vega shrugged and went in low.

Another mechanical *click* made Vega flinch and recoil, but this was no trap.

It was almost worse.

Black lights ignited and lit the room in a ghostly bluish-white glow.

The third corpse stood before them.

"Jesus Christ," Habst spat, and took a step out of the room. This was too much for him.

The second police officer stood upright, propped up by some mechanism neither man could see. Its arm held a small box out to its side. Suddenly, one of the black lights cut out—plunging the corpse's head into darkness—while another light turned on, illuminating the box in the thing's hand. Within could be seen the severed head of the first officer.

These two lights kept alternating, illuminating one head while obscuring the other in darkness.

It took Vega a few moments to realize that something was written on the floor in luminescent paint that glowed a bright fluorescent green in the glare of the UV lights.

TO FIND YOUR ANGELS, YOU MUST FOLLOW THEM TO HELL.
PLUMMET TO YOUR DEATH, AND LOOK FROM WHERE YOU FELL.
THE HEAVENS ABOVE HAVE MUCH TO TELL.

"Oh my god. Hatbox Ghost," Habst said, having reentered the room without Vega noticing.

"What?" Vega asked.

"Hatbox Ghost. Animatronic from Disneyland's Haunted Mansion. His head disappears from his shoulders and reappears in a box in his hand. That's what this is."

Vega had no clue what this Hatbox Ghost was, but it was too specific to be anything other than what Habst claimed. It was deliberate.

"Then what does this mean?" He pointed to the words on the floor.

Habst read silently for a few minutes before admitting that he didn't know.

"It has to mean something," Vega challenged. "Do any of those words have anything to do with this Hatbox Ghost?"

Habst was lost in thought for several moments before bursting out with: "Wait a minute!"

"I'm listening."

"Plummet to your death…." Habst recited.

"Yeah?"

"Well, there's a theory that at the end of the attic scene in the Haunted

Mansion, the bride pushes you out the attic window and you fall to your death. That's why the Doom Buggy turns backward and you can see the ghosts so well in the graveyard scene and, like, the caretaker and his dog are scared. You're dead—you fell to your death. You're a fucking ghost."

"But what does this have to do with this Hatbox Ghost?" Vega asked.

"Because you fall to your death right after you pass him."

"And Charlie threw Holloway out a window. He fell to his death, too."

Vega took a breath.

"Shit."

"Yeah."

"So, we have to ride this ride?"

Habst nodded grimly.

# TWENTY-SEVEN

CHARLIE STOOD ON THE EDGE of a precipice of dark stone, gazing out over a great plain. It was dusk and he was somewhere ancient and vast; perhaps Africa, perhaps somewhere else entirely. The dry yellow grass far below swayed and parted as various unidentifiable wildlife came out of their nests in preparation for a night of hunting, or took shelter to rest until morning. The sun was only now beginning to make its final descent below the horizon. Twin moons glowed red in the dying light, as if they were the eyes of some great demon watching him with malevolent interest.

This definitely wasn't Africa. This wasn't *anywhere*.

He stood in an alien land.

In his hand, he discovered a rifle: a pristine antique double-barreled elephant gun. This was a powerful weapon meant for only the most dangerous of prey.

Was he hunting as well?

*Charlie....*

He thought he imagined the voice—it came from all around him. Or was it inside his head? He couldn't tell.

*Charlie....*

He heard it again. This time closer, and from behind him.

He spun quickly, dropped to a knee, and shouldered the rifle, aiming toward the shadowy stand of gnarled black trees fifty yards away. The darkness between those trees was so inky and absolute that anything could have hidden within, watching him as he stood silhouetted by the dying sun.

He remained there, kneeling and aiming into the blackness for several minutes, but he heard nothing more. He thought he could see shapes moving

through the trees, but they were liquid and formless and he attributed them
to eyestrain from staring into the darkness for so long. Just as he was about
to stand and look out over the plain once more, the voice returned.

*Charlie....*

"What do you want?" he snarled.

*Everything....*

Charlie cocked back the dual hammers on the massive rifle and prepared
to fire on whatever emerged from the darkness.

*Oh, how I've waited for this, Charlie....*

It was a woman's voice. Familiar.

*I've waited for this moment. The moment I could take everything from you.
I can taste your fear, Charlie. You are afraid....*And he was afraid. He'd never
been so terrified. His heart thundered hard against his ribs as if it were trying
to kick its way free from his chest.

Suddenly he saw a grayness materialize out of the blackness of the trees.
His breathing quickened and he felt a tightness in his chest. Panic, he realized
too late. He knew that whatever was coming toward him was too powerful
for him to face alone. And yet here he stood, with nothing but this antique
rifle in his hands and an alien world full of strange creatures at his back.

*That's it, Charlie, give in to your fear. You cannot win. You will not survive.
Everything you love will wither and die. Do not resist.*

The gray shape became larger, brighter.

Closer.

And yet he did not lower the rifle; did not give up.

*Your bravery is a lie. You are no hero.*

He steadied his breathing as the grayness began to shimmer and take
shape.

Humanoid.

*Your fear sustains me. Strengthens me. I drink it in, and I gain power. I cannot
be stopped. You have no power here.*

"Fuck you," he growled, but his voice did not portray the ferocity that he
sought after. He could hear the fear in his tone.

*There is a price to be paid for the sins of the past. I will not yield until I have
consumed you and all you love. Give in. There is nothing you can do.*

Finally, the grayness fully emerged from the trees and drifted toward him.
It hovered several feet above the ground and jerkily glided to a stop twenty
feet from him. The grass parted beneath it as the force from whatever sorcery
propelled it flattened the blades.

*Look upon me, Charlie, for I am the end of everything.*

▼▲▼

Charlie woke with a start, his head throbbing. He'd felt like this only once before—when Spencer Holloway's men had injected him with a tranquilizer and brought him before their boss. Just as the anticipated thirst hit him, he noticed a water bottle had been affixed to the palm of his hand with a rubber band. He didn't bother breaking the band before removing the cap and eagerly downing the contents. Precisely as it had when Holloway had woken him years before, the headache subsided a few moments after the water had worked its way into his system.

*She used the same tranquilizer Holloway had,* he thought, recognizing the significance.

Finally, he glanced around at his surroundings, only to have a wave of panic hit him after realizing he had no clue where he was, but he was outside.

He took a moment to get his bearings before standing up.

He was between two small brick buildings that looked to have been abandoned for decades. Each had crumbling walls covered in moss, insects, lizards, and debris, hidden behind piles of palm fronds and detritus that had clearly not been attended to after years' worth of hurricanes and three-o'clock thunderstorms. Overgrown trees and other vegetation obscured much of his view beyond the buildings; however, he could see bright light illuminating the haze in the air off to his left.

Doing a fast equipment check, Charlie learned that he had been left with his entire kit; handgun, knife, watch, wallet, baton—even his phone.

*Bizarre.*

Given the fact that he'd been captured by the enemy, he thought it peculiar that he was left with all of his weapons and equipment. He couldn't decide whether to be relieved or concerned. He settled on wary.

Deciding to get a better idea of where he'd been abandoned, he moved toward the darkened doorway of the closest building—and immediately tripped over Kalani. Charlie went sprawling, but managed to catch himself on the doorframe after nearly trampling his friend.

"What!" Kalani barked, startling awake and snapping up to a sitting position. "Fuck!" he bellowed, the headache clearly hitting him hard. He shot his hand toward his brow, not realizing that he too had a water bottle banded to his palm. The bottle struck him on the forehead with a dull thud and a plastic crunch.

"Come *on!*" he whined, using his free hand to massage his brow instead.

Charlie quickly knelt beside him.

"Drink the water, the headache will go away fast," he instructed. Kalani agreed with a nod and, within a few moments, looked to be back to normal. Charlie pulled out his phone, turned on the flashlight, and shined it around. Sure enough, Victoria and Bell lay nearby—identically unconscious and equipped with water bottles.

"Wake these guys up," he told Kalani. "I'm going to try to get an idea of where we are."

Kalani nodded again.

"Be careful, man," he offered with a general wave of his hand. "Traps, you know?"

It was Charlie's turn to nod before heading through the doorway.

It only took a moment of scanning the building before Charlie knew exactly where he was.

The trashed filing cabinets, the bird nests, the abandoned freezers and fire extinguishers and old safety posters. This could only be one place: Discovery Island.

Discovery Island was once a self-contained destination that took up an entire island in Bay Lake. It was a walkthrough attraction that mainly dealt with observing the region's many species of rare birds. After a twenty-five year run, the place closed in 1999. The island had been abandoned and largely neglected ever since.

Several YouTube videos and blogs full of pictures had been posted by urban explorers in recent years, and they showed some admittedly disturbing things that one wouldn't expect to find on Discovery Island. Diet Coke bottles with the preserved corpses of small snakes sat on shelves intertwined with the nesting material of vultures that had moved in after the abandonment. Lights inside the outbuildings still functioned but seemed to serve no purpose. A wealth of strange things any urban explorer would love to encounter.

Habst had always wanted to see the island, but Charlie had refused to give him access.

Now, it seemed, Charlie would get to live out his friend's wish instead.

Habst would be furious.

Charlie shined his phone's light into the building, aiming at the floor to make sure he didn't snap an ankle on the uneven rubble.

Two steps into the building, Charlie's face hit something glossy and hard hanging from the ceiling. Assuming he'd just collided with a bat or some other form of wildlife, he recoiled in disgust and shined his light in the object's direction.

It was no animal—it was an iPad with a sticky note on the screen that said *Watch Me*.

"This just keeps getting weirder and weirder," he stated, shaking his head in exasperation.

"Kalani," he called behind him, glancing toward the big man as he woke Victoria and Bell. "Got an iPad in here. I'm going to grab it, but stay frosty. Could be another trap."

With almost no grace, Charlie hastily grabbed the iPad, breaking the cord that suspended it from the ceiling, and nearly dove out of the building expecting to be set on fire, shot with lasers, or creatively killed by any number of ridiculous traps. Sure enough, from somewhere deep in the darkness, a metallic *click* sounded followed by an unraveling rasp and a heavy thud.

Then the spectacle began.

Bright lights snapped on, bathing the room in a blazing white glow, very clearly meant to draw their attention to the only thing in the room.

A shirtless, unconscious man was strapped to a chair in the dead center, his head slumped forward over his chest.

Before anyone could react to the sight, a device on the man's arm whirred to life. It was some sort of hydraulic contraption connected to a syringe that had already been inserted into a vein. The device was simple enough in its purpose. As they watched, it steadily depressed the syringe's plunger and injected the man with an unidentifiable clear liquid.

Again, without giving anyone time to react to what they'd just seen, the iPad in Charlie's hand began furiously chiming. Message after message relentlessly appeared on the screen.

13: WATCH ME!
13: WATCH ME!
13: WATCH ME!

"Maybe we should just watch it, man," Kalani suggested, looking back and forth between the captive man and Charlie.

Charlie nodded and unlocked the iPad. It was already set to the video player, so he tapped the play button and held the device up so everyone could watch.

The video began with a close-up of a woman's icy blue eye. Even before panning out, Charlie knew who that eye belonged to.

Thirteen.

As the video panned out, they saw that Thirteen was inside the very same building in front of which they were now gathered. She wore full pirate garb, including a cutlass and an eyepatch. She hadn't bothered to cover up the split lip that Vega had given her. In place of a parrot on her shoulder, one of the island's numerous vulture inhabitants perched proudly, chewing on a piece of unidentifiable meat.

"You've got to be kidding me," Victoria grumbled.

"Welcome… to Treasure Island!" Thirteen announced on-screen.

"There's no way…." Charlie uttered.

"What?" asked Kalani.

"This place was called Treasure Island before it became Discovery Island," he told them.

Everyone glanced at Charlie and then back at the screen.

"Wait, you know where we are?" Victoria asked, but Thirteen continued before Charlie could respond.

"I'll shoot you straight, mateys," Thirteen swaggered on, using pirate lingo but not attempting an accent. "The grog you just drank was poisoned."

"What!" everyone but Charlie exclaimed at once. Charlie wasn't surprised, only irritated.

As if anticipating that reaction, Thirteen confirmed, "Yep. All of you just poisoned yourselves. Cool, right?"

She waited, grinning, before moving on.

"I guess you're wondering what the game is. Well, since you just poisoned yourselves, I should probably tell you that by grabbing this iPad, you also just poisoned *that* guy."

Thirteen stepped aside. A man in a chair could be seen behind her, out of focus.

*This couldn't have been filmed long ago*, Charlie reasoned.

"Breaking the cable's connection activated the injector. So, if you lose, he's fucked, too. And if you don't already know who he is… well… we'll get to that in a minute. He is the prize. See? I told you earlier the prize was shit."

She reached up with a gloved hand to pet the vulture, who nipped at her fingers affectionately, looking for food and finding none.

"The game is pretty simple. There are four of you and one of him," she leaned away and pointed to the unconscious man again before continuing. "There are five poisoned people, so that must mean there are five bottles of the antidote, right? All you need to do is find them. That's it.

"Now, who is this guy?" She jerked a thumb over her shoulder and the vulture hopped away, startled. "This asshole is the reason Charlie Walker is a glorified Rent-A-Cop and no longer a well-respected Murder City detective."

She walked over to the unconscious man, grabbed a fistful of his hair, and lifted his head for all to see.

"Shit," Charlie swore.

It was Harland Caulfield. The man who had leveled fabricated accusations at Charlie and had him ejected from the police force, consequently forcing Charlie's friend, Captain Pete Valdez, to resign on the spot.

"The *prize*, lady and gentlemen, is to decide whether this shitbag lives or dies. Like I said, the antidotes are on Discovery Island waiting for you. Can you find them in time? Will you give him a dose if you do find it? Who knows?"

She sighed and let Caulfield's head slump back down to his chest.

"I'll let you get to work in just a second, but I'll go over a few quick talking points beforehand just so that we're all on the same page.

"One: don't try throwing up. The poison has already been absorbed. You'll just look stupid and feel terrible.

"Two: there's a lot of real estate to comb through for five-ish tiny bottles, so I won't leave you empty-handed. In one of the nearby buildings there is an honest-to-fucking-god treasure map. And remember: X marks the spot.

"Three: While X *does* mark the spot for treasure, sometimes it also marks the spot for some other fun things. Traps—I'm talking about traps. They'll kill the shit out of you, so don't be wrong."

She laughed.

"Four: There *is* a time limit. Obviously—poison, that's kind of the point. However, I'm not telling you what it is. I figure, if you die you'll know you didn't win."

"And five: the antidote also contains another tranquilizer. If you pass out after drinking it, don't worry, that's part of the plan. It means you won. Make sure you're somewhere comfortable when you drink it because that shit works fast. When we see that you're all in dreamland—or dead—we'll come and get you and you can move on to the next round.

Good luck."

Thirteen pointed her cutlass at the camera and the screen went blank.

# TWENTY-EIGHT

ABST WAS WEDGED into the queue next to Vega and he'd never been more excited to ride the Haunted Mansion in his life. He realized the circumstances were grim, and that they had an unconscious combatant in the back of their vehicle, but he was still eager to be there.

He cleared his throat.

"Dude, I know the situation is super messed up, and this is really serious—but I'm excited for this," he declared.

Vega gave him an irritated glance but softened when he saw the smile on Habst's face despite the beating he'd taken earlier in the day.

"You really do love all this stupid Disney stuff, don't you?" he asked.

"Stupid? Man, look around you. Tell me this isn't amazing."

Vega looked around at the tombstones and up at the sinister mansion before taking a deep breath.

"I mean, yeah, it's cool and all... but this is little kid stuff."

"You take yourself way too seriously. You don't always have to be a hardass CIA murder machine, you know. You *are* allowed to have fun. Shit, how long have you worked here? Six months? You're telling me that in all that time you never rode the Haunted Mansion?"

"I never had time," Vega lied. "I was sent here to keep an eye on the Walkers and make sure nothing happened."

Habst, not as slow as Vega expected him to be in his condition, immediately called his bluff.

"So, all those times we sat drinking at Trader Sam's, you were watching the Walkers like a hawk? Right. *Somehow* you had time for that."

Vega didn't reply, so Habst did it for him in an awful mockery of his voice, "*No, Habst, I didn't have time for that, vato. I was way too busy lifting weights and hating fun and showing off how mature I am. I'm Hector Vega, I'm an adult and my dick is gigantic!"*

Vega tried to stone face him, but couldn't. He burst out laughing as the doors to the lobby opened and they were ushered inside. Habst watched Vega with interest as they made their way into the room. It was rare to ride with a true first-timer.

When they were able to enter the stretching room, Habst led Vega across the space and stood near the wall below a painting of a girl in a dress holding a parasol. There weren't many others in the eerie chamber, and nobody stood near them. Vega found it peculiar that Habst would lead them specifically to this spot, but he didn't bother to ask why.

From his left, closer than he'd expected, Habst's whisper had startled him.

"Fuck you, *cabrón,*" Vega whispered back, hearing Habst's laugh as he tried to stifle his own.

"Welcome, foolish mortals, to the Haunted Mansion! I am your host... your *ghost* host...."

The ethereal baritone voice boomed from all around them. Vega was surprised to find that he was completely enraptured. The dialogue continued, the room began to stretch, and Vega found he couldn't take his eyes off the spectacle.

Suddenly, lightning flashed, the ceiling became transparent, and a body could be seen swinging from the rafters before everything went back to normal again.

"Kid stuff, right?" Habst jabbed in a whisper.

Vega was silent even after the lights came back up. He felt a pressure change and a slight breeze and realized that the wall behind where he and Habst stood was opening and that there was a hallway beyond leading to the ride vehicles. Now he understood why Habst had brought him to this spot.

Begrudgingly, he was also beginning to understand why Habst and Charlie were fascinated by this place. If nothing else, it was an ingenious display of creative engineering.

"So what are we looking for?" Vega asked Habst as they waited to board.

"Well, like I said back at Charlie's, the attic scene is what we're waiting for. Hatbox Ghost isn't there, but the reverse fall from the window is. I've never thought about it before, but I don't actually remember what's above you when you descend. No time better than the present to have a look."

Vega nodded as they squeezed themselves into a Doom Buggy. After a moment, Vega reached out to grab the safety bar but Habst slapped his hand and pointed his finger in the air.

As if on cue, the host's baritone boomed, "Do not pull down on the safety bar, please. *I* will lower it for you."

Vega shook his head as he watched Habst lip sync the warning dialogue—including the Spanish. Sure enough, the bar lowered itself, slamming down on Vega's thighs and causing him to flinch, the motion irritating the slash on his chest.

A few minutes into the ride, Vega realized that he was enjoying himself. This truly was something else. He'd never visited a theme park in his life before his posting here. His mother could barely afford food on her meager El Paso barmaid's salary, let alone a trip to a place as expensive as this.

He found himself analyzing every scene, his brain struggling to come up with solutions for how each different act of wizardry could be achieved through contemporary engineering. He no longer felt the pain of his injuries; all he wanted was to see more of this place, to try to unravel more of the mysteries presented in these dark hallways.

He was so hypnotized that he didn't realize they'd reached their destination. Habst tapped him to remind him.

"Dude, attic," Habst whispered.

Sure enough, they were in the attic.

It was smaller than Vega had assumed; less cavernous than the set pieces that had come before. The scenery was close; he could have almost leaned out and touched the props if he'd wanted to.

"Here, on the right," Habst prompted.

Following Habst's pointed finger, Vega spied a large stack of dusty, unassuming hatboxes, as well as a rack with a few old hats covered in cobwebs.

"That's where Hatbox Ghost stands in California's version. We're about to turn around."

Habst had it down to a science. Almost instantaneously after the words left his mouth, the Doom Buggy began to slowly rotate. Eventually, the Buggy began to tilt backward and Vega was given no chance to wonder where he should be looking.

There was no need.

What Thirteen lacked in sanity, she made up for in spectacle—and this was a shining example of her madness.

A shriek sounded out, a ghostly purple light snapped on, and suddenly the "sky" was alight with fluorescent paint. Their next clue had been revealed.

SWINGING WAKE.
MIDNIGHT.
COME SOCIALIZE!

"That was it?" Habst asked, incredulous. "All that for *this*?"

"What the hell is a *swinging wake*?"

As Vega spoke, he heard the specters all around him singing about a swinging wake but it did nothing to clarify the situation.

"A wake is part of a funeral, isn't it?" Habst asked.

Vega shrugged, "I guess. But why would there be a funeral at midnight?"

"And where is this wake? It didn't tell us where to go."

Confused and irritated, Habst and Vega ended the ride in silence. The baritone voice boomed again.

"Now I will raise the safety bar, and a ghost will follow you home!"

As the bar lifted and they stood, Habst couldn't help but feel like the volume of that single line of dialogue was louder than it had ever been before.

Dejectedly, they elbowed their way through the crowds filing out of the park and headed back toward their "borrowed" truck, which they'd parked in the lot of the nearby Bay Lake Tower. They were silent, each pondering what Thirteen's vague clue meant—or whether they were even supposed to be able to work it out.

Habst felt a shudder pass through him as they stepped into Bay Lake Tower's lot, knowing how much death and violence had taken place here three years ago. He felt an unexpected sadness for Charlie; for the things that had happened to him, the things he'd been forced to do, and for whatever he'd be pushed to do now to get them all out of this mess.

When they reached the truck, Habst sighed and slumped into the passenger seat.

▼▲▼

*Fucking amateurs,* thought Joseph Reid, as he watched the CIA operative and his friend exit the truck and hurry off toward the Magic Kingdom.

Reid had been following the men since they'd left the Walkers' house. After the Spectres' attempted hit on the pair, Reid had found one of his men dead in the road and the other missing in action. He'd used his phone to track the GPS locator on the missing truck and found that it was three blocks from the Walkers' residence—and getting closer every second. So they'd killed his man, disabled the other, and stolen his truck.

That made him unhappy.

Reid had parked a good distance down the street from the Walkers' place, in a position to see the stolen truck, but not so close that he could be seen from the house. The entire area was bathed in a red-and-blue flashing glow from the police cruiser that still sat unmanned. He didn't need to get close to know what had happened here; he'd been there to help.

The Walkers' house was only somewhat isolated, however—this was still a neighborhood—and the Spectres knew that it would only be a matter of time before a neighbor drove by and called 911. They'd planned for that eventuality.

A few minutes later, he'd seen the pair exit the house, with the Company man pressing a bloody dishrag to his chest, but otherwise looking none the worse for wear.

*Must have found the clue,* he'd thought, after he'd put the car in gear and begun following their truck at a safe distance.

He'd followed them all the way to the parking lot of Bay Lake Tower. The trip had been uneventful aside from passing several police cruisers and ambulances speeding in the opposite direction.

▼▲▼

Reid casually strolled toward the large silver truck, pulled his phone from his vest pocket, and unlocked the doors.

Opening the back door, he found the rear seats folded up and his man face down on the floor.

"Cormac," Reid growled, slapping the younger man on his face to wake him. "Cormac, bloody hell, wake up!"

Cormac startled awake and looked up at Reid with abject confusion.

"Reid, what…." he trailed off, trying to move but finding his hands and ankles bound by his own flex cuffs.

Reid snapped open a folding knife and cut the kid's bindings. With one arm, he grabbed Cormac's vest and dragged him from the vehicle, depositing him roughly on his feet. He shoved a set of keys into Cormac's hand.

"Take my car and report in. Alfie's going to have your ass for this one, but you'll live. Now get the hell out of here."

"Reid—" Cormac tried to protest.

"Go! Now! I will handle things from here," Reid snapped.

When he was satisfied that Cormac was on his way, he climbed into the truck, closed the door, and sat cross-legged on the floor. He removed a small pouch from his belt and withdrew two autoinjectors.

He sat this way for nearly an hour, never taking his eyes off the path to the theme park. Finally, he saw Habst and Vega reemerge and took up his position, lying face down on the floor, exactly as he'd found Cormac. His idea would work, assuming they weren't coming directly to the truck to interrogate Cormac. Although that was a real possibility, Reid figured his odds were good. It was a safe assumption that they currently had other things on their minds. And even if they didn't, he was confident he could handle them.

They were never meant to *find* the "swinging wake." It wasn't exactly a *clue* that had been left for them this time, rather a promise of what was to come. Much the same as in the Haunted Mansion storyline, they had no choice but to attend and would be pulled inexorably forward by a ghostly hand whether they liked it or not.

If it had been Walker in their place, Reid was sure that the former detective would have made that connection, and it would have been interesting to have seen his reaction. However, the Company agent and Walker's friend arrived instead, but the end result was the same. Thirteen had built in many safeguards against countless variables like these. Her plan would succeed regardless of who went where—or who died in the process. It was a masterpiece that Spencer Holloway could only have dreamed of.

Moments later, he took a deep breath and held it as the pair entered the truck, sitting up front as expected and ignoring him for now.

For almost two whole minutes, there was no sound aside from the occasional sigh. They didn't even bother to start the ignition. Then the Company man spoke.

"Where the fuck are they, Habst?" he said, slamming the heel of his palm down on the steering wheel hard enough to make the vibrations reach Reid.

*Oh, big man's angry,* Reid mused, grinning. He tried his hardest not to laugh.

"I don't know, man," the other one, Habst, admitted. "Maybe we missed something somewhere."

"We didn't miss anything…." the Company man trailed off, and Reid knew that he'd just realized Cormac was still in the back of the vehicle—or so he thought. "Let's ask our passenger where we need to be," the agent suggested, confidently.

Reid chose his moment carefully and perfectly—he was a professional, after all. As Habst was opening his mouth to reply, and the Company agent's focus was on his friend, Reid sprang from his position, an injector in each hand.

He drove one injector into Habst's neck, and pressed the button that would force the tranquilizer into his bloodstream. Leaving the injector imbedded in Habst's neck, he rapidly turned to finish the job, but he found that he'd underestimated the wounded operative. A rock-hard fist crashed into his temple, and stars danced across his vision, but he'd taken hard hits before and shook this one off while thrusting the needle toward the big man's neck.

The agent threw a palm up, driving Reid's arm into the roof, while simultaneously going for his throat with his free hand. Reid twisted enough that the operative's hand went over his left shoulder instead of hitting home. Reid leaned his head to his left, squeezing the agent's arm between his head and shoulder, and threw his weight into the seat, effectively pinning the agent's arm in place while still leaving one of his own free.

With his free hand, Reid seized the opportunity and drove his knuckles into the bloodied area on the agent's chest. The pain caused the operative to loosen his grip on Reid's right arm, and, taking advantage of the opening, he tore his arm free, drove the injector deep into the big man's neck, and pressed the button.

He stared into the agent's eyes as he lost consciousness, laughing as he watched the realization dawn on the man that this was not the same person he'd left in the back.

Reid had succeeded where Cormac had failed.

After dragging the big man into the back, he got behind the wheel and took off.

*A ghost will follow you home, indeed.*

# TWENTY-NINE

EVEN WITH THE MAP—which they'd located almost immediately—they couldn't find anything on the island.

For too long, Charlie, Kalani, Victoria, and Bell had searched for the promised antidote vials, and come up empty-handed. They hadn't even come across a trap.

Oddly enough, they *had* found a brand new boat tied up near the dilapidated remains of what used to be the main loading dock. After a quick search of the craft, they learned there was nothing useful aboard—but the keys were in the ignition.

"We might be in trouble," Bell admitted, shrugging and looking toward Charlie and Victoria for guidance.

"No," Charlie disagreed, staring at the map. "We're just missing something. This isn't right—I can feel it."

"Maybe it's on some other island," Kalani joked, chuckling at himself.

Charlie's head snapped up suddenly, his eyes locking onto Kalani's.

"I was just kidding, *braddah*, don't kill me," Kalani joked. He put his hands up in mock surrender.

Charlie pointed at him.

"I think you're exactly right. And I'm an idiot."

Kalani grinned and shrugged.

"Genius does run in my family." He nodded, agreeing with his own statement. "So, if they aren't on this island, where are they?"

"Discovery Island," Charlie declared, hands spread wide.

"Isn't *this* Discovery Island?" Victoria interjected, exasperated that she may be stating the obvious. She felt a "Who's on First" scenario beginning to emerge.

"It *was*. Remember when Thirteen called this place Treasure Island? Well, she did it on purpose. That was a clue. And the map she left us very clearly says Discovery Island on top. Like I said, this placed *used* to be called Treasure Island, then they changed it to Discovery Island."

Victoria chewed her lip, "You're not really making this any clearer for us, bud."

Charlie nodded impatiently.

"I know; I'm getting to it. This *was* Discovery Island, but then they moved it."

"Moved it where?" Bell asked.

"Animal Kingdom. Discovery Island still exists, but it isn't here anymore. Thirteen was messing with us. Look," Charlie pointed to some roughly drawn structures on the map. "These buildings? These aren't the abandoned shacks on this island. These are the stores over at Animal Kingdom. I should have noticed immediately—we're in the wrong place."

"Good thing we found the boat that—now that I think about it—was absolutely left here for exactly this reason," Victoria deadpanned.

"How are we going to get there?" Bell wondered aloud. "We don't have a car."

Charlie sighed.

"You're not going to like this."

▼▲▼

After a quick back-and-forth about what to do with Caulfield, the decision was made to leave him behind. They couldn't carry a half-naked, unconscious man through crowded areas and expect it to go unnoticed. Bell called the sheriff's department to commandeer a boat and recover him. They were under instructions to bring him to Animal Kingdom's entrance and wait for Bell to retrieve him. They figured the deputies would be able to get to Caulfield and bring him to their location in the time it took them to recover the antidote. That was the plan, anyway. Bell also asked them to bring him a vehicle. They were reluctant about the whole situation, but they agreed.

Kalani was the only person who had any real boating knowledge, so he was elected as captain for their short journey out of Bay Lake and across the lagoon. At Charlie's request, he anchored the boat against the seawall just south of the Magic Kingdom's bus depot. After trudging through the landscaping and hopping over a railing, they landed smack-dab in the middle of the evening chaos. It was a mad rush for people to find their way to their resort's bus stop, and the lines looked as long as Charlie had ever seen them.

The line for Animal Kingdom's bus was not as painfully long as the ones for the resorts. With a small amount of luck, they made it aboard the very first bus. They sat just behind the driver but Charlie, being Charlie, stood to allow a pregnant woman to sit.

As the doors to the bus were closing, a man in a camouflage tank top, long black denim shorts, and slip-on sandals stepped aboard.

"Made it in the nick of time, sir!" the bus driver bubbled, jovially.

She made to close the doors, but the man casually held out his hand to stop her.

"No, no," he said simply, as if he were speaking to a disobedient dog.

"I'm sorry, sir, I—"

"Don't close them doors," he said, his low southern drawl remaining just this side of a growl. "My brother-in-law is on his way. He had to go buy a bubble wand for his kid and just texted and said he's almost at the park exit."

Charlie gritted his teeth. He turned to face the man and stared daggers into the side of his head. The camouflage man didn't seem to notice or care.

"Sir, I'm sorry, but I'm afraid he will have to wait for the next bus," the driver apologized.

"Nope. He's getting' on *this* bus and we're waitin' right here for him."

The man crossed his arms and stared at the driver.

"Sir, another bus will be along shortly, he can—"

The man took a step toward her, towering over her.

"Who knows when the next one'll be? I said that we are going to wait for him. So, we're gonna wait right here for him."

Charlie had had enough of this man and his false entitlement—this was far too common an occurrence in the parks and Charlie was in no mood to cater to idiots. Forgetting about his current crisis, he stepped forward and turned to the driver, giving her a little reassuring smile.

"Sharon, is this man bothering you?" he asked, recognizing her after seeing her face.

For a moment, the driver looked startled, but she quickly recognized him as well.

"Charlie! He, um, he...." she stammered, but Charlie nodded his head. He put himself between the man and Sharon.

"I need you to take a step back, sir," Charlie commanded. "This bus is leaving. Now."

"Who the hell are you, pretty boy? Sit your ass down and relax like everyone else."

"Take a step back."

Not a request.

The camouflage man simply snorted a laugh and turned to look out the window for his brother-in-law.

Charlie nodded to himself.

*So, this is how it's going to be.*

He'd done his due diligence and now he felt free to solve the problem as he saw fit. Slowly, he let his right foot slide back, shifting his center of gravity.

He leaned in, close enough that only the camouflage man could hear him.

"Walk off this bus or be thrown off. Your choice."

The camouflage man only registered his surprise for a split second before his hands came up in an attempt to shove Charlie away.

The idiot was sloppy and untrained, telegraphing his strike ages beforehand, and Charlie easily brought his guard up to deflect the attacking hands away. Without giving his assailant enough time to react, Charlie centered both hands and shoved the man with as much power as he could summon.

Unprepared for Charlie's retaliation, the man lost his footing and tumbled backward out of the door, landing flat on his back, the air bursting from his lungs. Before he could rise, Charlie was on him, hands knotted into his shirt. He roughly hauled the camouflage man to his feet and shoved him against a railing. The camouflage man feebly tried to throw a wild, wide right hook. Charlie easily swatted the blow away with his left hand and threw a quick two-knuckle punch that landed just beneath the man's sternum—a strike he used often and to devastating effect.

The camouflage man coughed sharply and doubled over, the air bursting from his lungs for the second time in a matter of moments. Charlie cut him no slack and roughly shoved him back upright.

"Listen to me," Charlie growled in little more than a whisper as the camouflage man struggled to draw breath. "I don't have time to deal with you, but if I find out that you gave anyone else *any* trouble for the rest of your trip, I will find you, and we will pick up where we left off. Nod if you understand me."

The camouflage man enthusiastically nodded.

*Nothing humbles a tough guy faster than an ass-kicking in front of a bunch of people*, Charlie thought.

Charlie reached down, snatched the man's MagicBand from his wrist, and held it up.

"And now I have your name," he snapped and stepped back onto the bus, oblivious to the stares of nearby Guests who'd just witnessed their scuffle. He could see people pointing their phones at him but couldn't care less.

This wasn't the worst thing he'd done on Disney property—or on video.

He grabbed the overhead strap near his friends and leaned his weight into it, feeling his exhaustion creeping up but not allowing it to take hold. It had been a long couple of days and things showed no sign of stopping any time soon.

"He's not going to be a problem anymore, Sharon, we can go now," he said, without looking over his shoulder.

"Uh, yeah! Absolutely," Sharon bumbled, startled into action. The bus rumbled off toward Animal Kingdom.

▼▲▼

"The map definitely looks more helpful now that we're on the right Discovery Island," Charlie decided. He leaned against a trashcan in front of the Island Mercantile shop and used a Sharpie to make X marks on copies of park maps he'd picked up on their way in. When he was satisfied his marks matched those on Thirteen's original map, he drew a line down the center of each map and then passed them out to the others.

"Okay," he began, "watch yourselves out there. I'd have liked us to stick together but for the sake of time—who knows how much we have?—we need to split up to cover more ground. Victoria, you're with me. Kalani, you and Bell take the left side of the map; we'll take the right. Call as soon as you find anything.

"Thirteen said there would be traps and I believe her. I don't want to state the obvious, but be smart about it when you find one of these things. If you can safely disable it, do it. If not, mark the location and we'll send someone for it later. Last thing we need is a Cast Member or Guest stumbling across a trap. Any questions?"

Heads shook. Charlie nodded.

"Let's get to it."

Once Charlie and Victoria neared the first location and were out of earshot of Kalani and Bell, Victoria spoke up and her voice reverberated off of every surface, sounding almost too loud.

—everyone

It was eerie how well sound traveled when the parks were deserted.

"Something feels off about this," she admitted.

"I know. I really don't feel like it's going to be as simple as 'find the antidote and avoid the traps.' There's another layer to this."

Victoria didn't respond, but Charlie could almost hear the gears turning in her head.

Oddly enough, they found the first dose of the antidote almost immediately. It was in a small bottle, roughly the size of an energy shot you'd find in any convenience store. It was taped unceremoniously to the back of the menu board in front of Flame Tree Barbecue.

Charlie leaned in close to inspect it and saw nothing that concerned him, so he reached up and retrieved it without issue.

"Huh," he breathed, turning the small vial over in his hands. "That was easy."

Victoria reflexively took a step back, expecting a trap. Charlie had more or less invited one with that comment.

"Don't jinx it," she warned.

Fortunately, there wasn't a trap. They moved on toward their next X unharmed, and with one-fifth of the antidotes in hand.

Soon after, they approached a large circular planter with a single tall tree in the center and shrubs filling in the rest. According to the map, another dose—or trap—was here.

"I don't see anything," Victoria admitted after a few moments of cursory inspection.

"Hang on," Charlie halted, noticing something strange.

Two floodlights jutted out from the foliage in the planter, aimed upward to light the tree at night. These lights, however, were not functioning. Carefully, Charlie knelt over the one closest to him and peered down into its enclosure. As he suspected, an antidote vial lay inside, beneath the glass. Quickly, he checked the other light and found another vial. Affixed to the side of the housings of each were what appeared to be service tags. He leaned in to read the text.

```
Time to choose! One vial of antidote, and one
vial of water on top of a vibration-activated
explosive device. Don't think too hard, you might
hurt yourself!
```

"Son of a bitch," Charlie sighed.

"What's up?"

"We need to break the glass to get to these vials. Sounds easy, but one of them is the antidote, and the other is a decoy sitting on a bomb."

"And they're identical?"

"Down to the very last detail, as far as I can tell."

Victoria moved to the opposite side and inspected the floodlight for a while, searching for any way to identify an explosive. She came up with nothing.

Suddenly, it came to Charlie. The nudge was right there in Thirteen's tag: Don't think too hard. He and Victoria were overthinking the scenario. It didn't take a detective or a Company agent's brain to solve this one—anyone could do it.

"Vee, go stand over by that bench. I've got an idea," Charlie requested, pointing to a seating area some thirty feet away.

"What do you have in mind?" she asked.

"Keep it simple, stupid," he said, rapping on the side of his head twice with his knuckles.

Victoria shrugged and decided to let it be.

Charlie headed over to a trashcan labeled "BOTTLES AND CANS ONLY." He reached inside and found a couple of Coke bottles that were nearly full.

"Brace yourself," he warned, and threw one of the bottles toward the closest light. He didn't have the best arm, but at this distance, it didn't much matter. The bottle bounced off the ground once then, with luck, sailed right into the side of the floodlight.

Nothing happened.

"Hmm," Charlie sighed, scratching his head. He picked up the second bottle, got himself in position to hit the other light, and loosed his next volley.

This time, it was a direct hit. The bottle landed directly atop the second light with a dull thud before tumbling into the foliage.

Again nothing happened.

"What the hell?" Charlie muttered. "I figured that would have—"

His vision went white.

A fraction of a second after the flash, the sound hit him like a tidal wave. He instinctively threw his arms up to cover his face, but any shrapnel was far too small to do any damage. After his vision cleared, he noticed that the light housing was gone, but nothing else nearby was damaged. Even the majority of the plants surrounding the light were fine.

"Flashbang," Victoria announced. "Loud and violent, but not lethal if you aren't laying on top of it."

Charlie didn't respond. He didn't have anything to say. He found it interesting that Thirteen would use a nonlethal charge. Weren't they meant to die if they chose incorrectly? Deciding that it ultimately didn't matter, he trudged over to the undetonated light and broke the glass with his foot, careful not to crack the vial within.

"Two out of five," he announced as he grabbed his prize.

Victoria was already checking her map for the next location.

"Hopefully Kalani and Bell have found something."

Almost as if she'd summoned it, there was a muffled pop from off in the distance and a small puff of smoke rose up from near Pizzafari. Without a word, Charlie and Victoria ran toward the sound just as Kalani rushed out into their path.

"Whoa!" he bellowed. "It's okay! It was a flashbang. Bell got most of it but he's alright."

Bell staggered over to them, rubbing his eyes. Victoria knew what he was feeling all too well. He was hurting and his ears were probably ringing something fierce but it would pass. She looked him over for shrapnel wounds and was relieved to find him unscathed.

"Son of a bitch!" Bell grumbled. "When we find her, let me shoot her first."

Charlie laughed. "Fair enough. Did you guys find anything?"

Kalani reached into his pocket and pulled out two vials.

"Yep," he announced proudly. "You?"

"Same. There's one left. Let's get this over with."

It took them twenty more minutes to check the most of the remaining spots—even forcing them to head into the Discovery Island Trails—and none of them produced vials of the antidote or even any traps. In all of these spots, Thirteen had left little jokes—AT-AT Walker figurines from *Star Wars* broken in various creative ways, as well as defaced surveillance photos of Charlie and his family. It didn't unnerve him as much as it irritated him—but he figured that was more than likely the point.

At the last possible location, they found the fifth and final vial. It was on a section of path near the bridge to Asia. Blue lanterns were hung on either side of the path, all illuminated except for one. Charlie approached the darkened lantern only to find that the vial had been mounted in place of a bulb. There was no trap, he simply removed the vial without incident.

*Too easy*, he thought, figuring something would soon go wrong.

Nothing went wrong.

Charlie felt a growing sense of dread. Thirteen said this "wouldn't be easy" but, so far, this had been the easiest yet. Why had she said that? She never did anything without a reason.

"What now?" Victoria asked, interrupting his line of thought.

Charlie turned to Bell who was looking at his phone.

"Your guys show up with Caulfield yet?"

Bell nodded.

"They're here. They've got Caulfield and a cruiser for us."

"Tell them to leave Caulfield and the keys in our cruiser and take off."

Bell did as instructed.

As they made their way back toward the exit, Victoria stepped in close to Charlie. She noticed he'd been uncharacteristically quiet since they'd found the last vial. It was a win for them, he should have been at least a little happy about it.

"You alright, old man?" she asked, giving him a light punch on the arm.

Charlie rubbed his eyes hard enough to summon bright pops of color that slowly faded.

"I'm just tired, Vee. I've had this feeling all night that even when this is over, it won't really be over."

She raised an eyebrow. "What do you mean?"

"When we finally deal with Thirteen, what happens then?"

Victoria pursed her lips and feigned deep thought.

"You, your hot wife, and your two crazy kids take a vacation. Maybe Universal Studios this time?"

Charlie laughed, but pressed the issue.

"I mean it, though. Who's next, Vee? Is Thirteen the last psychopath that wants a shot at me? Or is she just the next in line?"

This, Victoria actually considered. She tried a different tactic.

"So what if it isn't?" she asked. "Who cares? Are you dead yet?"

"*I* kind of care," he offered with a shrug.

"There are a few types of people in this world, Charlie. There are people that hide in their houses and let the faceless warriors do the dirty work to keep them safe. There are also people who prey upon the weak. Then there are people like us. We are those faceless, nameless crazies that go out and get elbow deep in it. We fix the problems everyone else is afraid to even acknowledge. But somebody has to do it, right? Face it, Charlie, you were born for this shit, and you *like* it."

Charlie sighed.

"As much as I have tried to fight it or deny it lately, I've realized you're right."

Victoria grinned.

"So, what's the problem? If Thirteen is the next in line then it's nothing more than a queue of shitty people who earned a pine box or an iron cell. Every time somebody comes after you, it's another chance to make the world a safer place. You signed up for it the day you put your name on the academy's paperwork back in Detroit."

Charlie nodded somberly.

"I know. *I* signed up for it. The problem is that I didn't sign up to put my wife and daughters in the path of psychopaths and terrorists. When I started at the academy, I hadn't even met Meghan. Then I did, we got married, and Violet and Katie showed up. My priorities have shifted to them now. If something happens to them, they might as well have killed me, because everything I've done will have been for nothing. I'm not a twenty-year-old single guy who can pick up a gun at the drop of a hat and go rushing off to fight the bad guys anymore."

Victoria didn't respond, so Charlie continued.

"Vee, I might be able to handle this shit, but can Meghan? I know she's tough, but she's a college professor, not a soldier or a cop. She's going to reach a point where enough is enough and she's going to take the girls and get as far away from me as she can. And could you blame her for that? Nobody wants to live every day looking over their shoulder."

"You really think that?" Victoria asked, caught off guard by Charlie's dark mindset. "You think she'd leave you? Charlie, she left her whole fucking life behind to come down here with you and didn't bat an eye. And that was *after* a bunch of mercenaries tried to kill all of you on your vacation."

Charlie spread his hands.

"I know, and she's never hinted at it as a possibility, but it's the most logical and reasonable thing she could do. Her first priority—same as mine—is to protect Violet and Katie. Their lives are worth a hell of a lot more than our happiness."

"I hate to break it to you, but do you think those crosshairs will just disappear from her and the kids the day she signs some divorce papers and moves to Alaska? Hell no. And who is the one person on the planet she trusts more than anyone else to keep her safe? Trust me, she's in exponentially more danger away from you."

She grabbed Charlie's wrist and showed him his own wedding band.

"You see that?" she asked, shaking his hand dramatically. "She gave you that to tell you that she knows what she signed up for and she's in it until it's over. She needs you, and you need her. And I need both of you because you're the only stable things in my life, and I have to live vicariously through you guys," she finished, joking.

Charlie laughed and nodded in agreement, but didn't speak.

"Am I making sense, though?" she asked. "You guys are a team. She's not going anywhere, and neither are you."

"You're right," Charlie admitted, begrudgingly. "I just feel like these people keep targeting Meghan and the girls because they know they're my biggest weakness."

"Not a weakness," Victoria corrected him. "They're your strength. You draw that famous Walker intensity from the need to protect them. You took a bullet from one of my dad's mercs and ignored it because your wife and kids weren't with you yet. Normal humans would have gone to the hospital after that, but you just reloaded your gun and pushed forward until they were safe. There are fourteen people who didn't live long enough to regret fucking with you that day. Eventually, either the rest of these idiots will get the message, or we'll keep cycling through them until the planet runs out of bad guys. Deal?"

"I can't argue with the logic of a crazy person," Charlie joked.

Victoria laughed but didn't deny anything.

"So, we've got to finish this. And we'll move on to the next one if that time ever comes. No use worrying about it until then," she offered. "Now, get inside your head, lock Whiny Bitch Charlie back up in his padded rainbow closet, and bring Warrior Charlie back—he's got work to do."

Charlie didn't respond, but Victoria saw his eyes harden and knew his head was back in the game. She made a mental note, however, to buy him a cup of coffee if she got the chance—he looked like he hadn't slept in the last decade.

Their conversation had eaten up the rest of the walk to the exit, and when they made their way through the gates, they saw the loaner cruiser parked at the curb just past The Outpost Shop. Sure enough, Caulfield was inside, slumped against the window in the back seat. Victoria laughed as she noticed the officers had left the windows cracked.

"So, what do we actually *do* now?" Kalani asked, his point valid enough.

They knew the antidote also contained more sedative, but they had no idea what would happen to them once they were unconscious.

"We get in the car, drink this shit, and see what happens. We have no other choice. I don't feel anything yet, but who knows how fast this poison works?"

They all climbed in the cruiser and Charlie got in next to Caulfield. Carefully, he upended the first vial into the unconscious man's mouth, making sure not to spill any. When he was sure Caulfield had swallowed all of the liquid, he turned to the group and uncorked his vial.

"Slàinte," he said, and downed it in one draught.

Faster than he expected, he lost consciousness yet again.

CHARLIE FOUND HIMSELF once more in that alien landscape, the antique elephant gun again clutched in his hands.

Materializing before him, he saw what could have once been a very beautiful woman. She was white from head to toe—hair, skin, clothes, everything.

Everything except her eyes.

Her eyes were blacker than the blackest darkness imaginable.

Her body was twisted and grotesque. Limbs shuddered back and forth blazingly fast and at impossible angles, almost seeming to change shape and instantly reform. Her mouth worked awkwardly, noiselessly, as if unsuccessfully trying to reseat a dislocated jaw—but her words were not spoken, rather they were projected. Black blood poured from her eyes, nose, mouth, and ears—and with every rapid jerk and jitter, droplets flew from her and spattered the grass to either side, landing with a sizzling hiss and destroying whatever they touched.

*Look at me, do not cower. Face your destiny with dignity....*

"What are you?"

*What are we?* she corrected, and suddenly the grass began to swirl violently around where her blood had tainted it.

Shadowy hands tipped with jagged talons punched through the surface of the bizarre landscape and frantically clawed for purchase in the alien soil. Two nightmarish and unspeakably monstrous beings pulled themselves free of the terrain and stood beneath their bloody, spectral mistress, ready to serve. Ready to kill.

She laughed, high and cold.

*We are the ones who spread the pestilence. We are the end, Charlie....*The creatures lunged for him.

Charlie ignored the charging abominations and, without hesitation, took aim directly at the apparition's center mass, and fired.

▼▲▼

When Charlie awoke, bright light filled his vision and the pounding in his head was worse than ever. He frantically and blindly felt around with his hands until he found the bottle of water he was looking for. He greedily downed the entire thing and, moments later, began to feel the pain subsiding.

He struggled to his knees, rubbed his eyes to clear them, and saw that the bright light came from the headlights of several black cars arranged in a circle around him, all pointed toward something in the center. As he looked around, he saw almost everyone he knew and loved in the circle of light.

To his left, Victoria knelt, looking uncertain. Kalani sat to his right. Meghan was directly across from him, flanked on either side by Violet and Katie. Zeus sat behind them, his teeth bared at figures Charlie couldn't see. Violet had a few fingers hooked around his collar, keeping him in place. McCoy, Bell, Jen-Jen, April, Vega, and Habst completed the circle around a central figure.

Thirteen herself stood in the center of the ring, her foot resting on the chest of Harland Caulfield, who was splayed out on his back, still unconscious.

"Welcome, everyone," she announced, her arms held out to the side as if she were an old-timey showman. "I'm so glad you could make it."

Nobody spoke, just waited for the inevitable.

"We are gathered here tonight in celebration and—soon—remembrance of a soul who is not long for this world. You passed the test, Charlie. You found the antidote and saved your skin. However, we still have to give you your prize before we can call it a night."

Charlie stared into Thirteen's eyes with an intensity that would have made a normal person cower. He hated this woman. He wanted her dead.

"There are thirteen of you here tonight—a fitting number—and it's almost midnight. I promised a swinging wake, and a swinging wake we shall have. Here's the deal," she said, as she removed her foot from Caulfield and began pacing slowly around the circle, gazing at all of her captives as she passed them. "One of you will not leave this circle tonight. The Mansion's thousandth spirit is one of yours, and the Master demands his sacrifice. My gift to you, dear Charles, is the gift of choice. I will leave it up to you to decide who dies tonight."

With that, she stopped in front of Charlie and bent over, bringing her eyes level with his. She was only inches from his face, cleavage spilling out of her shirt—intentionally, he assumed. He smelled alcohol on her breath and saw the cut on her lip courtesy of Vega. She knelt before continuing.

"You survived, Charlie, so the choice is yours to make. That is your prize."

Charlie snorted derisively, "*That's* my prize? Condemning one of my friends to death? You're insane."

She shrugged, agreeing with him.

"No. Your prize is *saving everybody else's lives.* You're welcome. Now, you have thirty seconds to choose, or I will choose for you. Spoiler alert: if you leave it up to me, I'll pick the blonde child. She's adorable."

Charlie lunged at her and almost immediately felt the cold steel of a gun barrel against the back of his head. He hadn't even realized there was someone behind him.

"Don't make this difficult, Charlie," Thirteen purred. "Just pick someone so I can kill them and then we'll all move on. Oh, time starts now."

She walked past him.

"Pick Caulfield," Victoria suggested simply. "He's already fucked you over and ruined your career."

"He's an asshole but that's no reason to kill him," Charlie shot back.

"It's him or Katie, goddamn it! This should be an easy decision," Victoria told him.

"I'll do it," Vega called out. "Pick me, Charlie. Don't let her hurt Katie. I volunteer."

"No!" April gasped. "You can't!"

"I have to." Vega shook his head. "I'm sorry, but it was my job to protect them and I failed. It has to be me."

"Hector, you can't—"

He held up his hand and she stopped talking.

"It'll be okay. I love you."

Charlie, for the first time in his life, was absolutely at a loss for how to proceed. There was no possibility in which he could make this decision and yet, if he didn't, Thirteen would kill Katie.

"No."

A deep voice. McCoy.

"It's me," he said, standing.

McCoy walked to the center of the ring and knelt beside Caulfield's unconscious form.

"I'm ready," he said, looking at Victoria and then closing his eyes. It broke Charlie's heart to see this man offer to give his life for the rest of them. In a bizarre way, though, he understood. McCoy wasn't saying he was ready to die, he was saying he's ready to finally see his daughter again. Still, Charlie couldn't speak, couldn't move.

"Aaaaaaaand time's up!" Thirteen said, stepping back into the ring. "So the choice is made, then? I have to hear you say it, Charlie."

"I—I can't."

"Bring me the blonde kid," she ordered.

"No!" Meghan screamed, and Katie began to cry as a tattooed man in a black vest dragged her into the center of the ring. Zeus growled and barked but held back, constantly looking at Charlie for reassurance or command.

Thirteen pulled a knife from her pocket and Charlie immediately recognized it. It was his Microtech Halo. The knife that had been used to murder Martin Ramos. The knife with Violet's prints. The knife that was missing from the evidence box.

She snapped the blade out and held it to Katie's throat.

"Charlie, please!" Meghan shouted. "You have to do something!"

Charlie shook his head to clear it. It was the most horrible decision he'd ever have to make, but it needed to be done.

Thirteen pressed the blade against Katie's throat and Charlie saw the skin dimple under the pressure.

"It's him," Charlie said, quietly. Those two words broke something in him. Something snapped and the pieces could never be put back in place.

"And so the decision has been made."

Thirteen pushed Katie back toward Meghan and turned to McCoy.

"You sure about this, big man?" she asked. "It's kind of permanent."

Wordlessly, McCoy tilted his head back, presenting his throat.

Thirteen checked her watch and seemed to be waiting for something. Counting down the seconds until midnight, Charlie guessed.

"Sit tight, big guy, still a couple minutes until midnight. Let's wake up our friend here and tell him he gets to live. Maybe he'll even thank you, but he doesn't really seem like the grateful type."

Thirteen pulled a syringe from her jacket and injected it directly into Caulfield's neck. He woke with a gasp and stared wild-eyed at the ring of people kneeling around him.

"Mr. Caulfield!" Thirteen exclaimed. "Welcome back. How do you feel? Bad? Don't worry, it'll all be better soon." She looked at her watch again.

"Why are you doing this?" Caulfield asked in a terrified whimper.

"Because I'm good at it and it's fun," she stated, offering no further explanation. She never looked up from her watch.

Caulfield saw Charlie for the first time and Charlie could see the recognition dawning on his face, even through the medicated fog.

"Walker? Walker! You have to—"

Thirteen put a finger to his lips.

"Shut up, guy. We're just getting to the good part."

Caulfield looked like he was on an alien planet, surrounded by monsters.

He had no clue what was going on. As much as Charlie disliked the guy, it was hard to see him like that.

Thirteen finally lowered her watch and stepped behind McCoy. The time had come. Charlie turned away as Thirteen knotted her fist into McCoy's hair; he didn't want to watch his friend die. Rough hands grabbed Charlie's head and forced him to look upon the scene before him.

"Eyes on the prize, mate," a gritty voice told him.

"And so the witching hour has fallen upon us," Thirteen began, tipping McCoy's head further back. "Nine hundred and ninety-nine souls gathered to welcome their newest companion and take him home."

A digital alarm started beeping to signal the start of the new day. Aside from the shrill tone, there was no sound. Nobody moved, nobody breathed. The sound of death's arrival was silence.

And then Caulfield vomited blood into the dirt before him. His skin had rapidly turned sickly pale, his eyes so bloodshot they almost looked entirely red. He retched again, splashing Thirteen's black leather boots with more blood. His body was racked by convulsions, every muscle strained so hard that Charlie was surprised his bones held up. He flopped over and hit the dirt, violently shuddering. He vomited again, blood splashing his own chest and neck. The bloody dirt had caked on his upper body in a black-red paste.

It seemed like the convulsions would never stop but, after one more violent retch that produced still more blood, he finally lay still and it was over.

Thirteen bent down again and looked into McCoy's eyes.

"Not today, Ginger Jesus."

She shoved his head away and approached Charlie.

"Why?" he asked, his voice hoarse.

"Because *this*," she waved a hand at the cooling body that was once Harland Caulfield, "is the prize I wanted to give you all along, but I knew you wouldn't be able to make the decision on your own. You're too good for that. You'd let one of your friends sacrifice themselves before condemning an unconscious asshole to death."

"I gave him the antidote myself," Charlie growled, enraged.

"What antidote?"

"Are you fucking kidding me?"

Thirteen laughed, high and pretty. "None of you were actually poisoned. Do you know how much work it would've taken to cook up a poison like that? One with an antidote that needed to be combined with a sedative that didn't kill you due to some crazy drug interaction? Fuck all that. You guys just went on a wild goose chase for a bunch of sedative shots. Hilarious."

"Then how do you explain Caulfield?"

"I haven't told you the whole story. That injector in his arm earlier? When you broke the iPad's connection, it dosed him with exactly enough sedative to keep him asleep without killing him—even after factoring in the dose of 'antidote' you fed him. One of our guys is fucking phenomenal at math," she looked over at someone Charlie couldn't see and grinned, "or *maths* as these British weirdos call it. But whatever. It worked flawlessly. Awesome.

"The poison itself, however? I did that myself just now. Neurotoxin mixed in with the stimulant I used to wake him up."

Charlie nearly shook with rage, but he didn't speak.

"Aren't you happy your friend is alive? I mean, you *do* have to live with the fact that you ordered his execution to save that useless meatbag, Caulfield. So, that should be an awkward conversation later, eh?"

Thirteen sighed, as if lost in thought. She put up a finger.

"There is one more tiny issue we need to straighten out before we part ways for the night."

"What now?" Charlie complained.

"My Spectres came to pick up your wife and girls. It didn't go well. Your friends killed two of them. If you don't believe me, you can currently find their bodies in your house along with the bodies of some cops who were too nosy for their own good. *Then*, big hombre over there killed another one of my guys out on the road. That can't go unpunished. Alfie, bring me the wannabe hero and his girlfriend."

The tattooed man that had grabbed Katie earlier now dragged Vega and April over and kicked them to their knees before Thirteen. They knelt on either side of her, facing each other. April was crying; Vega was stoic and unreadable. Charlie didn't know what to expect, but he knew it couldn't be good.

"What are you going to do?" April asked, timidly.

"Little girl," Thirteen hissed, "do not speak unless spoken to."

With that, she stepped behind Vega, looped an arm around his chest, placed the tip of the Microtech over his heart, and slid the blade in up to the hilt. When she pulled the knife free, Charlie watched as the life seeped out of Vega; saw his eyes lose focus. He was so close, he could hear Vega's final breath escape his lungs.

April screamed and lunged toward Thirteen but Alfie was too fast; he caught her and forced her back to her knees. Habst squeezed his eyes shut and gritted his teeth until they hurt. The sound of April's tortured wail was almost too much for him to bear after witnessing the death of his friend.

"Shame," Thirteen mused. "That was for my lip and my guy on the road. *You*, on the other hand, were there when my other two men died. Look at your hero, little girl. Look at him. He's not so heroic anymore is he?"

Thirteen stepped over to April.

"Stand her up. Let her go," she commanded, and Alfie did. She flipped the Microtech around and offered the knife to April. "Now, you can take this, kill me, and end all of this right here. However, if you do, everyone gathered around you will die. My men will execute every single one of them, and they will make you watch—just like you watched these pathetic morons die in front of you. But the decision is yours. Go on. Take it."

April looked shattered. Her eyes wandered from the knife to all of the faces gathered around her. Charlie wanted to help her, but there was nothing he could do. They had the upper hand. He was powerless to do anything but watch.

"Take it, bitch," Thirteen goaded.

April sighed, defeated. She wiped the tears from her eyes. Her eyes travelled down to Vega's body and Charlie watched as she took a deep breath to steel her nerves for what was coming next.

"No."

Thirteen shrugged.

"Fair enough."

In one fluid motion, she flipped the blade around and jabbed it deep into April's throat. She didn't stop there; she pulled the blade free and rapidly stabbed her over and over. She hit an artery and the blood sprayed out like a jet, splattering Thirteen's face and glasses. She drove April to the ground, landing atop her and continuing her relentless assault.

By the time Thirteen was finished, April's throat was nothing but a red ruin. She'd even left the Microtech embedded in the dead girl's neck as an added insult.

"Goddamn you!" Charlie barked, leaping to his feet. "Neither of them did anything wrong! They didn't deserve this!"

Thirteen wheeled upon Charlie. Covered in April's blood, she no longer resembled the pretty redhead with the glasses he'd seen in photos and videos—and even just moments before. Now she resembled something else. A banshee. A demon. A monster.

She wiped two fingers along the side of her face, collecting the blood, then pressed those fingers against Charlie's forehead, leaving two red dots— one for each of the friends he'd just lost.

"You're right. They deserved worse," she said, breathing heavily. "I'll keep that in mind for next time."

Charlie took a deep breath and held it, trying to calm himself.

Thirteen blew him a kiss.

"See you in the morning."

As she was leaving, she turned to him and, as an afterthought, added, "And don't think of leaving town before we speak again. If you do, there will be consequences that will make national headlines for years to come—I can promise you that."

Without another word, Thirteen marched off. Within minutes, her Spectres had followed her, leaving ten people, one dog, and three bodies behind.

# THIRTY-ONE

FTER THIRTEEN AND HER TEAM left them, shocked and reeling from the deaths of Vega, April, and Caulfield, it took Charlie only seconds to realize that they were inside the recently permanently shuttered *Lights, Motors, Action!* at Hollywood Studios. As much as it irritated him that Thirteen had been able to bring them all here completely unnoticed, he was not surprised.

The Spectres had recovered and left Victoria's Navigator for them, as well as Bell's replacement cruiser. Inside the vehicles, they found all of their weapons, gear, and technology. Thirteen's complete disregard for the fact that she'd continually left highly trained CIA operatives armed and alive bothered Victoria. She could have taken their weapons on several occasions, but hadn't, and that was distressing.

When the initial shock of the brutal executions wore off, Bell called LeCarre, who was just finishing up dealing with the scene of horror at the Walker house. He wrapped that up as quickly as he could and immediately ordered first responders to meet them at the Studios.

LeCarre arrived with the first responders, and the paramedics looked over the survivors. They gave the all-clear, but still wanted to take everyone to the hospital for monitoring. LeCarre quickly closed that avenue by claiming that they would all be needed for questioning and that they'd be brought to the hospital after that.

Victoria told LeCarre that she wanted the bodies held at the Sheriff's Department, but nobody—not their families or the Company—could be notified until after the situation was resolved. It was a cold and ruthless decision, but if word got out and somehow negatively affected the outcome, she wouldn't be able to live with it. Ultimately, it was safer to wait, and

LeCarre agreed. By that point, he fully understood that he was out of his league and took direction from Victoria without issue. He seemed almost relieved not to have to be in charge.

Once the scene was secured and all of the standard procedures were completed, LeCarre and Bell left along with the first responders, while the rest of them had to figure out what to do. Since the Walkers' house was currently an active crime scene, they needed somewhere else to regroup. Charlie suggested pulling a few strings to get them a suite at one of the resorts. After calling around, he was able to secure a two-bedroom villa at the BoardWalk that—if there wasn't a sudden rush of bookings—they'd be able to use free of charge for a couple of days. He hoped they wouldn't need it that long.

▼▲▼

Once they'd checked into the BoardWalk and settled into their villa, Charlie was able to spend a little time with Meghan and the girls. After a while, he left them so they could get some sleep in one of the bedrooms. He passed McCoy and Jen-Jen, who sat in silence in the living room—both staring at the floor. Kalani was with Habst on the balcony, smoking something that Charlie decided not to ask about. Victoria was sitting alone at the kitchen high-top, pouring from a bottle of Wild Turkey that had somehow materialized. When she caught him out of the corner of her eye, she poured a second glass and set it down next to hers. Charlie took the seat beside her and drained half the whiskey in one gulp. He set the glass down harder than he meant to and Jen-Jen looked up at him. She smiled sadly before resuming her inspection of the flooring.

"I'm sorry about April and Vega," consoled Charlie, catching Victoria's eye. "I liked Hector a lot. He was a good person. None of them deserved that, not even Caulfield."

"Thirteen's bluffing," stated Victoria, ignoring Charlie's sympathies and wiping a single tear from her eye with her fist. "We have to get you and Meghan and the kids out of here. Let me call the Company; they'll put you in a safe place until we can get this sorted out."

Charlie shook his head slowly but didn't immediately respond.

"I know she's bluffing," he agreed, calmly. "I think that whatever she has planned is going to happen whether I'm here or not—but I can't just run away."

He paused to take another sip, seemingly lost in thought.

"At first," he continued. "I stupidly thought this was just about us—about revenge—but it's not, and I don't think it ever has been. It's about attention. She wants to do everything your dad tried to do and more. She wants to do it bigger and better—and she wants the world to see it. These games are just distractions. She's going to hit the parks somehow and she's trying to keep us out of the way."

Charlie finished his drink.

Victoria looked defiant, but deep down she felt it was the truth. There was a storm coming and it wouldn't be like anything they'd seen before.

"So why hasn't she just killed us all?" Victoria countered, refilling both of their glasses. "At least then she could be sure we were out of the way. She's had plenty of opportunities, especially since she's been ten fucking steps ahead of us the entire time."

"She can't kill us—not yet. Think about it: Disney World's head of Security and his family go missing right after one of his employees was murdered? That would draw a lot of unnecessary attention to the area. On the other hand, if a park employee died and the head of Security was arrested for it, all of the attention would be on me. Nobody would be looking at the parks."

"But we got you out. Your name was cleared before it hit the press," Victoria countered.

"I know. And she was ready for that. She knew you'd come. If you got me out in time, then she had these ridiculous games on deck to keep us occupied until zero hour. If you didn't? Well, it just would have been that much easier for her. Once the charges got dropped—and they would because there wasn't enough evidence to lock me down—it wouldn't matter because she'd have already made her move and we'd be looking at another 9/11."

Victoria stared into her glass, unable to fathom the sheer scope of a tragedy like that occurring in the parks. It was a busy time of year, the population was dense, and the casualties would be high. It was the unthinkable made real. After the situation with her father, and the thought of the damage his single bomb could have done, the thought of an attack like that on a larger scale made her hands shake. She picked up the glass and drained it—it was her third, and only now did she begin to feel it.

"We're in over our heads," she admitted quietly, still staring into the empty glass. "We have to call in National Security and the Bureau. This is domestic terrorism. The entire resort needs to be evacuated."

Charlie put a hand on her shoulder and it startled her.

"Vee, we don't even know what they're planning. A full-scale evac would be national headlines within the hour. Whatever she wants to do, the damage will be multiplied tenfold if she does it during an evacuation. We're on our own here—at least until we know what we're dealing with."

Victoria hung her head.

"How the fuck are we going to get out of this one?" she asked.

Charlie laughed, "I don't know. But we will. We have to."

"What do we do next?"

"We wait for Thirteen. She said she'd see us in the morning."

"And then what?"

Charlie finished his second drink and stood.

"Then we play her game—whatever it is—look for an opening, and put a bullet in her."

Leaving Victoria to drink in peace, he walked back to the bedroom where his wife and daughters were sleeping. Climbing over Zeus, he laid next to Meghan, draped an arm over her, and kissed her hair.

Within seconds of his head hitting the pillow, Charlie Walker was asleep.

# THIRTY-TWO

ACK IN THE SPECTRES' SUITE at the Swan, Alfie sat on the balcony, his feet propped up on the railing, looking out over Crescent Lake. It was a different place in the dark. This early in the morning, there were no boats running, no people shopping or eating, no joggers circling the water. It was silent. In the distance, he could see the big, silver geodesic sphere that was Spaceship Earth.

"Hmph," he half-laughed to himself, thinking about how radically different this view would be twenty-four hours from now.

All of those people, going about their vacations, fat and happy. American greed and hubris in its highest form. He couldn't understand the appeal. What kind of arseholes would subject themselves to such monstrous crowds and irritation for so little return on investment? He and Thirteen were doing the world a favor, as far as he was concerned.

Today would be a day that would never be forgotten. History books would be rewritten. There would be hashtag movements, donation drives, and Facebook frames. Conspiracy theorists would flood YouTube and Reddit with speculation and fearmongering. Nobody would be able to pick up a phone, fire up a computer, or turn on a TV for months without seeing what the Spectres had done. It would forever be known as America's greatest tragedy, overshadowing everything that had come before.

And he would be one of the few who knew what really happened.

He heard the door open behind him and Thirteen stepped out onto the balcony wearing only a towel, her red hair wet and dark from the long shower she'd just taken. She sat on his lap, carefully avoiding his injured thigh.

"Look at that," she said, waving a hand at the view before them. "Do you know how much money people pay just to be here? I looked it up. Even at the entry-level resorts, it's borderline extortion. Some people sacrifice paying their mortgages to experience this. How does that equate to happiness?"

Alfie chuckled.

"You aren't exactly the authority on happiness, love."

She snorted, "You know what I mean, though."

He nodded slowly.

"You're sure you want to do this?" he asked her. "There's no coming back. You will be the world's most wanted terrorist. They'll hunt you forever."

"*Terrorist?*" Thirteen sneered, ignoring the rest. "You think that's what this is, Alfie? Terrorism?"

"You can call it whatever you want, love, but the media will label it terrorism from moment one. Do you think they know or care about your history with Chaos Squad? Even if they did, do you think they'll buy the revenge story? They'll see that for what it is—an excuse to do what we're here to do."

She turned toward him, the motion pulling the towel lower, Alfie couldn't help but notice.

"And what story is that?" she snapped.

"You might have the rest of the boys fooled, but you're mad if you think I believe you're here just because Charlie Walker and those CIA thugs killed some friends you hadn't seen in years. They've never had anything to do with this. They're just a convenient excuse to be here and the icing on the cake if they happen to die."

Alfie grinned. Thirteen studied him, then softened a bit.

"So tell me, why am I here?"

"You're here to let the world know who you are. You were forgotten once, when you left Chaos Squad behind, and you're here to make sure nobody ever forgets your name again. You're going to show them all that you can do everything that Chaos Squad couldn't."

She looked off into the distance.

"I left Chaos Squad because they were soft. Sure, they were ruthless and greedy, but there were lines even they wouldn't cross. Certain things were off-limits. Do you know how many jobs we could have completed in less than half the time if they'd let me kill a wife or a child to force a target into action?"

Alfie raised an eyebrow.

"Chaos Squad were the good guys, then?" he laughed.

"No. They weren't good guys, but they didn't have it in them to do what needed to be done. It got to the point that I had to start building machines that made it look like people killed themselves. What a pain in the ass *that* was, but I was fucking good at it. I hear they tried doing it themselves after I left and it didn't quite work out." She laughed. "Could have avoided bullshit like that if they'd just wiped the whole goddamn village out—no witnesses means no witnesses. Instead, we had to sneak in after dark and rig up suicide machines to keep their anonymity and *sense of honor* intact. What a fucking joke."

Alfie put a hand on her thigh.

"So it's revenge against *them*?" he asked, seeing a new side of her.

"Partly," she admitted. "If they're watching us from hell, then they'll forever know what a bunch of cowards they really were. But it's more than that. When we do this, everything changes. Not just America, but the whole world. We're not using guns or bombs or planes. All of the things these morons bitch about on the news: heightened airline security; *they're going to take our guns*; that kind of shit. It's all going to hit the backburner. Everyone's eyes will be right here. On us. You think America is still going to be at everyone else's throats when the hardest they've ever been hit is by one of their own?"

"Ah," Alfie scoffed, not without some condescension. "We're saving the world from itself."

"We're not saving it—you can't *save* it. We're making it *self-aware*. And we're also showing them that we are still out there. This might not be the last time we show up with a little reminder."

Alfie rubbed her thigh slowly, starting to move his hand up under the towel.

"Personally, I don't care why we're doing it," he told her. "You want revenge on Charlie Walker, the CIA, Chaos Squad, Holloway, America, the *world*—whatever. I'm with you no matter what."

She looked into his eyes with a burning intensity.

"You'd better be. If you weren't, I'd kill you."

"Promise?" he joked.

She pulled his hand out from under the towel.

"Let's get some sleep; it's going to be a big day."

Alfie stood, picking Thirteen up as he did, and carried her off toward the bedroom.

"I have plans of my own first."

# THIRTY-THREE

WHEN HE AWOKE, Charlie found Meghan watching him from her spot, just inches away.

"Good morning, Detective," she purred, smiling at him. Even though he hadn't been a detective in years, she still used that line from time to time. He liked it.

It felt like ages since he'd woken up next to her. With golden light framing her face, he figured that if heaven existed, this must be what it looked like.

He smiled back, but the smile quickly faded as he realized that the light was coming from outside. "Shit, what time is it?" he asked, starting to sit up. "Where are the girls?"

Meghan gently pushed him back down.

"Relax. It's eight thirty. Violet and Katie are in the other room playing with Victoria. There haven't been any developments yet."

He let his head fall back against the pillow with a sigh and pinched the bridge of his nose. He'd gotten a little over six hours of sleep, but his body felt like it had just woken up after a thousand-year hibernation.

"Are you okay?" he asked without looking at her.

"A few scratches, nothing major. And before you ask, the girls are fine. They didn't see what happened last night. Jen-Jen and I grabbed them and pulled them away. They *know*, but they didn't see. I didn't see it either. I couldn't watch."

Charlie breathed a sigh of relief. He'd seen a lot of death, but what happened in front of him would scar anyone. He was glad his wife and girls didn't have to see their friend die.

"I've missed you so much," she said softly. "I feel like I haven't seen you in a year."

"I'm so sorry," he apologized, looking into her eyes. He wasn't only apologizing for being away the past couple of days—he was apologizing for everything. "When this is over, I promise, I'm going to—"

She cut him off with a kiss. It was much deeper and rougher than he expected, but not at all unpleasant.

When she came up for air, he tried to speak again but she shut him down a second time.

"Shh." She gracefully moved on top of him, straddling his hips. "Everything is going to be okay. No more worrying."

Charlie looked up at his wife and then his eyes shot to the door separating their room from the main villa. He saw that the locks on the door were in place. Even the privacy latch was closed.

*Sneaky.*

"Here? *Now?*" he whispered, laughing quietly.

Meghan smiled, shrugged casually, and slowly pulled off her shirt, dropping it on the bed next to him.

"You're not serious," he stated, trying not to laugh again.

She raised an eyebrow as if challenging him, then undid the button and zipper on her jeans. Charlie's eyes fell upon the exposed triangle of red lace and knew it was all over for him—he never stood a chance. There was no defense against power like that.

"You *are* serious."

She fell upon him hungrily.

Forty-five minutes later, Charlie got out of the shower and dressed. Jen-Jen and Kalani had gone down to the shops on the BoardWalk and bought everybody clothes with a Company card, doing the best they could with the limited selection and guesstimated sizes.

Charlie had ended up with a black Adventurers Club T-shirt and a heavy, dark blue button-up. He was forced to wear his jeans from before, however, as the resort didn't sell men's pants. Regardless, he felt better than he had in a long time.

Stepping out of the bathroom, he found Meghan next to the bed with her back to him, bending over to pull up a pair of black Disney yoga pants and slipping on a long, grey Minnie Mouse tank top. The red lace nearly victimized him a second time, but he was able to keep it together long enough for her to get dressed.

"I love you," he told her, and slapped her lightly on the ass.

"I know," she said with a grin, throwing Han Solo's reply at him as she sometimes did. "I love you, too."

She handed him his gun and his watch.

"How about an outer space vacation after this is all over?" she asked.

He pretended to think about it as he holstered his weapon and buckled on his watch.

"Yeah, I think that sounds nice. Maybe Mars?" he suggested.

"Too close to Earth," she countered, shaking her head. "Fhloston Paradise?"

Charlie grimaced.

"I don't know," he cautioned. "Remember what happened to Bruce Willis last time he was there? How about a vacation with a little less gunfire this time?"

She laughed clumsily, realizing that while referencing the destination from *The Fifth Element*, she'd forgotten that it was immediately attacked by alien terrorists just after Bruce Willis' arrival.

Charlie shook his head and laughed with her.

"Come on, Leeloo; let's go check on our offspring. They've probably stolen Aunt Vee's phone and started hacking into CIA databases by now."

With that, they headed through the door into the adjoining room and saw the place in much better spirits than it had been in the darkness of the early morning.

Victoria sat cross-legged on the floor with Violet and Katie, holding an iPhone to her forehead with the name "Olaf" displayed on the screen. Violet and Katie were cracking up as they tried to describe the huggable snowman to her. Zeus was asleep on his back in front of the door to the balcony, snoring quietly.

McCoy sat in an armchair nearby, sipping coffee and smiling at the two little girls. Kalani and Jen-Jen were hovering over a spread of room service that had been laid out across the entire kitchen counter space. Even Habst was in a noticeably better state, although his bruises had deepened and he favored his injured side. It still didn't stop him from piling a plate with more food than the average mortal could eat.

Seeing Habst's mountain of food, Charlie realized he too was starving. He hadn't eaten in more than a day.

"Morning, everybody," Charlie called out, dodging Kalani and Jen-Jen to secure some of the food for him and Meghan before it all disappeared. Everyone acknowledged him in their own way and Charlie felt genuinely good, despite their situation and what may still lie ahead. It was nice to have everyone with him, even if it was just for the moment. This was the closest thing to a family gathering the Walkers had had since moving to Florida.

Jen-Jen handed Charlie a cup of coffee as he sat down next to Habst, and he watched his wife as she sat with Victoria and the girls. Maybe it was just recent events coloring his mood, but he thought to himself that he'd never been more attracted to his wife than he was right then. She constantly found new ways to surprise him. He caught her eye and she threw him a sly wink before returning her attention to the girls.

"You got yourself some this morning, didn't you?" Habst speculated, holding out his fist for a congratulatory bump.

Fork halfway to his mouth, Charlie stared at him. Deciding to throw the kid a bone, he leaned in close.

"You're goddamn right," he growled—in his best Walter White impression—and bumped Habst's fist before returning to his food and shoveling it into his mouth.

He'd never seen Habst laugh harder.

"How you holding up, brother?" Charlie asked him after his laughter had died away.

"Sore. Everywhere. But I'm good." His voice dropped to a whisper. "I still can't get that shit that happened to Hector out of my head, though. Every time I close my eyes I see it."

Charlie nodded solemnly.

"I will make her pay for that—I promise you I will," Charlie said, matching Habst's whisper.

"Are more people going to die before this is over?"

Charlie didn't know how to answer that, so he bought himself a little time by taking another bite. Eventually, he decided that honesty was his best course of action.

"I don't know. If I can help it, everyone will be fine—but I don't even know what's coming. All I know is that it's bad, and the only people who can stop it are in this room."

Habst nodded and took a deep breath, let it out slowly.

"I'm ready to do what I have to. This place is my home, I gotta do my part, too."

Charlie considered this. Habst was hurt. Sending him out into the field would only make it worse and maybe get him killed. He couldn't bring himself to do that to him; the kid had already been through enough. Suddenly, he was aware that everyone in the room was looking at him—they'd overheard the conversation. Charlie decided to address them all.

"I don't know what's in store for us," he admitted. "Thirteen and her people are everywhere, they're unpredictable, and they're invisible. They're winning. We've had our asses handed to us since the beginning, but that's taught us something, hasn't it? It's taught us that being on the defensive doesn't work. She *wants* us backed into a corner. She *wants* us off balance. It's what allows her to stay so far ahead of us."

He looked around at everybody, making eye contact with each person in the room—even Violet and Katie, because they were as much a part of this as anyone.

"We need to be proactive. Instead of just playing along and hoping we don't step into another trap, we need a plan of our own. This is a war now." Charlie waved a hand around. "This place—this room—is our headquarters now. It's our war room. This is where we start to fight back."

He stood, took a sip of his coffee.

"Since we don't know what Thirteen is up to, or when she's going to contact us, our first priority is to secure this place. Victoria, does that Navigator come with any party supplies?"

She pursed her lips, thinking about it. "It's on loan from the FBI—one of their field mules. It'll be Bureau equipment but, from what I saw, they had two Glock 19Ms, two Colt AR-15s with some fancy attachments, two Kevlar vests, and some other gear in a Pelican case under the seat. On top of that, we came down with our own personal kit. Reduced, obviously, with just our computers, sidearms, and ammunition. We do, however, have April's rifle, a CheyTac M300 Intervention. It's big, it's loud, and it's expensive, and it can punch a hole through a steel plate from over a mile away. I don't know what good it'll do us—if any—but we have it, just in case."

Charlie winced internally as he heard mention of April's name, but he pushed the memory aside.

"Good. At some point soon, somebody should grab a luggage cart and get it all up here. I don't care if Thirteen's people are watching. It'll show them it's a bad idea to try anything here."

He turned to McCoy.

"You any good with that M300?" he asked the big, red-haired agent.

McCoy nodded, and that was enough for Charlie.

"Then I want you stationed here with Jen-Jen. We have three balconies and the field of view is insane. If we need to use it, we're in the right place. You two will stay with Meghan, Violet, and Katie. Keep them safe. Zeus is a retired duty K9—you can use him, too. Habst, I want you here, as well."

Habst looked like he was about to protest when Charlie unclipped his Walther from his belt. He set it on the table in front of Habst.

"That's for you. No safety, a round already in the chamber. I showed you the right way to hold it that day we went to the range, remember? Thumbs forward. All you have to do is point it at the bad guys and squeeze the trigger until they go to sleep. No time to worry about their feelings. They step in this room, they die. Understand?"

Habst picked up the Walther, careful not to point it at anyone. He had a quick flashback of Vega handing him a pistol the night before.

Something hardened within Habst then. These were his friends, and they were in danger right along with him.

"I got it."

Charlie gave him a quick nod.

"I want that back when this is over."

Habst grinned.

"Violet, Katie? You know Zeus' bad-guy commands. I'll need you to show everyone what they are."

The girls nodded, eager to be able to help.

"Meghan," Charlie pointed to his wife last. "I need you to keep our girls safe. And I need you to keep yourself safe. Thirteen is going to spilt us apart again, and this will be the hardest thing we'll ever have to do, but I will not lose any of you."

Meghan smiled at Charlie, and all the anxiety he'd felt over whether or not she'd run from him to save herself and the girls faded away. He'd been so stupid to think she'd ever abandon him. They were a team, and tearing them apart was as good as killing them. Nothing was more important to him. Maybe Thirteen knew this. Maybe it was still a part of her plan. If so, they would be ready for it.

"Victoria, do you still have access to that facial recognition software?"

"Always," she confirmed.

"Good. I *could* grant you access to Disney's cameras, but not from here—so that's a no-go. Do you still have that backdoor you used three years ago?"

"Of course."

"Then use it to find Thirteen."

Victoria bit her lip.

"I'm sure her people are already linked in; they'll see us if we're accessing live feeds."

Charlie nodded, having predicted this.

"Right. So don't access live feeds. We have a separate cloud server that stores past footage. I don't want to know where she is now—that won't do us any good; I want to know where she's *been*. She *has* to be staying close by, and if we can refine the search area at all then we might be able to hit her at home. Her people shouldn't be able to see if we're accessing the feed history. I doubt they even care about the recordings."

Victoria nodded slowly, seeing the merit in this idea.

"That could work," she agreed. "Also, I can mask our IP address to look like it's coming from Security. Even if someone's looking, they'll just see one more machine in Security accessing recorded files. It would take *way* too long for someone to check into activity like that, so there's a solid chance they couldn't find us even if they were looking."

Charlie grinned. He always felt better when there was a plan of action. There were still a lot of variables and they had no idea what Thirteen was planning, but the pressure was on her now—and she didn't know it. If she made a mistake or didn't cover her tracks, then they'd gain a much-needed advantage.

Habst spoke up just then, looking at Victoria.

"That facial recognition software you're talking about—does it *only* work on faces?"

Victoria cocked her head a bit.

"What did you have in mind?"

"You know that douchebag hipster guy she's always with? Well, him and his buddies all wear ridiculous vests. They all have a big embroidered patch on the back with Hatbox Ghost. Could you run that logo through the system?"

She considered it. Charlie was impressed by his ingenuity.

"That might actually work. But we don't have the logo. I don't think a drawing would work—we'd need the exact image."

All of the pieces of the puzzle fell into place in Charlie's head.

"The bathroom near Splash Mountain last night," he began. "When they hit us, she had a few of those guys with her. Find that footage, screengrab the vest, and plug it in. If we can find that vest, we can find the faces of the guys wearing them, and then you can get us their names and files. If this works, we can learn everything we need to know about her entire team."

"The ones that wear vests, at least," Victoria added, but she was smiling.

"Those are her enforcers," Charlie told her. "They're the public face and the muscle. If anyone is going to carry out an attack, it'll be them. We need that intel."

Kalani headed for the door.

"I'm going to get the gear," he announced with a quick salute then disappeared through the door.

For the first time since Habst had called him about Ramos' murder, Charlie finally started to feel a sense of optimism. It wasn't much, but it was a start. With any luck at all, they could find a weakness and maybe cause Thirteen to slip up. If they couldn't find an opening, maybe they could gain enough intel to *create* one.

Charlie took a sip of his coffee. It was cold now, but he didn't care. Everything tastes better when you're in a good mood.

*Time to turn this thing around,* he thought.

Then came the knock at the door.

# THIRTY-FOUR

JEN-JEN OPENED THE DOOR to a pretty, red-haired girl in her twenties clutching an olive green duffel to her chest as if her life depended on it. She didn't resemble Thirteen, but her hair color put the CIA operative on alert regardless.

"There something I can help you with?" Jen-Jen asked, quizzically. The girl stared at her, seemingly confused, and then tried to look past her into the room.

"Is, uh, Charlie Walker here?" the girl asked.

"The only Walker here is Johnnie, and the bottle is almost empty. Sorry," Jen-Jen smiled politely and began to close the door.

"Please wait!" the girl blurted, and Jen-Jen paused. The girl leaned in close and whispered, "They said he'd be here. They told me if I didn't find him… it would be bad."

Jen-Jen leaned out into the hallway and looked in both directions. Seeing nobody but the girl, she quickly ushered her inside.

"Get in here fast, little girl," Jen-Jen muttered, and closed the door behind her. She drew her sidearm. "Try something stupid, and catch a bullet," she warned.

The girl spotted Charlie near the table and started toward him.

"Whoa, whoa!" Jen-Jen barked. "Hold on a sec. Put the bag on the counter and go stand against that wall." She pointed to the opposite side of the room.

Skittishly, the girl did as she was ordered. Victoria stood and approached the girl.

"I'm sorry about this, but we can't be too careful," she apologized, before thoroughly frisking the frightened girl. Finding nothing dangerous, she nodded. "You're good."

Charlie recognized the girl. She was a Cast Member, a face character. He didn't know her name, but he knew she was one of the actors that played Ariel in the Grotto at the Magic Kingdom.

"I know you," he told her. "What's your name?"

"Carina Whittaker," Habst spoke up, startling Charlie, who turned to him with a half-confused, half-amused look on his face.

"What?" Habst asked defensively. He was too tired for subtlety. With a wave of his hand, he said simply, "She's hot, dude. I know her name."

Grinning and shaking his head, Charlie turned back to Carina.

"Why'd they send you here, Carina?" he asked.

She swallowed hard, almost as if she was afraid of Charlie.

"They gave me that bag. Told me that if I didn't bring it directly to you— in this room—then they'd hurt my sister and me. I didn't know what to do."

Charlie put a reassuring hand on her shoulder.

"It's okay, you did the right thing. This is my problem; no need for you or anyone else to get hurt because of it."

"Oh, shit," Jen-Jen exclaimed, having opened the bag. She turned to Carina. "Did you open this after they gave it to you?"

Carina looked like she was going to cry.

"No! I didn't want any more trouble. I just brought it here as fast as I could. It's not a bomb or something, is it? Oh god."

"Come look at this, guys," Jen-Jen suggested, ignoring Carina's question.

Everyone but Carina, Habst, and the kids gathered around the bag.

"What the hell is this?" Charlie asked. The duffel was almost entirely full of painters' respirators. There were at least ten, including two small pink masks meant for children.

Charlie pulled the respirators out of the bag, setting each one on the counter. When he had them all out, he noticed a passport in the bottom of the bag. He retrieved it and flipped it open. As he suspected, it wasn't a real passport, but one of the souvenir World Showcase ones they sold at EPCOT Center's gift shops so that Guests could visit each country's pavilion and get it stamped as proof of their visit. Each country had its own page with information about the corresponding pavilion.

Charlie flipped through the booklet, noticing that most of the eleven pavilions had been stamped. The only one left unmarked was Canada. He couldn't deduce any significance from this, but he also understood that Thirteen never did anything without a reason. Other than this, there was no discernable information. No demands, no instructions—nothing.

"Not a lot to go on, here," he admitted after double-checking that the bag was empty. "Some respirators and a World Showcase passport. That mean anything to anyone?"

Victoria shrugged.

"You're the Epcot expert. If it doesn't mean anything to you, then none of us are going to know what the hell it means."

*Fair point*, Charlie thought with a shrug. He ignored this development for now, compartmentalizing again as he had earlier. There were bigger problems in the room that could be solved first.

"Jen-Jen, can you get a hold of Bell and LeCarre?"

She nodded and pulled out her phone.

Charlie approached Carina and spoke to her. "I need you to give Agent Jennings your sister's info. She'll have her picked up. Bell and LeCarre are friends of ours—detectives. We'll get you both put into protective custody while we deal with this. You'll be safe."

After telling Jen-Jen where her sister could be found, Carina stared at Charlie.

"It's not true, is it?" she asked, as if confirming something she'd thought earlier.

"What's not true?" Charlie asked.

"What she said about you. That woman. She said that you were a killer, and that you were going to kill thousands of people today."

"She fucking *what?*" blurted Habst from his seat at the table. Carina ignored him.

"She said that you were a bad guy and that you were going to cause a terrible tragedy today, and that if I brought that bag to you, I'd be helping to stop you."

While Charlie exchanged a concerned look with Victoria, Habst got up and walked over to Carina.

"Girl, you are smoking hot, but you have to be dumber than a bag of hammers to believe that bitch. Do you see this?" He pointed to his face; she'd have to be blind not to be able to see the damage. "*She* did this. She killed our friends. She's trying to kill us."

"Habst...." Charlie warned.

"No, man. I'm sick of this. How can Thirteen do all this awful shit and still try to convince people *we're* the bad guys? Carina, *everyone* in this room is trying to stop that woman. Charlie used to be a cop, these people are CIA agents, and they all stopped a terrorist from lighting up Space Mountain a few years ago. Those people that gave you that bag are the real bad guys."

Carina didn't say anything.

"Also," Habst continued. "You seriously believed someone would threaten you and your sister so you'd help them stop the bad guys? Really? *They* are the good guys?"

Charlie put a hand on Habst's back.

"It's alright, man—it's not Carina's fault," Charlie told him, calmly. This, Habst assumed, was his dad voice. "Thirteen is trying to cause chaos by turning everyone against us. You know that. We're going to finish this, and we're going to finish it soon."

Habst nodded apologetically, his frustration expended.

"Are you thinking what I'm thinking?" he asked.

"That Thirteen is planning an attack and that if I somehow survive it she's going to pin it on me?" Charlie theorized.

Habst pointed finger guns at Charlie.

"Exactly."

"Not going to happen," Charlie promised. "We're going to stop her. Step one is figuring out what that passport means."

Charlie walked over to the counter and retrieved the passport. He flipped through it again.

"One thing's for certain: we're meant to visit the Canada Pavilion. Maybe we won't find out why until we get there but at least it's something to go on."

Before anyone could respond, the door to the villa banged open and Kalani dragged in a luggage cart filled with black plastic cases of various sizes, as well as a few canvas bags.

"Uber Blaster Delivery, at your service," he joked, before pausing to stare at Carina with curiosity. "Aloha, little *wahine*. You look familiar."

Kalani, being as laid back as he was, asked no questions about Carina's presence. He assumed that if nobody was pointing a gun at her, then she wasn't a threat. He proceeded to pull the cart over to the dining room table and began offloading gear.

"Charles—here," he called, tossing Charlie a small black case.

Charlie opened the case to find an FBI-issue Glock 19M, and three loaded magazines. He accepted a slim Safariland paddle holster and placed it on his hip. It was the FBI's concealment holster, so it disappeared easily beneath his shirt, even with the Glock riding inside. The weapon was much larger than his Walther, but it carried more than double the ammunition, and Charlie feared he might need that extra firepower before the day was over.

"Who gets the other one?" Kalani asked, and Charlie pointed to his wife. The bulk of their firepower needed to be in this room. If Thirteen chose to hit them, they'd have to do it here—and Charlie wanted Meghan to be able to protect herself and the girls.

Meghan accepted the weapon graciously and checked the action. Satisfied, she holstered the weapon in a slim shoulder rig Victoria gave her. It was left unsaid, but Meghan assumed the holster had once belonged to April.

In the years since the Holloway incident, Charlie had given his wife and daughters frequent small arms training. Meghan, Violet, and Katie all understood safe firearms operation, and could each handle a nine-millimeter pistol with more than enough proficiency to save their lives. Violet, specifically, had impressed Charlie with her accuracy. He was more than comfortable leaving loaded firearms with any of them.

Charlie turned to Carina.

"Sorry if this is a little scary, but the people we're up against have much worse."

McCoy silently opened a large case and began assembling April's M300. Victoria hadn't been kidding—the rifle was enormous. The rounds he loaded into the magazine were massive. He unfolded and attached a bipod to the rifle's handguard, then set the entire weapon on a low table facing the doorwall. At first, the placement confused him, but then Charlie understood why. If McCoy needed to fire that weapon, he would do so from a position deep within the room. Shooting from eight or ten feet back would hide the muzzle flash from any counter-sniper spotters Thirteen may have in place. He would definitely be heard, but not seen—and that could save his life.

Victoria offered Charlie one of the two Kevlar vests but he turned it down, and instead had her give both to the kids. They were too large and didn't fit well, but they'd stop a bullet if worse came to worst.

"Okay," Charlie said when all were kitted out. "I'm going to have a look at this pavilion—see if I can't find a clue. Victoria, you all set with the cameras?"

"Five by five," she agreed. "I'll call you as soon as we learn anything."

"Big Kahuna, you with me?" Charlie asked, pointing to his friend.

Kalani scoffed, "Of course I am, little man. It'll be just like old times."

Charlie nodded; he would feel a lot more comfortable having Kalani watching his back.

"Jen-Jen, are the detectives on their way?" Charlie asked, wanting to be sure everything was taken care of before he left.

"They're inbound but need to make a couple of stops first. ETA is a few hours. They offered to post units here with us in the meantime but I declined. Didn't tell them our suspicions about Thirteen's possible attack. I figure either we stop her, or they can find out about it with everyone else. They'd just get in the way if they knew. And you better not tell them anything either," Jen-Jen said to Carina, pointing a finger at her.

Carina put up her hands in surrender and gave a weak smile.

"Good girl," Jen-Jen said, and winked at her.

Before leaving, Charlie made his way over to his wife and daughters. Meghan stepped in close and put her arms around him. He hugged her to his chest and put an arm around the girls as well. Zeus whined, upset that he'd been left out. Charlie scratched him behind the ear and it earned him a tail wag.

"Guard," Charlie told the big shepherd, and placed a hand on each of his girls in turn. Zeus licked Katie's face and she giggled.

"Be careful. Come back to us," Meghan whispered, letting him go.

"I promise I will. I love you guys," he told them, heading toward the door. With that, Charlie and Kalani headed out into the unknown.

# THIRTY-FIVE

ALFIE DROVE THE BOX TRUCK while Thirteen rode in the passenger seat. They were headed for Epcot, carrying the last pieces of her big surprise. Over the last several months, Thirteen had paid an exorbitant amount of money to have a designer neurotoxin developed that could withstand the Floridian ecosystem and maintain potency long enough to deal the desired amount of damage. Testing had shown that the toxin had an effective lethal duration of twenty minutes outdoors before becoming inert. The manufacture of the required volume and dispensers had cost her even more than the development. Still, at ten times the cost, it would have been worth every penny.

Using historical data and weather forecasts, as well as taking into account the heat, humidity, and light breeze typical of the season, Thirteen had calculated an almost universal spread. The toxin would disperse over nearly every inch of the park within fifteen minutes—more than enough time for the chemical to do its job. The death toll would be in the tens of thousands. She'd injected Harland Caulfield with that very neurotoxin mere hours ago and the effect had been dramatic, to say the least.

It was Friday, it was Earth Day, and it was Thirteen's plan to make sure the air itself would be the very thing that killed everyone in and around Epcot.

The previous afternoon, tanks of the aerosolized toxin had been loaded into the Smellitzers inside Spaceship Earth and Journey Into Imagination which she planned to deploy today at exactly three o'clock—the busiest time. She'd even planned to have it loaded into Soarin' before she found out it was closed.

The rest of the park, however, had required a little more creativity. She'd designed special dispersal units—two for each World Showcase pavilion, and one for each of the remaining Future World pavilions. They sat right out in the open as portable Smellitzers that were being utilized for the weeklong Earth Day celebration. She'd cleverly themed them to each area and collectively labeled them as the "Spring Scentsation Tour."

The dispensers had been in place all week and, much to Thirteen's surprise, people really seemed to enjoy them. Today, however, their payload would be something significantly more dangerous than themed aromas.

Thirteen smiled as she considered the irony.

It would be the most visible tragedy in the nation's history. Everyone's worst fears would be realized: the Disney bubble could be penetrated and its perceived safety was only an illusion. Thirteen would show the world that no one was untouchable.

A year ago, her plan had been solely to destroy Charlie Walker and X-ray Team. But it had evolved into so much more. What had started as a simple act of revenge had grown into something grand—something others had surely imagined, but hadn't had the stones to carry out.

Alfie had been half-right when he'd called her out on the balcony. Charlie Walker had become nothing more than a convenient "in" to give her a reason to come to this place. He would die by her hand, sooner or later, but he was no longer her priority—and he hadn't been for some time. Whether he died when the toxin was released, or after, didn't matter to Thirteen. Defeating Walker had been a way for Thirteen to publicly assert her dominance over both Walker and Spencer Holloway, but he had led her to an unexpected opportunity that would accomplish that goal exponentially more effectively.

Walker, in all his arrogance, was fully convinced that this was still all about him. He would soon learn that he was not the center of the universe— and he would learn this by seeing the people it was his job to protect dying all around him. It made Thirteen laugh. Charlie Walker's greatest failure would be his last. Depending on what she chose to do, the attack could be pinned on him but, if it wasn't, it would be his fault anyway. The hero that saved the Magic Kingdom and was later hired to protect the entire resort failed to stop the largest attack on American soil since 9/11. His face would be plastered across all media outlets as the greatest disappointment of his generation. All of his accomplishments would be erased in the face of this failure—and *that* would be how Charlie Walker would be remembered.

It's one thing to hurt a person, another to kill them—yet it was an order of magnitude greater to destroy a person's legacy. To eradicate them completely from the world's favor is better than pain, or death, or anything else. This would wipe away every good deed he'd ever done and turn his name to mud, because people these days only cared about what was current. Sure, Walker was a hero several times over, but in an age where social media focuses the world's attention on only the most recent events, all of his good deeds would be forgotten.

This line of thinking brought her back to the shipment she and Alfie now carried. Originally, she had intended to mix the nerve agent with helium to fill the balloons sold throughout the park, but she quickly learned that Epcot—Walker's favorite park—had no balloon vendors. Still, Thirteen hadn't become the person she was without a healthy ability to adapt.

Since she couldn't fill balloons and watch chaos spread outside the park as Guests took her neurotoxin home with them, she decided that she wanted to see her plan come to fruition from *inside* the park. Their truck carried flight cases packed with the highest-quality hazmat protection gear available on the planet. They'd stolen the suits and masks from a CDC viral weapons research facility and kept them for this very purpose. Just before they released the toxin, Thirteen and the rest of her team would don the suits and walk among the Guests as they died.

When all was said and done, a helicopter was scheduled to pick them up south of Innoventions. It would then fly them east to the coast where they would board a chartered yacht to abscond to Bermuda while the carnage unfolded behind them. Nobody would question a single helicopter flying away from the scene, as the eyes of the earth would be on the unthinkable tragedy she'd left behind. Sure, it was arrogant and risky—but it would work. She was sure of it.

Thirteen's team of Spectres, while almost supernaturally efficient, was surprisingly small. Taking into account the two dead men from the assault on Walker's house and the one killed on the road, she still had ten people, including herself. All of the mundane work—setting everything up, installing dispensers, rigging up traps, swapping payloads—had been done by locals that had been bribed, threatened, or tricked. Who better to carry out these various tasks than the people who knew the place best? It had been surprisingly easy to gain the cooperation of everyone she'd needed.

▼▲▼

"You really want to be *inside* the place when those dispensers go off?" Alfie asked her, not for the first time.

"Did you bring me subpar hazmat gear?" she asked in reply.

"Of course not, but there are loads of variables involved here. These people are going to be in a great deal of pain; they are going to be desperate and dying. What happens when they see us in our suits? You think they won't immediately try to take them from us? What happens when one of them grabs hold of one of us and rips a seal? Nobody is immune to the toxin."

Thirteen smiled sadly at him.

"Alfie, you will be armed. You are a trained killer. You've been in more combat scenarios than I can count. If you—or anyone else on the team, for that matter—can't stop a fat, dying vacationer from getting inside your guard then what the fuck good are you to me?"

For a split second, she saw a shadow of distrust pass over Alfie's face, but it was gone just as quickly.

"I'm just saying that this is risky. We should leave now. We can watch the coverage from the yacht."

"You want to watch this on *TV*?" Thirteen glared at him. "You're *here*, Alfie. You get to be one of the only people on earth to see history being written in front of you, and you want to watch it on a little screen like the rest of the world? I swear I don't even know you anymore."

Alfie sighed.

"It was only a suggestion. I just didn't want to take an unnecessary risk."

"*Unnecessary risk?*" Thirteen scoffed. "Alfie, your job is literally *only* unnecessary risks. The Spectres are professional unnecessary-risk takers. Do we actually *need* to do what we do? Absolutely fucking not. We do it because we're good at it, it's fun, and we're all crazy. Do you suddenly not meet the requirements of this team?"

"You know I'm willing to do anything for you."

Thirteen grinned.

"That's what I like to hear. Now, did the package get delivered to Walker yet?"

He nodded and grinned.

"Patrick just texted me. He says the redhead girl has entered the villa with the bag. You think Walker liked our little joke?"

As an added insult, Thirteen had sent a bag to Walker containing more than enough respirators to cover his family and the surviving CIA agents. The filters on those respirators were barely functional and wouldn't do them any good. She assumed he would be smart enough to understand that—and that he understood the joke. The bag also contained the "clue" that would send him into the Canada Pavilion and keep him in the park long enough to witness her surprise firsthand.

At this point, she'd dumbfounded the ex-detective enough times to where she was certain he would furiously pursue this game she'd given him until he was sure he'd figured it out. The joke, this time, was that there was no game. It was a wild goose chase that would lead him to make an impossible choice. He'd learn that there was no way out for him. She hoped he would bring everyone with him to the park, but even if he didn't the resort in which they'd set up camp was close enough to be hit by the toxin.

That was part of her plan as well.

The previous night, after she'd left Hollywood Studios, Thirteen had made a few phone calls. Having known that Walker's house would be uninhabitable—possibly forever, after what the Spectres had done—she'd assumed his first reaction would be to use his status as head of Security to gain the use of a room at one of Disney's resorts. Using her methods of coercion, Thirteen had made sure the only resorts that would offer Walker any availability were the Yacht Club, Beach Club, or the BoardWalk. This guaranteed that wherever he chose to house his loved ones, it would be within the kill zone. Even if he came to the park alone, anyone left behind at the resort would still perish.

That made her smile wider.

▼▲▼

Alfie parked the truck backstage alongside the World ShowPlace Pavilion and the pair stepped out, greeted by three of the remaining Spectres. The other five members of her team were already setting the day's events in motion, with two in the Canada Pavilion and the rest seeded throughout the resort area.

"Everything all set?" she asked.

"Everything's good to go. All systems are online and ready to be activated. The hot button is on your phone," said Greene, the man Charlie Walker had known as Murphy. "You just have to input the go-code and confirm. Then we can watch the show."

"Fan-fucking-tastic. Suits are in the back of the truck. Break them open and have them ready to rock. We'll be back in a few hours. For now, Alfie and I are going to spend some time in the park—maybe see why all these morons spend so much money to be here. It is more than likely, after all, that this will be the last day this place will ever be in operation."

Greene comically placed a hand behind his ear as if listening for something.

"I can hear the screams already!" he joked, grinning wide.

With a laugh, Thirteen and Alfie made their way into Epcot.

It was going to be an unforgettable day.

# THIRTY-SIX

CANADA, EH?" KALANI ASKED, nudging Charlie with an elbow as they entered the park through the International Gateway.

"Canada, indeed. Not sure where to start, though. We don't even know what we're looking for. Still, it's Thirteen, so I'm sure there will be something theatrical and threatening for us to find there."Joking aside, neither of them were comfortable with entering this next game blind.

"Do they sell those turkey legs here?" Kalani asked as they made their way through the United Kingdom Pavilion, his thoughts traveling back to the time they'd gotten them when hunting members of Chaos Squad at Hollywood Studios.

Charlie looked at him as if he was insane.

"Dude... you *just* ate."

Kalani grinned at him.

"That was, like, an hour ago. I'm a big boy. One day you'll grow up and eat like an adult, too. Maybe fill out that bird chest of yours."

Charlie laughed.

"Fair enough, Sasquatch. Closest turkey legs are in the American Adventure Pavilion, which is in the complete opposite direction from where we're headed—so you're out of luck."

"Bummer."

As they made their way to the Canada Pavilion, Charlie couldn't help but notice how busy World Showcase already was. The Flower & Garden Festival was in full swing, and with the added chaos of it being Earth Day, Charlie predicted the crowds would only get heavier as the day went on. Whatever Thirteen had planned, it would happen here, and it would happen today. The Canada Pavilion itself isn't very large. It consists of a Circle-Vision film called *O Canada!*, a restaurant called Le Cellier, a shop, and a small stage. Not much to go on.

"Let's try the store," Charlie suggested.

Kalani shrugged. It was as good a place to start as any.

Entering the store, they found it nearly empty. From experience, Charlie found that this was the case most of the time. For whatever reason, this shop never saw much traffic despite the fact that it had some really interesting and unique items. Aside from Kalani and Charlie, the only other occupants were a flannel-clad Cast Member and a family of three near the rear of the store.

Charlie sighed.

"I honestly don't know what I expected," he admitted.

"Remember the Pirates store? There were pictures of your family in a digital frame. Maybe we just need to look harder," Kalani offered.

Charlie nodded and began perusing shelves, but he had a feeling that he would find nothing out of the ordinary. Thirteen, he had come to realize, was a master of playing with his expectations. Any time he thought he had her figured out, she evolved. Now that he'd become acclimated to her games and how she presented clues and evidence to him, she'd changed the formula. Gone were the treasure maps and puzzles; now he was left with the bare minimum. From the passport in his back pocket, he could deduce nothing other than that she wanted him in this specific pavilion. There was nothing else, and that frustrated him.

Years without detective work had left him rusty. His security work in the parks hadn't amounted to much more than a few physical confrontations. Aside from Habst's situation, the attacker in the Haunted Mansion, and a couple of other minor instances, he hadn't needed to use his detective's brain—and he honestly felt out of practice. Still, as frustrating as this was, he couldn't shake the feeling that it wasn't his lack of detection skills impeding his progress. He simply felt that there was nothing to find. He couldn't help but feel as if the passport was a red herring, more misdirection meant to keep him out of the way.

He stopped searching.

*There was no threat.*

Charlie didn't know why he hadn't noticed this earlier, but it was true. Thirteen had given him another cryptic challenge, but she had alluded to no threat for failure, nor to any prize for victory. There was nothing. As it stood, he didn't feel that he was *required* to participate in this game. There were no stakes.

"Kalani," he called out. "Am I missing something? What's the prize for winning this game?"

Kalani ran a hand through his hair.

"There isn't one, as far as I know."

"And what happens to us if we lose?" he asked.

The big Hawaiian shrugged.

"Nothing? I don't know. I don't think she said anything about that either."

Charlie spread his hands.

"Then why the hell are we here?"

It was then that Charlie noticed the store was even emptier than it had been when they'd entered. They had made it to the rear of the store, and the family that had been there had left. Even the flannel-wearing Cast Member was nowhere to be found.

Charlie heard footsteps approaching. Two sets.

"You're here because *we* want you to be here," a voice spoke. Charlie couldn't find its source. "You'll find out the rules and prizes when *we* want you to. And you'll do as *we* tell you."

"Come on, show yourself. I don't have time for this," Charlie barked impatiently.

Two men stepped out from around a corner, both clad in dark denim vests.

Spectres.

One of them had an arm in a sling, while the other had a jagged scar along his jaw.

"That's better," goaded Charlie. "Now tell me what you want. Let's get this over with."

The scarred one spoke.

"Just the two of you, eh?" Scar said. "No matter, that's enough. Why don't you boys go see a film? I hear the one next door is worth a watch."

"You coming with us, big man?" Kalani shot back, his chin raised.

Scar grinned, "Not yet. But don't worry, you and I are gonna dance real soon."

With that, the Spectres turned on their heels and casually made their way out.

Kalani was startled to see Charlie hurrying past him, quickly but quietly moving after the Spectres. He had something in his hand that Kalani at first mistook to be a gun, but was actually a phone.

Charlie hurried after them, snapping as many pictures of their vests as he could, hoping to get something he could send to Victoria. Satisfied, he broke away unnoticed and headed back to Kalani.

"Not going to lie, *braddah*, I thought you were going to shoot them dead."

Charlie grinned.

"As much as I'd have liked to, we've got to play it a little smarter for now. I think I've got something we can use."

Looking through his burst of photos, Charlie found he'd captured an extremely clear photo of the vest logo. Immediately, he dropped it into a text to Victoria.

Our first lucky break, he said. Find them.

As he and Kalani headed toward *O Canada!*, Charlie got a response from Victoria.

Perfect! Your cloud server was a homerun. I've got her and the boyfriend leaving an executive suite over at the Swan and Dolphin earlier this morning. Room should be empty now. I'm going to head over there soon. I'll keep you updated.

For the second time in as many minutes, Charlie felt that their luck was changing. He was gaining the upper hand.

Watch yourself, he warned her. Who knows where the rest of her guys are?

Victoria simply responded with a wink emoji, and he decided not to further lecture a CIA field operative on how to do her job.

"Victoria found their base," Charlie told Kalani as they made their way into the show building.

"Finally some good news," Kalani sighed. "Still makes me nervous, though."

"Agreed," Charlie nodded as they approached the Cast Member outside the theater.

"Good timing, eh?" the Cast Member said in greeting. "Show's just about to begin and it looks like you gents have the place to yourselves."

Charlie nodded his thanks to the Cast Member as he and Kalani made their way inside.

"Here we go again," Charlie groaned, noticing the similarities to Holloway's hijacking of the Carousel of Progress in an empty theater. He found it peculiar that not a single person was waiting to see the show, but it wasn't unexpected. He'd seen entire sections of the parks cleared by people on either side several times.

Circle-Vision movies, unlike most shows, are shown in standing-only theaters. The action takes place on screens surrounding the room in a full 360-degree circle. Charlie had only seen the most recent version of this show once, and couldn't remember it being remarkable, but he had a feeling he wouldn't forget it this time.

"How do you think she'll try to kill us now?" Kalani joked. "Taco Neck Syndrome from trying to look at all these screens at once?"

Charlie laughed, but his laughter faded as the doors closed with a solid *clang*, a note that rang with an unsettling sense of finality. Even Kalani sobered up as the lights dimmed.

"Okay, not liking the feeling of all of this dark space surrounding us," the big Hawaiian admitted, gazing around at the blackness beneath the screens.

Already, Charlie could tell something was off. No Cast Member stood at the podium to recite the introduction. Still, he didn't feel threatened.

He shook his head.

"If she wanted us dead, we'd be dead already. No, this is something else. She's putting on a show for us."

As if Charlie had summoned it, Thirteen appeared onscreen. She didn't immediately take advantage of the full-surround capability, instead opting to use only a single panel. She was dressed in a red flannel button-up shirt, similar to the Cast Member from the nearby store, but unbuttoned halfway to expose a black bra and a healthy amount of cleavage. Standing before a dark backdrop—similar to Martin Short in the actual *O Canada!* film— she peered up over her thick-rimmed glasses as if she were truly making eye contact with Charlie. Charlie leaned forward, his elbows on the railing before him, preparing to absorb whatever theatrics she was about to put on display. Her lip was uninjured, he noticed, so this had been filmed far enough in advance that she hadn't yet encountered Vega and Habst.

"Well, you did it. You've made it here alive," she said simply. "But we all knew you would—right? The famous Charlie Walker wouldn't go out in an earlier round, would he? No. You're too good for that."

She shifted in her seat, more cleavage spilling out—a move that was clearly intentional; he'd seen her use it before.

"What if I told you that you *aren't* that good, though? What if I told you that you'd be here no matter what happened during any of those games? Would you believe me? You should. How about this one: this has never been about you."

Charlie nodded to himself, recently having guessed that this whole thing really had nothing to do with him other than a convenient connection to Thirteen's old team.

"But I'm glad you're here. You'll appreciate what I've created. Disney loves Preview Centers, right? Little rooms with videos and models showing you shit they're doing in the future so that you'll think all those price increases actually count for something. Well, let's temporarily call this theater Thirteen's Preview Center. You are going to get a never-before-seen preview of what *I* have planned for the future. Take a look at this sizzle reel really quick."

She snapped her fingers and the scene changed to a generic shot of scientists in a lab. Semi-transparently overlaid onto that scene was a montage of more stock footage and still images: pipettes, petri dishes, a biohazard symbol. These frames began to bleed over onto adjacent screens until the footage was completely surrounding them. Charlie recognized it as a distinctly Disney-esque presentation style despite the subject matter. Soon, pleasant music and a voiceover began, and Charlie was taken aback, as he was almost certain he recognized the voice of Mike Brassell, a narrator of Living with the Land and the Tomorrowland Transit Authority PeopleMover.

"The twenty-first century has brought with it an abundance of technological innovation. Everything—from cellular telephones, to medicine, to cars and cuisine—has benefited from this advancement." The stock footage changed to flyovers of farms and food production factories. Charlie found it hard to focus in any one direction, a problem he'd often had with Circle-Vision films. "Suddenly, we are using technology not only to create, but to *enhance*. Crops have been modified at a genetic level to improve flavor, nutrition, yield, and price. Even the medical industry has seen a boom, as new vaccines and medications are being developed every day, helping people across the globe defeat illnesses once thought incurable."

The music darkened and the shot changed to insurgents fighting in the Middle East and bombs being dropped on cities. It was strange to see all of these acts of violence on screens usually utilized for footage which is more positive and hopeful.

"As the old adage goes, there are two sides to every coin. With every humanitarian triumph, an opposite creation is born of malevolence. New advancements in weaponry and battlefield technology have come to a head; the future isn't in nuclear warfare—as originally expected—but in *biological* warfare. Battles are no longer being fought with the biggest bombs, but the smallest pathogens. Chemicals are being developed that can do more damage than blasts ever could.

"It is here our story begins to take shape. In an undisclosed laboratory, a team of biological engineers has undertaken the development of a designer neurotoxin called Spectre. This highly modified strain of synthetic tetrodotoxin is easily and quickly adaptable to different climates, populations, transmission vectors, and—most importantly—distribution formats. Across twelve iterations, this neurotoxin came close to, but could not meet, all of those criteria. Perseverance won the day, however, as the thirteenth iteration is nothing less than perfection."

The footage changed again, but something about it was different. The production values of the stock footage were gone, and the film had reverted to a single screen. The scene they now viewed was shaky handheld footage shot on somebody's phone.

This footage was of a different laboratory setting, with many people in lab coats celebrating and drinking champagne. After a few moments, one of the people attempted to excuse herself and leave the room, only to struggle to open the door. At first, she laughed, but moments later her laughter turned to panic as she realized the door had been locked. Other people joined in, trying to open any door or window they could to no avail. They'd been locked in, and Charlie assumed he was about to learn why. He didn't want to watch, but he forced himself to look.

"What the fuck is this?" Kalani asked, more to himself than anyone.

After what felt like an eternity, but in reality was less than a minute, the onscreen struggles and panic of the people in the lab turned to agony. One man fell to the floor, blood rushing from his mouth, ears and eyes. The woman who'd first discovered the locked door vomited blood into her hands and stared at it, disbelieving. One man fell and, reaching out for anything to break his fall, dragged a desk lamp down with him. The lamp's shade broke free and rolled away just as a woman in a blood-soaked lab coat fell backwards atop it, the glass shattering and cutting into her back.

All around the lab, people died grisly, violent deaths at the hands of the invisible neurotoxin. It didn't need to be said, but Charlie understood that this was the team that had developed the toxin. Thirteen had used the product on the people she had hired to create it.

"Spectre Thirteen," the narration continued. "The first wholly successful iteration of the Spectre toxin. It is odorless, tasteless, and invisible to the naked eye. It can be delivered in almost any form—liquid, gas, or aerosolized. It can be inhaled, injected, ingested, or even transmitted through abraded skin. Above all else, Spectre Thirteen has a one-hundred percent mortality rate. It is the perfect weapon for the modern age."

After the narration ended, the footage remained, but by this point, the person filming the scene had died and the phone camera was static, stuck facing the ceiling. This lasted only a few moments before the flannel-clad Thirteen reappeared.

"Do you like it, Charlie?" she asked, a genuine smile stretched across her pretty face. "What kind of dumb luck is that? The *thirteenth* iteration is perfection. Incredible!"

She took a deep breath, almost shivering with pleasure.

"So, now that you've seen Spectre Thirteen's private maiden voyage, how would you like to be at the public world premiere? If so, you're in luck—check this out!"

The shot switched from Thirteen to that of a YouTube vlog showing strange machines around World Showcase. Charlie listened closely as the vlogger, whose voice he recognized, narrated what they were filming.

"Look at these things," the vlogger said, pointing at the machines as he spoke. "Disney just installed these all over the park for the Earth Day celebration this week. They're portable Smellitzers that are pumping out all kinds of different scents! How neat is that?"

Thirteen came back onscreen.

"I had these installed almost a week ago. You've been on vacation so you might not have seen them. Don't worry—right now, they're only pumping out harmless scents, and people really seem to be digging them. That being said, later today, those babies will be spewing pure death. I've brought enough Spectre Thirteen to wipe the whole fucking place out. I've also got the toxin scheduled for dispersal from the existing Smellitzers in Spaceship Earth and Journey Into Imagination. Hell, I've even got dispensers all over Future World because Thirteen strives for perfection."

Thirteen winked.

"So, for our intrepid vlogger, at three o'clock today it really will be time to pay the price."

Thirteen actually laughed at this.

"Jesus, Charlie," Kalani whispered. "She's going to release it here—today. We might already be too late."

Thirteen took a deep breath, then continued.

"This is where you come in, Charlie. I emptied out this theater and brought you here to give you a choice. Once the doors open, you can hurry back to your family, pack them up, and get out of Dodge before the toxin is released. You'll live, obviously, but would you really want to?"

Multiple screens began to display various archived news clips of the aftermath of natural disasters, first responders, bodies covered in sheets, and candlelight vigils with dozens of people crying. Each one was overlaid with a CNN news ticker that read:

**THOUSANDS DEAD IN HORRIFIC ATTACK AT WALT DISNEY WORLD. CHARLIE WALKER SEEN FLEEING THE AREA WITH FAMILY HOURS BEFORE. AUTHORITIES ARE ON HIGH ALERT.**

Thirteen smiled.

"Pretty self-explanatory: you leave, it's your fault. They'll either think you did it, or you let it happen. You're probably saying to yourself, 'I'll just warn everyone and evacuate the park.' But that's a stupid idea, since I will know about it, and I'll release Spectre Thirteen immediately. So try not to do that.

"The second option is to stick around and be a part of the show. Of course, that means you die, but at least you die a hero. Or a martyr. Whatever. In any case, you'll be dead—that's the main point.

"I'll be sticking around for the duration. My team has brought hazmat suits capable of withstanding the toxin, so we'll be walking through the park and watching the carnage. After the show, a helicopter is going to fly right into the park and pick us up. Yes, it's dramatic. Yes, it's cliché—but I think it's fucking hilarious so that's what I'm doing. I hope you live *just* long enough to see it."

Thirteen sighed contentedly.

"Now, you might be thinking, 'Those aren't very good choices. There's no way for me to win!' Here's my favorite part: you are more than welcome to try to stop me. I won't be giving you any clues from this point on, and this will probably be the last time you'll see my face. You're probably asking yourself, 'Did she build in a way for me to stop this toxin from releasing?' And I know it'll piss you off, but I'm going to answer that with a maybe. *Maybe* I did install a way for you to be the attention-whoring hero you love to be, or *maybe* I didn't. *Maybe* I'm so confident in my plan and my designs that I'm going to let you bang your head against the wall until you fail. You'll never know unless you try.

"I'll leave you with this: False hope is still hope, but hope might just be the most dangerous thing in the world. Good luck, Charlie."

With an almost sad smile, Thirteen gave a little salute and the screen went blank. The lights came up and the doors opened.

Without pause, Charlie headed toward the exit in a hurry, already speaking.

"We need to get eyes on those machines. We need to see if there's a way to—"

"You need to slow right down," said Scar, as he walked into the theater through the exit door. "Now, Thirteen may have told you to try and stop her, but I don't think that was very smart of her. I think I'll just end you now and tell her you died from the toxin."

Kalani stepped forward.

"Charlie, go. I've got this," he said, pushing Charlie toward the door and rushing Scar.

Scar seemed to have underestimated the massive Hawaiian, as he was much faster than his size suggested. Kalani darted in, got inside Scar's guard, and delivered two quick right strikes to the Spectre's abdomen. Scar doubled over, but recovered quickly and kicked out toward Kalani's knee. Kalani, prepared for the strike, spun to the side, but not before Scar caught him across the jaw with a surprise left, spinning him off balance. Kalani went down to his knees as Scar rushed in, his arm cocked back for a fight-ending overhand right.

And then Scar's wrist shattered, as Charlie struck him from the side with his collapsible baton. Scar opened his mouth to scream but it was too late. Charlie already had a bicep locked around his throat in a viselike rear naked choke. Immediately, Charlie had cut off both Scar's oxygen supply as well as the blood supply to his brain.

Kalani recovered and opened his mouth to crack a joke, but something in Charlie's eyes gave the big Hawaiian pause. The Spectre had stopped struggling, but still Charlie held strong.

"Let him go, *braddah*, it's over," Kalani told him gently.

Charlie almost didn't register his friend's voice.

"*Charlie!*" Kalani barked, and Charlie snapped out of whatever trance he'd been in. He released the unconscious Spectre who fell limply to the floor.

"Thanks for bailing me out, but what the hell was that?" Kalani asked.

Charlie shook his head, not to answer, but to clear it of whatever had just possessed him.

"I don't know," he admitted, then realized that Guests or Cast Members could enter the theater any second. "But we need to do something with him before someone sees him."

Kalani considered it for a moment then spoke.

He grinned.

"I've got an idea. And you're going to like it."

▼▲▼

Three minutes later, Charlie calmly placed the lid back on the trashcan outside the theater. Kalani had used flex cuffs to bind the Spectre into something closely resembling a human ball, used a strip of the man's own vest as a gag, and then the pair of them had lifted the unconscious man into the trash. Luckily, the nearby Kidcot station was closed, so they'd been able to stash the sleeping Spectre unseen.

"Hey, Siri, remind me to send someone to pick this guy up... tomorrow," Kalani said to his Apple Watch.

When they had almost closed in on a dispenser placed near the entrance to Le Cellier, Charlie's phone rang. It was Victoria.

"I've got news," she told him.

"So do I," he countered.

"You first."

Charlie quickly recounted Thirteen's video presentation, and he was surprised to find that Victoria didn't immediately respond. When she did, she sounded afraid.

"God...." she breathed. "This is bad."

"It is," Charlie agreed. "We need to stop her. Kalani and I are heading to one of these machines now. We're going to take a look at it, but I'm not optimistic. I don't think she built in a way for me to stop these things from going off. We're going to need an alternative."

Victoria sighed.

"So what's your news?" Charlie asked her.

"Assuming we picked all of her people up on the facial recognition scans, she's got nine people left. X-ray killed two at your house, and Vega took one out last night."

"Make it eight," Charlie corrected. "Kalani and I just had a run-in with one of them. Guy with a big scar on his face. He won't be a problem anymore."

Charlie heard the sound of keys tapping and Victoria humming lightly.

"Yep. He's one of the nine. Good work."

"He's in a trashcan by *O Canada!*" Charlie said simply.

"Jesus. You shoved a dead body into a trashcan?" Victoria asked.

"No, he's not dead. But he won't be very happy when he wakes up."

Victoria laughed lightly.

"Fair enough. Listen, I'm going to head over to Thirteen's room at the Swan, but there's something I wanted to run by you first."

Charlie heard some shuffling and then the sound of a doorwall being opened and closed. Victoria must have stepped out onto the balcony for this part.

"Habst has volunteered to come with me," she told him. "I need X-ray here in this room, so he's the only one who can feasibly watch my back. *I* have no issue with it, but I wanted your thoughts."

Charlie considered it. Habst was volunteering to enter the hornet's nest. He had no training and was injured, but he was a spare set of eyes and ears, and that could make all the difference for Victoria.

"If he thinks he's up for it and you think he can handle it, take him. But don't let him get hurt. We've lost enough friends already."

There was a moment of silence before she responded.

"Roger that," Victoria confirmed. "We're going to head out now. Godspeed, Detective."

"And you as well, Special Agent."

With that, they disconnected and headed into the unknown. It was up to them to prevent one of the greatest tragedies in American history.

# THIRTY-SEVEN

KAY," VICTORIA BEGAN, as they exited the elevator at the Swan. "This is going to be the most dangerous thing we do all day. I have no idea if there are any Spectres inside, so we'll need to clear it room by room, the old-fashioned way. By that, I mean: *I'm* going to clear the suite, and you're going to stay here by the door to make sure nobody shows up to the party uninvited. If they do, make a bird noise or something."

"Understood, boss," Habst agreed, with a small salute.

"Before we bust in there, Charlie really trusts your knowledge of Disney property—is there anything I should know about this place?"

"Honestly, I've never been up here before," shrugged Habst, apologetically. "A little too rich for my blood, and technically this isn't owned by Disney so it's outside my realm. I've really only been to the lobby and the bars."

"Fair enough."

Quickly, Victoria and Habst made their way to the executive suite that Victoria had pinned down as the Spectres' base of operations. When they reached the room, Victoria put a finger to her lips to call for silence as she slowly pressed her ear against the door.

Ignoring the "Do Not Disturb" sign, she looked in both directions to make sure the coast was clear and drew her gun. From her back pocket, she pulled a cloned room key she'd been given by the Cast Member at the front desk per Charlie's request. When she was confident they were alone, she inserted the key, popped the door open, and took two steps back, aiming down her sights.

Believing the entryway to be clear of hostiles, Victoria quickly made her way inside, cutting angles and clearing areas as she went. Methodically, she cleared each room—a process she'd done many times in her career. It took her three minutes, but by the time she returned to Habst, she was absolutely positive they were alone in the suite. Before they'd left the BoardWalk, she'd seen security footage showing all Spectres leaving the room, with none returning. But anything could have happened in the time between that footage and her arrival. In her field, redundancy meant safety, so she cleared the place regardless.

"We're good here," she told Habst. "Come on in."

She holstered her weapon as Habst followed her inside. For a split second, he stopped in his tracks as he saw the state of the room. This place didn't resemble a vacationer's suite—it was a war room, plain and simple. Weapons were scattered around haphazardly. Body armor and tactical BDUs were laid out on tables. Blueprints for various machines, as well as aerial photographs of the parks and resorts were posted on walls and many other flat surfaces. In the center of it all, on the dining table near the balcony, a massive computer workstation was set up.

"That's what we're looking for," Victoria told him, taking a seat at the keyboard.

"This is insane," Habst insisted. "How did they get all this in here without anyone noticing?"

"A giant Hawaiian just hauled a small army's worth of weapons into our villa at the BoardWalk without so much as a second glance. *This* surprises you, though?"

Habst chuckled, "Well, when you put it like that...."

Victoria nodded absently, tapping keys and searching the computer for anything useful.

"With any luck," she began, "there will be something we can send Charlie to help him disable those plague machines... and look what we have here!"

With a few mouse clicks, Victoria pulled up the Spectres' live feeds. They were patched into the security system, just as she'd suspected. Looking more closely, if she'd accessed the live feeds herself, they'd have seen her immediately. Using the historical footage was a stroke of genius.

"We have full access to security cams now. You know what that means?"

"We can revive Flash Mountain?" Habst joked.

"What?" Victoria asked, not understanding the reference. "No. It means that I can use my facial recognition system to see where her people are in real time. Nobody's watching, so nobody will know."

"Awesome. Looks like we finally caught a break. Let's get these fuckers and—"

Suddenly, Victoria cut Habst off with a raised finger. She thought she heard a noise from the hall. Sure enough, seconds later a lock clicked and she heard one of the entry doors swing inward.

"Bedroom—now!" she whispered, shoving Habst toward the nearby room and hurrying after him.

They huddled against the wall behind the door, and Victoria listened closely. She heard footsteps and muffled voices, but could not make out what was being said.

"Two people," she murmured to Habst. She holstered her weapon and drew her knife. She could not risk firing shots here. It would cause too significant a disturbance, police would be called, and Thirteen would certainly be alerted. These two Spectres had to be eliminated, but it had to be done quietly.

"What are you going to do?" Habst whispered.

"My job. Stay here."

Silently, Victoria cracked the bedroom door open and spotted both Spectres. They sat almost exactly where Victoria and Habst had been moments before—one at the computer and the other on the couch nearby. Luckily, both had their backs to her.

"Honestly, I'm countin' the seconds until this whole thing is over," the one at the computer was saying, in a thick Irish accent.

"You're telling me," the one on the couch responded. "I can't take much more of this fucking place. It's miserable."

With practiced ease, Victoria approached them, using their voices to mask the sound of her footfalls, until she was directly behind the Spectre on the couch. She waited for him to finish speaking, clamped a tight hand over his mouth, and buried her knife to the hilt in the base of his skull. He died without so much as a gasp.

"What? You don't like the magical home of Mickey Mouse?" the other one joked, laughing.

When he didn't respond, the Spectre at the computer turned, only to find Victoria's gun leveled at him.

"Hands high, partner," she ordered, quietly. "Make a move I don't like and end up like your buddy. Tell me if you think I'm lying to you."

The Spectre, shocked into cooperation, slowly raised his hands, unable to look away from the dead man who had been commiserating with him mere seconds ago.

"Habst," Victoria called out, never taking her eyes off her captive. "We're clear, come out here."

Habst hurried out of the bedroom, his eyes widening as he saw the dead Spectre on the couch.

"Fuck me," he gushed. "You are a badass."

Victoria winked at him, grinned, and pulled out a few sets of flex cuffs with her free hand, offering them to Habst.

"Pat him down," she directed. "Take everything he has. Don't leave so much as a ball of lint in his pockets. When that's done, cuff him tight with these."

Without complaint, Habst did as he was told. By the time he was done, he'd made a pile of weapons and technology on a nearby table, and he'd cranked the cuffs down so tight on the Spectre's wrists that he was sure he'd cut off circulation, which was fine with him.

"I have some questions," Victoria told the Spectre, pulling up a chair to face him. "If you don't answer them, lie to me, fuck with me, or do *anything* I feel is uncool in *any* way, I'll kill you. No warning, no second chance—just a knife to the throat." To punctuate this, she leaned back and crudely retrieved her knife from the skull of the dead Spectre. She didn't even bother to clean off the blade. "Be aware: I don't need you. However, you can make my life easier and, by doing so, maybe make it out of this alive."

The Spectre swallowed hard, then nodded.

"Let's start with your name. First name only, I don't give a shit about who you are; I just need to know what to call you."

"Pat—um—Patrick."

"Very good, Patumpatrick. Next, I need you to tell me how to disable the dispensers Thirteen has placed in the park next door."

Patrick sighed and lowered his head.

"There is no way to disable them."

"I really don't like that answer," Victoria told him. With a sad shake of her head, she leaned forward, bringing up the already bloodied knife.

"Wait!" Patrick blurted. "There might be another way. They can't be disabled—they weren't designed with a shutoff—but they need to be activated to release the toxin."

"You must have had your Lucky Charms this morning, Paddy—you're starting to redeem yourself," Victoria declared. "How are they activated and how do I stop that from happening?"

Patrick hesitated, torn between betraying his team and dying a painful death. Eventually, the need to survive won out, and Patrick told her everything.

The activation would be done using a numerical PIN entered into a custom app on Thirteen's phone. She would enter this PIN, then have access to a literal "go button" which she would press to release the toxin. Preventing the release, Patrick told her, would be as simple as stopping Thirteen from entering the code and pressing the button.

"So where is she?"

"Honestly, I don't know where she is," he admitted. "But I'm guessin' you CIA spooks have the ability to track GPS signals. I have the necessary data to track Thirteen's phone, as well as trace her calls, but she didn't allow me to bring that technology for this very reason."

Victoria grinned, pulling her laptop from her bag.

"I have that technology. Give me the info, please," Victoria demanded, and Patrick walked Habst through pulling it up on the computer system. "Now, Charlie told me that you all plan to ride off into the sunset in a helicopter. What's that all about?"

Patrick explained the logistics of the helicopter getaway, and Victoria asked him what the point of it was—it was unnecessarily risky and kind of stupid. Patrick agreed with her, telling her that several members of the team had voiced their concerns about the dramatic exfiltration and had been shut down immediately or ignored. A backup escape route, Patrick told her, was planned using the box truck they'd used to haul all of the hazmat suits. Habst, having plugged Thirteen's phone data into Victoria's system—which, to his surprise, had been extremely simple and user-friendly—interrupted them.

"Uh, Victoria, what does this little red blinking light mean?" he asked, pointing to her laptop screen.

"That means there's currently activity on Thirteen's phone! Quick, click that 'Access' button!"

Habst did as he was asked. The system took an uncomfortably long time to connect, and both Habst and Victoria held their breath, hoping they would be able to listen in before the call was over.

"—and everything is going fucking sideways! I've lost contact with three of my team members," they heard Thirteen growling into the phone. "I need you to get here ASAP. I'm not fucking around with Walker and his friends anymore, we're getting out of here early."

"Affirmative. I'm inbound now. See you soon, boss."

"Good. The faster you get here, the more I'll pay you. Hurry your ass up."

On that note, the call abruptly ended.

"Shit, she's calling the chopper in early. Patrick, do you have contact information for that pilot?"

"I do," he confirmed hesitantly, but again walked her through locating it.

For a few moments, Victoria scanned satellite topography of the area, and then looked Patrick directly in his eyes.

"Do you know this pilot personally?" she asked him.

"I do," he said again.

"Then you're going to make a call for me. Get him on the line and have him change his approach to this heading."

She showed him her laptop screen.

"What if he asks why?" Patrick asked.

"Height test balloons," suggested Habst.

"What?" Victoria and Patrick asked in unison.

"Height test balloons," Habst repeated. "When Disney is planning to build something new, they fly these brightly colored balloons at the exact height of whatever they're planning. They use them to get an idea of how the height of new structures will affect sightlines across the property. Tell the pilot that he needs to change course to avoid the height test balloons."

Victoria punched him lightly on the shoulder, smiling.

"You're two for two, kid. Keep it up. Paddy, make the call," she said to Patrick, dialing his phone and holding it up for him.

As it rang, Victoria whispered to Habst.

"I'll finish up here and seal the place. Head downstairs and meet me by the fountain in the lobby. I have an idea. We're going to fuck some shit up. It'll be fun."

"I like the sound of that," he agreed, heading toward the door. "You sure you don't want me to stick around?"

Victoria shook her head.

"Nope, I'm all good here. I'll be down soon."

Habst gave her a nod and headed out.

Patrick did as he was told and the pilot agreed to change the approach heading to the new one Victoria had created. He then gave her the location of Thirteen's box truck, containing all of the hazmat suits.

"Are we good now?" Patrick asked as Victoria stood. "Would you mind loosening these cuffs? They're makin' me bloody hands numb."

Victoria slowly moved around behind Patrick.

"What are you doing?" Patrick asked, fear creeping into his voice. "I thought you said you'd let me go."

Victoria took a deep breath and knotted her fingers into Patrick's hair.

"This is America, motherfucker. We do not negotiate with terrorists."

With a quick flick of the wrist, she took another Spectre out of the equation.

▼▲▼

In the lobby with Habst, Victoria called Charlie to apprise him of the situation. He wasn't shocked to hear that Thirteen was calling the helicopter early.

"The only way to stop these things from going off is to find her and make sure she doesn't input that code."

"Where is she?" he asked. "She could be anywhere."

Victoria flipped open her laptop and pulled up her locator.

"GPS tracking on her phone shows her in the Norway Pavilion. Looks like she's in or around the Kringle... uh, Kring—the fucking bakery, you know what I'm trying to say. Are you anywhere near there?"

"Not even close. We're still in Canada looking at one of her machines. We've been at it since I last talked to you, and it's impenetrable. I can't even see a way to access it, let alone shut it down."

"Then abandon it. Thirteen is your priority now. You've got to get to her."

"What about her chopper?" he asked. "If that thing is coming, then we don't have much time."

"Don't worry about the chopper; I'll make sure it's taken care of."

"Taken care of?" Charlie asked, prompting her to elaborate.

"I don't have time to explain, but needless to say, that chopper is never going to arrive. Should buy you time to get to her."

"I hate to be a nitpicker, but what about the hazmat suits? If she suits up, it doesn't matter whether her ride is here or not; she can release the toxin whenever she wants."

Victoria laughed; Charlie was definitely being Charlie.

"Don't worry about the suits either—Habst and I are about to handle that. Give us twenty minutes and the suits won't be an option. At that point, if she releases the toxin she'll kill herself along with everyone else. You'll have all the time you need to get to her."

Charlie laughed.

"You are one of my favorite people on this planet, you know that?" he told her.

"Easy, killer—you're married," she joked. "Remember, twenty minutes and then she's stuck here with us. She'll be playing *our* game then."

After she hung up, she told Habst what needed to be done.

"Man, you are an evil genius," he laughed.

Habst knew exactly where they needed to go, and the fastest way to get there.

Victoria smiled at the thought that Thirteen would soon be trapped in Epcot, and that *she* would be the prey.

# THIRTY-EIGHT

JEN-JEN'S PHONE BUZZED and she answered it on the first ring. It was Victoria.

"Everything going smoothly over there, Vee?" she asked.

Victoria gave her a quick recap of what she'd learned and done, and quickly outlined her plans for the future.

"McCoy's got that M300 set up, right?" Victoria asked,

Jen-Jen leaned around the kitchen counter to see the large black rifle balanced atop its bipod on the coffee table. McCoy was near the doorwall, scanning the grounds with a pair of binoculars, searching for the Spectres' logo wherever he could.

"Yep, it's ready to rip."

"Fantastic. Put me on speaker; I need him to hear this."

Jen-Jen did as Victoria asked and and McCoy turned to listen.

"Can you hear me? Good. Thirteen and the gang have themselves a getaway bird inbound. It was scheduled to swing in from the east, but I convinced them to change their approach heading. Now they're going to be coming in directly over Crescent Lake lake—right through your field of fire. McCoy, I need you to peel that thing out of the air with April's rifle. You'll have to drop it right in the center of that lake where it's not going to hurt any civilians. Can you do that?"

McCoy took a moment and glanced at the lake. It was sizable, and he'd certainly made more challenging shots throughout his career.

"Yep," he announced, and that was all Victoria needed to hear.

"Perfect. Bad news is: I have no idea when it's coming in, so you'll have to watch for it."

"When will you be back?" Jen-Jen asked.

"A little while yet," Victoria admitted. "Me and Habst are going to take care of something first. Keep that place locked down tight until we get there. And McCoy? Keep in mind, that chopper shot is critical. I need that bird in that lake. If it makes it inside the park, we're all fucked."

"Understood," McCoy said with a nod.

"Then I'll see you both soon. Stay safe."

▼▲▼

It didn't take long. Less than fifteen minutes had passed since Victoria's call when McCoy spotted the large black helicopter a few miles out.

Moving targets were never easy to hit, but McCoy had the advantage of a superior angle. When the chopper was over the center of the lake, McCoy would be able to see the pilot not quite head-on, but near enough to significantly reduce the difficulty of his shot. Drawing from his past experiences with crashing helicopters, and the current speed of Thirteen's bird, he'd have to take the shot a few seconds before it was over the center of the lake to give it the best chance of landing where it wouldn't hurt anyone. Luck was on his side, as there were no boats on the lake.

"Ear protection," he barked at Jen-Jen.

Hurriedly, she tossed McCoy a set of cans before ushering Meghan, the kids, Carina, and Zeus into the other room and shutting the door. As she wadded up a towel and shoved it against the gap beneath the door, Jen-Jen informed everyone that they needed to keep their ears covered tightly until after McCoy took the shot or they'd more than likely be permanently deafened. She didn't sugarcoat it—the firing of a .408 CheyTac round in a room of that size without hearing protection would cause enough pressure to burst anyone's eardrums.

Jen-Jen went so far as to open every window in the villa, and had even cracked the doors to the corridor. They only had two sets of ear protection, and McCoy would need one since his hands wouldn't be free to cover his ears. The other set went to Meghan, who was covering Zeus' ears.

Huddling behind the door to the adjoining room, Jen-Jen stayed close to Violet and Katie, making sure the girls didn't remove their hands from their ears for even a second. She glanced over at Carina, who was sobbing in the corner. The poor girl was terrified. Jen-Jen could only imagine what was going through her head.

Meanwhile, McCoy, having adjusted his windage and elevation satisfactorily, lined his crosshairs up slightly ahead of his target, compensating for airspeed and direction.

And when the chopper reached the spot where it needed to die, he simply squeezed the trigger.

The blast was so cataclysmically powerful that it knocked pictures from the walls, ruffled curtains fifteen feet away, rattled glasses, sent plates of food crashing to the floor, and closed the doors to the corridor. The blast, redirected by the massive muzzle brake, burned twin scorch marks into the carpet on either side, and left the coffee table smoking.

The harm done to the villa, however, was nothing in comparison to the damage the round had done to its intended target.

McCoy was a world-class marksman, and his first and only shot struck true. The .408 CheyTac round punched into the pilot's head and cracked it open like a watermelon at a Gallagher show. The projectile continued on, pounding into the engine block and hitting hard enough to wobble the entire aircraft. As the contents of the pilot's head splashed around the cockpit, his body pitched forward against his controls, dragging the chopper immediately down and to its left. The chopper turned around to face the opposite direction, and McCoy momentarily worried it would veer toward the shore near the Beach Club, but it suddenly angled straight down and crashed into the surface of the lake with a huge splash.

Unlike in the movies, the rotor blades didn't break free from their mounts and fly away dramatically; they simply encountered resistance from the water, slowed, and finally stopped as the smoking wreck sank into the depths.

The whole event was over in a matter of seconds.

# THIRTY-NINE

ET'S GET BACK TO THE TRUCK and get our suits on. Put the word out to the team that the party is starting a little earlier than planned," Thirteen told Alfie as she stood, abandoning her second glacier shot on the table.

They were in the Norway Pavilion drinking Aquavit when Thirteen had realized that three members of her team had stopped reporting in. Somehow, Walker or the CIA had found a way to either kill or disable them. Despite this development, she was confident that her plan was still in good shape, but she refused to let them press their advantage and decided it was better to be safe than sorry. She called the helicopter in early and would activate her dispensers as soon as her team had all put on their hazmat suits.

It took them some time to make their way through the ever-thickening crowds in World Showcase, but eventually they arrived at the bridges between the France and United Kingdom Pavilions. Halfway across the second bridge, Alfie stopped and grabbed Thirteen by the arm.

"What the—?" Thirteen complained.

Alfie held up a hand to silence her protests.

"Do you hear that?"

Thirteen listened hard, concentrating, and before long she could detect the low thump of rotor blades. Her helicopter was coming, much sooner than she'd expected. She was going to give that rock star pilot a *massive* bonus.

Looking in the direction of the sound, over the trees she spied the helicopter in the distance. For some reason, it was coming in low over Crescent Lake—the opposite direction from which she'd expected it—but there was no mistaking that this was her ride. Ignoring the questionable approach, Thirteen beamed.

She looked up, smiling wide at Alfie. She leaned in and kissed him hard.

"We did it!" she exclaimed. "Alfie, my love, we fucking did it. Nobody will ever forget this. We're going to be—"

She stopped mid-sentence, unable to process what she was seeing.

Without warning, the helicopter wobbled, canted to its left, spun 180 degrees, and dropped from the sky. She heard a sharp, reverberating *crack* echoing off the trees shortly after the helicopter dropped from sight. It was the unmistakable sound of a distant high-caliber rifle.

Thirteen's jaw dropped. What she'd just witnessed was so unexpected, so shocking, that she didn't know how to react.

"What... what...?" was all she could manage. She gripped the bridge railing so hard her knuckles turned pure white.

How could this have happened? She had laid her plan bare before Walker out of vanity, yes, but only because there was nothing he could do to stop her. It wasn't a challenge, it was an insult. She was spitting in his face one last time before he died. He wasn't supposed to be able to intervene. How could he have brought down her helicopter? How could he have even known when it would be coming? How could he have known *where*?

"Wait...." Thirteen trailed off, the horrifying realization hitting her all at once.

He hadn't simply *known* where and when the helicopter would be coming, he had *decided* it. She should have known something was off the second she saw that chopper approaching from the opposite direction. She scolded herself for her oversight—but she'd been overcome with delight thinking that her grand plan was finally coming to fruition. She was wrong, and that stung the worst of all. She was *never* wrong.

Walker and his CIA friends had done something; they'd found some gap in her armor and struck fast. She didn't care how they'd done it, but she would make them pay for it.

She growled with rage. Alfie placed a hand on her shoulder to reassure her. Normally, she'd have thrown his hand away with fury, taking his gesture as an insult. This time, however, she had ascended past that petty mindset. She was in a new plane of existence, transported by this unexpected failure. Nothing but Walker mattered to her now. He would die, and he would die *hard*.

"We still have the truck—and the suits," she offered, trying to keep her voice level and steady. "Let's get back there, get suited up, and fuck this place up. The sooner we release the toxin, the sooner Walker and his friends die a horrible death."

"Listen, this is getting out of hand, love. I think it's time we—"

"It's time we *what*, Alfie? Run away?!" she screamed, drawing the attention of people nearby. She looked around and saw that the people who weren't looking at her were staring toward Crescent Lake. The trees near the International Gateway blocked their view, but a thin column of smoke rose above the them. Thirteen couldn't be sure, but she swore she heard the faint sound of sirens in the distance. Even if the helicopter had gone down in the lake, as she suspected it had, the arrival of authorities was inevitable. If she didn't move quickly, she may have no avenue of escape—even with the truck.

"No, I...." Alfie stammered, but couldn't finish his thought under Thirteen's withering stare.

"There is nothing left for us to do but get to the truck and finish what we started. Now *move*."

Thirteen stalked off, nearly jogging, toward the World ShowPlace Pavilion. By the time they'd made it backstage to their truck, Thirteen and Alfie were sweating profusely beneath the hot April sun.

They expected to see Greene sitting in the cab of the truck—drinking or smoking or whatever he did in his spare time—but the door was shut and nobody was around. It was peculiar, but Thirteen was past caring about small details. She and Alfie would don their suits, and if Greene decided to show up he was welcome to join them.

Before she could reach the rear of the vehicle, she noticed the puddle spreading on the ground. She didn't have to bend down to know what it was.

It was fuel.

"Petrol line's been cut," Alfie told her, kneeling to look beneath the chassis. "Shit."

Thirteen gritted her teeth. *Walker's crew has been busy*, she thought as she rounded the rear of the truck.

Climbing onto the rusted diamond plate step, Thirteen grabbed the handle to the huge roll-up door and yanked it open.

The dank, coppery smell hit her before the door was even open enough for her to see.

Blood. She could smell it even over the pool of diesel fuel spreading beneath their feet.

When the door was fully open and the early afternoon Floridian sun flooded the cargo area, she was again shocked into silence by what she found.

Greene lay on the floor, dead. His throat had been savagely cut from ear to ear. The cut that killed him was so deep that vertebrae were visible beneath the flayed muscle and severed trachea. He had died with a look of absolute horror on his face, as if one of hell's demons itself had come to claim him.

*Maybe they had*, Thirteen thought, sadly. Greene had been one of her oldest friends, and she was genuinely hurt to see him left in this condition.

However, it wasn't the grisly condition of her friend's body that had affected her the most—it was what surrounded him.

In tatters, like an assortment of obscene party streamers, lay the Spectres' hazmat suits—or what was left of them.

Thirteen knelt and grabbed a fistful of the shredded material. Inspecting the cuts, she was easily able to piece together the scene. Somebody had cut their fuel line, killed Greene, and then destroyed the suits—all of them. Looking at the edges of the slashes, stained with blood, the killer had not even bothered to clean their blade after slaying her friend before starting in on the suits. Upon further inspection, she realized that this had happened *very* recently. Greene's blood wasn't even tacky, it was *fresh*. This happened while she and Alfie stood on that bridge, watching their exfiltration vehicle dive headfirst into the lake.

For the first time since she could remember—possibly ever—Thirteen felt her heart thump hard against her sternum; she was *nervous*. The ruthlessness and speed with which her entire operation had been attacked was unexpected. Walker and the CIA operatives had ruined their avenues of escape, killed or incapacitated several members of her team, and stranded her here. In a true reversal of recent events, *they* had forced *her* into a situation for which she was not prepared.

She sat down heavily on the rear step of the truck, staring at the bloodied scraps of hazmat suit clutched in her fist.

Alfie, wisely, remained silent.

"Walker has issued a challenge," Thirteen declared. "He has spilled the blood of our family, and we will make him pay for that."

Alfie nodded.

"What's the plan?" he asked.

In reply, Thirteen pulled out her phone and pressed the button that would connect her to all of her remaining Spectres at once.

"Check in," she said simply.

"Reid, checking in."

"Cormac, checking in."

"Summers, checking in."

"Frost, checking in."

And then silence. Four team members were all that remained.

"Charlie Walker and his friends have hurt us," she told them. "You are all that is left of our team. Our helicopter is at the bottom of the lake, the fuel line to our truck has been severed, and our hazmat suits have been destroyed. We have no avenues of egress left to us, unless you boys fancy calling a Lyft. But fuck that. We're not dead yet, so we'll keep moving forward.

"Alfie and I will find Charlie Walker. I need the four of you to make your way to his room at the BoardWalk and kill his entire family and every one of those fucking CIA assholes." She read off the room number. "Make a scene. Make it violent. Make it dramatic. Fuck his wife, eat his dog, piss on his friends' corpses—I don't care. Whatever you do, I want it to be a scene of carnage like the world has never seen. When we find Walker, we'll bring him to see what you've done, and only then will we kill him. After that, we'll activate these dispensers, get out however we can, get to our yacht, and get the fuck out of the country. Sound good?"

"Affirmative," replied Reid. The others echoed his response.

"Get to work, then."

She disconnected the call.

It was a full minute before Thirteen looked up at Alfie.

"I need you," she said to him.

"I'm here," he said, calmly.

"We need to finish this."

Alfie nodded. As much as he loved Thirteen, he did not support her plan to capture Walker and parade him before the corpses of his family. Walker and his Company friends had already proven too dangerous to play with.

No.

When Alfie and Charlie met, he would kill the bastard on the spot and deal with the consequences after.

# FORTY

VICTORIA AND HABST HEARD the vicious bark of McCoy's rifle and the sound of the helicopter crashing into the surface of Crescent Lake as they made their way down the backstage road near the World ShowPlace Pavilion. This is where Patrick had said Thirteen's truck would be, and he'd assured her all the hazmat suits would still be inside.

Sure enough, the truck sat directly alongside the pavilion, guarded by one Spectre. Victoria's lip curled in disgust as she realized who that Spectre was: Greene, AKA Murph. The monster that had killed an entire family and taken their place.

Victoria's snarl turned into a wicked smile as she realized that she had been given an opportunity to avenge the Murphy family. It wasn't much, but she was more than happy to have the opportunity.

Quietly, she whispered her plan to Habst, who sullenly nodded. Having seen the bodies of the real Murphy family, Habst wanted to see Greene brought down just as much as Victoria did.

▼▲▼

"Hey, man," Habst said, approaching Greene from his left. "I'm looking for my friend. Have you seen him? Little purple dragon. Kind of an asshole, smells like a skunk. That ring any bells?"

Greene eyed him cautiously and stood, flicking his cigarette into the road.

"The fuck are you talking about? Wait. I know you, you're—"

Before he could finish his sentence, Victoria slammed into him from the opposite side, catching him unaware, and sending him crashing into the back of the truck. Greene's head connected hard with one of the cases the suits were stored in, dazing him. He had no time to react before she was kneeling on his chest, a knife in each hand.

"Robert Murphy sends his regards," she said, and slit his throat with both knives at once. She leaned all of her weight into it and could swear she felt one of the knives scrape bone. Good.

Wasting no time, she stabbed a knife into the wooden floor of the truck's cargo area, allowing the struggling Spectre to bleed out without another glance.

"Take that and start cutting these suits up. Fucking shred them to pieces."

Habst, deciding not to argue with a woman that had just slit a man's throat, got to work, using the bloody knife to saw through the heavy rubber of the suits. Victoria headed around the side of the truck, reached beneath the running-board fuel tank, and severed the fuel supply line. Satisfied that the truck was out of commission, she helped Habst finish his task. It took them only two minutes to destroy every single one of them. When they were done, she closed the roll-up door, sealing Greene's body in with the remnants of the hazmat gear.

"What now?" Habst asked.

"Now? Now we let Charlie do what he does best. Thirteen is trapped on his home turf with no way out. Charlie will hunt her down, and he'll finish this."

Habst nodded. He knew what Charlie would do to Thirteen when he found her. He just hoped that, when the time came, Charlie wouldn't underestimate Alfie as Vega had.

# FORTY-ONE

'M SORRY—YOU'RE GOING to have to repeat that. A fucking *what* just dumped into Crescent Lake?" LeCarre barked into his radio as the dispatcher notified all units.

"Repeat: an unmarked helicopter has just crashed into Crescent Lake. All available nearby units please respond."

Bell looked over at his partner with urgency.

"The Walkers are staying at the BoardWalk, which is *on* Crescent Lake. This can't be a coincidence—maybe the situation is a little hotter than they let on. We need to get over there fast."

LeCarre nodded to his partner, took a deep breath, and keyed his radio once more.

"Belay that, dispatch. This is LeCarre, I'm in the area with Bell and we will respond."

LeCarre knew he couldn't hold back uniformed officers from responding to an actual helicopter crash on Disney property, but he hoped his seniority would at least buy him enough time to get to Walker's family first and make sure they were safe.

Earlier, Bell had received a call from Agent Jennings asking him to arrange the pickup of two people she needed placed in protective custody: a girl named Carina and her sister. He'd sent a black-and-white to grab the sister, but he and LeCarre had hadn't yet headed to the BoardWalk for Carina, as Jennings had said the matter wasn't urgent. Now, however, it was a different story. Something bad was happening over there.

LeCarre pressed the accelerator to the floor and sped off toward the BoardWalk with his siren screaming and flashers blazing.

Bell pulled out his phone and called Victoria.

"Bell?" she answered after a few rings. He could hear sounds of shuffling and wind, as if she were moving very quickly through a wide-open space.

"Agent Holloway, we've just heard a report of a helicopter crashing down into Crescent Lake. You have something to do with that?"

"Yes," she said without elaboration.

"I won't waste your time asking about it, but were any civilians hurt?" he asked.

"Negative. Only casualty was the pilot, and he was working for the Spectres. That was Thirteen's getaway bird. As of now, she is trapped on property with us. I don't have time to explain, but we've thinned out her team a little bit. Thirteen, her boyfriend, and four others are all that remain."

Bell hesitated.

"Is there… is she planning an attack?" he asked.

"Yes," Victoria confirmed. "She's planning to release a modified neurotoxin into the park at three o'clock. Nobody inside the gates would survive it. She was going to put on special hazmat suits, watch the toxin do its thing, and then take off in that helicopter. It's why we risked shooting it down. If she has no escape route, then she can't release that toxin without killing herself."

"She's still got the suits you mentioned," he ventured.

"Nope. Destroyed. She's got no air exfil and no protection, so the only way she can release that toxin is if she's willing to kill herself and her whole team. I don't *think* she's that desperate, but I can't know that for sure."

"We need to evacuate the park," Bell stated, plainly.

"No. She's already warned that she'll deploy it at the first sign of an evacuation."

"Then what do we do?"

"Charlie and Kalani are currently tracking her down. We've learned that she has to manually activate the dispensers by inputting a code through her phone. Don't worry, Bell, I know Charlie, and you can trust me when I tell you that he *will* get that phone from her. His family is in the kill zone, so he won't stop until this is over. We just need to keep his family safe until he can—"

Gunfire cut her off mid-sentence.

Bell flinched away from his phone, as the sound was loud enough to hurt his ear. He couldn't be sure whether Victoria was firing or being fired upon.

"Agent Holloway? Victoria?"

No answer.

"Victoria!" he yelled into the phone.

The last thing he heard before the line went dead were the terrified screams of dozens of people.

# FORTY-TWO

W E JUST NEED TO KEEP his family safe until he can—"

And then somebody shot her.

Victoria did not cry out as the bullet tore into her hip. Her training kept her mind where it needed to be, scanning for her attacker even as she spun and fell to the ground.

She landed hard, thankfully on the opposite hip from the one in which she'd been hit. The pain was nearly blinding, but she fought through it.

She'd been on the BoardWalk with Habst, rushing past carnival games and surrey bikes to return to their villa, when someone had opened fire on her. The crowds were heavy, with Guests lining the railings to stare into the lake, searching for any sign of the helicopter that had gone down. A crowd of innocents was no place for a gunfight, and that single shot caused pure chaos among the gathered gawkers.

As more gunfire rang out, she tried to stand, but her hip gave out on her and she went down again. She still couldn't spot her assailant, and by this point the BoardWalk was in a blind panic. Guests were screaming and running in all directions, trying desperately to get away from the scene of an active shooting.

Before Victoria could try to stand once more, a hand gripped her by the bicep and helped her to her feet. It was Habst. He had Charlie's Walther in his opposite hand and was scanning the crowd frantically, looking for anyone with a gun.

"Come on, we gotta move," he grunted, pulling Victoria's arm over his shoulder and supporting her the best he could.

"Did you see... did you see where that came from?" she asked, the pain causing her to wince.

"I couldn't see anything. Especially with all of these people—it's a fucking madhouse out here."

Hurriedly, Habst pulled the limping Victoria through the courtyard, and up the stairs to the BoardWalk's lobby terrace. He was terrified, fully expecting to be shot in the back at any moment. But the shot never came. They made it to the lobby alive, but only just. Habst noticed the trail of blood Victoria was leaving behind and it scared the hell out of him. She was in bad shape, and he didn't know what he could do for her.

A throng of panicked vacationers was forcing itself into the hallway on the Villa side of the lobby, which was where they needed to go. But they also needed to keep moving, so Habst pulled Victoria into a hallway on the Inn side of the resort.

To their left, against the windows, was a pair of antique mutoscopes—large, cast-iron, early motion-picture devices that worked on a hand crank. Habst had always been fascinated by the machines. Any other time, he'd have stopped and watched the simple little flip-film within. Now, however, he watched as Victoria collapsed against one of the machines, her back to the window.

Over the years, Habst had heard stories about Victoria Holloway. He'd heard what she'd done to help Charlie when her own dad tried to kill him. He heard about some of the less-classified things she'd done with the CIA. By any definition of the word, this woman was a complete badass. Until the previous day he'd never actually met her, but she'd nonetheless become a sort of larger-than-life figure—a legend. Anyone Charlie Walker admired as much as this woman deserved respect.

That's why it scared him so much to see her like this. Her face had become ghostly pale, and he could see tears welling up in her eyes that she repeatedly blinked away. She coughed once as she leaned back against the window. Shakily, she drew her gun and let it rest on her lap.

"You gotta go, Habst. They're going to follow that trail of blood and when they get here they'll kill us both."

"I'm not just going to leave you here. Come on, let me help you back—"

She held up a hand to quiet him, resignation in her eyes, and shook her head slowly. She blinked, and one of those tears she'd been holding back finally broke loose and tracked its way down her cheek.

"No. You need to go. Now. Before they get here."

"And what are you going to do?"

"Take as many of them with me as I can."

The hair on the back of Habst's neck stood up. In the stories Charlie told, Victoria had been ready to give her life to buy him the time he needed to save his family. In fact, she almost *had* given her life, but Charlie had saved her.

He usually downplayed that part of the story, but Habst had heard it from other people who had been there on that terrible day in Bay Lake Tower's parking lot. Charlie had executed the mercenary that was going to kill her. Shot him in the head with a gun just like the one Habst held in his hand. It was one of the things that made Habst trust him as much as he did. It made him respect Charlie and fear him in nearly equal measure.

And here was Habst, in an almost identical situation. Special Agent Victoria Holloway lay bleeding and nearly helpless on the ground. This time she wasn't out of ammo, she was critically wounded. The people who shot her were doubtlessly coming to finish the job. Maybe she'd get one of them, but she looked as if she didn't have the strength to even raise her weapon. And she was telling him to leave—to save himself. How could he do that?

*Don't be a hero*, Charlie had told him the day before. Against his friend's warning, he'd tried to be a hero and had taken the most thorough beating he'd ever received in his life. Charlie had been right. But what of the alternative? Just let people die? Fuck that.

"Go!" she barked. "Now!"

Startled into action, Habst backed around the corner and into the path to the Belle Vue Lounge. As he rounded the corner, he spied a man dressed all in black, wielding an assault rifle and wearing an all-too-familiar vest approaching slowly from the lobby. People ran from him, still screaming madly, but he ignored them. He was laser-focused on Victoria.

*Spectre.*

"Fuck," Habst spat, staring at the gun in his hand. "Fuck, fuck, fuck, fuck, *fuck*."

Could he really use it? Could he really kill somebody?

There had only been one Spectre shooting at them. Even so, he knew Victoria didn't have the strength to defeat him. He had to make a decision. He had to either take this man's life, or watch a legend die. And he would have to live the rest of his life knowing he'd been the coward that didn't try to help her.

*I'm here for a good time, not a long time*, he thought.

"Goddamn it. He had an idea.

▼▲▼

"Well, look at you," the Spectre laughed. "The mighty Victoria Holloway bleeding to death in a hotel hallway. You know, they warned me about you. Said you wouldn't be easy to kill and that I shouldn't underestimate you."

He laughed again.

"Get on with it," Victoria spat, interrupting his self-congratulating monologue. Her gun lay limply in her lap; she didn't have the strength left to bring it to bear.

"Feisty to the bitter end," the Spectre commented. "I like your spirit. I just wish you'd have put up more of a fight. Would have been a better story to tell my mates back in Blighty."

Suddenly, Victoria's head snapped to her right—the Spectre's left—the expression on her face shocked, focusing on something behind him, near the lobby.

Confused, the Spectre raised his rifle and turned to see what Victoria was looking at.

Habst slammed into the Spectre from the opposite site, driving a shoulder into the man's hip with all of his weight. The Spectre was lifted off his feet and he crashed into the heavy iron mutoscope, his head hitting the rim of the viewport with a sickening crunch. Habst tumbled safely to the side and the Spectre crashed headfirst to the floor, facing Victoria. She could see the gaping wound on the side of his head, beside his eye. It was gruesome, but it wasn't fatal. In his eyes, she saw the look of shock and defeat—and she grinned.

"That's what an ambush feels like, motherfucker," she rasped.

With that, she turned her gun a few inches and put a single round through the Spectre's forehead, spraying the hallway with blood, hair, bone, and brain.

She let the weapon fall from her hand to clatter noisily on the floor.

Habst knelt before her.

"You're a bad boy," she said with a weak smile. "I told you to leave."

"And I told you I wasn't going to leave you here."

Victoria's smile turned sad.

"Don't know how much good that did. I don't have much left in the tank," she said, taking her first good look at the bullet wound in her hip. It was bad, fatal if she didn't get medical attention soon. The blood had begun to pool around her, soaking through her entire pant leg.

"Somebody on your team's gotta be a medic, right?"

Victoria nodded.

"She got stabbed to death last night."

"Well you're not fucking dying here!" Habst nearly yelled at her. "Get up, come on."

Habst grabbed her arm again and she winced. Sirens sounded in the distance, but they were too far away to give him any hope. He didn't know what he was going to do, but he wouldn't let her die here. He led her back into the lobby, uncertain where he'd go from there. His heart beat hard in his chest and he was carrying more and more of Victoria's weight as they went—she was fading.

When they reached the lobby, Habst yelled, "I need a goddamn doctor! Come on! Is anyone a doctor? Nurse? Vet? Fucking *anything*!"

At that point, the doors burst open and two men entered, guns drawn. Habst nearly resigned himself to death before he realized who he was looking at.

Bell and LeCarre.

"Bell! LeCarre! Over here, quick!" he yelled, catching their attention.

At first, they didn't recognize him in the panic, but when they saw him they sprinted to his side, each detective taking one of Victoria's arms and carrying her over to a white couch that sat between two tropical plants.

LeCarre was on his radio before her head had even hit the cushions.

"All available units, I need an ambulance to the BoardWalk lobby—I repeat: BoardWalk lobby—for a gunshot victim. This is priority one."

Bell took off his jacket and folded it up into a tight square. He pressed it hard against Victoria's wound. She winced, but didn't cry out.

Bell grabbed Habst's hand and put it on the makeshift bandage.

"Put pressure on this. I don't care if it hurts her—or you—but *keep* that pressure on it or she dies. You understand?"

Habst didn't speak, just looked at the detective with steely determination and nodded.

Victoria looked up at Habst and Bell as LeCarre barked into his radio, challenging and insulting any first responder that claimed to be too far away.

"Thank you guys for trying," she said weakly. "I mean it."

"Trying?" Habst chuckled. "Woman, you're not dead yet."

Victoria laughed at that, and that laugh turned into a violent cough. More tears streamed down her cheek, mingling with the blood staining the white fabric of the couch. Habst winced; she was dying.

He was doing his best, but he was holding her life force in with a wadded-up jacket—it was a losing battle, but he would fight it until the end.

Victoria's eyes unfocused then, seeming to look at nothing.

"No, no, no," Bell said hurriedly, lightly slapping her cheek to focus her. "You've gotta stay awake. You've gotta stay with us. You're not going anywhere. You're going to be okay."

Victoria smiled weakly.

"You're a bad liar," she told him.

"And I thought you were tougher than that," he shot back, taking hold of her hand. "What? You've never been shot before?"

"Oh, and *you* know what it's like?" she challenged with a weak chuckle.

Bell scoffed and waved a hand dismissively.

"Of course, I get shot all the time. Haven't you ever heard of Florida Man?"

Victoria laughed silently, her chest shaking and more tears falling from her eyes.

"You're alright, Bell," she told him. "You're going to make a fine detective someday."

"Yeah, we'll see about that."

Habst frantically looked around the room for something—*anything*—that could help him save this remarkable woman's life. But there was nothing. It was hopeless. The terrified Guests and Cast Members had vacated the area, and the lobby was deserted. From far off in the distance, within the resort itself, he heard muffled gunshots. He knew that the other Spectres had made it to the villa. He closed his eyes, squeezing them tight. He prayed to whatever cosmic entity would listen that McCoy and Jen-Jen would be able to defend Meghan and the kids. Carina, too. He definitely wouldn't mind seeing her again.

Just when Habst had completely run out of hope, the impossible happened.

The doors burst open and two paramedics rushed in, dragging a stretcher between them. Immediately, they rushed to Victoria's side as LeCarre barked orders. Gently, they took over for Habst as Bell guided him backward.

The paramedics were absolute professionals, doing everything they could to save Victoria's life.

Using shears, one of the medics cut her pants away and carefully inspected the wound while the other inserted an IV into her arm to give her fluids. Carefully, the pair transferred Victoria to the stretcher. The one who'd inspected the wound approached Bell and Habst while the other strapped Victoria in and applied a clotting agent and bandage.

"Tell us," Bell demanded, not beating around the bush.

"If we'd gotten here ten minutes later, she'd be dead. Bullet went through and out. Doesn't seem to have clipped any organs, but it did hit her hipbone, and I imagine she'll need surgery for that. She might walk with a bit of a limp for the rest of her life, but she's not going to die today. She'll be in surgery over at Celebration within the hour."

Habst had never felt more relief in his life—and he'd been through some shit.

LeCarre finally stopped yelling orders as the paramedics wheeled Victoria out to the ambulance and.

"You did it, buddy," Bell told Habst, slapping him on the shoulder. "You saved her."

He almost tried to deflect the attention with a joke about his prices being reasonable should his help ever be needed again, but his words caught in his throat as he heard the muffled *snap* of another gunshot from deeper in the resort. "Fuck," he gasped.

"What is it?" LeCarre asked, stepping in close.

"The rest of the Spectres, they're in our villa. We have to go—now!"

Habst sprinted toward the stairs, with LeCarre and Bell hurrying to keep up.

# FORTY-THREE

AFTER THEY'D LEFT the Canada Pavilion, Charlie and Kalani had
gone directly to the Norway Pavilion, where Victoria had mentioned
spotting Thirteen on the GPS tracking. Not having had any luck,
Charlie had approached a Cast Member—Kathryn—that had been working
at the bakery. He knew Kathryn and hoped she would be able to help him
out.

Earlier in the year, Kathryn's car had been broken into by another Cast
Member, and her laptop had been stolen. She was terribly broken up about
losing the computer, and Charlie initially couldn't fathom why. Regardless,
Charlie had almost immediately caught the man who'd done it and recovered
the laptop.

It was only when he'd returned the computer to her that Charlie had
learned the significance of the item. The computer had contained the single
remaining copy of a video message Kathryn's sister had left for her just before
passing away the previous year. Charlie had opened his desk drawer, pulled
out a flash drive shaped like the old CommuniCore icon, and tossed it to her.

"Make copies of that video, Kathryn," he'd told her. "You can always
replace the laptop, but you can't replace that video."

She'd hugged him tightly before thanking him and leaving his office in
tears. Since then, every time she saw him she greeted him more cheerily than
anyone else who worked for Disney did. He was hoping to cash in a little of
that goodwill now.

"Kathryn," Charlie greeted her pleasantly. "How's work today?"

"Charlie!" she blurted in a high pitch. She ran out from behind the
counter to hug him.

"Walk with me, yeah?" he asked, gesturing to some tables outside the bakery. "This is my friend Kalani; he works for the CIA. We're looking into something pretty important and I think you can help us."

She looked nervous at the mention of the CIA, but Kalani gave her a bright grin and she relaxed a bit. They all took a seat at one of the tables outside.

"I'm not sure what *I* can do, but I'd be happy to help if I can," she offered. Charlie had always been impressed by how mild her accent was, considering she was a native Norwegian and had only lived in the US for six months.

"About half an hour ago, do you remember seeing a red-haired woman with thick-rimmed glasses and a cut on her lip? She would have been with a man about my height, thin, covered in tattoos, and wearing a dark denim vest?"

She only took a moment to think about it.

"Yes, they bought four glacier shots and they sat at this exact table. Why?"

Charlie glanced at Kalani, who caught his eye.

"I have to find her. She has something important that we need. Do you know where she might have gone after she left here?"

Kathryn nodded.

"She made a phone call before she could drink her second shot. They left two full shots on the table and hurried away. I didn't hear everything and I wasn't really paying attention, but I heard her mention a truck and I also heard them talking about the ShowPlace Pavilion. It's not open right now, is it? Why would they want to go there?"

Charlie stood. He knew where she was going. The truck with the hazmat suits would more than likely be parked right next to the World ShowPlace Pavilion. She was headed for those suits. Hopefully Victoria had dealt with them in time.

"Maybe she doesn't know what festival this is?" Charlie mused with a forced smile, gesturing at the Flower & Garden Festival decorations nearby. "Thank you, Kathryn, you gave us exactly what we needed."

Charlie and Kalani began to head out, and then stopped, turning back to the girl.

"Hey, Kathryn? Take the rest of the day off, alright? I'll make sure you get paid for it. Just a little 'thank you' for helping us out today."

"Are you serious?" Kathryn asked, smiling. "Thank you *so* much, Charlie!"

Charlie grinned, threw her a wink, then turned back to Kalani as he pulled out his phone. While they walked, Charlie sent a quick text to Melissa Valiquette, telling her that he'd given Kathryn the rest of the day off with pay and that he'd be putting in an Applause-O-Gram for her having gone above and beyond her duties to help him out. The response was one of surprise, but people rarely questioned Charlie.

"You sure that was a good idea, *braddah*? We weren't supposed to evacuate anybody."

Charlie glanced at him sideways.

"We're not *evacuating* anybody. She was rewarded with paid time off for a job well done. Besides, her parents have had a hard enough time. If we fail, I don't want them losing another daughter."

Kalani didn't respond, but he saw the intensity return to Charlie's eyes. Kalani knew that Charlie was thinking of his own daughters then. He understood why Charlie had told Kathryn to leave; he'd put himself in the place of her parents and wanted to spare them additional pain if he could.

After walking a while in silence, Kalani spoke up.

"So, when we find Thirteen, what are we going to do? I mean we can't just shoot her in the middle of a crowd."

"I don't know," Charlie admitted. He truly had no plan. "We have to find her first. Then we'll figure it out."

Subconsciously, Charlie felt in his pocket for his knife. While his new Glock was too dangerous to use out in the open with all of the crowds milling about, if he could get close enough he could end Thirteen's life with one thrust of that blade.

Distractedly, Charlie noticed Kalani staring longingly at the turkey leg booth in the American Adventure Pavilion as they passed through. He almost laughed—such a simple thing, to laugh in a time of crisis. He tried his best not to look at the toxin dispenser sitting idly by, not ten feet from that very booth. Without a doubt, it was already loaded with the neurotoxin that would kill everyone within a mile of this place. Kalani had referred to these dispensers as "plague throwers" and, while not technically accurate, it was as good a name as any.

Without thinking, Charlie quickened his pace.

▼▲▼

When Charlie and Kalani finally found Thirteen, she and Alfie were in Future World. Having found no sign of them near the World ShowPlace Pavilion, Charlie pulled aside three separate Cast Members before one finally recalled seeing someone fitting Thirteen's description heading out of World Showcase.

Charlie spotted Thirteen and Alfie as they were headed toward Spaceship Earth. It looked to Charlie as if their intention was to head out the front exit. If the pair could catch a cab or a bus or a Lyft, they could theoretically still carry out their plan.

"Kalani, look. One o'clock."

"Son of a bitch. How often do we get *this* lucky?"

Without responding, Charlie took off, dodging and weaving through the crowds while drawing the knife from his pocket. He held it in a forward grip, ready to drive it into Thirteen's neck the moment he was close enough. He noticed that her phone was in her hand, hanging loosely at her side. She seemed agitated and walked so quickly she was nearly running—Victoria must have been successful in taking care of those suits.

When Charlie and Kalani were ten feet away, their luck turned on them.

The sound of sirens wafted through the air, coming from the direction of Crescent Lake. It was distant, and barely audible above the hustle and bustle of the crowds, but Thirteen had heard it.

And she turned around.

When their eyes locked, her expression was one of shock, and Charlie's was one of pure rage.

Disregarding his loss of the element of surprise, Charlie charged Thirteen, driving the knife toward her throat with a savage thrust.

And suddenly he was no longer facing her.

In his fury, Charlie had completely forgotten about Alfie, who had simply stepped in, spun Charlie away, and stripped him of the knife.

Charlie barely had time to process what was happening before he was forced to dodge a vicious counterattack. Alfie slashed at him with his own knife, catching him across the left shoulder and sending ruby droplets of blood spattering onto nearby Guests. Some screamed, some gasped, but all fled when they saw the man with the knife and the blood on its tip.

Charlie lunged for Thirteen once more but connected hard with a Guest who was trying to drag his young son out of the danger zone. Rebounding off the man, Charlie was knocked back toward Alfie, who stepped in with another blinding cut.

Just as Alfie started the blade on an arc that would have slit Charlie's throat from ear to ear, he was knocked nearly off his feet by a massive fist. Kalani had delivered a crushing haymaker that caught Alfie hard across the jaw from the side. The impact twirled the slim Spectre around and he lost his grip on the knife, which sailed off into some nearby landscaping. As hard as Kalani's blow had been, Alfie recovered with an almost supernatural quickness.

Kalani stepped between Charlie and Alfie, and Charlie used the disruption to charge Thirteen again.

This time, he caught her.

Charlie, chivalry abandoned, threw a fist as hard as he could into Thirteen's stomach. He put every ounce of strength he had into the shot, pivoting at the hips and twisting into it for added force. It connected exactly where he'd been aiming and nearly lifted the redhead off her feet. She doubled over immediately, vomited up her Aquavit, and lost her grip on her phone.

Unable to breathe, she dropped to her knees, sucking in shallow, wheezing, panicked breaths, and retched once more, unable to stop Charlie as he grabbed her phone, pulled the battery from it, and shattered the device on the pavement. He threw the battery over the railing and into the nearby water.

Thirteen's eyes widened and she reached a hand out futilely.

"Not today," Charlie told her, slapping away her outreached hand.

And it was done.

The control device for the toxin dispensers was destroyed, Thirteen's plan was completely dismantled, and the park was safe. It was over.

Charlie breathed a sigh of relief.

His relief lasted only a fraction of a second, for that was when he saw his friend struggling with Alfie twenty feet away. Kalani was an experienced combatant, but he was losing this fight. Alfie was something else—a killer. Alfie never fought to protect, only to kill; to destroy.

Charlie gave Thirteen one last glance as he sprinted toward the melee.

All around, people were running away from the fighting, and Charlie dodged them as he ran to aid his friend. He could feel the knife wound on his shoulder starting to burn, but he ignored it. His job was not yet done.

"Charlie," Thirteen rasped from behind him, and he stopped. "Your family is already dead."

She started to laugh, and it was no longer the high, pretty laugh from before—this was a laugh of pure evil.

"What?" he snarled, torn between helping his friend and hearing news of his wife and kids.

"Why do you think there are only two of us here?" she asked, still laughing. "Those sirens aren't for *us*. The rest of the Spectres are slaughtering your slut wife and your irritating kids. *God*, I hope they make her watch while they kill your kids."

Charlie started toward her but the realization hit him that she was lying—stalling for time so her boyfriend could defeat Kalani, and then he'd be outnumbered.

"Fuck you," Charlie growled, turning once more toward Alfie and Kalani.

By the time he reached them, Kalani had been driven to a knee and Alfie was winding up for a hard overhand right.

Charlie drew his Glock and fired.

The shot was wild—and pure reflex—but Alfie had his back to a slope covered in landscaping so there was little danger of injuring a civilian if he missed. The bullet struck Alfie on the side of his head and knocked him away from Kalani.

The shot, while effectively saving Kalani's life, sent the surrounding Guests into a flurry of panicked motion. Anyone who hadn't run from the knife fight now fled the gunfire with all haste. Charlie didn't risk a second shot now that Guests were running unpredictably by, but one shot had been enough to cause everyone nearby to rush for the exits.

As Charlie closed in on Alfie, intending to finish the job if his first round hadn't done it already, Thirteen once more called his name.

"Charlie!" she yelled, and he stopped again. "You think you've won?"

Charlie turned halfway to her, not letting Alfie out of his line of sight.

"Oh, you *do*," she laughed, stood. "You thought I was going to input the go-code on my *personal* phone? Not quite."

She giggled as she pulled a small rectangle of black glass from her pocket—a second phone.

He hadn't destroyed the right device.

Instinctively, he raised his weapon to fire on her, but she drew her own and fired first.

Unlike the last time he'd been shot on Disney property, Charlie did not get lucky. This was no grazing of the ribs. Thirteen's round struck him square in the abdomen, just above his belt line. The impact, though sharp, was not as forceful as he'd expected. It staggered him just a bit, and only caused minimal pain.

All of those years ago when he'd faced off against James Holloway, the pain of that bullet tearing its way into his throat had been excruciating. This? This was strangely tolerable. He shook it off with almost no interruption. Looking down, he noticed something stuck to his shirt, above his hip.

It was a tranquilizer round—Thirteen had shot him with the same type of pistol used on him at the Magic Kingdom the previous day. Luck was on his side, as the tranquilizer had struck his spare magazine carrier and the round hung from his shirt by the bent needle. He pulled it free, thanking the stars for his luck—if he'd been hit, he'd have rapidly lost consciousness and it would have all been over.

Charlie fired two rounds at Thirteen in retaliation, but he was too late—she was already on the move. She was sprinting toward the exit as fast as she could.

"Alfie, move! Get up! Let's go!" she screamed as she ran, and to Charlie's surprise, the slim Englishman scrambled immediately to his feet—despite the bullet he'd taken to the head—and sprinted after her.

Charlie was momentarily stunned into inaction. A man he'd just shot in the head had stood and run from him. In his career as a Detroit police officer, he'd seen instances of officers shooting suspects and the bullet ricocheting off the skull instead of penetrating. It took incredible luck, but it was very possible.

The sound of Kalani's weapon being drawn from its holster snapped him out of his daze and he leveled his own pistol at the backs of his enemies.

They were fifty yards away by the time he was able to place his front sight over Thirteen's back—a difficult shot even for a competition shooter. By that time, Thirteen and Alfie had made it close enough to a group of running Guests that if Charlie missed his shot, he would certainly hit an innocent civilian. He refused to take that risk, and was relieved to see that Kalani felt the same.

"Damn it!" Charlie growled, taking off after the fleeing Spectres as fast as he could. He heard Kalani hot on his heels.

"They're headed for the front exit!" Kalani yelled, and Charlie agreed.

If Thirteen and Alfie could get out of the park and get clear of the kill zone then they could enter that go-code and kill everyone inside Epcot. Thirteen's goal was still within reach and she knew it.

"They're not going to make it out of this fucking park," Charlie shot back, determined. They were coming up on the backside of the massive geodesic sphere that was Spaceship Earth, one of Charlie's all-time favorite attractions, regardless of the narrator or sponsor. "Go right, meet me around the front. I have an idea! Go fast!"

Kalani did as asked and sprinted off down the path to their right while Charlie pursued Thirteen and Alfie to the left. His hope was that he could gain enough ground to force the pair to run head-on into Kalani. At that point, they would have only one escape route: directly into Spaceship Earth itself.

Charlie—who was no fan of running, let alone sprinting—put every ounce of energy into his stride and gained significant ground on Thirteen and Alfie. They refused to look back, so he needed to force their attention away from the park gates, which were just a couple hundred yards away. Thinking quickly, Charlie fired his gun into the sky—low enough to clear the underside of Spaceship Earth, but high enough to sail away into the distance without endangering anyone on the ground or Monorails.

Thirteen made the mistake of looking back, and it slowed her pace just enough for Charlie to gain the remaining ground he needed. When he was nearly within arm's reach, she dodged away from him and nearly collided with Kalani, who blocked their path. Just as Charlie predicted, they fled up the ramp, directly into the loading room of Spaceship Earth.

Reloading his Glock with a fresh magazine, Charlie grinned.

*You're in my world now, bitch.*

# FORTY-FOUR

WHEN THE THREE REMAINING Spectres assaulted the Walkers' villa at the BoardWalk, they did so with an air of absolute professionalism. Their approach spoke of years of experience carrying out coordinated and synchronized assaults on interior locations, and the efficiency of it scared the hell out of Jen-Jen.

The two-bedroom villa had two doors leading to the hallway and three balconies, each with its own glass doorwall. The Spectres seemed to come from everywhere at once.

Both hallway doors were kicked in simultaneously and another Spectre came in from the left-hand balcony, having climbed over from the unit next door. It was top-tier shock and awe, and it was something she'd only ever seen her own team successfully utilize.

Bullets were flying before the doors had even settled back into their frames.

Jen-Jen was immediately struck in her left arm. A deep graze, but still painful and disorienting combined with the thunder of the muzzle blasts in the tight quarters. She ignored it, because there were two little girls behind her that needed to be alive when all this was over.

Zeus growled furiously as he put himself between Violet and Katie and the attackers. Jen-Jen heard McCoy's AR bark several times as he engaged the Spectre that had entered the room on his side. Jen-Jen fired toward her attacker, but she missed wide and to the right, shattering a lamp on a nearby table. The Spectre on the balcony stepped through the threshold and closed in on Meghan.

Before Jen-Jen could turn toward him, he grabbed hold of Meghan and dragged her outside.

The Spectre that remained in the room with Jen-Jen wore a sling on one arm, and she recognized him immediately. He'd been one of the men that had attacked the Walkers' house the night before—the one whose arm Zeus had brutally crushed. In his uninjured hand, he held a short-barreled shotgun, which he aimed straight for Jen-Jen's head. She had no time to raise her weapon—he was going to kill her.

"Zeus!" she heard Violet yell. "*Hit!*"

This time, the German shepherd didn't simply grab the Spectre by the arm—he went for the throat. One hundred and ten pounds of furious, protective, combat-trained German shepherd latched onto the man's throat and dragged him to the ground. In his scramble to free himself of the dog's mauling grasp, the Spectre let go of the shotgun, all but forgotten. Zeus did not let up, however, and it wasn't long before the Spectre's terrified screaming turned into a wet gurgle as the shepherd tore his throat to shreds. After sustaining that much trauma, it took only seconds for the Spectre to die.

It was the first time Jen-Jen had seen the true outcome of what happened when a threat came between a shepherd and his family. She shivered as she looked into the animal's eyes. There, behind all the blood, were the black eyes of a savage wolf—a predator, not a family pet.

"Zeus, come!" Violet commanded, and the eyes immediately lost their predatory gleam. The dog lovingly bounded over to his people, having done his duty to protect them.

From outside, on the balcony, Jen-Jen heard two loud pops.

Gunshots.

▼▲▼

The Spectre had Meghan by the wrist, dragging her out onto the balcony, when she heard Zeus growl and snap. Anything else was cut off by the grunting of the man who'd pulled her out into the afternoon Floridian sunshine. In his opposite hand, the Spectre held a short assault rifle—however, it wasn't pointed at her. It was pointed toward the sky, as if he didn't intend to use it yet. She could still hear the sounds of struggle and gunfire from inside the villa, but out here it was strangely peaceful. Absently, she noticed people on the BoardWalk below running in every direction, as well as police officers trying their best to keep the peace.

"I'm disappointed my team didn't get you at your house, but I promised I'd eventually have you," sneered the Spectre. "Although, you may have been a bit sleepy when I made that promise."

Summers, Meghan remembered. Summers, the leader of the Spectre assault team that had turned her house into a warzone the previous day.

He threw her down into a deck chair, hard.

"We're going to have some fun, you and I. First, I'm going to make you watch when we kill your kids, then your friends. Then, when all that's over, maybe you and me...."

He didn't finish his sentence, and instead threw her a wink that she did not like one bit. He still held his assault rifle pointed skyward, and it was then that Meghan felt the cold iron digging into her hip. In the panic of the last few moments she'd forgotten all about the handgun that Kalani had given her. Having abandoned the shoulder holster, she'd tucked the gun into the waistband of her yoga pants for easy concealability.

"What do you want?" she asked timidly, playing the victim.

"That's obvious, don't you think? I mean, look at yourself," he laughed again, clearly enjoying himself despite the sounds of ongoing struggle within the villa.

She stood, moving close to him, and he allowed it. She ran her hands across her thighs and hooked her fingers beneath the hem of her tank top.

"Is this what you want?" she asked, slowly pulling it up. It seemed to confuse the Spectre, who clearly expected her to put up more of a fight.

"Well, uh, yeah?" he stammered.

Continuing to pull her tank top up with her left hand, Meghan's right hand slid into her waistband and found the grip of the FBI Glock. In one fluid motion, she drew the weapon and fired twice into the Spectre's gut.

The look of shock on his face was absolute. The force of the rounds punching into his abdomen staggered him back two steps, and he dropped the rifle.

"Wha...? What?" he coughed, blood seeping from his mouth. "What did you do?"

"That's obvious, don't you think?" she shot back, grabbing him by the vest. "I mean, look at yourself."

Then she shoved him with all of her strength and the Spectre tumbled over the railing, falling three stories to land headfirst onto the BoardWalk below.

▼▲▼

When Jen-Jen stepped into the adjoining room, she found that McCoy had disabled the last remaining Spectre, and had the man on his knees. McCoy sat on the edge of the coffee table clutching his side. his His Sig P229 was pointed at the back of the Spectre's head. Jen-Jen noticed that the CheyTac had been knocked over and lay on the floor next to a bloodied fixed-blade knife.

Jen-Jen already knew where the Spectre had made his fatal mistake. McCoy was deadly at long range, but unstoppable at close range. The Spectre had come at him with a knife, closing the distance as McCoy fired on him with the AR. At that close range, the carbine-length rifle had trouble tracking targets, so it didn't surprise Jen-Jen that the shots she'd heard had missed. All said and done, McCoy knew well the golden rule of knife fighting: you will get cut; expect it; accept it.

Jen-Jen stepped up to the Spectre and towered over him. She didn't speak; instead, she removed a RATS tourniquet from a small pouch on her belt and tied it tightly above the gunshot wound on her arm, staring into his eyes the entire time.

"You look familiar," she told him, using a rag to wipe away the blood that had streaked down her arm.

"You killed my brother," he spat.

"Did I?" she asked, feigning ignorance. "Was he a murdering shitbag like you?"

The Spectre breathed deeply and gritted his teeth, but didn't respond.

Jen-Jen heard footsteps behind her and saw Meghan approaching the doorway. Holding up a finger, she smiled a silent apology and closed the door.

"What's your name, shitbag?" she asked, turning back to the kneeling Spectre.

"Reid," he growled offering nothing else.

Jen-Jen nodded, glancing at McCoy. He nodded back.

"I remember now. Say hi to your brother for me."

She drew her Sig and executed the Spectre on the spot.

Over the ringing in her ears, she heard a startled yelp from Violet, Katie, and Carina in the other room.

"Come on, big guy," she said to McCoy, as he slowly got to his feet. "Let's get those girls out of here."

▼▲▼

The last thing Jen-Jen expected to see when she returned to the room next door was a fourth Spectre holding a gun to Carina's head—but that's exactly what awaited her. Jen-Jen recognized him from the surveillance footage; a large man with a jagged scar running along his jaw and one wrist clearly broken. He fit the description of the man Charlie and Kalani had disabled in the park and tossed into a garbage can. Somehow, he'd escaped his bonds and made his way here.

He was slowly backing away, dragging Carina toward the hallway door, holding her with his injured arm.

"Whoa, whoa," Jen-Jen cooed, holstering her Sig. "Slow down, friend. Let the girl go."

McCoy took a menacing step forward but Jen-Jen placed a hand on his chest when Scar cocked the hammer on his pistol. Carina let out a single choking sob and tears rolled down her face. Jen-Jen felt for her; the poor girl was having a *very* bad day.

"What do you want?" Jen-Jen asked him calmly.

"Pick up the phone, call Charlie Walker, and get him here. Now!"

He shook as he spoke Charlie's name. This man was clearly out for blood.

"Can't do that, bud. He's a little busy right now."

Scar's eyes shifted around the room until they landed on Meghan. Suddenly, he threw his left arm around Carina's neck in a chokehold—he didn't apply pressure yet, but Jen-Jen knew he could put her to sleep in seconds if he wanted to. At the same time, he aimed his gun at Meghan, who froze in place.

"Do it, or the wife dies," he demanded. "You call Walker here or I kill his wife. Then his kids. I'll kill everyone in this room if you don't bring him here."

Jen-Jen sighed. It wasn't the first time she'd been in a situation like this, but it was the first time the people whose lives she'd be forced to sacrifice were people she actually cared about. As harsh as it was for her to admit, it was the truth, and it truly did make her position more difficult. Still, this was her job, and she'd do as she would have done any other time.

She tilted her head and shrugged her shoulders as she spoke, "I'm not going to lie to you. You're not in the best bargaining position. If Charlie abandons what he's doing, tens of thousands of people will die. Do you see the dilemma that puts me in? My job is to protect American lives. At the same time, if you shoot her, you won't get the chance to take a second life. McCoy here will drill a .357 Sig hollow point through your brainpan the second you pull that trigger. If you think he can't do it, take a second to consider the helicopter at the bottom of the lake behind me. McCoy put a single round through your pilot's head at eight-hundred yards *while the chopper was in motion.*"

The Spectre seemed to deflate, but only slightly. He wasn't about to budge.

"Call. Charlie. Walker. *Now!*"

Jen-Jen was about to speak, but everything changed in an instant.

At first, Jen-Jen couldn't see why, but then she spotted the shadows behind Scar in the doorway to the hall.

"Drop your gun, asshole," she heard a voice say. It was a familiar voice, but she couldn't place it.

Slowly, Scar turned around and Meghan got her first glimpse of the voice's owner. She had to admit, it was the last person she expected.

Habst stood with Charlie's Walther aimed at Scar's head. Behind him, just outside the doorway, stood Bell and LeCarre with their service weapons drawn and aimed. Both Habst and Bell were covered in blood and Victoria was nowhere to be found. Her heart began to beat faster.

"What are you going to do, little man—shoot me?" Scar challenged, turning completely around so that Habst was aiming directly at his forehead.

"If I have to, yes. Drop the gun, it's over."

Jen-Jen couldn't see his face, but she knew the Spectre was smiling.

"It's over when I say it's over," he barked, raising his weapon.

McCoy, seeing the Spectre bringing the gun to bear, fired twice. From the hall, more shots rang out as Bell and LeCarre fired into the Spectre.

All of Bell and LeCarre's shots connected center mass, but it was McCoy's first shot that put the final Spectre to bed for good. As Jen-Jen had foretold, McCoy's .357 Sig round punched into Scar's skull and switched off his lights instantly.

Interestingly, Jen-Jen noticed, Habst had neither flinched nor fired his weapon. Throughout the firefight, he'd stood statue still, willing to accept his fate or spit in the face of the gods. She respected that. He had balls.

"Damn, kid," she said to him as he slowly lowered the unfired weapon. "You just saved the fucking day."

He grinned, but she could see in his eyes a sadness. Something bad had happened.

"Victoria," Jen-Jen prompted. "Where's Victoria?"

Habst took a deep breath.

"There's something I need to tell you."

# FORTY-FIVE

HIS GAMBIT HAD PAID OFF. Charlie and Kalani chased Thirteen and Alfie up the ramp to Spaceship Earth, knowing that they had made a mistake coming here. She'd only had two options if she didn't want to turn and fight them head-on: hop cars back toward the unload area and make a break through Project Tomorrow, or head into the ride itself. Either way, Charlie knew the lay of the land better than she did. If she headed into Project Tomorrow, he'd simply double back, head down the entrance ramp, and meet her at the exit. If she headed into the ride itself... well, that was Charlie's domain, and there was no chance of escape for her if she chose that route.

Thirteen and Alfie had a decent head start on Charlie and Kalani, but as soon as they'd pushed past the few people waiting on the loading platform, they saw Thirteen's red mane disappearing into the darkness of the ascent tunnel.

So, she'd chosen the ride.

Charlie grinned. Even in the darkness, this was his kingdom—and she would never leave it.

Charlie didn't recognize either of the Cast Members working the loading platform, but they clearly recognized him.

"Charlie! Should we shut down?" one of them asked, gazing into the ascent tunnel where two armed people had forced their way onto the ride.

"No," he responded. "Let it run. But don't load anyone else. I also need you to get on the phone and have Project Tomorrow evacuated immediately. Ask everyone still in line to leave as quickly as possible. I'm headed after them, and I want this line empty when I get back, understood?"

"Absolutely, sir," the Cast Member nodded and immediately got to work, radioing unload to apprise them of the situation. Charlie respected his work ethic. He couldn't see his name tag from where he was, but he vowed to learn the man's name after this was over so that he could reward him.

"Alright," Charlie told Kalani, "we're going in. Move when I move, step where I step, and don't fall off. If you do, the whole ride stops and we lose a huge advantage. Also, you could get *really* fucked up if you fall between the cars so stay *extra* frosty, alright?"

Kalani nodded, stepping into the moving car next to Charlie. With Kalani's sizeable bulk, the pair of them barely fit, but they made it work.

For the first little while, they didn't exit the car.

"We need to wait until we're out of this darkness," Charlie whispered over the narration dialogue. "It's too dangerous to move. If I had to guess, Thirteen and Alfie are ducked down in a Time Machine somewhere not too far ahead of us. They won't risk it either. We probably won't be able to get to them until we get to Rome."

"I love your enthusiasm, *braddah*, but I have no fucking clue what you're talking about."

Charlie laughed and nodded.

"I'll let you know when the little hand says it's time to rock and roll."

Kalani laughed at the reference, but Charlie was already staring ahead of him. Every few seconds, a light flashed as a picture was taken of the occupants of cars ahead of them. Charlie was looking into the light to try to spot Thirteen or her boyfriend.

After a few seconds, Charlie spotted a flash of red hair. It was her! She was maybe four or five cars ahead of them. A good lead, but nothing they couldn't make up. Thirteen might still believe they'd gone the other way. If he hadn't seen her red hair disappearing into the darkness, he may well have gone in the wrong direction.

"Here, in this hostile world, is where our story begins," spoke the narration.

Along the walls, moving illustrations drawn by primitive civilizations were barely visible in the dim caves.

"We are alone, struggling to survive until we learn to communicate with one another. Now we can hunt as a team and survive together."

As they moved through the scene and into the next, the atmosphere brightened as they transitioned out of the primordial darkness.

By the dim glow of the cave fires Charlie could just make out Thirteen and Alfie ducking down in their car ahead.

"Now, let's move ahead to ancient Egypt," Dame Judi Dench's narration continued, "because something is about to happen here that will change the future forever."

Thirteen and Alfie stayed low throughout the Egypt scene, but started to shuffle upon reaching the burning of the Roman Empire. To Charlie, they appeared to be getting ready to move. It occurred to him then that Thirteen possibly knew more about this attraction than he had anticipated. She had mentioned in her video manifesto that one of the locations for dispersal of her toxin was the Smellitzer on Spaceship Earth—in this very scene.

Charlie was aware of an emergency evacuation route just around the next bend. If Thirteen knew as much as Charlie now believed, then she would go for that exit. If she made it, then she'd be able to gain too much ground. He had to move.

"We're getting off right around the corner. There's an emergency exit under a balcony up ahead, we need to stop her before she gets there."

Kalani nodded, eyes still on Thirteen, who hadn't yet moved. He was disappointed that he couldn't simply shoot her, but there were far too many Guests in the surrounding cars, and he refused to take the risk.

When they rounded the corner, Kalani saw a small, half circle-shaped stage with three animatronic men seated on their right, and the balcony Charlie mentioned jutting out over the far end. The ride vehicles snaked around the perimeter of the stage, and Kalani could see Thirteen and Alfie on the far side. Unexpectedly, Charlie jumped out, landing on the stage. He ran at a full sprint toward Thirteen's car, which was almost rounding the corner.

At nearly the same moment, Thirteen and Alfie leapt out onto the stage, more than likely intending to make a run for the exit before they saw Charlie inbound. Kalani was only a few steps behind.

Without breaking stride, Charlie threw a quick punch toward Alfie—not necessarily to do damage, but to distract him so that Kalani could get around and catch Thirteen. Kalani understood what Charlie was trying to do but so, apparently, did Alfie. The Spectre lieutenant swatted Charlie's strike aside, and lashed out with a swift forward kick, catching Kalani on the front of the thigh and throwing him off balance. Without missing a beat, he threw two quick punches into Charlie's abdomen, the second of which the ex-detective was able to block.

"Rebecca, go! I'll handle this," Alfie commanded.

Thirteen, standing a few steps behind him, seemed plagued by indecision. If she left him, her plan would succeed and she would live, but Alfie would die either by Walker's hand or the toxin. If she stayed, the two of them may be able to defeat Walker and the Company operator, but she ran the risk of her phone being destroyed in the conflict. Or worse—they could lose.

The regretful feeling in her chest infuriated her as she left Alfie to his fate. She loved him, but she hadn't come this far not to succeed. She'd lost her entire team, but she wouldn't fail.

Turning on her heel, she ran for the emergency exit, hidden in the darkness, as Alfie squared off with both opponents.

"Your girlfriend left you. Bummer," Kalani goaded, as the darkness behind Alfie momentarily lit up with the fluorescent lights from the opening door in the hallway beyond. As the door swung shut, the darkness settled back into place.

Alfie smiled sadly at them.

"I don't need to beat you, gentlemen—just have to keep you busy long enough for Rebecca to win. Shouldn't be too difficult."

The ride vehicles that slowly passed them as they stood facing each other were empty now, the last of the Guests having moved deeper into the ride. Charlie decided that it was safe to go weapons-hot; he didn't have time to play games with Alfie.

Rapidly, Charlie drew his Glock, intending to end the threat permanently and immediately—but Alfie was just too fast. He stepped inside Charlie's reach, twisted his wrist and relieved him of the Glock, which fell to the floor nearby. Kalani used this opportunity to draw his weapon, but again Alfie was a blur. He knocked Kalani's pistol into a passing ride vehicle, which wasted no time in carrying it away.

Angrily, Charlie threw an elbow straight up and connected with the Spectre's chin and heard his teeth click together hard. But it didn't seem to faze him in the slightest—even with the gushing head wound from Charlie's bullet. Kalani stepped in with a meaty right hook, and Alfie ducked beneath it, while swatting away another of Charlie's strikes. Charlie and Kalani were stunned, unable to damage this lone, slim, injured Spectre.

Alfie took this opportunity to go on the offensive. He lashed out with an open hand and caught Charlie on the ear, dazing him and throwing off his equilibrium. The former detective crashed down to a knee and Alfie almost laughed, having expected Charlie to be tougher than that.

Using Kalani's size against him, he got low and inside his guard, throwing quick, sharp punches into his thigh, groin, forearm, and bicep. He stamped down on the Hawaiian's foot and guided him to the floor as he fell, using the big man's falling weight to launch himself through the air toward Charlie, who knelt near the edge of the stage, facing him.

In mid-air, Alfie arced his fist back, preparing to knock Charlie unconscious with a crushing overhand right—when he realized he had been tricked. In the span of a split second, Alfie knew it was over, and horror dawned on him as he understood that there was nothing he could do. Charlie hadn't taken a knee because he was injured; he had done it to position himself for what came next. Charlie had known that whatever happened with the Company agent, Alfie would have to come at him high and from this exact angle. He'd set a trap, and Alfie had jumped right into it.

Charlie saw the Spectre streaking down toward him—fist raised for the knockout blow—and knew his play had paid off. He suddenly shifted his weight backward, grabbed Alfie by the vest, and used the man's own momentum to send him headfirst off the stage.

With nothing to stop him, Alfie rebounded off the corner of one of the ride vehicles and fell between it and the one behind it. The Spectre's arm, shoulder, head, and neck slipped below the level of the track and his ribs landed painfully on the rail. His pain didn't last long, however, as the Omnimover did what it did best and continued ever forward.

Charlie watched with sickened awe as Spaceship Earth itself literally pulled the Spectre apart at the shoulders. Even over the music and narration, he could hear the wet sounds of meat tearing and bones cracking as the ride vehicle relentlessly fought its way forward, ignorant of the obstruction on its track.

Spaceship Earth dismembered Alfie as quickly and efficiently as a butcher quartering a chicken. The bright blue shell of the ride vehicle appeared purple as it shone through the slick layer of blood that had been splashed across its surface. Charlie couldn't look away as what was left of Alfie's body slipped off the railing and fell to the floor with a heavy, wet *thud*.

"In the meantime, here in Europe," the narration continued ahead relentlessly, "monks toil endlessly, recording books by hand—but that is about to change."

*Well, that's for damn sure*, Charlie thought, morbidly.

Snapping back to reality, Charlie reached over, grabbed his Glock, and sprung to his feet.

A quick glance showed Kalani already up and following close by—albeit with a bit of a limp. Neither of them remarked on Alfie's gruesome end as they made their way into the evacuation stairwell and took the stairs three at a time. They weren't far behind Thirteen; the fight had lasted only a few seconds, though it had felt like an eternity. In fact, they were so close behind that the door at the bottom of the evacuation route that led out to the loading platform was still open. Charlie rushed across the threshold and hopped across the ride vehicles that were still in motion, very aware of what would happen should he slip.

"Which way?!" he yelled at the Cast Member he'd spoken with before boarding the ride.

"There!" the Cast Member shouted, pointing back down the entrance ramp. "Five seconds ago."

Charlie nodded and sprinted down the ramp, Kalani hot on his heels. The brightness of the daylight temporarily blinded him, but he ran anyway, determined not to let Thirteen slip away. If she escaped, everything he'd done—everything he'd *been through*—would have been for nothing.

Charlie's eyes had adjusted to the daylight by the time he'd made it around the mirrored pillar and he immediately spotted Thirteen, roughly a hundred feet ahead of him, just in front of the fountain. She wasn't running—only walking—but she was focused on something in her hand.

The phone—she was inputting the code!

"STOP!" he commanded. "Now!"

She ignored him.

Charlie was fifty feet away when he stopped, took aim, and fired on Thirteen. The round caught her on the shoulder and spun her around, and the phone sailed away and crashed down to the pavement. Thirteen fell, bounced off the rim of the fountain and landed hard, but rebounded quickly and struggled to her feet. Hand pressed to the gunshot wound that was seeping blood, she tried to limp to the phone, desperate to release the toxin.

"Stop and turn around—*now*—or I will shoot you dead," Charlie warned, now only thirty feet away.

Thirteen ignored him again.

When Thirteen was only a few steps away from her phone, Charlie took aim for her center mass and squeezed the trigger once. He was close enough that he knew his aim was true. The round struck Thirteen between her shoulder blades and sent her skidding past her phone to land face first on the pavement.

She didn't—or couldn't—try to stand again.

Hurriedly, Kalani ran to retrieve the phone.

As Charlie hurried to Thirteen, weapon still at low-ready, Kalani yelled to him, "She didn't send the code. We did it, *braddah!*"

Charlie sighed with relief, feeling a lifetime's worth of stress melting away. After everything he'd been through, he expected to feel happiness, but as he approached Thirteen's unmoving form, all he felt was rage.

This woman had threatened everyone and everything he loved and had come within a few keystrokes of accomplishing her goal. This monster that lay before him was a psychopath and a terrorist, and Charlie had never felt such deep hatred for anyone or anything.

When Charlie reached her, he could see that she was alive. He noticed the shallow movement of her breathing. Blood still seeped from the wounds on her back and shoulder, but she did not move.

Roughly, Charlie grabbed her by the wounded shoulder and rolled her onto her back. Strangely, she did not cry out—did not even react, as much as it must have hurt her.

When he looked into her eyes, he saw nothing but fear. Tears spilled from her eyes beneath her cracked glasses, and she did nothing but blink. Charlie knew what had happened.

"C—congratulations," she rasped. "You're a hero again."

Charlie said nothing. He simply stared into her eyes.

"Alfie? Is… is he—?" she asked.

Charlie shook his head.

Thirteen sighed, and Charlie could hear the rattle of a punctured lung.

"I can't move, Charlie," she sobbed. "I can't fucking move. I just feel cold. What did you *do?*"

Kalani came to stand next to Charlie.

"Jesus, *braddah*," he said.

"Charlie, why can't I move?" Thirteen cried, afraid.

"You're paralyzed," he informed her. "I'd imagine there's a bullet lodged in your spine. From the looks of it, there'll be no fixing that. Not for you."

Charlie knew it was brutal, but it was the truth. It would be a difficult and expensive surgery, and nobody would waste that much money, time, and effort on a terrorist. They'd stabilize her and call it a day, at best.

Thirteen closed her eyes, squeezing them tightly in fear and anger.

"Finish the job," she asked him, pitifully. "Please."

Charlie looked at the gun in his hand and aimed directly between her eyes. He'd sworn that when he got the chance, he would kill Thirteen for what she'd done—for what she'd planned to do. Killing her would be merciful—an end to her suffering.

He holstered his weapon.

She didn't deserve mercy.

"No," he told her harshly.

"Kill me, you fucking coward!" Thirteen shrieked, with all the power her ruined body and punctured lung could muster.

"You don't get to take the easy way out," he said, matter-of-factly.

Thirteen's eyes fell on Kalani.

"Then *you* do it, big man. Be the hero—kill me!"

Kalani folded his arms in front of him and slowly shook his head. She'd taken two of his friends from him right before his eyes; he had no sympathy to give.

Charlie knelt over her, his face inches from her ear.

"Living your life in that body, never being able to move or *feel* ever again? That would be a lifetime of torture for anybody—especially you—and I'm going to make sure you live a *long* life," he promised in a cold whisper only she could hear. "I will never let you forget how you failed here today. See you real soon."

Charlie stood, pulling his phone from his pocket. For the first time since Wednesday, he could call his wife with good news.

The Spectres had lost.
Thirteen lay broken, defeated.
The nightmare was finally over.

# EPILOGUE ONE

THE SURGERY HAD GONE WELL. The doctors were able to repair her hip and, after a few blood transfusions, she was transferred out of the ICU into a room of her own.

It had only been a month, but the progress she'd made had impressed even the more experienced doctors. Charlie had joked that she was so stubborn that even the laws of science couldn't control her.

He had visited Victoria in the hospital daily. At first, he'd worried about her ability to pull through—he'd seen people in far better shape never recover—but, over time, the old Victoria slowly came back.

Bell and LeCarre had visited often, too. They'd gotten in a little bit of trouble for helping Charlie and X-ray but after a full review of the circumstances—as well as a consideration of the results—they were commended instead of punished. They'd even become national heroes. Every news outlet in the country had broadcasted the story of the brave men and women that had prevented one of the most horrible attacks in the country's history.

Kalani, McCoy, and Jen-Jen had flown home a few days after Victoria's surgery, taking with them the bodies of April and Vega to be laid to rest. The deceased agents would be two more anonymous stars on the wall in Langley—same as Mason years earlier—but their sacrifice would never be forgotten by their friends and teammates.

As luck would have it, instead of being reprimanded, X-ray Team had also received commendations for their success. Since they'd worked with Bell and LeCarre—and, by extension, the Orange County Sheriff's Office—they were technically attached to a domestic agency, which meant they were legally able to operate on American soil. X-ray Team, for the second time, had prevented a terrorist act inside the United States by taking advantage of a loophole.

▼▲▼

Finally, the doctors had signed off on her release, and Charlie had come to the hospital to take Victoria home. The doctors had not, however, cleared her for air travel and the Walkers had volunteered to take her in until she could fly back to Virginia, even though they'd been staying in a rental house on account of their own home becoming a warzone.

"Well, good morning, Grandma Vee," Charlie teased, offering Victoria a hand to help her out of her wheelchair. "Oh—do you have her cane or walker or whatever?" he jokingly asked the orderly who had wheeled her out. Victoria laughed and punched him in the shoulder.

"You're my Walker," she shot back. "Now come on, help an old lady to the car."

She'd struggled a bit to get to her feet, but surprisingly walked with only a hint of a limp as they made their way to Charlie's car. The doctors had said that with physical therapy, she would be nearly good as new in a few months.

"Oh, damn," she whistled, eyeing Charlie's black muscle car glistening in the sun. "You came to pick me up in the Shelby?"

"I know you're an old lady with a bad hip and all, but I figured you'd appreciate it. Damn kids and their loud cars."

She laughed and elbowed him in the ribs before they got into the car. Charlie fired it up and Victoria chuckled again as the throaty engine growled its way to life.

"This thing is badass," she told him. "Probably too badass for you, you fuckin' nerd."

Charlie shifted gears, barking the tires as he pulled out of the parking lot.

"If you lived nearby, you could borrow it. But I don't want this monster up in Alexandria—the fucking wheels would be stolen in an hour."

Victoria smiled, but she didn't laugh. He expected another comeback, but she seemed lost in thought. For a moment, Charlie figured she was simply lost in the fog of her pain medication, but she surprised him.

"Maybe I'll move," she said, suddenly.

"Where?" Charlie asked, taking a curve faster than he probably should have and enjoying it.

"Here," she said simply.

"Not sure there's a Company branch around these parts."

She shook her head.

"I had a lot of time to think when I was lying in that room for the last month—and I don't believe I want to work for the Company anymore," she admitted.

Charlie threw her a glance.

"Seriously?" he asked. "But you love it."

"I *used* to love it," she countered. "But it's a lonely, miserable life up there. I've got a one-bedroom apartment, no friends because I'm out of the country all the time, and when I'm home, everyone else in X-ray disperses to all ends of the globe to blow off steam."

Charlie nodded; he could understand.

"What makes you want to come here of all places?" he asked her.

"You. Meghan. Violet and Katie. Zeus. Mickey," she smiled. "I don't have any family left. My adopted mom and dad died a long time ago. My *real* mom and dad... well, you know what happened to them. You guys are the only family I have."

Charlie smiled, touched by his friend's honesty.

"What would you do for a living, then?" he asked. "I could set you up with a job in Security, but I think you're a little overqualified."

She laughed. "Actually, I've had several offers from the FBI over the years, which I've always turned down. They have a field office in Tampa with satellite offices all over. One of which is in Orlando—same guys that loaned us the Navigator. I called them up a week or so ago to ask about the operation. As it stands, they need investigators. I had my file sent over to them and they extended me an open offer the very next day."

Charlie was shocked.

"Really? Are you sure about this?"

"Nope," she admitted with a laugh. "But who's ever sure about things like this? I'm going to do it, Charlie. I'm sick of long plane rides and cold fucking winters."

"What about X-ray Team?" he asked. "They'd be lost without you."

"They'll be fine," she countered. "They're the best in the world. They don't need me barking orders to stay on top. Jen-Jen is bossy enough for all of them."

Charlie didn't protest. After a while, he nodded.

"I'm on board. You know... the girls are gonna lose their minds."

Victoria grinned, "I'm counting on it."

As they passed by condos and neighborhoods and apartment complexes on their way to Charlie's rental, he was already scanning lawns for sale and lease signs for her.

"How long until the doctors say you're cleared to fly?" he asked.

"Two weeks, if nothing goes wrong."

"Then we've got two weeks to find you a new place to live."

Victoria smiled and leaned back in her seat, relaxed. This was exactly what she wanted, and for the first time in forever, she was happy.

▼▲▼

Habst had made a complete recovery—much faster than he'd expected. After all was said and done, he'd had three cracked ribs and a hairline fracture on his left orbital socket. He'd had headaches for five weeks, but the wild cocktail of pain meds the doctors had prescribed him had almost made it worth it.

All in all, things could have gone a lot worse. He'd lost a good friend, but he could have lost so much more. He'd frequently daydreamed about scenarios like the Spectres' attack, but it had always been in the vein of "wouldn't that make a cool movie?" He'd never expected something like that to actually happen, and—now that it had—he wished he'd never fantasized about anything even remotely close. That much violence was cool on film and on paper, but in reality it was a whole other story.

Any normal person would have been marked by the things Habst had been through—but he refused to let it get to him. Yeah, it sucked, but it was the past. You gotta move on.

"Not bad, right?" he asked, looking off toward the sunset. He held out a hand to his companion, who grabbed it, reluctantly accepting his help.

"Are you kidding?" she whispered, as if there was anyone else around to hear. "It's terrifying. I'm not coming up there. I can't believe I even came this far with you. We're going to get in a lot of trouble."

"By who?" Habst laughed. "Charlie? He's off playing Mr. Mom. Come on. It's safe. I got that piece-of-shit scissor lift fixed just for you, and it wasn't cheap."

Habst sat next to the open hatch.

"Come on," he cooed. "It's safe… ish. I'll make sure you don't fall off and die."

Laughing, Carina took his hand, climbed up, and sat down beside him.

"How cool is this?" he asked her.

Habst spread his hands wide; they were atop Spaceship Earth, one-hundred and eighty feet above Future World, watching the sunset on a cloudless spring night.

Of course, it was horribly dangerous, but after what they'd been through, it didn't much matter.

Habst had no complaints. He was somewhere he'd always wanted to be, he was alive, and he had a hot—non-evil—redhead with him.

Life was good.

# EPILOGUE TWO

COUPLE OF MONTHS AFTER the incident, an envelope containing a set of keys showed up at the Walkers' rental house. The only other item in the package was a piece of heavy white cardstock with an address on the front. Charlie immediately recognized the neighborhood—Golden Oak.

On the back of the card, a small message was printed in the style of old dot matrix printers.

YOU KNOW WHAT THEY SAY ABOUT A KICK IN THE TEETH.
HERE'S A LITTLE SOMETHING FROM US TO SAY THANKS.

The card was unsigned, but Charlie suspected he knew exactly who had sent it—and whose idea this "little something" had been.

The "little something" turned out to be not so little at all. As Charlie pulled up to the address on the card, his mouth hung agape in pure shock.

It was by no means the largest or most extravagant house in the Golden Oak community, but it was absolute perfection in Charlie's eyes. Just viewing it from outside, it looked like the details for the perfect home had been pulled directly from his mind and into reality. Knowing who'd given him this house, it wouldn't surprise him in the least if that was the truth.

As he unlocked the front door, the first thing he noticed was the state-of-the-art security system that had been installed. The front door was heavy, with a bulletproof weightiness Charlie recognized from the armored doors of his old police cruisers. Several cameras watched as he pushed the door open, which glided easily on well-oiled hinges.

A small table stood just inside the entry and upon it sat a towel-animal

Mickey head with another dot matrix card that simply said:

WELCOME HOME, CHARLIE.

Right around the time Charlie got the keys for their new Golden Oak house, Victoria had finalized her transition to the FBI and moved into the condo she'd picked out—which was just a couple of miles away from the Walkers' new house.

Only a few weeks later, Victoria's section chief, a decent man named Ben Townsend, had informed her that three transfer requests had come through, and that he'd like her to review the applications before he responded to them. He grinned knowingly as she looked over the paperwork and laughed as her eyes widened when she read the names.

Jennings. Kalani. McCoy.

"Are you kidding?" she asked Townsend.

He shrugged.

"Came across my desk an hour ago. They used you as a reference. What do you think—let 'em in?"

Victoria couldn't help but laugh.

X-ray Team was not prepared to let their squad dissolve without a fight.

"Deny them," Victoria joked, tears in her eyes. "These guys are the worst."

December came along, and by that point, X-ray Team had been back together for a few months—albeit no longer officially under the X-ray name and carrying Bureau shields. The Walkers had been settled into their new house for a while and every trace of the Spectres' attack on the parks had long since been scrubbed away—including the helicopter at the bottom of Crescent Lake. They were simply able to relax—something neither the Walkers nor X-ray Team were used to.

For a while, Charlie found it strange to have X-ray Team living less than twenty minutes away. He had a hard time getting used to the fact that Kalani and McCoy could simply meet him for a drink at Trader Sam's, or Victoria and Jen-Jen could spend a day in the parks with Meghan and the girls—and they did, often. Eventually, Charlie acclimated to having his friends around and found a certain comfort in having these warriors nearby. In the back of his mind, he still couldn't help but think that a new threat was inevitable, and it made him feel a little better to have X-ray close at hand.

Still, today was a day he had been looking forward to for quite a while. It was Christmas Day and everyone had gathered at Charlie's new house—even

Bell and LeCarre had promised to stop by later in the evening. It was in the mid-seventies, sunny, and everyone was outside on the patio enjoying the day. The turkey was in the oven; it was peaceful and quiet.

Or as peaceful and quiet as any given day could be in the Walker household.

"Golden fucking Oak," Habst shook his head and took a sip of his beer. "You get six stitches and they give you a brand new house in Golden Oak."

It wasn't the first time Habst had been to their new house—nor was it the first time he'd expressed his astonishment on the subject.

"We also had our house assaulted and destroyed by mercenaries," Meghan reminded him with a wink. "But we'll just pretend that didn't happen."

"Fair enough," Habst laughed. "Tell the fridge to bring me another beer."

Charlie scoffed as he poured Lagavulin for himself, McCoy, and Pete Valdez—who'd been in town with his wife looking at retirement properties.

"It was seven stitches and they put the first one in before the lidocaine fully kicked in," he deadpanned. With over-exaggerated seriousness he added, "It stung pretty bad. I'd say this almost makes up for it."

Pete drained half his Scotch in one long pull, as he'd always done, and said, "How the hell do you keep getting into these situations, Walker?"

Charlie shrugged, sipping his own whisky.

"People like me."

Jen-Jen hurried past in a tiny black bikini, hoisting a squealing Katie over her shoulder and tossing the girl into the pool before jumping in herself. Victoria was already swimming—in an only marginally less-revealing swimsuit. They'd embraced the Floridian state of mind very quickly.

"Six to midnight," Habst mumbled and Carina slapped him on the arm.

Charlie laughed.

"No privacy at all around this place," he joked.

"You really think *that* is appropriate holiday attire, Charlie?" Habst said with mock sternness, throwing a sideways glance at Carina.

Charlie glanced over at him before draining his glass.

"You go right ahead and tell those two you don't like it, bud," Charlie offered, patting him on the back as he passed by.

"And ruin the scenery?" he shot back, which earned him another slap from Carina.

"You two just going to blatantly stare at Jen-Jen's ass all day or what?" Meghan joked.

"Jealous?" Habst laughed. "It's seventy-five degrees outside, and you're out here in a damn cardigan. If you really wanted to be included in the ogling, you're not trying very hard."

"This is my life," Carina sighed and then giggled.

Charlie shook his head—once Habst was on a roll, it was hard to stop him.

Violet, who was speeding by with Zeus on her way to the pool, stopped dead in her tracks and stared at her mother. The shepherd, oblivious, continued on and launched himself into the water, splashing Victoria, Jen-Jen, and Katie.

"Have some wine, Mom," Violet offered, motioning to Carina's bottle. Her mischievous smirk told everyone around that she knew something no one else did. It was a Violet Walker trademark—she took after Charlie a bit too much.

"Violet, you know I can't have—"

Suddenly, Meghan stopped speaking, her face flushed.

Violet grinned an evil grin.

"Tell everyone why."

Meghan, caught off guard, stammered a few times before looking around at everyone. Violet had pieced together Meghan's secret on her own and for weeks had been using that information for blackmail. Up until now, that arrangement had been working out.

Compliments of Violet, Meghan now had everyone's attention.

She stood and took a deep breath.

"Um. I'm pregnant," she announced, timidly.

Violet, smiling knowingly, dove gracefully into the pool, ignoring the shocked reactions from the guests—including Charlie.

"I'll be damned," he smirked, laughing.

Before anyone could congratulate them, Kalani spoke up.

"Does anyone else smell smoke?" he asked.

Suddenly, the smoke alarm started blaring its shrill tone.

"Oh, come *on*," Kalani moaned. "Am I about to get screwed out of turkey *again?*"

Charlie could hear everyone laughing as he rushed through the smoke toward its source: the oven.

The turkey did not survive.

# CREDITS

THE ONE HUNDRED AND THIRTY-EIGHT minutes of film you've just experienced wouldn't exist without the collaborative effort of over eighteen-hundred hardworking professionals including VFX artists, cinematographers, stunt persons, camera people, catering personnel, sound designers and mixers, body doubles, firearms trainers, animal handlers, producers, and—

What?

Oh—hold on a second, everyone, my assistant is frantically waving his arms trying to get my attention for some reason. Let me just see what he wants.

Eduardo, can't you see I'm in the middle of—wait, this is for the book version of *Spectre Thirteen*? There *is* no movie version? There never will be?

Come on, that can't be right. What about that huge check from the studio? Is *that* made up? Jason Momoa literally *just* texted to thank me for giving him the role of Kalani—are you saying I made *that* up, too?

None of that actually happened?

Oh.

Well, shit. Okay.

Let's try this again.

# ACKNOWLEDGEMENTS

THE STACK OF PAPER you hold in your hands (or the collection of ones and zeros taking up space on your hard drive) wouldn't exist without the collaborative effort of a small handful of people who are, honestly, absolutely fucking crazy for enabling me to do this a second time.

Let's talk about these psychopaths.

Naturally, we'll start with the big boss himself: Leonard Kinsey. This guy, for some reason I'll never be able to comprehend, adopted me into the Bamboo Forest family when all I had was a weird idea for a story that shouldn't exist. That idea eventually turned into *Hollow World*, the bane of pixie-dust-snorting mommy bloggers everywhere. Here we are again, almost seven years later, and he's still telling me it's a good idea to keep doing what I'm doing. He rolled the dice on a brand new writer and for that I'll be eternally grateful.

Next on the list is the madman from across the pond: Hugh Allison. This is the chap that willingly spends months of his time arguing with me (for money). For the love of Cthulhu, why would you want to put yourself through that kind of trauma? That said, he's a bloodhound who refuses to let me look anything less than an absolute professional, no matter how hard I try. Nobody does it better.

Aside from the aforementioned, only one other person was subjected to an early draft of this ~~movie~~ book, and that was Jeff Heimbuch. Jeff has spent the last six-plus years heckling me; insulting me; slandering me across Twitter, Facebook, and Instagram; making TikToks; taunting me; and threatening me, all in an attempt to get this project made. We can look at this in one of two ways:

A) It's thanks to his unwavering persistence that this book was even finished at all.

or

B) It's his fault it took six years because his constant verbal assaults took a toll on my mental wellbeing and put a damper on my creative process.

I'll let you decide.

Time travel isn't easy, but here I am writing this from the past. That said, I can't finish these ~~credits~~ *acknowledgements* without a round of applause for Jeff Delgado, who handled the fantastic cover art wrapped around these pages. It's great, isn't it? I mean, I *assume* it's great—I haven't seen it yet. Here in the past, it hasn't even been started, but I've been a huge fan of his work for years and was genuinely surprised when he agreed to do the artwork. You're from the future, will you let me know how awesome it is? Also, do we have flying Deloreans yet?

Obviously, I need to mention my wife, Laura, our brand new son, Jack (who, being stuck here in the past, I have not yet met), and the Giant German, Grimm. Can't have a book without talking about Dad, Mom, Jake, and Savanah. These poor people are stuck with me forever—sucks to be them.

All of these fine people aside, there's one more psychopath who bears mentioning—and that person is you. You made *Hollow World* a success and raised your voice loud enough in reviews and across social media that I couldn't help but heed the call: Give us more of the Walkers and X-ray Team!

So, inevitably, when the mommy bloggers and forums filled with oversensitive control freaks break out the pitchforks and torches to hunt me down, I'll tell them it's your fault their virgin eyes were despoiled by the swear words, nudity, carnage, and violence in these forbidden pages.

Thank you all, and I'm sorry it took so long.

PS: NO thanks to Eduardo, who is going to regret quitting his job at the Magic Kingdom locker rental. I'm looking for a new assistant.